LIMERICK CITY LIBRARY

Phone: (061) 407510
Website: www.limerickcity.ie
Email: citylib@limerickcity.ie

The Granary,
Michael Street,
Limerick

This book is issued subject to the Rules of this Library.
The Book must be returned not later than the last date stamped below.

Class No. .... Acc. No. ....

Date of Return	Date of Return	Date of Return	Date of Return
0 MAR 08	20. NOV	1 2 OCT 2016	
03. JUL 08	27. JAN 10.	2 1 OCT 2016	
03. NOV 08	28. OCT 10	2 7 OCT 2016	1 DEC 2017
17. DEC 08		1 6 NOV 2018 2018	
0: JUL 09	1 4 DEC 2010	1 3 MAR 2019	
	1 2 MAY 2015	- 8 FEB 2020	
	2 3 JUN 2015		
	- 8 JUL 2015		

Forgotten Faces

Jeannie Johnson

First published in Great Britain in 2005 by Orion,
an imprint of the Orion Publishing Group Ltd.

1 3 5 7 9 10 8 6 4 2

A CIP catalogue record for this book is
available from the British Library.

ISBN 0 75285 344 9 (hardback)

Typeset at The Spartan Press Ltd,
Lymington, Hants

Printed in Great Britain by
Mackays of Chatham plc, Chatham Kent

All the characters in this book are fictitious, and any resemblance
to actual persons living or dead is purely coincidental.

The Orion Publishing Group Ltd
Orion House
5 Upper Saint Martin's Lane
London, WC2H 9EA

www.orionbooks.co.uk

For Rachel Leyshon – a much-appreciated copy editor

Chapter One

One last, painful contraction pushed Isaiah Thomas Strong onto fine linen sheets. Dr Owen, a dapper man in a burgundy waistcoat, the buttonholes of which strained over a spreading waistline, snapped orders at a midwife, two nurses and a wet nurse who hadn't yet taken off her cloak.

Beyond the bedroom door, fifty household servants carried out their duties. Outside, a team of gardeners tended flowers, fruits and vegetables for consumption by the occupants of Marstone Court, a palatial residence of castellated turrets and large windows surrounded by acres of parkland. Two men and two boys, hired from the village, looked after the sheep and deer which kept the grass short beneath the stout oaks and majestic elms.

Those that heard the newborn's cry raised their heads, wiped the sweat from their brows and murmured a swift 'God bless' for the latest addition to the Strong family.

Squalling and wriggling, the baby was snatched by the midwife, bound in red flannel and covered with a soft white shawl.

Horatia Strong arched her back in an effort to endure the fading pains of a long labour, the room around her a blur of opulence and activity. Silk hangings floated from the tester bed but she might just as well have been in a barn or a miserable cottage of damp walls and rotting thatch. All she cared about was that the pain was over. Nothing else mattered.

'A fine boy,' exclaimed Dr Owen, overbearingly attentive and as charming as a courtier. Leaving the babe to the women, he absorbed himself in checking the mother's heartbeat and pulse. She was his most affluent patient, and he had every intention of taking care of her and his income.

Collapsing back on her pillow, Horatia vowed this son would be the last child she ever brought into the world.

'Would you like to look at him?'

Her eyes flashed open. Of course she would!

She was forty years old and had carried fear as well as a child during this pregnancy. From deep within she found the strength to push herself up from the pillows, her heart thudding with trepidation.

If anything was wrong with him, they'd say so . . .

She looked with relief upon her son's crumpled face as he mewled like a kitten in the arms of the midwife. Labour had lasted thirty-six hours, twenty hours longer than with her daughter, Emerald. But that was eight years previously and she'd been younger then. This baby had taken his time. Endless pain, endless pushing and the feeling that her body was being ripped in half had left her wanting to sleep for a week. But when the midwife showed her his bundled form, the tension – far more intense than the pain she had endured – left her body. She touched his head with her fingertips. He was dark-haired and there were no unwanted physical characteristics. She was safe. Her arm fell exhausted to her side. The old secret that had so long niggled at the back of her mind, no longer mattered. No one would ever know about Max Heinkel, her father's chosen heir in the event that she did not marry Tom. He would never be acknowledged and now she would make sure he never would.

'You must rest,' said Dr Owen.

'I intend to.' Her eyes closed, as fresh linens were applied to stem the bleeding. At the same time, strips of linen were wound around and around her stomach.

'Tighter,' she murmured.

The nurses paused and exchanged hesitant glances.

Horatia's eyes flicked open. 'Tighter,' she repeated. 'I'm not a sow who doesn't mind a flopping belly. Tighter! As tight as you can!'

To most women, the birth of a child was compensation enough for the loss of a few inches of waistline, but not Horatia. Being swollen with impending childbirth had been bad enough. Hating her bloated body, she had stayed indoors during the latter months of her pregnancy, determined she would not venture out again until her belly and her bloom had returned to normal.

The women carried out her orders and the doctor attempted to soothe her with platitudes – as if she needed any.

'Leave me to sleep.'

The doctor leaned over her, his words silky. 'The wet nurse will ensure your son is properly fed.'

'So she should. That's what she's paid for,' she murmured before falling asleep.

She needed rest, but her sharp mind had not entirely shut down. Released from a secret worry she'd been nursing for months, her mind turned to the subject that was closest to her heart: the Strong Empire. She couldn't wait to get back to the cut and thrust of city commerce: the sugar, shipping and property interests, a solid base laid down in the eighteenth century on which future business could and would be constructed.

The Bristol sugar trade was not what it was. Horatia had known that for a long time. Thanks to Napoleon's encouragement, Europe was growing field after field of sugar beet. Transport costs were minimal compared to importing cane sugar from Barbados. The writing was on the wall.

Obsessed with what she would do once she was up on her feet, she gave little thought to her child, safe in the knowledge that he was being properly taken care of and that he was everything she'd hoped he would be. The boy would fill her husband with joy, and would be a bridge between them. Tom would be thrilled when he got back from Barbados, his expression bright with wonder. She remembered that he'd been tongue-tied when he'd first seen his daughter. Emerald had been a little mite with a screwed-up face, her complexion red with anger as she screamed her way into the world. Her fists had been clenched and had reminded Horatia of Tom in the days when he'd indulged in bare-knuckle boxing. But a son? Imagine how he would be with a son!

Isaiah Thomas, the only name she had ever contemplated calling her newborn baby, had been less vocal when he'd been born than Emerald had been, though his skin had seemed redder and his hair, a black thatch, had curled like tiny feathers all over his head. The dark hair had worried her a little. But each time a nagging doubt threatened to rise, she reassured herself again that Tom had very dark hair, that the child's hair was just like his.

Five days later she was ready to see her son again. Sears, her personal maid, entered with the breakfast tray and beamed when she saw she was awake.

3

'You do look well, madam!'

'I feel well. In fact, I feel quite marvellous.'

Glowing with satisfaction, she pushed herself up against a mountain of crisp linen pillows. She patted her bound stomach and eyed it thoughtfully. She wanted to look her best when her husband returned, to preen like a peacock, all shiny and svelte, bedecked in fine clothes and jewels, having produced the most precious jewel of all. What should she wear for his homecoming? In her mind she ran through the contents of her wardrobe: the silks, the velvets, the linens; the tartan, the cream, the royal blue and the yellow. Mentally, she chose a violet taffeta that fell in velvet-trimmed frills the colour of wild blackberries. Would it still fit her?

'Sears, my stomach is like a wobbly blancmange. It cannot be allowed to stay that way. I want you to get my corset ready. I want to try it on right away.'

Sears, a thin-faced woman with high cheekbones who might have been beautiful if she wasn't so gaunt, looked aghast. 'Madam! You have only just given birth. Surely you should be staying in bed for fourteen days at least.'

Horatia was adamant. 'Nonsense. Isn't it true that the washerwoman who comes in from the village had her baby on Monday and was in here at the scrubbing board by Wednesday morning?'

The fingers of her personal maid folded tightly over the breakfast tray on which an invalid's breakfast of salted porridge, a boiled egg, half a kipper and a glass of milk had been placed. 'But she's used to such exertions,' said Sears, her attention fixed on the job in hand as she set the tray down on the side table. 'I do believe that was her fifth confinement, if my memory serves me correct.'

'Hardly a confinement if she was scrubbing my laundry just a few days later,' said Horatia. 'Nevertheless, I will get into those corsets. There will be celebrations when my husband gets back. He has a son. We must both look our best.'

'Indeed, madam.'

'Every man wants a son. And now he's got one.'

'He will be pleased, madam. Judging by his lusty cry, he's a very bonny baby. No doubt the doctor will allow you to see him today?'

'I see no reason why not. I am completely recovered. You haven't seen him yourself?'

4

'No, madam. But I have heard him cry. The nursery is only just below my room.'

'Good.'

Sears dropped a swift curtsey. 'I'll be back for the tray in a while.'

Horatia's thoughts were suddenly elsewhere. When Emerald was born, it had been twenty-four hours before she held her, and over a month before anyone else except the doctor, the monthly nurse, the wet nurse and her husband saw her. It was normal for a child to be secluded during its first months of life. Even so, a mix of impatience and nervousness crept over her as she waited, her eyes fixed on the bedroom door. She began to tap her fingers on the quilt and vowed to give Dr Owen a piece of her mind. Perhaps he was merely being considerate. She had been in labour thirty-six hours – twenty hours longer than with Emerald. But she was impatient to hold him again, to bond with a son who was also a weapon in her war to gain, and even maintain, her husband's interest. She knew that, deep in his heart, Tom's affection lay with Blanche Heinkel, with her stone-grey eyes, honey-coloured skin and luxurious black hair. Horatia's half-sister. In the past, it had been hard to avoid Blanche and her husband Conrad. They had attended the same society events and even if Tom's acknowledgement of Blanche had not gone beyond the normal niceties, she had felt his passion for her burning like an unseen flame. Now Blanche was a widow and this worried Horatia. Only a son, a legitimate son, she had told herself, would ensure Tom did not stray.

It was no good. She couldn't wait any longer and the gold tassel of the bell pull was within easy reach. Sears answered it.

'I want to see the monthly nurse.'

Sears bobbed one of her deep curtseys and went off to tell the nurse she was needed. It was ten minutes before she heard her footsteps and the thud of a fist on her bedroom door.

'Enter.'

Horatia folded back the silky blue coverlet as the nurse approached. The woman's reticence annoyed her.

'Well, come along,' she snapped. 'It's been five days since my son was born, I want to see him. I want to see him *now*!'

The nurse seemed nervous. 'The doctor said—'

'Yes! Yes! To wait until he got here. But I've waited long enough. Now, give me my child.'

The woman looked perplexed, her breasts rising and falling with the rapidity of her breathing. When she turned to go, her progress across the room seemed unnecessarily slow.

Horatia frowned impatiently. 'What's the matter?'

The nurse had seemed a jolly character before the birth, her cheeks as ruddy as autumn apples, and a crescent smile permanently dimpling her face. Now she seemed pensive, as though she wished she was elsewhere, anywhere except in the presence of a mother wanting to see her son. She opened her mouth to say something then shut it quickly and left the room, returning ten minutes or so later with the baby. Her fat face screwed into a nervous smile, she handed Horatia the child then stepped away from the bed.

Bursting with joy, Horatia turned the corner of the shawl away from the child's face and was instantly aware that something had changed. Her worst fears, the terrible doubt that had clawed at her pregnant body, were now laid bare in this child.

The black thatch of hair was more crinkly than she'd thought. The pink face had turned brown, the colour extending all over his body – except for the palms of his hands and the soles of his feet. Her smile froze as she stared at the rosebud mouth that sucked the air, hoping to be fed.

'I don't understand . . .' she began.

Before she had chance to say more, the door opened. Sears showed Dr Owen into her room. He looked nervous, his deep-set eyes, like buttons in his face, darting about the room as if seeking some way of escape.

Horatia looked up at him and winced when she saw the wary look and the way his mouth moved as though he were trying to form the right words.

Her voice was cold as ice. 'Tell her to go,' she said, her face straying briefly from the doctor to Sears, who was beaming from ear to ear and obviously hoping to linger and catch a glimpse of the new baby.

The doctor nodded at the lady's maid. Her smile dissolved like melted snow. She knew when her mistress meant what she said.

Without any trace of her former joy, Horatia glared at the doctor, her jaw set and her eyes hard. In her silk-edged peignoir and Chinese silk shawl in jade green decorated with flowers and birds of paradise,

6

her hair hanging loose, she should have looked radiant. Instead she looked as if she'd been carved from rock.

'Go away, woman!' Horatia barked at the nurse who hadn't moved fast enough for her liking. 'Leave us alone!'

The nurse scurried away, her head bowed all the way to the door.

Horatia felt sick. Her heart thudded against her ribcage and her tongue stuck to the roof of her mouth. At last she said, 'This is not the child I saw the other day. This child is dark. Mine was not dark. It was red when I saw it. What is this?'

In her heart of hearts, she knew the truth. The child had African blood. But she wanted it confirmed. She wanted to hear the doctor explain to her that her eyesight was out of focus, that the child was a foundling, that there'd been a mix-up . . . anything but the truth.

The doctor cleared his throat, hitched his thumbs into his waistcoat pockets and frowned thoughtfully as he considered his explanation.

'I find this very difficult, Mrs Strong. But please be assured, you can trust me to be discreet. This is not the first time I have come upon such an occurrence in those families with interests in the West Indies . . .'

She was quick to interrupt. 'He wasn't this colour when he was born.'

Dr Owen rubbed at the nape of his neck. 'Apparently, it's quite usual. They're born quite light but . . . discolour gradually.'

'*Discolour*! Hardly an appropriate term, Doctor. As though he is not quite perfect or has become stained by tea or coffee or even tar!' She realized her voice verged on hysterical, but it reflected how she was feeling.

'He is still your child.'

'Really?'

He was offering her a very reasonable excuse. Many families with interests in the West Indies did indeed have African blood, which did, on occasion, lead to dark-skinned throwbacks.

But what if Tom saw the truth in her eyes? What would she do then?

She decided on attack and outright denial.

'And what do you think my husband will say about that? And other people, my friends, relatives?'

How will *I* cope? she thought. The small form snuggled

contentedly in her arms. The consequences of giving birth to a coloured child appalled her. She dragged her gaze away.

'He can't be mine!'

Embarrassed, Dr Owen looked at the floor. 'The child definitely has African antecedents. As I said, it is not unusual in families with West Indian connections, especially when families are separated . . . white men separated from white wives. Men have needs, and throwbacks have been known to occur, thus reflecting those previous . . . ah, indiscretions. He is your child, though born two weeks earlier than he should have been.'

Horatia felt herself turning cold. 'You know this?'

'Of course. The fingernails are the commonest giveaway.' He went on to explain certain other points, but she wasn't really listening. Two weeks made all the difference. Two weeks in her life, nine months ago.

Ancestry was the obvious excuse, the one she would have to give Tom. She thought of her father, of her half-sister Blanche, daughter of a former slave. She had accepted Blanche as an error on her father's part. Men behaving like men, she could understand. And men could get away with having tainted blood, but giving birth to a coloured child? A woman would be ostracized. Tom would be devastated. Could she be sure that he'd accept the doctor's explanation? Could she chance that he'd accept it?

Imagine seeing this child every day. Imagine how you will feel each time you see him. The child will remind you of what you are and what you have done. Can you really look Tom in the eyes and tell him what the doctor said?

All her dreams crashed earthwards but her mind was made up. A mistake had been made and, regardless of the cost, it had to be rectified.

Placing the child on the bed, she clasped her hands tightly in front of her and stared at the patterns on the bedspread as she considered her options. A host of satin roses danced before her eyes. She imagined the gossip, the cruel remarks and the slurs on her honour. The gossips would have a field day. No matter how much a son would mean to him, she could not, indeed she *would* not, present Tom with a coloured child.

'I can make arrangements for him,' said the doctor as if reading her thoughts.

Horatia's nostrils flared and her throat juddered. She t[...] breath and made a conscious effort not to look at the [...] formed face, the tiny hands and the rosebud mouth, pu[...] waiting to be kissed.

Her son began to cry, a demanding yell of a hungry child [...] his mother's warmth and sustenance. She would not pick him up. If she did, she'd be lost. Emotion would override common sense.

'I cannot keep him. It wouldn't be . . .' She searched for the appropriate words. It wasn't easy, and the word she chose seemed less than adequate. 'Acceptable,' she said, and felt her blood turn to ice.

The doctor paused as he too considered what the most powerful woman in the city wanted him to do. Horatia Strong, although married to an adopted orphan who had become a Strong, had inherited the family fortune in her own right. Her father had recognized that she was his most talented child and had, in his Will, overlooked his sons in favour of his daughter. Horatia was respected by those of influence in the city and known to be as ruthless in business as any man. He could well understand her reasoning. She could not allow anyone to find out that she had given birth to a coloured child, and certainly not her husband.

'Are you quite sure?'

She refused to look the doctor in the eyes, clenched her jaw and closed her heart. Tight-lipped, she said something then that she would regret for the rest of her life:

'I don't want him. Take him away.'

The doctor eyed her speculatively. The Strongs paid well for his services, and he had no intention of losing their patronage. 'Do you want to know where he'll go?'

She shook her head and turned her head away, as the bundle squirmed beside her, his small movements travelling through the bedding in soft little flutters.

'The nurse can be trusted,' the doctor said. 'I'll get her to come with me now on the pretext that there is something amiss with the child, but I will keep his face covered. Luckily the wet nurse has very poor eyesight so is easily deceived. Your servants will learn via a message I send that the child has died. You'll see neither the nurse nor the child again. Will that suit?'

Horatia kept her gaze fixed on the window and the garden beyond.

9

he trees were swiftly turning green. Spring was coming. Everything was bursting with life. Birds were building nests, lambs were being born; the world was busy renewing itself.

'I will write to my husband in the West Indies. I will tell him his son did not survive.'

'He will be disappointed, I take it?'

Horatia nodded and her jaw trembled with the effort of keeping it firm. 'Very. He wanted a son.'

'They'll think him very well dressed, sir,' said the nurse, as the doctor's gig rattled down the road towards St Philip's Marsh.

'You know what to say?'

'Yes, sir. That the child is of a good family, but the daughter got involved with a foreigner of Middle Eastern extraction.'

'Very good, Daisy.' Dr Owen gave her a few coins. 'Two sovereigns for your silence. Two sovereigns for the warden of this establishment. They won't ask any questions.'

'No, sir.'

The nurse secreted two of the coins in her apron pocket and tied the other two in a corner of the shawl.

The doctor caught hold of her shoulder. 'And neither will you. Do you understand? No questions. None at all!'

'Yes,' she said, nodding vehemently, her eyes never leaving his face. 'Yes. I mean no, sir. No questions at all, sir.'

Dr Owen pulled his chestnut cob to a halt at the corner of the stony road leading to St Philip's Workhouse. He watched thoughtfully as Daisy made her way towards the gate. It would have been easier to have pulled the bell and left the child outside, but leaving a little money might help the child survive. The mortality rate of babies left in the Workhouse was exceptionally high. There were few survivors.

Days went by and the parkland surrounding Marstone Court was sprinkled with wildflowers, an abundance of white, yellow, pink and blue. There was emptiness in Horatia's heart, although she convinced herself she'd done the right thing. But it wasn't easy to forget. As her strength returned, she reconsidered what she had done and whether she could go some way to improving matters. She was having terrible dreams, and in the morning the pain and regret remained. Her hand shook when she wrote to Tom. She kept her words plain. It was better that way.

When Dr Owen called to check that she was fully recovered, she gave in and asked him where he had taken the child.

He looked surprised. 'Do you really want to know?'

'I have to,' she said softly. 'It is my guilt, and my family's guilt. Though I would still swear you to secrecy.'

He told her.

'You may go,' she said without giving him chance to examine her, then turned her back on him and looked out on the verdant parkland.

'You have done the right thing,' he said in an obvious bid to reassure her.

She did not answer and he knew better than to pursue the matter.

Once the door was closed behind him, Horatia tore open the lid of her writing desk. After writing the most important note of her life, she sealed it in an envelope, called for a carriage and then sent the butler to call for Sears.

'I need to take some air,' Horatia said to her maid. 'Fetch my walking-out bonnet and my cape. Gloves, too.'

Sears, who usually accompanied her on shopping trips and general carriage rides, immediately fetched Horatia's walking clothes and also brought her own.

'You can hang your things up, Sears. I am going out alone.'

The corners of her maid's mouth drooped downwards and her cheeks sagged.

Sears watched the carriage leave, Horatia stiff and upright, staring straight ahead. The maid's bottom lip trembled. Her mistress was her life.

Sears busied herself tidying the contents of drawers, layering lavender bags between underwear, smoothing dresses and polishing her mistress's shoes and boots, the latter usually collected by an undermaid and cleaned by a boot boy. Filling her time helped keep her from feeling slighted. After all that she'd done! Nothing had ever been too much trouble, she thought as she rearranged shoes into colours and polished the silver knobs on the many bottles of creams Horatia used. Between each task, she got up and peered out of the window in case she had not heard the sound of horses returning.

She couldn't understand why Horatia had gone out alone. No lady of position ever went out without a chaperone. It just wasn't done.

Sears could not help but believe that her mistress had a secret mission and wondered what it was.

She dare not ask, of course. On Horatia's return, Sears fell on her, taking her bonnet, smoothing her cloak, telling her that everything was in order in her room, and that she trusted she'd had a good day.

But Horatia brushed aside her questions and retired to the study with orders that she was not to be disturbed.

Sears ran all the way up to the top floor, hid herself in an end room and burst into tears. Once she had regained her self-control, she went downstairs and waited for the moment when she could ask the only other person who knew where her mistress had been.

Later, when the coachman was rubbing down the horses, she asked him where he had taken Mrs Strong. She felt her face reddening in response to his scornful grin. It was well known that she doted on her mistress.

'Jealous, are you?'

Sears was indignant. 'I just asked you a question. I wondered if she was all right. She's had a baby, you know.'

'We all know,' he said disdainfully.

Sears felt as though she were going to cry. 'And the poor thing died. You can't possibly imagine how sad that makes a woman feel.'

Her ruse worked. The coachman, unwilling to be faced with a grizzling woman, relented. 'If you must know, she went to the Post Office in Bristol.'

Sears looked at him as though he'd just told her he could fly. Her sobs ceased immediately. 'The Post Office? Why would she want to go there?'

'To post a letter?'

That wasn't what she meant, but she wasn't going to bandy observations with a common coachman. The fact was that post at Marstone Court was usually given to a junior footman to take to the Post Office, perhaps once a week. No member of the Strong family ever went to the Post Office in person. It just wasn't done.

As she walked back to the house, her wide skirt bouncing as a result of her small, jerky steps, she decided she would not mention the matter to her mistress. Of course she wouldn't! Losing the baby and having to organize its funeral had upset Horatia. She'd had to do everything by herself and had felt a need to share the event with her husband by letter.

'It's only natural, my poor sweet,' she murmured, and dabbed at her nose, satisfied that she'd guessed correctly.

Horatia's heart felt more at ease after posting the letter. All she had to do now was lie to her husband. In the meantime she concentrated on regaining her strength, threw herself into business and social matters, and practised in private what she would say when Tom returned: 'We've lost a son, but still have a daughter. Let's be thankful for that.'

Chapter Two

Moonlight shone through the slatted shutters, throwing alternate bands of black and silver across the rich rugs and curtained bed.

Tom Strong was surfacing from a half-remembered dream, crossing over into that nebulous state where reality takes over and waking up is not too far distant. On the other side of the world, his wife was giving birth to his son. Only in dreams could he see the child, the years to come when he would grow big and strong, learn to ride, to sail and to box, just as his father had done.

Although he tried to hold onto it, the dream would not stay and he began to awaken.

Through half-closed eyes he saw the familiar bars of light and dark. He liked this room, and the way the moon bathed it with light.

He would normally have drifted back into sleep, but instead he jerked awake, aware that something had happened, though not quite sure what.

A rustling sound. Perhaps trees dancing before a sudden breeze, or sugarbirds disturbed from their night-time slumber. Alert now, he opened his eyes. The bars of light were suddenly interrupted by a flitting shadow.

He sat up.

Something or someone had rushed past the window.

He leapt from his bed and threw open the shutters. The shadow of Rivermead House, built by the Strong family in the previous century, fell over grass and gravel, giving it the appearance of a great, black lake.

The trees were still. A flock of birds circled overhead. Every so often they dived towards the trees, fluttered and took flight again.

Someone had disturbed them. Someone was still out there.

He reached for his clothes and headed outside.

The whole house was sleeping, and although it occurred to him to wake someone, he decided not to. It would take too long and by then whoever was lurking outside would be gone.

Trusting to his fists for protection, he ran outside, the grass wet beneath his bare feet. Ahead of him a figure moved into the moonlight before disappearing in the trees.

Avoiding the gravel path, Tom ran in that direction, legs made strong from years at sea propelling him swiftly over the ground. Clenching the fists that had put pay to many a fighter's dream of a good purse, he reached the wood.

The figure had vanished. The world seemed still, glades speckled with moonlight; he heard more rustling. He stopped and peered into the foliage, which wavered as though disturbed by a light breeze. Tonight there was no breeze.

'Who's there?'

Whoever hit him came from behind. His knees crumpled. He fell to the ground.

'Kill him,' he heard someone cry.

Then there was blackness. He heard nothing more.

'He's coming round.'

Tom opened his eyes then swiftly screwed them shut again. 'Oh my head!'

'It's a wonder you weren't killed.'

He recognized the voice of Rupert, managed to open his eyes a fraction and saw the gleam of his brother-in-law's complexion and the corn-coloured hair. Blue eyes came into focus. Dr Penfold, who owned a small plantation on the north of the island, stood next to him.

Attempting to raise his head proved a bad idea. He groaned as he fell back into the pliant goose down. 'What happened?'

'That's what we were going to ask you,' said Rupert, concerned.

'I heard someone outside. I went down to the copse and someone hit me over the head.'

'You were lucky,' said the doctor as he snapped the clasp of his black medicine bag. 'You have the skull of a coconut – perhaps even harder.'

The smell of lavender water filled Tom's head as Rupert leaned closer – his brother-in-law had grown into a fastidious adult. 'We can see what happened to you, my dear Tom, but how did you get back here? You certainly couldn't have walked.'

Tom frowned as he realized he was back in his own bed. Had he walked back? No. 'Where did you find me?'

He fully expected Rupert to say that he'd been laid out on the porch or propped up against the front door.

'Someone put you to bed and left a note with one of the servants.'

Again he attempted to raise his head. 'Who in hell—' The pain as he brought his head up from the pillow was unbearable. His head sank back again. He looked at the window then. As usual, the shutters were wide open.

'No,' said Rupert, reading his thoughts as the doctor was shown out. 'You didn't climb over the sill by yourself and, before you ask me how I know that, it's because someone was seen running away.'

'Did you see who it was?'

Rupert shook his head. 'Not me. Old Trevor saw a figure, but he's keeping quiet. I can't help thinking it's a relative of his. But you know how these people are . . .'

Tom sighed. He knew what Rupert meant. There was a lot of unrest on the island. There were ongoing feuds between rival factions, a struggle for power amongst Barbadian men and women drunk on a hard-won freedom and determined to gain more say in island affairs. But there were also jealousies amongst would-be leaders and some had a thirst for blood that no amount of freedom would ever assuage.

It was a few days before he recovered and during that time he contented himself with thinking of Horatia and the new baby. He hoped it would be a son. He knew she did too. He tried to imagine how it would look. Like him? Or like Horatia? His wife would be unbearable if it was a son. Like a noose around my neck, he thought, but a very nice one, and he smiled. Soon, he would receive news.

Marrying her had not been the best thing that had ever happened to him, but there it was. He'd vowed to be faithful, just as he had to his first wife who had died in Boston over ten years ago. Vows and promises were not made to be broken.

As he dozed off into fitful sleep, the vision of his wife stayed with him. He was trying to remember the night the child was conceived, but he couldn't quite grasp the details. Each time he reached for the warmth of her body, the ample roundness of her breasts and the inviting moistness between her loins, she began to move and, as she moved, she changed.

Horatia never moved when they made love, but merely lay there. Sometimes, if the lamp was on or the room was flooded by moonlight, he could see her expression and he'd automatically tense. If she caught him looking at her, she would smile and pretend to be aroused, but he knew she wasn't. She loved him and wanted him, but had acquired him just as she might a painting or a splendid piece of sculpture, something to be admired. She had always seemed incapable of sexual enjoyment, which is why a second child had taken so long in coming. She was satisfied that he was her husband, like the chestnut gelding who just happened to be her favourite horse. In bed her air of non-participation was akin to being drenched in cold water.

In his dream the body that moved beneath him had a different face, grey eyes and a dark complexion. The woman of his dreams was not his wife, Horatia, but Blanche Heinkel, his wife's half-sister and the widow of a man who used to be his friend.

The dream did not easily disperse. He tried to push it away, to supplant it with a vision of Horatia and his new baby, but it kept coming back.

A week later he cornered Trevor and asked him who he'd seen running away from the house on the night he'd received the hefty crack over the head.

'I'd like to thank him,' he said. 'He saved my life.'

'I don't know who it was, Mr Thomas.' Trevor, who was surely in his mid-eighties, shook his head, but Tom didn't believe him. His eyes were round with worry, and he looked in any direction rather than meet Tom's eyes.

'Trevor. Trust me. Please!'

Something in Tom's tone had an effect. Trevor squirmed and thought about it.

'I can't tell you for sure,' he said eventually. 'You know how it is. There's some who would kill him for what he done.'

Tom frowned. 'For saving my life?'

Trevor nodded and licked his lips. He was obviously nervous about saying anything. There were some dangerous people on the island.

'Now they want to kill him. They're calling him a white man's washcloth. Says he might be free, but in his head he's still a slave.'

Tom sighed. Intimidation hadn't ceased with slavery. Humanity put up its own barriers to true freedom. Toe the line or you cease to belong.

'So he's hiding?'

Trevor looked away. 'You could say that.'

'Will you at least tell me his name? Perhaps I can help him.'

Trevor shook his head. 'Best if you talk to someone they wouldn't dare kill.'

'Like whom?'

'Talk to Desdemona DeWitt.' He lowered his voice. 'His grandmother. They won't hurt her. She's too old and knows too much about the old ways. They're frightened of her. She lives in the old slave compound near Cleveland Rise.'

Tom knew it. Shacks that had once housed slaves were slowly being reclaimed by the wilderness. The trees were thick there, the last remnant of an ancient forest.

'I thought that place was long abandoned.'

Trevor smiled and admiration shone in his eyes. 'Not by her.'

Rupert insisted on coming with him. 'You need me to look after you. See?' He held up his fists and posed like a bare-knuckle fighter.

Grinning broadly, Tom took hold of Rupert's hand, forced it open and fingered the unblemished palm. 'As soft as a baby's bottom.'

Rupert looked peeved, but quickly recovered. 'I'm still coming with you.'

The old slave compound at Cleveland Rise was approached by a narrow path that wound through thick undergrowth.

Little sunlight penetrated through the overhead canopy of tangled branches. Brightly coloured birds and butterflies flashed through the gloom and Rupert chased them with his butterfly net, the true reason he had wanted to come.

Desdemona DeWitt's house was built of rough stone, with a roof of thatched palm leaves. A plume of smoke crawled skywards from a single clay pot that looked as if it had been stuck on as an afterthought. It seemed far too grand for such a shabby hut.

The lizards sunbathing on the roof fascinated Rupert.

'We're not here to study the wildlife,' said Tom with an air of impatience.

Instantly taking the criticism to heart, Rupert poked his nose forward and shouted, 'Is anyone there?'

The silence was strangely deafening. Tom kept his gaze fixed on the lop-sided door of odd-sized planks, which were nailed together in haphazard fashion.

'Perhaps she's dead,' whispered Rupert.

Tom told him to be quiet.

'You be members of the Strong family?' The voice was high-pitched, oddly attractive and took them unaware.

Rupert looked at Tom astounded. 'How did she know that?'

Tom shrugged. 'Can we come in? I mean no harm. I just want to thank your grandson for saving my life and perhaps save his, but I can't find him.'

Again a pause. 'Come in, but be careful with my door.'

There was no sign of wavering in her voice, no thin wail of old age.

Tom opened the door carefully, catching a piece of wood as it slid off its frame. He leaned the whole thing against the side of the hut, bent his head and entered. Rupert followed.

The hut was small, the floor packed mud and the shutters woven grass. There was a bed made from saplings, its mattress a single blanket tied with string to the frame. A cooking pot hung from a tripod over a bed of glowing embers. A curtain of mauve muslin hung from the wall, though on closer inspection Tom saw it was a dress of the style women wore at the turn of the century. The cloth had yellowed in places and it looked in danger of falling to pieces, but at one time it had been beautiful.

Desdemona DeWitt was tiny. She was sitting in an armchair that might once have graced a plantation mansion. The wooden arms were shiny from years of use, their lion heads polished by years of restless hands. The old woman's bare feet hung ten inches short of the floor. Her eyes were like glossy black buttons gazing out from sunken hollows, and her face was a mass of wrinkles, like the tough skin of an old russet apple.

She waved her hand as though bidding them to sit down.

Tom barely glanced around him before hunkering down in front of her. Rupert still looked for a non-existent chair.

19

Desdemona looked amused. The only chair was the one she was sitting in.

Tom began to explain. 'I owe your grandson my life. I feel I have to do something for him.'

'Hmm!'

He spread his hands to emphasize the point. 'I wouldn't want to think he put himself in any danger at my expense.'

'Hmm!'

Tom exchanged a look with Rupert. He wasn't getting anywhere, but if he expected any help from Rupert, he was very much mistaken. Rupert seemed as stuck for words as he was.

He persisted. 'Does he lack for anything?'

Desdemona closed one eye and fixed him hard and fast with the other. 'Lack fer anything? We darkies have *always* lacked, Master Strong. Know what an in'eritance is?'

Tom nodded. 'Yes.'

'No!' Her voice rang like a bell. Wings in the nearby thicket fluttered and took off. A lizard lazing in the sunlight that fell through the door scurried into the shadows.

'No,' she said again. 'You knows yer own, but you don't know ours.' She waved the stem of her pipe at him.

Resting his elbows on his knees, Tom clasped his hands together and considered what to say. He also considered leaving and was aware that Rupert was fidgeting. We can't face what an old woman has to say, he thought. Why is that? Rupert coughed and excused himself.

The silence, the sound of insects and birds and the rustling of dark-green foliage in an itinerant breeze made the heat seem more than usually oppressive. Unblinking, her gaze stayed fixed on his face.

'I'll tell ye of my in'eritance,' she said then. 'There was a woman of Africa, brought 'ere to be a slave. One day, she wanted fuel for her cooking pot and didn't have any. Nor did she 'ave the money to buy any. Desperate she was, and 'er children were hungry, so she stole some fuel and got found out.'

The old woman paused, took a puff of her pipe. Tom heard Rupert kicking at dust and stones outside.

'This woman was fierce for her children. Fierce for their lives. When she got found out, she proclaimed she didn't care; that she'd die for her children if need be. It was the worse thing she could have said. She wadn't regretful about what she done, you see. She wadn't regretful at all, and the master, Mister Oliver, he was angry. So they cart-whipped her.'

A kind of adverse loyalty to plantation owners, and more particularly to the Strong family, made Tom want to protest that this couldn't be true, that no man could do this to a mother who simply wanted to feed her family. But the words stuck in his throat.

'You know what that means?' she asked him.

He nodded. 'That means they tied her to a cart-wheel to whip her.'

The pipe wobbled at the corner of her mouth but her eyes held no hate.

'They stripped my ma naked in front of everybody.' She shook her head. 'Nothing shames a woman more. Her body's only fer her family and her man to see. But they didn't care. They whipped her. Thirty-nine times. Her back was a mass of red stripes after that. The next day they asked her whether she repented her sin and would never do it again. My mother refused. She swore at them and told them she'd do anything for her children.' The old woman shook her head again. 'So they decided another thirty-nine stripes might make her more repentant. By the following day her back was a mass of blood and she could barely stand. But that wadn't good enough for them, no, sir it wadn't. They said they didn't believe she wadn't fit to work, so to prove it one way or t'other, they boiled up pepper and poured it over her back. If she jumped up she was fine for work. But she didn't jump up. The shock killed her.'

Tom felt his stomach churning. 'I'm ashamed,' he said, his hands clasped between his knees.

Tilting her head to one side, the old woman looked at him speculatively, as if she didn't quite understand why he should say that. 'You weren't there. T'ain't nothin' to do with you. It's my in'eritance and my grandson's in'eritance and I'm tellin' you all about it. Ain't very pretty, is it?'

He shook his head. 'No.'

'That's why he's gone and shifted fer 'imself. Had enough of all this . . .' She took the pipe from her mouth and waved at her surroundings. 'We DeWitts is a bit of everythin', not just African. Dutch, British, African; we got a bit of everythin' in our blood.' She chuckled wickedly to herself. 'Men is men. Hot climates, hot men.

My grandson – his name is Samson, Master Strong – he gives respect to his African ancestors and his English ancestors. He'd always felt split in half like that and he was tired of the plantation.' She shook her head again. 'It ain't what it used to be. So he's gone to England. Once he's there he'll find his aunt's cousin. She married a sugar refiner. Don't know her married name. Don't know where he come from. Just know she's there and that Samson is set on finding her.' She chuckled again. 'But there, you knows how this Strong family is; and my Samson, like his aunt's relative and a few other of us, got more than a cupful of Strong blood in our veins.'

Tom heard his heart ticking, louder and louder, rising up through his body and thudding behind his aching eyes. Samson's relative in England was married to a sugar refiner. Dare he ask her name? His throat was parched and he was sure that if he got to his feet too quickly, he'd fall down again. Although he was sure he knew the identity of the woman Samson sought, he wanted it confirmed in the dank, shadowy surroundings of the mud-plastered hut with its roof of leaves and twigs.

'This relative. What is her name?'

Desdemona tapped out the contents of her pipe on the flaking plaster of the hut wall. 'Blanche,' she said with an air of affection. 'Blanche Bianca, and a pretty little girl she used to be.'

With the name ringing like a bell in his head, Tom got to his feet and thanked her. 'One more question,' he said, his muscular frame filling the doorway. 'Were you ever whipped?'

Her eyes glittered as she stared at him. She seemed to weigh him up with unblinking eyes before she slid down from her chair, turned her back on him and lifted the worn cotton bodice she wore with a blue skirt. Her back was a mass of healed stripes, a welter of raised lines criss-crossing and scaly, like the skin of the lizards that ran over her roof and bathed in the sunlit doorway.

'Do you believe that?' Rupert asked him as he mounted his horse.

'You heard?'

Rupert shrugged. 'I didn't like hearing all that about whipping. It makes me feel uncomfortable.'

Urging his horse forward, Tom nodded grimly. 'It should make us all feel uncomfortable. A civilized man shouldn't have such a thing in his history. It's a blot on the soul.'

Rupert fell silent. He clearly didn't want to be reminded that the Strong wealth was based on sugar and enslavement of others.

Tom's brow was furrowed as they rode back through the lush green vegetation that divided the old compound from the biggest cane field. Powder-puff clouds spilled from the interior into a sky so blue he wanted to dive into it. The sun was warm, and vivid birds skimmed the tops of the cane spears.

If the Garden of Eden had ever existed, it would have looked like this, thought Tom, yet even now, some sought exile in a land of grey skies and gales. Samson's running away to England troubled him. Escaping his problems was understandable, but arriving on Blanche's doorstep could cause enormous problems for her. Things had changed since the young Blanche Bianca had first arrived in England. At the beginning of the century, so long as a person had money and a family name, he or she would be accepted despite their origins. The burgeoning of a mighty empire had changed all that.

'Will you tell her?' Rupert asked, reining his horse alongside that of Tom's on their arrival back at Rivermead House. The same thought had obviously occurred to him.

'So you heard that, too?'

Rupert nodded. 'Look, Tom. I know how you felt about Blanche.'

'It was a long time ago. We both married.' Tom avoided looking at Rupert.

'You don't need to see her to warn her. You can just send word. I won't have you slighting my sister, but I have an affection for Blanche too, you know.'

'As a servant.'

Rupert seemed stuck for words at first. 'Well . . . yes. She was our nanny when I was young.'

Tom shook his head. 'What good would it do?'

Rupert scratched at his forehead with the butt of his riding crop. 'At least she'd be forewarned and could ensure the matter was dealt with as discretely as possible. Perhaps I should tell her. You know most people think her dark colouring is due to Spanish descent not Negro. She could never be accepted in polite society again if her true origins were known.'

Tom stiffened, dismounted and loosened his horse's girth. Rupert's words were like splinters piercing his heart. Exasperated, he leaned his head against the saddle, breathing in the smell of leather and sweating horseflesh. He had an overwhelming urge to turn round and fling another truth into Rupert's face: *She's your half-sister. Your father raped her mother*. It would be possible that Rupert would never speak to him again. If the episode in Desdemona's hut was anything to go by, Rupert could not cope with unsavoury truths.

Despite the attack and warnings from Dr Penfold that it was dangerous to be out after sundown, Tom walked through the darkness towards a house where climbing plants had run riot over a wrought-iron veranda. He settled himself in a rickety chair and eyed the dark silhouettes of trees against an indigo sky.

This was the old house where Blanche Bianca had grown up. He closed his eyes. The feeling of peace here was extraordinary and the night breeze was cool on his face. The sound of singing insects and rustling leaves was hypnotic.

One day I will bring my son here, he thought, opened his eyes and caught a glimpse of the sparkling sea through the black curtains of foliage.

One day, my son will go to the best school in Bristol. I will teach him to box, to ride and to sail.

And we will be happy, he thought as he drifted into sleep. We will all be happy.

Chapter Three

The cough had started in the spring. The doctor prescribed rest and suggested a stay in the city of Bath and the drinking of its famous water.

Feeling pressurized, and not liking it one little bit, Blanche had protested that she was not an invalid.

The doctor had adopted a fierce look and peered at her over the top of his pince-nez. 'You will be if you ignore my advice.'

She'd acquiesced, but only on the understanding he would not tell her family just how sick she was. The waters would cure the little tickle she had . . .

To her great surprise, she enjoyed the genteel atmosphere and old world charm of a once-fashionable city. There was less traffic than in Bristol and besides the imposing crescents, quaint alleys and walk-throughs designed for sedan chairs, there were open spaces of grass and well-tended gardens.

Her cough improved with the spring sunshine and the blossoming daffodils, narcissi, tulips and lilies-of-the-valley.

The Ambassador Hotel, recommended to her by the doctor, became like a second home, and she enjoyed watching people, passing the time of day with both the residents and the staff. It became an antidote to the silence of her home in Somerset Parade where she had only servants for company.

The house in Bristol once rang with the sound of happy children and the big, bluff presence of Conrad, her husband. Now it seemed so empty. The children were grown and married, all but Lucy, the youngest, and Max, her eldest son. Lucy attended a ladies' college and Max had stepped into Conrad's shoes, which he sometimes found far too big, though would never admit it. He was very protective of the Heinkel family interests and was determined to be accepted on equal terms by the older, more experienced men with whom he did business. Sometimes his intensity clutched at her heart because he still seemed so boyish, a minnow striving to be noticed in the pond where the big fish swam.

The Ambassador Hotel had spacious rooms, attentive staff and an aloof clientele, which suited her well. She did not seek company, only the sights and sounds of people bustling around her, confirmation that life went on regardless. In her solitude, she had time to think and ponder on life, death and eternity.

A fellow guest nodded and doffed his hat now as she entered the hotel. Blanche smiled at him. He winked. She feigned embarrassment and looked away. Middle-aged ladies no longer attracted the attention of men – at least that's what she'd come to believe on reaching her fortieth birthday. Her cheeks dimpled as she smiled into her gloved hand and caught a glimpse of herself in the glass of the hotel's revolving door.

Black suits me, she thought. I might never return to wearing violet, pink, lemon and powder-blue again. But I would definitely like a new hat. Despite the lack of sunshine and her illness, her complexion was still darker than average and glowed against the blackness of her clothes.

'Your tea is served, madam,' said the concierge, inviting her to take it in the lounge.

The hotel's lounge had comfortable chairs and huge glass windows overlooking Pulteney Weir. The view was splendid. A painting of the Rialto Bridge in Venice hung in close proximity to the windows, its position, obviously in a bid to elicit a favourable comparison, making Blanche smile.

She didn't accept the chair offered in a quiet corner, but chose one with a good view of the bridge. The tea tray followed, the waiter trying to maintain the waxwork disdain his employer preferred, though his eyes shone with admiration. Solitary females usually opted for seclusion behind a potted palm or a strategically placed Chinese screen, a kind of imposed purdah if they had no chaperone or man to keep them company. Mrs Blanche Heinkel pleased herself.

'And how is your daughter Mary, Sam?' she asked the concierge as he personally poured her tea.

'Very well, madam. She has only been working here just one month, and has already made her mark.'

Blanche smiled in a way that some might construe as being too friendly towards a servant. But she liked Sam. He'd always taken care of her and there had been a mutual warmth between them from the first time they'd met.

'You're lucky she has found an appointment so close to home.'

'I'm most grateful, madam. She enjoys looking after children.'

The years fell away, and Blanche remembered when she'd first come to England and, to her great surprise, ended up as the Strongs' nanny at Marstone Court. 'I trust she is well treated?'

'Very well indeed.'

Sam took his leave and said he would pass on her good wishes to Mary.

Other eyes studied her, perhaps disapprovingly, as she sat sipping her tea. It was hardly her fault. She wasn't old and neither was she ugly.

She had not expected to become a widow before she turned forty. But Conrad had been a big, bluff man with a hearty appetite and, as his weight had soared, his heart had given out.

She settled back into her chair, a gilt-edged cup and saucer in her hand, and eyed the recently built carbuncles hanging from the back of the buildings that lined Pulteney Bridge. They were hideous and spoilt the Italianate architecture the designer had sought hard to achieve. She turned her attention to the painting and smiled again. Bath was a vain city, albeit a beautiful one.

She was still smiling when she heard a voice that fixed her smile to her lips.

'Blanche?'

Her eyesight was not quite as good as it was, and for a split second she thought Nelson Strong was standing there, which was quite impossible. Nelson, her half-brother, was dead, swept overboard in a terrible storm. But the man standing there had the same corn-coloured hair, the same build and the same merry twinkle in his eye. The face, however, was plumper and unsullied by dissolute living, as Nelson's had been.

Setting down the teacup, she rose to her feet. 'Rupert! How nice to see you.'

'I hope you don't mind my intrusion.'

'No. Please. Sit down.' She gestured to a chair close to her own. 'Would you like tea?' She raised her hand to summon a waiter.

'No . . . oh . . . perhaps . . . yes.'

The waiter went to fetch another cup and saucer.

They talked first about the family and his marriage to an heiress that had doubled his fortune, and finally the situation in Barbados. They spoke as friends. Rupert was ignorant of their relationship. She would not enlighten him of the family's dark secret.

Blanche felt instantly homesick, something she hadn't felt for years. White sand, a warm sea and white-topped waves breaking over glistening rocks, she remembered them all. The old memories got the better of her and she couldn't help interrupting.

'Did you notice the sky?'

'The sky?'

'It's so very blue. Didn't you notice that? And the clouds are like fat sheep skipping over the sea. Surely you noticed?'

Rupert looked nonplussed. He was used to people asking him about what it was like to live there, if it was worth holding onto sugar plantations now that sugar beet was being refined in such quantities and whether the country was going to the dogs in the aftermath of slavery, but no one had asked him about the sky before.

They talked more of the family over tea.

'I heard of Horatia's loss.'

Rupert looked at her blankly as if he had something else on his mind though, goodness knows, what could be more important than a baby dying shortly after birth? Thank God, she thought, that none of mine died as babies, although Anne, her eldest daughter, had passed away at the age of eight from cholera. The loss still pained Blanche.

'The baby,' she said simply. 'I sent my deepest sympathies.'

'Oh yes,' he said. 'Of course.'

'I take it Tom was devastated by this terrible event.'

'Yes,' he said, and lowered his eyes.

She knew immediately that this was not just a chance visit. He had something important to say to her. He seemed nervous about it. She wondered what it could be and decided she didn't want to wait. If he needed a nudge, then a nudge he would get.

'Why are you here, Rupert?'

He bit his lip and was a boy again, a mix of bravado and hesitation. He gave a tight, nervous laugh. 'Must I be here for a reason?'

28

Blanche sat back in her chair and looked at him accusingly. 'Only my family knows that I'm here. You have obviously made enquiries of them and taken the trouble to travel here to see me.'

'I do have some business in Bath,' he blurted. 'My wife and I were thinking of buying a house here.'

'But you've sought me out. What is it, Rupert? What is so important that you made enquiries and travelled here to see me?'

Rupert took a deep breath. 'You have a nephew named Samson.'

She shook her head. 'I think you mean my cousin. His father was my mother's half-brother.'

'Ah!'

'But he's younger than me. He always called me aunt.'

Rupert nodded and couldn't find the courage to raise his eyes and look at her. 'He's come to England and is looking for you.'

Although the news startled her, Blanche regarded him silently, waiting for him to continue.

'I don't think I need to point out what this might do to your standing in the city if the truth became known.'

Her nostrils flared and she clenched her hands tightly together in her lap. She knew immediately what he was getting at, and imagined the sniggers, the asides, the innuendoes such knowledge might attract. Invitations to soirées, dinners, balls and seats on charity boards would dry up because of her West Indian origins. She could live with that, she decided. But what about Max? What about her daughters Adeline and Lucy? How would they cope?

'I promised Tom I would warn you,' Rupert went on, diverting his gaze to a potted palm.

Despite her annoyance, her heart fluttered. 'Thank him for me, will you?'

'I am here looking for a house, so it was no trouble to—'

'Don't lie, Rupert.'

Her perception took him by surprise. 'Goodness,' he said, shaking his head and smiling. 'You brought me up short then – just as you used to when I was a boy. Shouldn't be surprised, of course. You always were one step ahead of me.'

'Especially when we flew kites in the park,' she said, a nostalgic sparkle brightening her eyes.

Rupert had been a boy when she'd first arrived at Marstone Court.

She remembered him climbing trees and his devotion to Tom Strong. It still showed in his eyes, and she was glad it did.

But he was no longer a boy. Day by day, the British Empire was expanding its territory and its influence. Young men like Rupert were ruling that world and had firm views on what was and was not acceptable.

What he said next surprised her.

He leaned closer, an intense expression hardening his eyes. 'The best thing you can do is to get a servant to answer the door and tell Samson and his family to go away.'

She was speechless.

He reached for his hat and got up. 'You should be thanking me for telling you. I promised Tom I would and that the information would go no further. We accept you for who you are, but you have to understand that not everybody—'

'I'm tired,' she said suddenly, her face burning with fear and confusion. 'I think you should go.'

She stayed staring out of the window onto Pulteney Bridge long after Rupert had left, thinking about what she should do if Samson and his family came knocking at her door. Her children knew nothing of their West Indian ancestry or that Emmanuel Strong was her father. They knew of her maternal grandfather, the sea captain, who, she told them, had married a woman of Spanish origin. Conrad had advised her to concoct an alternative story when she'd been younger and at her lowest ebb. It had been all part of his plan to ease her transition from daughter of a slave to a lady of status. It had worked. So why was she feeling so angry?

Conrad was no longer there to curb her impetuousness or emotions. Rupert would never have noticed it, but she'd felt angry with him for reminding her that she had lied to her children. And what if she did tell them the truth? She refused to accept that her children, who had been brought up in the Christian household of Conrad Heinkel, a leading light in the Unitarian Church, were likely to condemn her for her ancestry.

Once the anger had subsided, she began putting her thoughts in some sort of order. She thought of Lucy's finishing school, Adeline's marriage and Max's enthusiasm for being accepted as an equal by the businessmen of Bristol. His youth already counted against him. Could she really gamble his future against her principles?

That night she slept badly, her heart and her head battling. Perhaps she might have accepted the news more calmly if Tom had brought it. She wished that he had, but could understand his reasons for not doing so.

She was now a widow, but Tom was still married. One breath of scandal, and Horatia Strong would make their lives a misery.

Chapter Four

Like a thousand, thousand tears, the rain dripped from overhead branches where springtime buds sprouted like small green hearts. Between tilted gravestones, long grass lay flattened into damp mattresses of last year's stalks and this year's shoots.

Her face stiff with tension, Horatia Strong watched from beneath a black umbrella as Tom approached the family mausoleum. This was the moment she'd been dreading. She hated herself for what she had done. What kind of woman would deceive her husband into thinking that their son was buried here?

Tom would despise her if he ever found out the truth. It must *not* happen. She had made arrangements to guarantee it. She pushed away her guilt with all her might. It was like pushing shut a heavy oak door.

The rain dripped from the brim of Tom's hat and down his neck as he gazed at the words engraved in gold block lettering:

Isaiah Thomas Strong
Born 12 February
Died 17 February
In the Year of Our Lord 1848

Hesitantly, he reached out, his fingers tracing each letter of their son's first name. Then his arm fell to his side. He bowed his head and turned away.

Watching him do it made her heart flutter and her limbs tremble. She slipped her arm into his. 'We could try for another baby.'

It was nonsense of course. Dr Owen had told her to refrain from bearing another child.

'There are ways, my dear lady,' he had told her, his eyes suitably downcast as though he were prescribing nothing more than a stomach powder, instead of abstinence from sexual relations.

Tom didn't look at her. She felt terribly hurt. She so wanted him to move closer to her – not in the physical sense, although heaven knew, the act of marital intimacy did not happen very often – but emotionally, a sharing of sorrow.

'Did you hear what I said? We could have another—'

'I think not,' he said, his tone deep but distant.

Her chest tightened. The air felt colder when she breathed it, and not just because of the rain. Although he walked beside her, it was as though her husband, Tom Strong, were somewhere else, somewhere warmer and happier, and with someone for whom he felt true passion. Without a moment's hesitation, she mentioned the one subject that would bring him back to her side.

'We still have Emerald. We have to remember that.'

His tension eased, his eyes flickered and he gave her a curt nod. 'Yes.'

He took hold of the umbrella and Horatia hugged his arm more closely to her side.

They were as one, locked together in grief. He would be presuming that her thoughts were as sad as his, which, in a way, they were. The child was gone.

But the closeness was good, and she found herself wishing they could be this way for ever.

They walked back to Marstone Court. The rain that had poured since breakfast finally stopped and the sun shone through. A bright rainbow pierced the clouds, an arc of colour ending somewhere towards the Avon Gorge, just below where Mr Brunel had built a brick tower that would eventually form part of the new bridge.

They stopped and silently admired it.

'We have to be thankful for what we have and cease grieving for what we have lost,' Tom said at last.

Horatia caught her breath. The lie had worked. She should have felt relief, but didn't. The guilt lay more heavily. She had told the most terrible lie to the man she loved. He didn't deserve to be deceived so badly, and in her heart of hearts she believed she would live to regret it.

33

*

Samson Rivermead, his wife and two young children spent most of the time being sick on the crossing from Barbados to Bristol. The journey had taken longer than anticipated on account of bad weather. Pitching and rolling in the fast race that runs between the rump of southern Ireland and the Welsh coast, the ship had run for Queenstown where it had stayed until the wind had died and the waves diminished.

The sun was shining and a rainbow spanned the Avon Gorge as the ship made its way upriver.

'Look,' said Samson. 'A rainbow. That means no more rain. God Almighty sent a rainbow after the great flood, his promise that there would be no more rain. It's a good omen,' he said, mostly to himself. The storms, the journey, the food and the general conditions had made him question his decision to leave Barbados. If he'd stayed he might well have been killed, purely for disagreeing with a plot to attack civilians rather than the military garrison. There had been times in the midst of the Atlantic when he swore that some old witch had stirred up this storm to get him anyway.

'The rainbow's a good sign,' he said again.

The sky had turned grey by the time their ship docked.

The customs officer asked for their names and Samson eagerly replied. Out of habit he called the man 'sir', and felt no different for doing so.

The officer adopted a disbelieving expression. 'That's a fancy name for a black man. You sure you didn't pinch it?'

Samson frowned. 'No, sir! My family used to work for the Strong family. They comes from Bristol, but their plantation in Barbados was called Rivermead, so we got given the name Rivermead, too.'

Surprised, the customs officer looked him up and down. 'Is that so? Would they be the Strongs who live at Marstone Court?'

Samson shrugged. He'd never heard Marstone Court mentioned by anyone he knew. All he'd ever known was that the family hailed from the city of Bristol in England. Its exact position on the west coast he'd worked out on their journey across with the help of the sun, the stars and the sight of land after they'd crossed the Atlantic Ocean.

Assuming the man would at least be polite, he said, 'I'm looking for an aunt of mine. Her name's Blanche Bianca. Would you know where she lives?'

The officer smirked and winked at his colleagues. 'Well, she wouldn't be living at Marstone Court, would she? Not if she speaks and looks anything like you anyways!'

There were chortles from others gathered there, and perhaps the things they said might have become more cutting, but a crowd of people were pouring off an adjacent ship, falling to their knees and kissing the ground, some crossing themselves.

The customs officer frowned. 'Bloody Irish!' he muttered under his breath as he stalked off towards them. 'Let's hope the wind changes soon and they're off again to America. Best bloody place for 'em!'

Samson thought of the big houses back in Barbados. He'd always avoided them. They were too intimidating. He'd avoid this one too and look for a lead elsewhere.

Samson's wife, Abigail, took in the bustling seaport, its tall buildings surrounding the quays and the others that pressed behind, like an army trailing over the hills around them. 'What do we do, Samson?'

He tucked his son, Hamlet, beneath his arm and stroked his chin. There were so many buildings and so many people. Where did they go? What did they do?

He looked behind him at the filthy water. In Barbados the water had been blue. Here it was almost black and didn't smell too good, and yet he felt loath to stray too far from it.

'Follow the river,' he said, picking up one of the six bundles they'd brought with them. 'We'll find somewhere to stay first. There's sure to be somewhere beside the water.'

Samson did not know it, but he'd soon strayed from the river and branched off along the towpath beside the canal. Waterside cottages, their front gardens thick with cabbages, raspberry canes and gooseberry bushes, bordered its banks. Older houses, built before the canal, leaned against each other. Some were derelict, their gables gaping and roofs open to the sky. A man with white whiskers supping ale outside an ancient inn watched him with narrowed eyes.

Samson gave him no regard. His priority was to find a bed for the night.

Those lodging houses that did look fairly decent had no vacancies, and those that looked dark, dirty and slowly decaying, he refused to consider.

His daughter Desdemona began to drag her feet. 'I'm wearied.'

'I know, I know,' he said in a way meant to chivvy her that bit further. 'We come a long way. Come all across the ocean, so we ain't gonna let a bit of walking get between us and a bed for the night, are we?'

Desdemona grunted a half-hearted agreement.

Dusk was falling. The heart of the city was behind them, although the smell of soot hung in the air, and he reckoned they'd walked at least a mile. The water had swerved between the left and right of them and it no longer looked like a river. The banks were without undulation, the sides rigid with brick or stone, and foliage hanging wetly over the water.

By the time they came across the narrowboat, the lamplighter had started his rounds and an isolated gas lamp popped into existence.

Samson had never seen such a boat as this, a riot of colour, and the light falling from its tiny window proclaimed a general air of cosiness. A ginger cat curled around the smokestack and bluebirds and roses cavorted around the castles painted on its side. It was moored close to a narrow bridge, only wide enough for pedestrians. He smelled tobacco, saw it glimmer and stepped closer.

The smoker moved slightly. She was sitting close to a small door where the smell of greasy bacon and stewed tea drifted out into the night.

Samson put down his bundles and rubbed his sweating palms down his trousers. He approached the woman nervously. 'Excuse me, missus.'

Although the light was fading and her features were indistinct, he knew she was looking at him.

'I'm looking for a room for the night for me and me family.'

He heard her lips smacking as she took the stem of a slow-burning pipe from her mouth. 'Come to the right place, then.'

Her voice was cracked, though strong, and her accent was similar to some he'd heard so far, though not exactly the same. He'd become aware of the strength of his own accent and that some people did not understand him very well, so he'd modulated his voice. Speaking more slowly seemed the best way forward.

Assessing the length of the boat and the fact that most of it was taken up with cargo, he took it she was not offering to share her home.

'You know of somewhere, missus?'

'I do. Four of you, is there?'

'Yes.' Pausing, he thought of the grim places he'd passed where the dirt on the windows matched the scum floating down in the harbour. 'Don't mean to be disrespectful, missus. But is it a clean place?'

'Course! 'Tis me sister's place. Right there. Right there behind yer.'

The house she pointed at was thin as a reed and squashed between two larger buildings, one of which was a public house called The Three Horseshoes.

'Ellbroad 'ouse. That's what me sister calls it. On account that the bridge is called Ellbridge, and the lane running at the side of the 'ouse is called Broad Passage.'

Although he felt like throwing his arms around the woman's neck, Samson's gratefulness sang through his voice. 'I am truly very grateful to you, missus,' he said, taking extra care to talk slowly so there would be no misunderstanding.

'She charges one and six a week for a room. Go knock on 'er door. Tell 'er Aggie sent you.'

Round-eyed with apprehension and shaking with exhaustion, Samson and his family approached Ellbroad House.

'It looks clean.'

Samson glanced at his wife. Inwardly, he sighed with relief. Abigail had been miserably sick on the journey over and sullen since their landfall. A good sleep and a good meal and all would be well. They'd stay here until he found his Aunt Blanche.

The *Demerara Empress*, the biggest ship built for the Strong Shipping Line, was being unloaded of her cargo of sugar. All of it was destined for the riverside wharf of Heinkel's Sugar Refinery, which was situated on a stretch of the river called The Counterslip that was too narrow for seagoing vessels. Onward transition required the use of a fleet of barges, a tiresome task costing both time and labour.

Four hogsheads to a net were being swung over the side by quayside cranes, which were operated by a hand-cranking mechanism. Each cask was then lifted onto the brawny backs of dockside labourers. In an unending crocodile, they heaved and puffed their way to a waiting barge.

Tom Strong frowned. He didn't like his ships entering the narrower parts of the city docks, and he knew it couldn't go on. Something had to be done if Heinkel's was to survive. Max was young and Tom convinced himself that he'd be open to suggestions. It was just a question of persuading him to see sense.

He eyed the young man who stood next to him, the stubborn set of his jaw and the quickness of his eyes counting the barrels as they were taken from one vessel to another. There were so many things he would have liked to say to Blanche's son – who was also his son – but he could not. Few people knew that there was any connection between them, and certainly not Max. All he could do was try to reason with him, to guide him as best he could but without arousing his suspicion.

'This is a very big problem,' he said, measuring his tone so he wouldn't sound overbearing.

He knew he'd failed when he saw Max's features set like cement. 'It's your ships that are too big.'

'They'll get bigger; and not just ours. It's progress. Nothing can stop it from happening.'

'I intend to try.'

Although exasperated, Tom maintained his equilibrium. This job had been foisted on him. Neither his shareholders nor his insurers were prepared to entertain the risk of berthing larger and larger steamships here for any longer. Much as it might dent Max's pride, his inexperience was showing through.

'I know how you feel, Max. It saddened me to see the demise of sail. You can't imagine how it felt in the days when there was no steam pouring from a blackened stack, no smell of soot, just the wind in our sails, the cry of seabirds and the rush of water against the side of the ship. All those things are gone, and much as I would like to, there's no turning the clock back. Steamships are getting bigger; that, I am afraid, is a fact.'

He waved a silver-topped cane at the ship, the toiling men and the barge needed to take the cargo from ship to refinery.

'This is too slow a process, Max. Why don't you reconsider a new property at Avonmouth where our ships can unload directly into the refinery? It could very well increase your output and make Heinkel's the main refiner in Bristol.'

'We do not restrict ourselves to Bristol!'

Tom looked at him, his stomach tightening when he saw his own blue eyes looking back, the dark blond hair streaked by sunlight, the handsome profile and the dusky complexion that would never pale with the years.

'I'm sorry if I sound sharp, but do bear in mind that I am not the sole inheritor of this business,' said Max. 'My brother Hans handles the London side of the business in Limehouse and also our new refinery in Hamburg where we use both cane and beet products.'

Tom fixed his eyes on the activity before him rather than on Max's worried frown. Persuading Max to make the move to Avonmouth was preferable to forcing him. He thought of Horatia's grim determination to be bigger and better at everything they did: to own the largest plantation, the biggest shipping line – and become the one and only sugar refiner left in the city. It was not an impossible task; so many small refiners were shutting their doors because of transport, port and growing costs. Emmanuel Strong and Conrad Heinkel had formed a partnership over ten years before. If Max didn't acquiesce, Horatia would brush him aside. They were her shares; a controlling number and, by her father's will, her money was her own. The boy could end up ruined.

'I trust your new refinery in Limehouse is going well?' he said instead.

'Very well, thank you. In fact, we may expand our operation there, although,' he shrugged his broad shoulders, 'Hamburg may be a better option. Carts from the fields rather than ships on the sea.'

Tom sensed that here was a chance to encourage the boy – he could still not quite see him as a man – in a direction more likely to reap success than staying in the old premises. He nodded affably. 'That makes good sense, perhaps a better idea than transferring your operation to a new location in Bristol, given the tidal problems we have here—'

'I will not neglect this place. My father built this business up from nothing when he first came here from Hamburg. This building was his dream. I will not close it and, despite the fact that you and your wife own shares in the company, I will fight you tooth and nail rather than close it down. I owe it to my father.'

It was like being hit hard in the face. Tom recognized his own stubbornness, and recalled the days when he'd been a bare-knuckle boxer. Hearing Max put his loyalty to his father before business sense was bad enough. But it was hearing him referring to Conrad as his father that really hurt. Yet what could he do? Conrad had brought Max up as his own. To tell him the truth would put a rift between them that might never heal.

'I intend doing exactly as my father did,' the young man added. 'I intend that what my father left me will be left to my children, and to their children, and to their children's children, all the way into the next century.'

Tom grasped the opportunity to change the subject and smiled. 'It takes two to make children. Do you have a young lady in mind?'

The serious expression that Max always adopted when faced with older business associates vanished and a wide smile brightened his face.

It was his mother's smile, and a feeling of great pride, great love and great passion made Tom's blood quicken.

'Not yet,' said Max, his cheeks colouring to a russet red. 'But I will marry in time, I assure you of that. And then I shall have a son, perhaps many sons, and I will teach and guide them in the same way that my father did me. I cannot better him. He was a good man, a very good man, and I miss him very much.'

Again overcome with the pain he could never admit to, Tom turned his attention back to the quayside where the last of the hogsheads were being loaded into the barge. It would have been a dream come to true to admit his paternity. Instead, one son was dead and buried. The other didn't know that his father lived, and circumstances would never allow him to find out.

Chapter Five

Horatia's eyes glittered with excitement; the City Corporation's plans for the new port at the mouth of the River Avon were spread out in front of her.

'All this area here, here and here,' said Septimus Monk, her lawyer. He pointed with a meticulously manicured finger. A single red ruby shone from the ring he wore.

'How much land is available?'

She flung the question at him sharply and he was glad he'd pre-empted her interest. 'All of it at present. Some of it would be very suitable for a sugar refinery.'

'I don't doubt it.' She straightened and looked thoroughly pleased with herself. 'Though a refinery is not part of my ongoing plans.' She turned to him, smiling in the same way as some mothers when their young attain great things above their fellows. 'I want that land.'

'For a refinery?'

'Certainly not. Thanks to our slow-acting City Corporation, the sugar trade will shortly be relocating to London. If I invest in a refinery at all, that is the place for it.'

'And your shares in the Heinkel establishment on The Counter-slip?'

'I will sell them in order to buy the Avonmouth land.'

'As you wish.'

The river, the sea and the land: at present mud flats, a shallow pool on a tidal river, with ducks, seagulls and all manner of other wild-fowl. The present-day scene fell away. In years to come there would be a mighty dock there and the Strong family would control it.

'Do you not approve?'

Laying down his quill pen, the lawyer clasped his hands in front of him, the fingers of one hand tapping lightly against the other. 'On the contrary, I admire your foresight.'

Most men were wary of a strong-minded, clever woman. Septimus was not like that.

She smiled. 'I knew I could count on you.'

He shrugged. 'It makes sense. There used to be almost a hundred sugar refineries in this city. Now there are what – fifty?'

'And becoming less. The river that used to be our lifeline is now our downfall. Ships are getting much bigger. I fear the Corporation may indeed have missed the boat. London is not tidal and the ships do not have to wind their way up a narrow river where one slip means catastrophe. London already has some of the biggest refineries in the country. Bristol's time is at an end – at least for now.'

'Hence a future port and future traffic?'

Face glowing with ideas, she said, 'The land will be valuable. I shall be able to name my price. There is still a market for the importation and refining of cane sugar in the Bristol area, but one refinery will be enough given the improvements in refining methods in the past few years. Strong money will not be involved – except with regard to the land and buildings.'

'Your foresight, as always, is impeccable – especially as you also own a shipping company. The transportation of merchandise is a very lucrative business.'

Their eyes met in mutual understanding.

'You intend selling your property in Barbados.'

She looked delighted. 'You *do* read my thoughts.'

On leaving the office of Septimus Monk, Horatia felt better than she had for a long time. Dealing with new ventures while trying to juggle the shortfalls of the old obliterated most thoughts of the child she'd named Isaiah.

But in the early hours of the morning, while the rest of the house slept and Tom snored gently beside her, she would suddenly awaken from dreaming of the child. In consciousness, her thoughts of him continued. How was he? Was he feeding well? Had he put on any weight?

The spring sunshine had brought out a number of nursemaids into the vicinity of the 'Barton'. The sound of babies crying, gurgling and laughing was like the water of a running brook; a tinkling mix of happiness, humour and sadness.

She closed the blind of her carriage as she headed back to Marstone Court, but the sound of the babies still rang around the flimsy window covering.

Behind her closed eyelids the visions of a new dock and a baby vied for space in her mind. The new development won. The world was moving on, and so was the Strong family.

Following Conrad Heinkel's death, one of his colleagues, with whom her husband had served as a magistrate, asked if Blanche might like to become an official visitor of St Philip's Workhouse. At the time she'd declined the suggestion and had stayed in mourning for two years, as her family flew the nest. Now, thanks to her doctor's advice, and her stay in Bath, she coughed less, felt better and had become restless. This mood coincided with a visit from the wife of the magistrate, advising her of a place on the Board of Governors of St Philip's.

She asked Max for his opinion. 'Do you think I should?'

'What if I said no?'

'I think I'd like to do something.'

Max had smiled knowingly. 'Mother, you will do whatever you want to do, no matter what I say.'

Dimples dented her cheeks. 'Edith refuses to call it charity. She says I'm just being nosy.'

His amusement reflected her own. Edith, their housemaid, was also a very old friend. She and Blanche had been in service together at Marstone Court.

'I suppose it is being nosy – but nicely so.' His expression turned more serious. 'And your cough?'

'I'm perfectly well. I drank enough hot spring water in Bath to wash away a lifetime of infirmities.'

A worried look creased his brow. 'Are you sure you shouldn't continue the treatment?'

With a disarming smile and a pat on each of his strong shoulders, she reassured him that she would go back to Bath the minute her throat began to tickle.

'Do you want to come with me, Edith?' she asked her on the day she was to present herself at the Workhouse.

Edith turned pale. 'No, I bloody don't,' she muttered, and made a dash for the warm kitchen where a pot of tea and two buttered teacakes awaited her.

43

It had been a long time since she'd heard Edith swear, but Blanche understood her reasons. There'd been times when Edith hadn't been far from destitute, and she had certainly known people who'd entered the Workhouse.

Blanche braced herself for the inevitable and dressed accordingly. She chose to wear a navy blue dress with a black velvet trim around the hem. Her cape and bonnet were also suitably sombre; navy blue and black velvet to match her dress.

Widows' weeds and black bombazine had been her sole garments for the past two years. In her heart she would have loved to wear something in yellow or red, or she thought she would, until she had tried both colours on. Black, she'd decided as she'd reached for the navy blue, had become a habit. Progress towards brighter colours would come only slowly.

Edith came in to put the dresses away and Blanche studied her reflection in the full-length mirror, which was set into the main door of the wardrobe. Usually Edith chattered like a magpie, but today she was silent.

'Edith?'

'Yes?'

'What's wrong?'

'Nothing.'

'I've known you for years, Edith. I know when something is wrong.'

Edith's face, then her body seemed to collapse. She sank onto the bed. 'It's you going to that place.'

'I'm only going to see if I can help in some way – just as a visitor.'

'No one can help those poor sods. Do you know that they separate husbands from wives, mothers from children?'

'I had heard.'

'And then there's the babies.'

Blanche felt her blood turning cold. 'What about the babies?'

Edith shook her head. 'No matter. Anyway, you shouldn't be going there. Your chest could get worse visiting a place like that.'

Blanche had told herself that she was completely recovered from her illness and did not want to be proved wrong. Perhaps Edith had heard her coughing during the night. Blanche sank down onto the bed beside Edith. They'd known each other for many years. There were few secrets between them.

44

She looked down at her gloves and fiddled with her fingers. 'I have to admit that I feel a little nervous. I've never done this before and I'll be all alone.'

She raised her eyes into Edith's face. Eyes downcast, Edith was still grim-faced.

'Are you sure you won't come with me? I would be less nervous if you were there.'

Blanche really did feel nervous, but this was also one of those times when Edith needed taking out of herself. Her second husband, Jim Blackcloud, had not come home from sea. His ship had foundered off the coast of Canada. A few of the crew were picked up, but not him. Edith had taken it hard. Two widows together, they had given support to each other.

'I do need new hats,' she added. 'I thought I would call in on Madame Mabel's first and you could give me your opinion.'

The effect was instantaneous. 'About time!' Edith's face brightened and she got to her feet. 'I'm sick of seeing you in that wretched black bonnet.'

'I haven't got just one bonnet.'

'Those that ain't black are old-fashioned. It's time you had new ones.'

Henry McDougal, the coachman who'd taken over after John had retired, was outside waiting for them.

By the time they reached Madame Mabel's, Blanche's stomach was tight with nerves and she was glad for the respite of such a trivial pursuit as trying on hats before reaching her destination.

A brass bell jangled as she opened the shop door. The décor was dark pink, the floor polished pine scattered with rugs. The walls were decorated with gilt-framed mirrors, and huge peacocks' feathers in olive green vases sat in corners and alcoves. The intention was to resemble a mughal's palace, or at least Madame Mabel's interpretation of one.

'Perhaps your maid could wait in the assistants' room,' said Madame Mabel in an affected French accent.

'No. I very much value my maid. She has an eye for fashion.'

Edith took a seat and Madame Mabel's disdainful look disappeared quickly once it became apparent that Blanche wanted more than just a single hat.

'You are out of mourning, *madame?*' the milliner trilled,

her eyes sweeping over the navy blue outfit as she took Blanche's order.

'I am.'

'It is still too dark, *madame*. You have been in mourning for too long and have grown accustomed to darkness. But soon you will have light. *C'est bon! C'est bon!* But this veil . . . ?' Madame Mabel turned critical eyes on the stiff veil that fell from the back of Blanche's bonnet. 'This is no good. It should be much longer, at least reaching halfway down *madame*'s back. The Queen favours such a length, I believe. If you will allow me to alter it, I am sure you will be very pleased with the result. Shall I arrange for it to be collected when Magdalene delivers your new bonnet?'

Blanche agreed it to be a very good arrangement and glanced at Edith, who was now beaming from ear to ear, her lips compressed as though she were suppressing a huge fit of laughter. Her shoulders shook as they headed for the door and once they were outside, she burst into laughter. 'French? French? She's about as French as my Aunt Fanny. Her name's Mabel Pudding – or at least I think it is.'

'Pudding?' Blanche chuckled. 'How can she possibly have a name like that?'

Edith took off her bonnet and scratched at her bun with a hatpin. 'Don't know whether it was her real name. It was just that her mother was in the pudding club all the time, so everybody called her Mrs Pudding.'

'And her father?' asked Blanche between giggles.

Edith shrugged. 'He went to sea a lot. Never knew his real name.'

She fell to sudden silence, the mention of a seaman clearly bringing back old memories. In the case of her first husband, Edith had enjoyed her best times when he was away at sea. In the case of her second husband, she'd preferred the times when he was home. Losing Jim had been a heartfelt loss.

They were still brooding by the time they arrived at St Philip's Workhouse.

Edith glanced out of the window of the carriage at the grim walls surrounding the place. 'Rather you than me,' she said, then gathered her cloak more closely about herself and looked the other way.

Taking her courage in both hands, Blanche got out of the carriage and was at once struck by the brooding height of the Workhouse walls and the black shadows they cast. She shivered as she imagined the thoughts of a penniless pauper about to enter the high wooden gates, studded with black nails and as formidable as any prison.

McDougal, the coachman, hovered at her side, his voice quivering with concern. 'Will you be all right, ma'am?'

She took a deep breath. 'I think so,' she said to him, then mostly to herself added, 'After all I shall be coming out again in less than two hours. Not so the inmates of this place.'

Henry McDougal tugged the iron bell pull. A dull tone sounded just beyond the gate. She heard coughing and the sound of heavy boots, then the grating of iron against iron as a bolt was drawn.

One half of the gate opened. The man standing there had a red face and wore a confused mix of more than one military uniform. The Royal Navy was represented by his trousers, which were of the baggy type and made of canvas. His jacket was green and trimmed with a little gold braid; his hat was blue and trimmed with a lot. His boots were of the cavalry type. She noticed that one was brown and one was black.

'Madam,' he said, bowing slightly without removing his hat.

'I am attending the Board of Governors' meeting,' she explained.

His watery eyes stayed fixed on her face and his tongue swept along his lower lip. She took it he was wondering at her colouring, though God knows she was paler nowadays than she'd ever been, thanks to the climate and her chest condition. He opened the gate wider and she found herself in a yard about twenty feet by twenty feet and surrounded by buildings that threw inky black shadows. The main entrance was straight ahead of her and was far less dour than she'd expected. The door was imposing, approached up a flight of three stone steps and flanked by two rather grand Doric columns, their whiteness bright against the dull red brick.

'This way, me lady,' said the man in the odd uniform. He gave another awkward bow before striding off in a lop-sided fashion by virtue of one leg being stiffer than the other. He dragged it behind him as if it were cast in lead.

As she followed, she noticed there were gates to either side of her. Above one it said 'Men' and above the other 'Women'.

She hadn't wanted to believe all that Edith had said, but this was evidence enough. She could barely drag her gaze away from the sight of the signs. What a terrible thing! Husbands separated from their wives and children. She thought of Edith waiting in the carriage outside and how she had turned away from the austere building.

'This shouldn't be,' she whispered to herself. These people were being punished for being poor. The thought appalled her. How do you know for sure? she asked herself then. You know nothing about this place. You've never been in a workhouse before. Guard your tongue and delay your judgement.

Her attention was drawn to a set of stocks beside the gate leading to the men's quarters. She frowned. Surely they weren't used nowadays? She found herself unable to accept that they had any use, convinced they were merely a leftover from earlier times when another building had been on this site.

The man in the muddled uniform rang a bell by the Doric-columned entrance before limping back across the yard. The door was opened by a wan-faced girl with pale blue eyes.

'Ma'am,' she said, bobbing her a curtsey.

An attempt had been made to hold the girl's fair hair into a bun at the nape of her neck. Some of it had escaped and hung like limp feathers around her face. Her dress was shapeless, mostly grey but with a yellow stripe down the front.

Blanche smiled at her. 'Good morning.'

The girl kept her eyes downcast and whispered a swift, 'Good morning, ma'am.'

It was reassuring, but also unsettling to see that she'd already met someone more nervous than she.

'I am come for the Board of Governors' meeting.'

'Yes, ma'am. Follow me.'

She accompanied the girl down a long corridor. Two women were on their hands and knees scrubbing the floor and the skirting boards, their hands red raw. The pungent smell of carbolic lay heavy on the air. They did not look up as she swept by, but attended the floor, their faces hidden by the flapping frills of their cotton bonnets.

She was shown into a room with big windows. There were no pictures, no soft furnishings and no curtains. A dining table was set out at one end, a dresser at the other and a number of chairs around the walls. The only decoration, if it could be so called, was various religious texts written in green paint on one cream-coloured wall.

One read:

> *Who best can drink His cup of woe*
> *Triumphant over pain,*
> *Who patient bears His cross below,*
> *He follows in His train.*

The smell of steak and kidney pie and other delicious foods seeped through from some other room she could not see. Her stomach rumbled. The food smelled as good as anything her own cook could prepare. Perhaps the inmates were fed better than she'd been led to believe.

A door in the far corner opened and a man entered, dressed in the drear black of a minister. She guessed that this was the chairman of the Board of Governors.

He extended his podgy hand. 'The Reverend Godfrey Smart, at your service, my dear Mrs Heinkel. I have heard so much about you from Justice Booker-Green. How nice of you to come.'

He held her hand very tightly and tried to clasp it to his chest as his eyes bored into hers, travelled as far as her waist, then returned to her face.

'It was the least I could do,' she replied once she'd snatched back her hand, barely managing to hold onto a very tight smile. 'This room is so light.'

She purposely turned her back on him and began walking around the room, as though it really was of great interest. She didn't stop until the whole length of the dining table lay between them.

'So we may all see each other as we are,' he exclaimed, his hands clasped as if in prayer and took a step closer.

'And those smells,' she said, sidestepping around the end of the table in order to keep the same distance between them.

'Man shall not live by bread alone.'

'Of course,' she said, and remembered a fairy tale about a girl, a grandmother and a wolf.

He took a step closer; she took a step back.

Blanche thanked heaven when the door at the far end of the room opened again and in walked the other members of the Board: six gentlemen and a plump woman wearing a yellow wig under her bonnet.

The Reverend introduced her as the widow of Conrad Heinkel – 'A great benefactor to the poor of this city,' he added. 'She wishes to become an official visitor.'

She was also introduced to the warden, a Mr Tinsley, who wore woollen mittens and had a slight stoop. His wife was taller than he, with a strong face, a too-long chin and eyes set wide apart. She explained she acted as matron for the women.

'And the children. Do you care for those too?'

'Indeed I do, ma'am,' said Mrs Tinsley, bobbing a quick, polite curtsey. 'I don't say I'm soft with them, but I do say I'm fair, as the Reverend gentleman will vouch.' She bobbed another curtsey and aimed a greasy smile in Smart's direction.

Smart radiated cordiality. 'Very commendable,' he exclaimed. 'Mrs Tinsley keeps everyone on the straight and narrow.'

Blanche managed a thin smile and warned herself to be careful of these two. Smart looked as though he revelled in Mrs Tinsley's servility. Mrs Tinsley's smile never wavered, yet her eyes were constantly on the move as if searching for any sign of disagreement or distrust, and alighted on the Reverend more than they did on anyone else. Blanche sensed conspiracy and secrets.

'With the agreement of my fellow members of the Board of Governors, I think it would be sensible if I take you on a tour of our fine establishment, so you can see for yourself what St Philip's Workhouse is doing to alleviate poverty in this area.'

The other members of the board nodded their approval and Blanche felt their eyes on her as the Reverend Smart cupped her elbow and guided her to the door. No one was fooled, she decided. They all knew he was a lecher and that she'd have to watch her step. No matter how innocent she was, they would gossip among themselves whilst she was gone, smearing her reputation whether she deserved it or not.

Purposely treading on the Reverend's toe, she turned round suddenly and smiled affably at the warden's wife. 'Perhaps Mrs Tinsley would like to come with us? After all, it is the needs of the women and children that concern me. I have strong views on family ties, and perhaps Mrs Tinsley could elaborate on some of the finer detail more astutely than can a man.' Sugar, never mind butter, could not have melted in her mouth when she smiled.

Mrs Tinsley looked ecstatic. Obviously, she trusted the Reverend gentleman no more than Blanche did.

The Reverend took on a pained expression that ebbed and flowed, then burst like a river flooding its banks.

Blanche congratulated herself too soon. The Reverend's mind was as nimble as his hands.

'I'm afraid that won't be possible, not if we're thoroughly to enjoy the sumptuous meal that's been prepared for us. I believe we're out of port, Mrs Tinsley,' he said, pointing a fat finger to where the decanter sat in a red stain. 'Would have helped if Sir Bertram hadn't upset it,' he chortled.

A man with a red face and a perpetual grin raised his empty glass. His buff waistcoat bore a streak of red over his rotund belly.

Mrs Tinsley pursed her lips, threw Blanche a jealous glare and obeyed.

The Reverend Smart again cupped her elbow and manoeuvred her to the door. The heat of his palm burned through her sleeve.

'I used to preach in Bath,' he said, smiling smugly. 'A very genteel, cultured place, with an aura of the classic cities of antiquity.'

Ah, thought Blanche, the man was a pompous ass as well as a lecher.

'I was also attached to a number of similar institutions to this,' the Reverend continued, as they walked along a dark panelled corridor. 'Some had been set up by certain august personages, whose names of course I cannot possibly reveal, to care for the more infirm and aged of our society. I was appointed as chaplain to a number of alms-houses where the elderly poor were housed following a lifetime of diligence and righteousness. We investigated their backgrounds most thoroughly before accepting them as possible residents.'

His arm went around her back, as though to chivvy her protect-ively through the door ahead of them, and he chuckled into her ear. 'It was a lustful city at one time, a Sodom and Gomorrah in this England of pleasant green fields and uplifting virtue. Have you ever been to Bath, Mrs Heinkel?'

'Never.'

There were times when the truth would not do at all, and this had been one of them. It was very likely she would be visiting Bath again. The thought of the Reverend Smart offering his services as a guide was utterly repugnant.

The air became colder as they turned into a stone-floored passage that he told her led to the women's dining room. She'd managed to keep ahead of his arm, so his hand had returned to her elbow.

'Tell me, dear Mrs Heinkel, how long is it since your husband departed this world?'

'Two years,' she said abruptly.

'My dear lady.' His voice dripped like rosehip syrup.

'And I am loyal to his memory,' said Blanche.

'Ah yes. Of course.'

Row upon row of trestle tables filled the dining room. Bench seating was set on one side so that all the inmates faced the front. The women ate silently without raising their eyes. Their grey clothes matched their complexions. The ceiling was high and interspersed with curved beams, each boasting a biblical text: 'God is Love'; 'Trust in the Lord'; 'Narrow is the Path of Righteousness'; and 'The Meek Shall Inherit the Earth'.

Blanche turned a jaundiced eye on each one in turn, as Smart's arm again began to slide around her back. She took a step forward.

'We endeavour to encourage our charges to live by such creeds, dear lady,' he said, his face shining with false conviction. 'The meek *shall* inherit the earth.'

'Hardly the earth, Reverend,' she said cuttingly, 'just the workhouse. Shall we see the accommodation?'

'We have three different forms of dormitory,' he said obsequiously, his chastisement unnoticed.

Blanche gritted her teeth. Already she was beginning to see herself as a bulwark between the needful poor and the sanctimonious patronage of people like Smart. God knows, but it seemed the poor needed a champion.

The first dormitory was depressing, dark and lined with troughs.

Blanche frowned when she saw there were lids hinged at the back of each trough.

'Those are beds for the casuals,' he explained.

'Beds? But why do they have lids?'

'In case they die during the night. We just shut the lid and have them taken out in it. That way no one is upset by the sight. Once they're buried – or whatever – the bed is brought back in to be used again.'

'Whatever'? The sheer inhumanity of what he had just described appalled her. And yet the Reverend seemed unperturbed by the arrangement, blinded by functionality and apparently oblivious that even the poor deserve some respect.

He took her to see other sleeping areas, one of which was merely a platform designed to sleep twenty. Others were stalls, similar to those used for horses. The bedding too was the same. The inmates slept on straw like animals. The smell was terrible.

Hidden by shadow, a woman nursing a child crouched in the corner of one stall. The child was obviously ill, its breathing rasping and loud.

Smart frowned and his voice altered, no longer the slippery-tongued, would-be seducer. 'What are you doing here, woman? You should be working with the others.'

The woman lifted her head.

Blanche clutched at her stomach on seeing the exhausted face and the deep shadows beneath despairing eyes.

'My John is sick.'

'Well, nothing you can do is going to make him better, is it? Leave him there, get to your work and I'll get Mrs Tinsley to fetch the doctor.'

The woman shook her head and began to cry. 'He's dying. Please, sir, I want to stay with him 'til he's gone.'

Smart puffed out his chest and his face reddened. 'Any excuse to get out of work,' he said in an aside to Blanche.

Before he could say another word, she was at the woman's side amongst the sour straw. Ripping her glove from her hand, she laid her cool fingers on the child's forehead and put her hand inside the thin garment that covered his chest.

'His skin burns like fire and his breathing is shallow.'

She shouted at Smart. 'We must have a doctor!'

His face turned redder and for a moment it seemed as though he too was unable to breathe. At last he managed an awkward smile. 'If it pleases you, dear lady, I will get Mrs Tinsley to send for Doctor Pettigrew.'

'Now!' she said, her expression and tone of voice leaving him in no doubt that she would stay by the woman's side until assured it had been done.

'Of course, of course,' he said, nodding emphatically before dashing to a door, hauling it open and bawling for someone called Betty. She heard him giving orders, heard someone reply, then his voice again: 'Get back here as soon as you've done it. No slacking.'

His shadow fell over her. 'Mrs Heinkel, we shall be late for our lunch . . .'

Deeply moved and angry at what she'd seen so far, Blanche did not move, but addressed the woman. 'Have you eaten today?'

The woman shook her head. 'I couldn't go to where we eats. I couldn't leave my John.'

'Food should have been brought to you.'

Trembling with emotion, Blanche got to her feet and turned to face Smart. 'She needs food.'

'Yes, yes,' he said, nodding vigorously in the vain hope that it might enhance her opinion of him. 'I will get some porridge brought immediately. There's sure to be some left from this morning.'

Sensing she could get her own way in this, Blanche resolved to push the repulsive creature as far as she could. 'I fear the child may not last, but perhaps he will take some of the porridge. His mother, on the other hand, needs something more substantial.'

The nodding continued. 'Of course, of course. Cheese, dear lady, and bread.'

'She needs meat and vegetables, perhaps a pudding too. I smelled something quite delicious cooking when I was upstairs. Perhaps she could have some of that.'

Smart's eyes fluttered like bats' wings. He was trapped. 'I will tell Betty to fetch it.'

He was true to his word. When Betty appeared, wearing the dull grey uniform with the yellow stripe, he ordered her to do all that Blanche had asked for.

The doctor would take a little time coming, but Blanche insisted they wait until the food arrived before departing to eat their own.

Betty returned with a bowl brimming with meat and vegetables plus a hunk of bread.

Blanche lingered until the bowl was half empty, the smell of rich gravy hanging in the air.

On the way back the Reverend took a different route, which skirted the men's quarters and had an open aspect over a yard. The odour was like nothing she'd ever experienced. It was so offensive that she covered her nose and mouth with both hands.

'What is that terrible smell?'

'You'll get used to it. It's only old bones being crushed.'

'What old bones? What do you mean?'

Smart did not notice her appalled expression. 'Old bones are brought in from the slaughterhouses, broken and smashed and ground into powder, then sold as fertilizer.'

She noticed he had finally ceased calling her 'dear lady', his solicitous attitude gradually diminishing since the incident with the woman and child.

The full stench hit her in the face as she leaned over the parapet. An orchestra of hammering also arose, along with a grinding sound from a machine that looked like a large cider press. A steady shower of matter fell into troughs around its base. Small children, some hardly big enough to tie their own bootlaces – if they were lucky enough to own boots – were scooping the ground bone into metal buckets, which in turn were tipped into a series of sacks hanging from nails. Each full sack was then taken down and replaced with an empty one. She saw a child hiding away where he thought he couldn't be seen, gnawing on a bone that might once have belonged to a horse. Whatever it was, it was days old and turning green. Some instinct warned her not to bring the child to the Reverend's attention. In good time she would look into the truth of what went on here. Until then she would bide her time, get to know those working here and those on the Board. Her comments would carry no weight until they had accepted her.

'A most enlightening morning,' she said, offering her hand to Smart before they entered the room where lunch was to be served. 'Your comments have been most illuminating. I can see I am going to have some interesting times serving on the Board.'

And my face might very well crack, she thought, as she forced the widest smile she owned across her mouth.

The smile, the comment and the offering of her hand had the desired effect.

'My dear lady,' he gushed, his oily voice returning. 'And now we shall dine and you can tell us all about yourself.'

Blanche cringed at the thought of telling him or the Board too much about herself. No, as always, she would edit the truth. Being of Spanish extraction was barely acceptable in these days of empire. If they should ever find out the truth, almost every door in the city would be barred to her.

She was invited to sit between the Reverend and Mr Tinsley, the warden. Mrs Tinsley's chair stayed empty as she oversaw two inmates who had been chosen to wait on table that day.

Blanche eyed the magnificent lunch. The table was spread with a sparkling white cloth and groaned beneath cold chicken, steak and kidney pie, bread still warm from a local bakery, Double Gloucester from Minchinhampton, Cheddar from Somerset, cream from a local dairy, a pork pie with a shiny crust, and a huge fruit cake, sultanas and cherries falling from its cut side. Bottles of wine, port, brandy and whisky were set out on a side table, trays of good quality glasses laid out around them.

Her stomach churned more vigorously than before. The bone yard had been enough to turn anyone's stomach, but the thought that here they were, sitting in comfort before a table piled high with food, while a child gnawed on a rotten bone, was obscene.

She was so engrossed in the unfairness of it all that she didn't notice the Reverend Smart's hand on her knee until he proposed grace, and his hands became clasped in prayer.

As he intoned a rambling thanks to the Almighty, her eyes stayed open and fixed on the food. All this for the Board, while the inmates, the poor whom they were supposed to serve, ate a thin gruel.

The sound of cutlery accompanied resumed conversation. Blanche picked up her fork and she studied the well-fed, self-satisfied faces around the table.

Above the heads of those sitting opposite her was another of the ubiquitous texts: 'Lead us not into temptation'.

The gentleman opposite noticed her interest. 'A commendable sentiment, don't you think, ma'am?' he said.

'Yes,' she replied, feeling the Reverend Smart's hand wander back onto her leg. She smiled and discreetly took her fork onto her lap. 'Very commendable.' She stabbed it into Smart's thigh.

Smart dropped his knife, gasped and leapt from his chair.

'Good Lord! What's wrong, man?' someone asked.

'Gravy! Some gravy slopped on my hand.'

'Rachel!' Mrs Tinsley grabbed the arm of the girl who'd been serving at table and shook her so hard the girl's mob-cap fell off. 'You clumsy, stupid girl.'

'It wasn't her fault,' said Blanche.

Her smile dared the Reverend to disagree.

He looked at her, the shape of his mouth altering from accusation to amiability as he fought to regain his self-control.

An enormous amount of food and drink was left on the table after they'd finished. The men asked to be excused and went out to smoke as Blanche took tea. Mrs Tinsley made her excuses to join them, armed with bandages and ointment, determined to stick to the Reverend Smart whether he wanted her to or not. The woman with the wig disappeared muttering something about knitting needles. She had looked as though she were going to be sick.

Blanche was left alone and went to use the water closet about which the warden had boasted in much detail.

On her way back, Blanche peered out of windows into the grim yards below, saw women hanging out washing in one yard, children stacking sacks and boxes in another and men heaving bags of used bones into a long trough. Walking slowly back, she thought about what she'd seen, how she felt and what she intended to do next.

When she got back to the dining room, the door was open. She could see Rachel hanging over the table and presumed she was clearing dishes. But she couldn't hear the sound of crockery being gathered.

Tip-toeing slowly so that her skirts wouldn't rustle, she edged forward and stood in the doorway, watching as Rachel tugged pieces from the chicken and the ham, tore chunks of cheese and bread, and shoved it all down the front of her apron.

Her chest infection still lingered and, after the dust of the bone yard, Blanche couldn't stifle the cough that came.

Rachel spun round and Blanche took in the pale face, the dire uniform, the stiffness of the girl's shoulders. She pointed at the girl's mouth. 'Your lips are greasy. Wipe it off or Mrs Tinsley will know what you've been up to.'

Rachel wiped her mouth on the back of her hand. 'You won't tell on me, will you, missus?'

'What would you normally have for lunch?' Blanche asked her.

'Soup.'

'But not today?'

The fear returned. 'Please, ma'am. I ain't took too much, just enough to keep us going. My grandmother's here, and she ain't had a bit of meat for days. I thought just a little, not enough for Mrs Tinsley to notice . . . anyways, I can't carry much.'

Blanche eyed the girl's apron bib. 'Not much at all. You need something to carry it in. Have you a teacloth?'

The girl shook her head. 'No.'

Blanche tried the dresser. There were no cloths in the first drawer, but plenty in the second. 'Here's one,' she said, bringing out a piece of red checked cotton.

'She counts them,' groaned Rachel. 'I can't.'

Blanche put the cloth back and closed the drawer. She didn't want to get the girl into trouble. Her eyes went to where her coat and bonnet had been hung. The veil of her bonnet, which Madame Mabel had referred to in disparaging tones, trailed down over her coat.

'This bonnet is out of fashion,' she said taking hold of it by its brim. 'My milliner says so.' With fierce determination, she tore the veil from the back of the bonnet. 'This will do nicely,' she said as she spread it out flat on the table.

Rachel stood open-mouthed. 'Ma'am?'

'Come on,' said Blanche as a piece of pie, followed by half a pound of cheese, half a loaf, a pound of ham and the bits of breast from the chicken carcass were bundled into the net that had once adorned her bonnet. 'This should keep your grandmother going. Take it now, but be quick. I'll be here when you get back and I'll make excuses for you, but if you can, try to get back before the gentlemen return then no one will be any the wiser.'

Rachel was swift on her feet. She paused by the door. 'You're a very kind lady, ma'am. There's many 'ere that will be thankful.'

Once she was alone, Blanche sank into a chair, her chest aching with effort. She was not as strong as she used to be. Should she be here at all? She could see it all now: she would get terribly involved, perhaps upset some of the stuffed-shirted patrons of this place, and even annoy her family. Was it worth it?

Staring out at the grim buildings, their roofs shiny now following a downpour, she thought it through.

Here, but for the grace of God, would have been my home too, if it hadn't been for Conrad Heinkel, she concluded. Life, she decided, was very full of 'ifs'.

Her musings were interrupted by the return of the men, Mrs Tinsley right behind them, her upper arm brushing that of the Reverend Smart.

No one noticed that the leftovers were not so abundant. Blanche congratulated herself that she'd got away with it.

Only Mrs Tinsley, sharp-eyed despite her fat cheeks, frowned at her as though something was not quite the same.

'Will we see you next Wednesday?' asked the Reverend Smart, who seemed quite recovered from being stabbed by her fork.

'If that is when I am expected, I will be here.'

'It is likely that there will be a new intake of wretches in need of bed and board. Perhaps you would like to see how these people are assessed? It's amazing how many say they are destitute in order to obtain entry.'

'I find it hard to believe,' she replied, thinking that she'd prefer to take her chances on the street rather than enter this place.

Smart misconstrued. 'Do believe it, my dear lady. It is indeed the truth. Some people prefer to throw themselves on the parish rather than do a good day's work.'

Sitting in the carriage, Edith tapped her feet impatiently and tried not to look at the forbidding walls of St Philip's Workhouse.

The day was warm. The sound of steam hammers sounded from the ironworks. Flies buzzed in black clouds around damp manure, the sound accompanied by the snores of Henry McDougal dozing up in his seat. Suddenly she heard someone singing, the words at first incoherent then becoming clearer as the singer came closer:

> *Another little gin, another little gin,*
> *Penny a mug,*
> *And twopence a jug,*
> *Now get thur and get me another little gin . . .*
> *Another little gin, another little gin . . .*

Recognizing the voice, Edith poked her head out of the window.

'Daisy Draper? You sings like an earwig!'

The singer, her straw bonnet askew, staggered as she came to a halt and looked up at the sky. 'Who said that?' she asked, scratching at the tufts of hair that stuck out from beneath her bonnet.

'Well, thee's bisn't gonna find me up thur!' said Edith as she got out of the carriage.

The heavy Bristol accent brought Daisy's wobbly gaze back down to earth. She blinked as she attempted to focus her eyes on Edith, then her whole face puckered with concentration, as though a terribly important thought had crossed her mind.

'Earwigs don't sing.'

'No, they don't,' said Edith, taking hold of her arm and sitting her on the side of a horse trough. 'And neither should you.'

Daisy attempted to push her bonnet straight, but only succeeded in making it flop the other side of her face. She suddenly noticed Henry who was still snoozing up on his perch, his chin fallen onto his chest.

'Do you know that bloke thur?'

'Course I do. That's the coachman.'

Daisy burped. 'Posh carriage. Fancy you riding in one of them. I rides in posh carriages too, you know.'

This didn't come as a surprise. Edith had known Daisy when she'd been little more than fourteen and lifting her skirts for anyone with the price of a meal. It was only natural, as well as more financially rewarding, that she'd gone upmarket.

'Oh yeah?' said Edith with a wry smile. 'Pays better, do it?'

'Not what yer thinking, Edith Clements what was. I've got a proper job. I've 'ad training, I 'ave.'

Edith was bemused. 'And what might that be?'

Daisy pulled herself up as straight as she could, which resulted in a succession of sharp hiccups. Then she gave Edith the shock of her life. 'I'm a nurse. Even got a proper uniform – well, a big white apron and a cap anyways . . .' Her expression changed suddenly. 'So what you doin' yur?'

Although she couldn't believe that Daisy would take it in, Edith explained the reason for being there.

Once she'd finished, Daisy tapped at the side of her nose, and said, 'Well, I've had reason to go in that place, though not on account of being destitute, you know. Oh no! I went in there on business, for which I was paid a princely sum – a *very* princely sum.'

Edith tried not to breathe as the woman's gin-laden breath assaulted her nostrils, then paled as Daisy went on to tell her all about the dark-skinned baby born to Horatia Strong. At the end of it, unaware that the colour had drained from Edith's face, she added, 'I was supposed to keep it a secret, but there . . . two sovereigns only keeps body and soul together for a while, don't it? And nursing don't pay that well, though it's usually an easy job. The wet nurse suckles the newborn in these rich houses, and I do the looking after, though that ain't hard. I swear by laudanum. I put a tiny spot on me finger and let 'em suck. I promise yo' it keeps the little mites quiet.'

Edith was hardly listening. It was bad enough to learn about the fate of Horatia Strong's baby, without hearing this. Poor as she'd been back when she'd lived in the Pithay, she'd never administered anything that might put her babies to sleep so they wouldn't bother her. It just wasn't right.

'Best be going,' said Daisy, staggering to her feet. Patting Edith on the shoulder, she leaned close to her ear. 'And I've a mind to earn a bit more if I can. Wonder what that Horatia Strong's husband would say if he knew that there ain't no baby buried in that graveyard out near Marstone Court. That the little nigger brat ended up in here . . .' She jerked her head at the Workhouse. 'Wonder what he'd say that his milk-white wife produced a dark-skinned son? How much do you think he'd pay to keep it secret?' She nudged Edith's arm a bit too aggressively and almost fell over. 'Poor little soul might even still be alive, though I doubt it. They don't last long once they go in there.'

Edith's first instinct was to grab the drunken Daisy by her bonnet strings and throttle her if she dared go near Tom Strong, whom she had once loved. Instead she was glued to the spot. There was so much at stake and too many courses of action she could take. Should she tell Blanche about the baby? Should she tell Captain Strong?

Engrossed with myriad concerns, she hardly noticed Daisy bidding her cheerio and staggering off in the direction of the Bath Road. Once she became aware of her disappearing figure, she shouted, 'Say nothing, Daisy. Say nothing!'

Whether Daisy heard or took it in, she didn't know. But her shout roused Henry who jerked awake and asked her what was wrong.

'Nothing,' Edith snapped, folding her arms and rubbing them as if they'd suddenly turned to ice. 'Nothing. Just a drunken woman who shouldn't be out by herself.'

Chapter Six

Horatia watched Tom wash himself. He was naked, the light from the window outlining the perfection of his physique, which was still firm despite him being in his forties.

He straightened suddenly, as though he'd just thought of something. 'What did he look like?'

She became as stiff as the starched nightdress she was wearing. 'I don't want to talk about it.'

'It? Surely, the word is "he"?'

She felt her jaw clenching as though she were going to retch. Her hands became clasped in her lap. 'Don't!'

He was silent and still for a moment. 'You never want to talk about him.'

'What good does it do?'

'I wish you would.'

'Well, I won't. Is that clear? I won't.'

She sensed his disappointment; perhaps he was even a little angry. She vowed to make it up to him, but not by talking about the child. She couldn't possibly do that. Perhaps in bed? Wasn't that the best place for a wife to please her husband?

Last night she had almost reached for him, but found that she couldn't. It wasn't in her nature to make the first move, not because she didn't desire him, on the contrary she loved him madly, but she was used to being adored. She'd been treated like a goddess for most of her life. When she'd grown into an intelligent woman who knew how to take advantage of her classic good looks, men had willingly fallen at her feet. Not once had she ever had to declare her adoration for them. Her heart wouldn't let her, and she really hadn't needed to. But Tom had always been different. She had always wanted him to make her feel desired, to have him pleading for her surrender. But he never did that and so, just like the space between them in their big double bed, there existed a cold emptiness that neither was willing to cross. Tom, she knew, perceived her stiffness as indifference and, unless he was very desperate, refrained from bothering her.

There would be no more babies. Her fertile years were coming to a close. In one way she was glad; the monthly interruption would not be missed, but the fact she had not presented Tom with a son – his own son – filled her with regret.

He'd been too long away in the West Indies. She'd sometimes wondered whether he was unfaithful, but didn't want to know. The fire of jealousy would be too all-consuming.

She felt her stomach tightening more forcibly than any corset, touching him in her mind; feeling the tautness of his muscles, the outline of his body against the cold greyness filtering through the window.

God, how she wanted him to want her! To really want her! Perhaps if she widened the gap between them . . . Absence, or at least a separate bedroom along the landing, might make the heart grow fonder.

As he began to dress, she pulled her gaze away and swung her legs out of bed.

'I've arranged for your things to be moved into the west wing; you always said you liked that wing best.'

She'd said it nonchalantly before sitting down at her mirror where she studied his reflection, waiting for a reaction.

To her consternation, he appeared unmoved. 'Let me know when it's done. I wouldn't want the servants to see me wandering the landing in my nightshirt.'

'You don't wear a nightshirt.'

He grinned. 'That's what I mean.'

Despite the signs of middle age creasing the corners of his eyes, his grin made him look boyish.

Horatia fought the urge to throw herself upon him. She began vigorously brushing her hair and changed the subject.

'I've decided to sell our share in Heinkel's Sugar Refinery.'

'For any particular reason?'

The question sounded casual, but Horatia was not fooled. Tom cared about Max. With a pang of regret, she knew he would have cared about the son she'd given him.

'I've decided we should invest the money in the land around the new docks being planned at Avonmouth by the City Corporation. It makes sense to have direct access to the sea rather than meandering all the way up through the Avon Gorge and into the city. You've said yourself that ships can only get bigger, too big to come up the river. Bigger ships carry a larger cargo and thus refineries need to be bigger. Which means Heinkel's is too small and in the wrong place. Isn't that so?' She smiled sweetly.

'Yes,' he said. 'It is.'

'So it makes sense to invest in the future. There can be no compromise. I for one have never entertained sentiment in business.'

'No,' said Tom, a little too grimly for her liking. 'No. No one can ever accuse you of being sentimental.'

She stiffened, one sleeve of the expensive lace-edged nightdress falling down to reveal a gleaming shoulder. Her look was frosty. 'I will not forsake my heritage, Thomas. My father willed the bulk of the Strong fortune to me rather than to my brothers, because he trusted I would run it as well as he did.'

Now fully dressed, Tom stretched out one arm, leaning on the window surround with his back to her. 'Your father left quite an inheritance. What would you have done, I wonder, if I hadn't carried out my part of his will, the part that insisted you would not inherit unless you married me? What would you have done if everything had gone to Max Heinkel?'

He turned towards her. Tom had always had a direct way of looking into her eyes, as though he were trying to catch her true feelings before she had chance to hide them away.

Like a young girl, she found herself blushing. 'He's the grandson of a black slave!'

'He's also your father's grandson, and therefore your nephew.'

'I won't have you blackening my father's name.'

Looking bemused, Tom shook his head. 'I think your father was quite capable of besmirching his own name without my help.'

'It is my family name.'

'Horatia, there's a painting of your grandmother in the attic. It's no accident that she bears a strong resemblance to Blanche Heinkel, and not just through your father. Did you ever wonder about her breeding?'

'You're accusing her of being a Creole! A mulatto! A nigger!'

Horatia was shouting now, barely able to control her anger and at the same time sounding unnaturally defensive, as though the fault were hers.

He shook his head. 'No, I'm not. She's dead and can't answer for herself. I'm merely pointing out to you that as plantation owners, the men of the Strong family had unlimited access to their female slaves. Don't be surprised if another skeleton falls out of the Strong closet. It's only to be expected.'

He didn't look back when he left the room. If he had, he would have seen her ashen complexion. Dark hair and a small, soft body; flesh of her flesh, how could she have done it? How could she?

Stiff and unyielding, she sank into a chair, her jaw aching with the effort of holding back the sobs that jerked at her throat.

No one he passed would have guessed from Tom's profile what was going on in his mind. No one knew Horatia as well as he did. People could fall dead by the wayside so long as she got her own way. She was plotting something big, determined that the Strong family would be the winners. In that event, Max Heinkel could only be the loser.

He frowned. Max was a grown man and, hopefully, could look after himself and his widowed mother. Tom cared for them both, but he also loved his little daughter, Emerald. For her sake, he had to make the best of his marriage. He couldn't condemn Horatia for throwing herself into the development of the new port with such enthusiasm. She'd lost a baby. It helped her cope. That was why he had not objected to moving into a separate room. She needed time to get over the birth. At least, that was what he told himself.

'It really suits you, Mrs Heinkel,' said Magdalene Cherry, the milliner sent by Madame Mabel with Blanche's new hats.

The first bonnet was mauve, its silk covering sewn into tight concertina pleats all around the brim and bunches of violets fastened over the place where the strings were sewn in. A long veil of fine French lace hung from the back.

Blanche eyed herself in the mirror.

'Very nice,' said Edith who was sitting in on the session, her head tilted as she considered each one.

The next bonnet was of blue velvet, and the third of green and red tartan.

'That 'un looks like a drum,' said Edith of the latter with a sniff of disdain and a slip into Bristol dialect.

'That's a daft thing to say,' chirped Magdalene. 'Oh. Sorry, Mrs Heinkel. Didn't mean to speak out of turn.'

Blanche smiled and shook her head. 'Why not? Edith does.'

She found herself liking the girl. She was small and dark, her eyes large and brown. There was an alertness and a quickness about her that reminded her of Edith in her youth, except that Magdalene didn't tell tall stories.

It came as a great surprise when a knock came at the door and Max entered.

'Very nice, Mother,' he said, nodding at the tartan bonnet, his eyelids flickering briefly before his gaze settled on Magdalene Cherry.

'No, it isn't,' said Edith. 'It looks like something a regimental drummer might beat with a couple of sticks.'

'Yes, of course,' said Max, who was clearly not listening.

Via her reflection Blanche exchanged a smile with Edith. Max's eyes were fixed on Magdalene.

The milliner, if she noticed at all, remained aloof, busily adjusting ribbons, putting in an extra stitch or a chalk mark here and there where alternations were needed.

'Mother, I'm off for a meeting at the coffee shop near the Corn Exchange, then to the refinery,' Max said, bending down and kissing her cheek.

'Yes, dear.'

Again she saw his eyes slide sidelong to Magdalene, fancied a faint blush came to his cheeks and imagined the quickening of his heart. She sometimes worried about the air of self-importance Max had adopted since his father's death. It could so easily lead to arrogance, but now she saw that his heart, for once, was ruling his head. From the look in his eyes, she could see that Magdalene Cherry had captured his heart. Whether the girl knew it or not was beside the point. Max was enraptured and Blanche was glad.

*

The smell of freshly ground coffee was conducive to the warm atmosphere of Carwardine's Coffee Shop. The walls, floors and furniture were of dark wood, enlivened by brass rails along the backs of the booths. Conversation hummed like a well-oiled machine, punctuated by the clink of silver spoons against fine ironstone china.

Heads nodded in greeting as Captain Tom Strong entered. Although there had always been comments about him marrying into money, they'd come to respect his firm manner and obvious integrity.

'Did you know he used to be a bare-knuckle bruiser?' they'd say one to another, then chortle and express their intention never to give him cause for anger.

In the wake of Horatia's news, he'd sent a note to Max Heinkel inviting him to an urgent meeting at the coffee house. He had considered going direct to the factory, but hoped the more congenial surroundings might help Max see sense.

'Fill two cups,' Tom said to the waiter on seeing Max come through the door. 'With cream and sugar.'

No one that Tom knew of had ever questioned Max Heinkel's paternity. Judging the young man by looks alone, it was easy to believe that the darkness of his hair was inherited from his mother, and its inclination to acquire blond streaks in strong sunlight was inherited from his father. Conrad had been a big, blond German with an easy smile and a congenial nature. He and Tom had liked each other, and both had loved Blanche.

They shook hands, and Max sat down.

He was wearing a dark coat with a lighter collar and cuffs and matching buttons. His trousers and waistcoat were beautifully tailored, and a gold chain crossed his chest, no doubt with a handsome half-hunter swinging on the end of it.

Tom was about to ask whether Max had given more consideration to his suggestion that he transfer the refinery to the new port, but Max got there first.

'I've fully considered all you said about the shortcomings of our original site on The Counterslip, and I agree with your observations.'

Tom felt his whole body relaxing. 'I'm glad to hear it.'

'I have thought long and hard, and have decided that in order to compete in this fast-changing world *and* maintain or increase profit at The Counterslip premises, we must look to increasing our investment in steam processes and vacuum driers.'

Tom looked at him in dismay. 'That won't solve your transport problems.'

Max tilted his head and looked at him with eyes that were the same pewter grey as Blanche's. It was impossible not to be affected by them. 'I have done some preliminary sums and am sure that one will compensate for the other.' He spoke with self-assurance, his face bright with youthful zeal, and a sudden intensity firmed his handsome features. 'I have to do this, Tom. You don't mind me calling you Tom, do you? Only my father and my mother always referred to you by your first name—'

'I don't mind at all.'

The truth was that his sudden intimacy affected him greatly. He felt an instant need to balance the situation. 'How is your mother? I haven't seen her in quite a while.' After saying it, he took a sip of coffee and looked into its dark surface as though he were seeing something more than was actually there, just in case Max, his son, their son, could read the look in his eyes.

'You know she hasn't been well?'

Tom shook his head. The news shocked him. 'Is she well now?'

Max smiled with the typical confidence of a young man for whom illness and death seem too far removed to worry about. 'It comes and goes. At least, that's what she says.' He grinned amiably. 'Sometimes I think it's just an excuse to stay a few days in Bath. She has a favourite hotel there. And she has come out of mourning at last. In fact, I left her trying on some hats . . . which reminds me . . .'

His confidence seemed to falter suddenly, as though he'd been found out to be only a boy pretending to be a man. He scrutinized the fine face of the half-hunter he pulled from his pocket, put it back in his waistcoat pocket and drained his cup. He got to his feet. 'Do excuse me.'

Tom felt sick at heart. Max did not have the experience to fight Horatia, and he knew that any advice to the strong-headed young man wouldn't work. Max was too like his father.

He could have told him of Horatia's plans, but he knew her too well. She'd destroy him, but most importantly, she'd destroy Max.

He left the coffee house feeling far less hopeful that Max Heinkel would survive in this fast-changing world. Although he would try to convince Horatia not to sell the shares held by the Strong family, he couldn't stop her – unless he bought them himself, or got someone else to buy them.

Perhaps out of respect for her father's wishes, she had always resisted selling the shares. But since the death of their son, she had thrown herself into business and had become, if it were possible, more ruthless and ambitious, and less inclined to follow family sentiments.

He gritted his teeth, waved his carriage away and turned onto the cobbled towpath that would take him eastwards out of the city. He needed to clear his mind. Was there any way he could persuade Horatia to reconsider?

The cobbles turned to gravel and crunched beneath his feet. Tufts of grass and bright yellow weeds jostled for space with purple buddleia, each bush dappled with tortoiseshell butterflies. The air was fresher here and although the city was encroaching along the side of the canal, there were still fields on the other bank curving out towards St Anne's.

A family of ducks scurried from the weeds and scooted off across the water towards a pair of brightly coloured narrowboats, lines of washing fluttering over their cabin roofs.

Up ahead, moored opposite a redbrick boarding house, was a gaudier boat, a ginger cat curled around its smoke stack, the name *Lizzie Jane* painted on the side. The cat got up at Tom's approach, stretched then lay down again, licked its mouth and closed its eyes. The boat looked familiar. A feather of white smoke curled from the stack and the smell of black shag tobacco and suet pudding hit his nose before he saw her.

'Aggie!'

On hearing his voice, a woman wearing a black bonnet and smoking a pipe squinted at him as hard as she could.

Aggie's eyesight is going, thought Tom, and was saddened. They'd arm-wrestled many a time at The Fourteen Stars tavern. Aggie had usually won.

Once he was up close, she recognized him. 'Tom Strong? Well, you old rum-wrencher. Come on aboard and I'll get thee a drink.'

The words and the way she said them were like music to his ears. It seemed an age since he'd seen her or heard those words spoken in a Forest of Dean accent – an odd cross between Gloucestershire dialect and Welsh.

She forced him to sit down and accept a drink from a chipped enamel mug decorated with yellow and red flowers.

'Now tell me all what you bin doing. How's that dark beauty you was so fond of? Blanche, wasn't it?'

'I married Horatia Strong, Aggie. I told you that years ago.'

She waved his protests aside. 'Yes, yes, and you live at that posh place out at Ashton, but I know you, Tom Strong. A ladies' man you are and always will be. So what 'appened to her then?'

'She married Conrad Heinkel and lives in Somerset Parade, Redcliffe. I believe I told you that, too.'

'Memory's not so good,' she explained and wiped a dribble of snuff with the corner of her apron.

'I thought you'd be retired by now, Aggie,' he said after they'd clinked mugs.

Aggie laughed and Tom noticed she'd lost more teeth. She was more hump-backed than when he'd last seen her, thinner too.

'This is me home, old butt.' She patted the boat's roof with a nut-brown hand, the skin shiny and thin enough to see the veins through it. 'I've lived on the *Lizzie Jane* for most of me life. Only way you'll have me off yur is in a box!' She laughed again, her teeth wobbling.

Tom leaned well back. Aggie had never boasted the sweetest of breaths.

'That's me sister's place.' She nodded at the brick boarding house.

The windows shone, the paint was fresh and although flowering weeds grew from the foundations and around the chimney, they made it cheerful.

'I gets all me water from there fur me cooking and me kettle. I could have enough to bathe in if I wanted, but I ain't goin' to change the habits of a lifetime at my age. Shock of cold water might kill me.'

'So you're not moving in with her,' said Tom.

Aggie shook her head. 'Not bloody likely. All them people coming and going at all hours, making a lot of noise, snoring and shouting in the next room to mine? Oh, no, no, no! I likes me independence, I do. Always have.'

'Not your sort, then, Aggie?'

'Well, what do you think?' She nodded to where the towpath and the narrow lane met the dirt-packed road. Two adults and two children were walking towards the boarding house. Their hair was woolly, their skin dark brown and their clothes a mismatch of texture and colour. The man had a determined expression, but Tom could see there was fear in his eyes.

He waved and Aggie waved back.

'They was looking for a place to stay, and I sent them over to my sister. Nice family. Straight off a boat from Jamaica or some such place.'

'Barbados,' said Tom. He didn't know why he said it, but there was something about the man that was vaguely familiar. Perhaps they'd met out there at one point.

'Do you know the bloke?' asked Aggie.

Tom shrugged. 'It'll come to me later.'

Aggie's sister-in-law waved from across the road as she opened the door to let in her guests. Even from that distance, there was no mistaking the delicious smell of West Country faggots – oozing with juices and sizzling in a hot oven. He guessed it was one of the better boarding houses in this part of the city.

The door slammed shut.

'They're looking for their relatives. Something to do with the sugar trade, of course,' said Aggie.

'Most people in the West Indies have something to do with the sugar trade,' Tom said.

Aggie was only half listening. 'I think she's too late bundling them in and slamming that door,' she said, and nodded towards two cottages, which leaned against each other for mutual support. People had emerged from the tumbledown doors and gathered on the corner. 'They noticed they was niggers,' Aggie said as she relit her pipe. 'There'll be trouble tonight.'

'Because they're different?'

Aggie nodded. 'It's all right for them to be a different colour in their own place, but not here. And they've travelled all this way on a fancy ship, which means they had the money to pay for it, and why should black folk have more money than white folk? That's the way they'll be thinking.' She pointed with her pipe, her voice turning a mite angrier. 'That lot over there ain't got two ha'pennies to scratch their asses, never have and never will. But they're down on anyone who's different and likely does have a few bob. There'll be trouble tonight, you mark my words!'

He hoped Aggie was wrong, but he understood her reasoning. There was a great deal of inequality in this world and, even in the minds of those that had nothing, there was still a need to believe that there was always someone one rung below you on the ladder.

He promised Aggie he'd see her again and said goodbye.

His confrontation with Max, combined with his grief at the death of his newborn son, weighed him down. A great tiredness seemed to overtake him as he made his way back to the coffee house, his fine horses and his equally fine carriage. All courtesy of the Strongs, he thought, and caught his grimace reflected back at him from the carriage window.

Where would he be if Jeb Strong, Horatia's uncle, had not found him licking sugar from a barrel as an urchin and adopted him? Dead? At sea? Married? Unmarried?

And what if he hadn't married Horatia? What if his first wife had not died in Boston? What if he had married Blanche?

Tom closed his eyes and leaned his head back against the rich comfort of the leather upholstery. There were too many questions and too many permutations of what his life might have been. The past was gone. Regrets were irrelevant, though he wished things could have been different. He wished many things had been different.

Chapter Seven

Septimus Monk cultivated an air of exquisite taste and used his hands stylishly, as if his cuffs were dripping with lacy frills. He sat at this moment behind his cherry wood desk, his head bowed over a share certificate, reminding Horatia of a portrait she'd seen of Charles II, though without the long hair, the garter or an insatiable lust for anything with a cleavage. In fact, the lawyer had a preference for young men.

Horatia cared little that his passions deviated from what was regarded as normal. He was an invaluable asset to her ambition, the best legal mind she had ever known.

His office near Stokes Croft reflected his learned profession, the walls gleaming with gilt lettering. Row upon row of law books rubbed alongside those of a more dubious – and collectable – nature. But although erudite, Monk sat like a spider at the centre of a web of information. Ten years ago he'd been useful to Horatia when Tom had been accused of murder. And he'd been useful many times since. No piece of gossip escaped him; no stone would be left unturned in the pursuit of information. Money talked in the twilight world where the wealthy dared not sully their name.

He looked up at her now, his pale eyes momentarily catching her unawares. 'You wish me to sign on your behalf?'

'Yes.'

Monk knew better than to ask her if she was sure. Horatia was always sure, more certain of her business than many men of greater years and experience. With a flourish of his unblemished hands, he signed the certificate, blew at the ink, then dipped his fingers into a bowl of lavender water and dried his hands.

Horatia was unfazed by the proceedings. Monk had always been fastidious. 'Good,' she said, feeling as pleased with herself as the day she had delivered a son, though perhaps more so. That event had not turned out to be as successful as she'd hoped. This present business venture would endure for years to come.

She paused by the door. 'Are you not going to ask me why I wish to own a bank?'

He looked at her as if surprised. A hint of a smile appeared. 'No.'

'Are you not curious?'

His smile broadened. 'Of course not. I am discreet in the extreme.'

Their eyes locked in such a way that an observer might have thought they were lovers. They were far from that, but each realized they were two of a kind. Deviousness led to success, and they both knew it.

'So you know why.'

'Of course I do. Whoever controls the bulk of the city's finance will end up controlling the new docks, and possibly the land around it. Thus, buy the bank that has locked its finance into the venture. I hear both the City Corporation and private individuals are indebted to the bank's absurd generosity.'

'That is exactly it,' she said as she pulled on a pair of blue kid gloves, buttoning them at the wrist and flexing her fingers. 'I want all of it.'

He nodded. 'Of course you do.'

'Let me know when you find a buyer for Rivermead.'

'There is some difficulty at the moment. I think things will improve somewhat once the insurrection there is under control. Free people are more difficult to control than those held in slavery. It never ceases to amaze me that those who were the masters actually went out of their way to educate these people.' He shook his head at the absurdity of it.

She made no comment. Like the child she had given away, Barbados was something she wished consigned to the past. Selling the plantation would help her forget.

It was only a few steps to her carriage, but before she reached it, a figure drifted like a wraith in front of her.

'Mrs Strong?'

The woman was drab rather than dirty. Her face was red and there was a marked bleariness to her eyes.

Presuming she was a former servant who had fallen on hard times, Horatia dipped into her reticule for a few shillings.

'I want more than shillings,' said the woman, but shoved the coins inside her blouse anyway.

The way she smiled made Horatia frown. She found herself overwhelmed with a feeling of threat and looked to her coachman. He was standing by the carriage dutifully, waiting to open the door for her. Behind her, Septimus Monk watched from his office door, a concerned look on his face.

Normally, she would have signalled for them to come to her aid, but something about the woman made her hesitate.

'Do I know you?' she asked.

The woman's smile widened, exposing a total lack of teeth from the bottom row and just a few pegs hanging on at the top. Horatia winced as she leaned forward. Her breath stunk of gin.

'Course you knows me. I'm Daisy Draper. I was there when your son was born.'

Horatia tensed. There'd been a midwife, a nurse, a monthly nurse and a wet nurse. She didn't recognize this woman and presumed she was the minor nurse, brought in to take away the soiled linens and dispose of the afterbirth. 'I don't remember you.'

'There was just me and a half-blind nurse left. But my eyes was alright, missus . . . oh yes . . . my eyes saw things the way they was.'

Again she rummaged in her reticule, apprehensive that the woman was there for a specific purpose, but keen to settle before anyone within earshot heard a word. 'There you are. Five shillings then for your trouble . . . My son died, you know . . .'

The woman's grubby fingers folded over the coins and she kept smiling as she shook her head. 'No, he didn't. I know where he is, 'cos I took him there.'

Horatia's features turned as hard and as pale as marble. A dozen possibilities of how best to deal with this situation wreathed like smoke in her mind.

'You were well paid,' she said, her voice low and her lips tight with intent.

'But not enough. I wants more, otherwise your husband's going to know that he mourns an empty grave. Wouldn't want him to know that, would you now?'

Horatia shuddered at the prospect. Tom must never know. *Never.*

The remaining coins in her reticule proved elusive; she wanted to take her time, to think. 'Here,' she said eventually, and handed over five sovereigns.

Daisy's smile broadened, her shrewd eyes narrowing as she counted the coins with blackened fingernails. 'That'll do,' she said menacingly, her mouth folding inwards as though she were sucking on a straw. 'Fer now. But I'll be back when this runs out. After all, you've sent the boy to a rotten place. Only fair that you does penance for what you've done.'

Horatia pounced, her fingers tightening around the woman's wrist and her eyes glittering with threat. 'Have a care, Daisy Draper. Should you approach me again, it will be the worse for you.'

Daisy sucked in her lips and hissed like a snake as she struggled to break away. 'What can a lady like you do?' she snarled, rubbing her wrist where Horatia's grip had left an angry mark. 'The likes of you run to law to sort the likes of me. But you can't do that, can you? That would mean yer husband finding out, and you wouldn't like that.'

Horatia stood frozen to the spot, watching as the woman wove along the pavement towards St Augustine's Reach, finally disappearing behind a coal dray pulling out from Denmark Street.

She sensed Monk at her side. 'I presume this was not a social encounter. The drab looked a nasty sort. I would guess from the emptiness of your reticule and the pallor of your face that the woman is causing you some concern. Am I right?'

Horatia nodded dumbly.

'Would I be correct is guessing that you would prefer her not to trouble you again?'

She knew what Septimus was implying.

'Yes,' she said.

Hands clasped behind his back, Monk nodded curtly. 'As you wish.'

Max Heinkel walked up and down between the Shakespeare Inn and the turning to Temple Church. The church cast a long awkward shadow, its lop-sided tower leaning over the roofs of the houses in Victoria Street.

Luckily, there were quite a few people out shopping, taking the air, or going about their daily business, so his promenading outside Madame Mabel, Milliner to the Gentry, failed to arouse suspicion.

He felt foolish, but couldn't stop himself. Each time he passed the milliner's window, he looked in, hoping for a glance of Miss Magdalene Cherry. He'd fallen in love with her when she'd delivered a hat to his mother just a few months before his father died. The hat had been cherry red and the slim, brown-eyed girl who'd delivered it had told her mother her name. They'd both laughed, and Max had stood tongue-tied in the doorway, holding his tennis racket and feeling stupid.

Two years ago! He'd thought never to see her again, and there she was again delivering hats to his mother, including a tartan one that Edith had compared to a military drum.

He knew little about making hats, except that it was hard work, the apprentices labouring all hours in dim workrooms, sewing and steaming and sticking on feathers beneath the wavering glow of a spluttering gas lamp.

He remembered she'd looked at him disdainfully, as though he were little more than a boy. In fact, he was certain he was older than her. She couldn't have been more than sixteen at the time, but like all women of her class, there was a worldly look in her eyes as if to say, 'I know what you want, but are you old enough to give it?'

Before his father's death, he hadn't dared admit his interest to anyone or even to her face. Now that he was more mature, he'd told himself that he could tell her what he was feeling, and that she would be inclined to listen.

At his mother's this morning, he'd merely nodded a greeting in her direction, had hung around outside in case she came out before he set off for Bristol. He'd waited fifteen minutes then checked his watch. He couldn't wait. Damn Tom Strong. Damn his meeting at the coffee house. And what was the point of it? No one had gained anything. He'd stated his position and Tom, it seemed, had finally accepted his decision.

Once that was out of the way, he made his mind up to seek Magdalene in her workplace. With that in mind, he walked up and down Victoria Street in the vain hope that she would pop out on another errand. He considered entering the shop, but found he didn't have the courage. All those women – the sales assistants, the customers and the girls in the backroom – peering up from their work at the sight of him and tittering amongst themselves.

He took deep breaths as he paced up and down, the air seemingly untainted by industrial fumes and the ripe pong of horse droppings. A weak sun was attempting to force its rays through flocks of fluffy clouds and the smell of hops rose in steamy warmth from the brewery.

A bell jangled as the shop door opened, and there she was, the girl of his dreams standing before him and bringing him to an abrupt halt.

Magdalene Cherry, demurely dressed in the blue and white uniform of Madame Mabel's and wearing a pale blue hat with a purple feather, swung briskly out onto the pavement, a hatbox swinging from each arm.

Smiling knowingly, she glanced his way, then tossed her dark curls, her small nose rising. Once she knew he was watching, her step became more bouncy, her hips wiggling beneath the prim uniform, her shoulders swaying and her bosom thrust forward against the tight buttons of her bodice.

Max was lost. 'Good afternoon,' he said, blushing and remembering to raise his hat as he stepped in front of her.

He'd presumed she'd act coyly, her cheeks turning rosy pink, and be too embarrassed to speak. Instead, her mouth dropped open and she looked bemused.

'Has your mother sent you?' she said in a cocky, forthright way.

Max was mortified. 'Of course my mother hasn't sent me!' He sounded and felt hurt. 'I came here of my own accord.'

'Why?' The way she said it was like a shot from a gun.

'That's none of your business.'

'Yes, it is. You've been following me. What are you after?'

'Nothing!'

'That's what all you rich gents say to us poor girls. Well, I know what you want, and you aren't going to get it here.'

Her accusation was like a slap in the face. He didn't see himself in the same mould as the wealthy gents who pursued the likes of her purely for sexual advantage. He felt genuinely offended and said so.

'How dare you suggest such a thing!'

She eyed him mockingly. 'Well, how dare *you*! Who do you think you are?'

'How can you talk to me like that?'

'I have every right to. You're the one accosting me, mister, and don't think I ain't seen you before – walking up and down the street, gawping in the window each time you pass. And don't deny it. We've been watching you. What you hoping to buy? And don't tell me you want a bonnet for your mother. She's quite capable of picking out her own bonnets, so go on, tell me before I send for the beak – what do you want?'

'Nothing! I mean—'

'Oh, yeah! I've met your sort before. Dressed like a gent, but not much of one underneath. Well, take note, mister, this is a milliner's not a knocking shop. We supply hats, not a bump and a grind against a warehouse wall. If you want that, you need to head down towards the docks. Ask any Bristol sailor and he'll tell you where to find it.'

Tossing her head, she spun on her heel and headed towards Bristol Bridge, the hatboxes banging against her hips.

Jaw slack and ego dented, Max watched her go. He hated being put down by anyone. What was worse he'd been most firmly put down by a milliner and a woman.

By the time he reached his club, he was slightly recovered and resolute in how he would deal with women like her in future. He made a huge effort to forget her heart-shaped face, her pert nose and her large brown eyes. And she is also very short, he reminded himself, hardly elegant.

He called for a drink, slugged it back, then called for another. The brandy burned in his throat but the vision in his mind refused to go away. What the devil is wrong with you, man? he asked himself. He'd never felt like this before. He couldn't concentrate, he couldn't think straight half the time. The business of sugar refining mostly dominated his life, and rightly so. But this slip of a girl, this milliner's assistant with her sassy walk and beguiling ways . . . He threw back the next drink, put the glass down and sighed. There was something about her. She was so alluring; a pocket Venus who held him spellbound.

Aggie Beven liked moonlit nights when the canal looked like a strip of silver and the sky turned turquoise. Tonight there was no moon. If there had been she would have stayed up top, sampling the fresh air along with a hot toddy and a fresh pipe, and she would have seen the shadowy figures creeping towards the boarding house, staves over their shoulders, dipping every few steps to pick up stones from the towpath. Instead Aggie drank inside the boat's cabin and, what with the drink and the warmth, fell swiftly and soundly asleep, her snores setting the china rattling.

Inside the lodging house, Samson woke from a worried sleep, his senses sharp and instantly alert. Instinct born of experience told him that something was wrong. In his childhood, overseers and those who'd sold their souls to the sugar planters had come creeping in the night, following a riot or a walkout in the fields by men who had once been slaves and had become poorly paid labour. Then there'd been the infighting amongst the various factions that had sprung up in the emancipated communities. He had had to be on his guard all his life. Here in England was no different.

Abigail stirred beside him. 'What is it?'

'Sshh!'

Keeping low, he crawled across the bed to the window and his heart leapt into his throat when he saw what was outside.

'Down,' he shouted, dragging his wife and children from the bed and diving under it. It was not a moment too soon. The windows came flying in, pane after pane spraying the room with splinters of glass. Rolling onto his side, he did his best to act as a barrier between the glass and his beloved family. What have we done to deserve this? he asked himself.

'I want to go home,' wailed Desdemona.

Much to his credit, his son, Hamlet, stayed silent, though his eyes were round as saucers. 'What shall we do, Pa?' he said eventually. His bottom lip quivered.

'Just stay down. Stay down!' his father replied in a hushed voice.

The door to the room suddenly opened. Samson covered the bodies of the children with his own.

'Come on. Out of there!'

Rosie, Aggie's sister and their landlady, filled the doorway.

'Down to the cellar. Quick!'

Hamlet bobbed up, ready to run. Samson grabbed the back of his pants and brought him down again. 'Crawl on your belly.'

The sound of staves beating on the front door echoed along the passageway.

'That's an oak door,' said Rosie, sounding more confident than she actually felt. 'They won't get through that.' She bustled them along to a door beneath the stairs. 'Lock it behind you,' she said.

'What about you?' Unlike her sister-in-law, Rosie was tall and angular, her clothes hanging like curtains on her lean frame. 'I'll talk to them. Don't you worry, me dears, I'll give 'em a piece of my mind. I'm good at talking.'

Samson was doubtful their attackers would listen. 'I can't leave you here alone,' he said.

She brushed him off. 'Don't you worry about me, ole butt. I won't be entirely by meself.' Rosie reached up behind his head and took something down. 'I've got Bessie,' she said in a determined, though cheerless voice. 'I'll shoot the bloody lot of 'em if I've got to.'

The fat muzzle of an ancient blunderbuss grazed Samson's ear.

'Now get down them stairs,' ordered Rosie.

Samson did as he was told, though he couldn't help worrying. She'd been very kind, had fed them simple but nourishing meals and, as they had spooned the thick mixes of potatoes and meat into their mouths, had regaled them with stories of her life in the Forest of Dean.

Once she was sure they'd bolted themselves in, Rosie made her way towards the oak door, her old knees creaking but her long legs swiftly covering the ground. She was feeling more jittery than she'd let on to Samson, but had convinced herself that she was still the woman she'd always been, the sort who could lay out a man with one blow of a fierce right hand.

The sight that met her eyes made her feel more worried. Much as she'd put her faith in the oak door, the old surround was made of a softer wood and was splintering around the locks.

'Get away from my door, or I'll blast the lot of ye!'

'Give us the niggers!'

'Damned if I will!'

The hammering continued. The doorframe splintered.

Rosie loaded the ball in the old gun, sharpened the flint and heaped powder in the pan. John, her late husband, had taught her how to use weapons when they'd been stationed in India – in case of need, he'd told her. A large number of Afghan tribesmen had been slain by John's army rifle. A few more had been blasted by Rosie's blunderbuss when they'd attempted to steal her donkey. That was in the days when they'd all been younger– including the blunderbuss.

The hammering was deafening. At last the wood splintered with a thunderous wrench and the door caved in.

Dark figures waving weapons charged then jammed in the door as three of them tried to get in at once.

There was a blinding flash as Rosie opened fire. The lead man screamed and grabbed at his chest. The weight of those behind pushed him forward. He fell flat on his face, stone dead.

'Get out of my house,' Rosie shouted as she swiftly reloaded. Usually she poured the exact measure into the pan, but there was no time.

'You've killed him,' the lead man shouted, pointing down at his colleague.

'And you be next, ole butt if you don't get out,' she shouted back, her gun cocked and loaded. 'This used to be a respectable area before the likes of you came along.'

'Call yourself respectable?'

The hallway was dark, so she couldn't see his expression, just the outline of his body. He smelled of sweat, dirt and mildew. She had to rely on movement, so she narrowed her eyes, winced as she bent her knees and waited.

'Come on, boys! You ain't afraid of an old woman, are ye?'

There was a flurry of movement as one man was pushed forward, a stave raised above his head. Rosie fired.

The flash was fierce and accompanied by a terrific burst of noise. Rosie had no time to scream. The old blunderbuss fondly christened Bessie had grown rusty and weak. In Rosie's haste to reload, she had tipped too much powder onto the pan and Bessie had exploded in her face. She saw no more, tasted blood in her mouth and heard heavy footsteps, the last sound she would ever hear.

'She's dead?'

'So's Smithy. Serves the old cow right.'

His colleague was more cautious and sounded nervous. 'That ain't the way the peelers are going to see it.'

'Then they ain't goin' to see it. We takes what we can then set the place alight. No one's gonna be any the wiser then, are they?'

'What about them niggers?'

'They can burn, too.'

Beads of sweat running down his face, Samson pressed his ear against the door. He'd heard the smashing of wood, the blasts of fire from Rosie's old gun. Now he could hear the trampling of boots – many boots – running through the house, up and down the stairs, tearing apart the room he and his family had been in.

He rummaged in his pockets, found nothing and grimaced. Every penny they had, every item they owned, had been left in the room.

Behind him, the children were beginning to whimper. 'I want to go home,' said Desdemona again, rubbing at her eyes. 'I don't like it here'.

Samson exchanged a swift look with Abigail as she attempted to calm the children's fears.

'We'll go back to bed soon,' she said.

'I don't want to go to bed. I want to go home,' Hamlet murmured.

Samson's body ached with tension. 'Go away,' he whispered through the door. 'Go away, go away.'

The sound of his racing heart echoed in his head as he waited, his fists clenched, ready in case they were discovered. Backwards and forwards, up and down stairs, cupboards opened, crockery crashing, things being dragged across floors, bumped down stairs. Each time the sound of boots came close, his mouth turned dry and he prayed as he'd never prayed before.

Religion had never figured large in his life, but someone must have been listening. At last the sound of voices and boots retreated. Then he smelled something.

'Are they gone?' asked Abigail.

'I'm not sure.'

He heard a crackling sound before the smoke filtered beneath the door, its fumes stinking of burnt varnish and lead paint.

'Fire,' he said in a low voice, his gut churning with apprehension. 'Get back down the stairs,' he barked. 'Take the children with you and get into the farthest corner. Don't move till I tell you.'

With the aid of the one and only candle they had, Abigail did as ordered, ducking her head against the curved ceiling of the cellar.

Samson took a shovel from behind the door. He couldn't be entirely sure that the gang had left, but he was ready to strike in case someone had stayed. Carefully he pulled back the bolt, and opened the door.

'Oh God,' he murmured.

A curtain of heat took his breath away. Flames soared ceiling-high down the narrow passageway and smoke billowed into the cellar.

Samson peered through the inferno, his eyes watering, choking on the fumes, wondering whether they could run to the front door,

perhaps if they draped themselves in wet clothes. But where would they get the water? Besides, the children would be terrified.

It's too late, he decided as panic gripped his mind. It's too late!

The wood that panelled the long passageway was spitting and crackling, the stairs above him burning as well as the old furniture, dried out and past its best, the varnish blackening and stinking.

There were two humps of what looked like scorched clothing beneath the flames and between him and the front door. He recognized Rosie's blue skirt, torn and blackened now. Even as he watched, the flames engulfed both shapes, the heat intensified and he was forced to retreat.

He slammed the door shut, wrenched the bolt across. Clasping his chest, he coughed the smoke from his lungs and breathed deeply. Surprised that the smell of singed fabric was still so strong, he touched his head and realized his hair was gently smouldering.

'Samson!' Abigail had noticed, too.

He hit at his head with his bare hands. Charred hair fell in a shower of sparks and smoking flakes.

'Samson?' Abigail called again, her voice trembling with fear, her eyes big with one unspoken question.

'She's dead,' he said, and shrugged. 'I don't know how.'

Once he was sure he was safe, Samson turned to his family, who were cowering in the far darkness, their terror accentuated by the light of the candle.

'We have to get out.' He looked back up the steps to the door. It was cloaked in darkness, but he was sure it was turning black and beginning to smoke. There was little time.

'Give me that candle, and stay there.'

'Pa!' Desdemona wrapped her arms around her father's legs.

Samson unwrapped her and pushed her back to her mother. 'Stay here. I'll find us a way out. But I shall need the candle. You will have to cope with the darkness for a while.'

Abigail gathered the children beneath her arms, her hands around their foreheads. 'Stay alive, Samson.'

Samson would have smiled to himself if the situation hadn't been so dire. Abigail had not told him to be careful, but to stay alive. Trust his wife to get to the heart of the matter.

He left them in total darkness. There was only half a candle left, so he had half an hour at the very most, he thought.

His first inclination was to head to where the coal was stored. In large houses, most coal cellars were accessed through wooden shutters set into the pavement or immediately against a house, separate entrances from the rest of the property.

Hopefully, the cellar would be empty.

He stumbled through the gloom until he heard the sound of something crunching underfoot. Hopes rising, he lifted the candle. Coal glistened, caught in the flickering glow. Like a small mountain, it was piled high.

Originally, he had planned to smash open the dual doors, get Abigail to stand on his shoulders so she could get out, pass the children up to her, then climb out himself purely by bracing his arms against the opening and heaving himself out. He had initially thought that too much coal would be an obstacle. Now he counted it a blessing. We can climb up over it, he decided.

He was just about to go back to Abigail and tell her, when something caught his eye. Bringing the candle to bear, he studied the heap of coal. Smoke filtered through and over the mound. Fear once again clawed at his heart. The cellar had become hotter. Sweat dripped from his forehead, nose and chin. To his horror, he realized that the cellar walls and ceiling were conducting heat from the fire blazing above them. He had no doubt that soon the pile of coal would ignite, the fumes killing them before the fire did.

Then he noticed that only one side of the coal heap seemed to be steaming. On the other side, the smoke seemed to be less virulent; in fact, he decided on closer scrutiny, it was a different colour.

Frowning, he swiftly considered the reasons for this. Perhaps it was the candle. Perhaps it was different coal causing a different colour. He sniffed. It smelled damp, not the dampness of coal, but the mildewed dampness of wet walls, a river . . . a canal! It wasn't smoke he could see and smell, but steam. The walls were wet!

Scrabbling over the coal, he dug with his bare hands, praying that the wall would be so wet he could dig through. He dug with his bare hands, his fingernails bloodied as they snapped off against the rough stone, more blood trickling from his knuckles and fingers. And yet he made little progress. It was useless. He needed something to dig with, and instantly remembered the shovel at the bottom of the steps.

He immediately felt his way back and retrieved the shovel, before turning to Abby and the children. The relief shone in their eyes.

'I think I've found a way out.' He thrust the candle into his wife's hand. 'Follow me. And keep close together.'

They made their way to the coal mound.

'This wall,' he explained. 'It's wet. We may end up in the river on the other side, but I'm betting we won't.'

Wife and children watched as he swung the shovel. Its sharp edge smashed into the wall. He had expected the coal dust with which it was coated to fill the air, revealing the bricks or stones beneath. Once they were revealed, he would have chipped at the mortar joining them with the sharp edge of the shovel. It would have been a long task without the use of a pickaxe, but it would have been their only hope. But there were no bricks or stones. To his great surprise a low wooden door, unrecognizable through years of disuse, sprang beneath the first blow, then splintered.

'It's a door,' he cried, and rained blow after blow until it was no more than matchwood.

'The candle,' he shouted, flinging the shovel to the ground.

Abigail passed it to him.

Samson held it out in front of them, saw the flame flicker in a cold draft of air.

'It's a tunnel,' he said, swallowing his relief and wiping the tears from his face. 'It's a tunnel.'

Toilet facilities on Aggie's boat were pretty primitive, consisting as they did of a large enamel bucket with a lid. She never bothered with it when travelling the more secluded canals, merely lifted her skirts over the side of the boat after making sure no one was around. But moored at a city berth was different.

She'd awoken from her sleep needing to go, used the bucket, then went out of the door. The clouds had disappeared and the moon was out. After she'd tipped the bucket over the side, she settled herself down on top and lit up her pipe.

She sighed contentedly as the sweet-smelling smoke of black navy shag curled up into the night air, then she settled herself into a comfortable corner. The only sound was the hum of the distant city and the snuffling and shuffling of small creatures running through the reeds or slipping into the water, their entry barely disturbing the surface.

She sniffed the air pleasurably, sensed something was different and frowned. There was too much smoke in the air and it certainly wasn't coming from her pipe.

Her gaze was drawn to the windows of her sister's boarding house. The downstairs window glowed orange. As she watched, a cloud of black smoke poured out of the door.

'Rosie!'

Despite her painful knees, she struggled over the side of the boat and onto the quay.

She shouted again. 'Rosie!'

She became aware of people jostling her, pointing and shouting for a fire engine to be called. Someone suggested forming a human chain of buckets, taking water from the canal to throw onto the flames.

A few men hung back. One of them, a nasty type named William Summer, whom Rosie had warned her about, had a gloating look about him. She recalled seeing him follow the West Indian family earlier. His sneer melted when he saw her looking.

Aggie's eyes watered as she stared at the flames. No matter that she and her sister were getting old and likely to depart this life before very long, they'd both hoped to die in bed, or at least doing what they'd always done. She knew, somehow, that Rosie was dead, and that it was no accident.

Chapter Eight

Daisy Draper left The Three Tuns in the early evening, her mood as foul as her breath. She'd run out of money and the landlord had refused to put it on the slate.

'I'll remember you,' she'd shouted at him as he'd seen her off the premises. 'You'll see!'

To anyone listening, her threats sounded hollow. To anyone who knew her, including the landlord, they were anything but. Daisy had a reputation for retribution. Cross her and she would take revenge.

There was a yard at the back of The Three Tuns. A wooden gate with peeling paint was set into the brick wall surrounding it. Before entirely taking her leave, Daisy eased it open.

A line of fresh white washing was blowing on a clothesline: two sets of combinations; three pairs of drawers almost big enough to be tablecloths; a few shirts; and some children's clothes.

She pinched the latter, stuffing them into her blouse. There was always a market for kiddies' clothes. But her thirst for revenge was only half assuaged. Pausing, she eyed the landlord's combinations and his fat wife's voluminous drawers. Her eyes went from there to a smouldering dung heap made more obnoxious by the contents of last night's chamber pot.

Using a pair of dock leaves, she formed glutinous balls from the sticky mass. Each completed ball was placed on the ground in front of her. Once she had six, she found a metal bucket, put them inside then took them over to the washing line and smeared every item with a glutinous mess of brown excrement.

With a swift 'up yours' sign, she closed the gate behind her, smiling to herself as she went on her way.

A summer fog had descended, a yellowish soup of heat haze mixed with the smoke, steam and gases spewing from tall brick chimneys around the city docks.

Her sojourn at the tavern had started mid-morning, so neither her legs nor her eyesight were up to the job of peering through the haze and negotiating the ancient cobbles, which were made of wood rather than stone. Many had been dug up during cold spells and used as firewood so the road was peppered with holes.

Daisy, being a bit more than tipsy, caught her foot in one and fell flat on her face. Muttering a host of obscenities, she struggled to her feet, straightened her hat, and continued on her way.

Despite her drunken state, the matter of money stayed uppermost in her mind. Although it may not have seemed so at the time, she had been a little intimidated by Horatia's attitude, though not enough to put her off the idea of extorting a few guineas. In fact, Daisy blamed the likes of Horatia Strong for her fall from grace. In her younger days she'd enjoyed a good reputation for reliability and consideration of mothers-to-be. Her downfall had been Dr Owen, who had a lilting ring to his voice and a roving eye. A few years ago, she'd been quite good-looking and had fallen for his charms. A child was conceived, but Dr Owen had seen to it that it was born dead. After that, she'd taken to drink, financed mostly by the guilty doctor, who also arranged for her to attend a few lying-ins. Before each one he would ensure she was sober, usually having her sleep in a room above his surgery the night before. Not that he ever joined her there now. At thirty-nine, she was too old to attract his attention any longer, and the drink had taken its toll. He had another lover now, a young woman with a tiny waist and a pert bosom, fresh to the city from a Welsh town named Aberystwyth. She looked little more than sixteen years of age.

People hurried past her in the darkening evening, heading for a hot supper and a warm fire. 'Get off, all of you,' she shouted.

No one stopped to challenge her and soon the street was deserted. Ordinary shadows became grotesque and sounds seemed hollower. There were few lights at windows or at the brooding façades of warehouses, where wine, sherry and port were stored.

The silence deepened. That was when she heard the footsteps.

She stopped and tilted her head to one side in order to hear more clearly. There was nothing. Perhaps she had imagined it. Pulling her shawl more closely about her, she staggered on.

But there were the footsteps again. Were they hers? Was she hearing her own boots tripping along over the cobbles?

She stopped. The footsteps stopped, too.

'Silly cow,' she muttered, and shook her head.

He sprang on her where a narrow alley erupted like a black hole between two buildings.

'This is for not minding yer own business.'

She heard the clink of a blouse button bouncing on the ground. Fresh air hit her chest as the two folds of her blouse fell apart, the stolen children's clothes following the bouncing button. Something flashed like silver before her terror-filled eyes.

He had a knife!

With no other option, she began to fight and scream at the top of her voice.

'Shut up!'

He grappled with her, tried to stab her at the same time as clapping his hand across her mouth. She kicked out behind her and he yelled as the heels of her boots met his shins.

Somehow, she managed to get out from under his arms, the last of the children's clothes scattering behind her as she ran across the road and into the alley.

In her heart, she knew she wouldn't get far. She was drunk and hampered by her skirts.

It turned out luck was on her side. The sound of hooves and the clatter of wheels suddenly rang down the street. A dray was returning to the brewery, the driver late and wanting to get home, his whip singing over the backs of the galloping shires, giant horses of over seventeen hands, their hooves the size of dinner plates, tons of muscle on the move.

The driver, having supped a few ales at the end part of the day, would see no more through this smog than she did. Even if he'd seen her assailant, he could not have stopped the horses in time. She heard the man cry out. The thud of wheels against something solid, the neighing of horses as they thundered over him.

Shivering with terror, and sweating with relief, Daisy hurried to her lodgings.

When the church clock of nearby St Stephen's chimed midnight, she was still awake, sitting in her room and wondering at what had happened. The man had not been out to rob her. He'd wanted to kill her. Thanks to the bundle of children's clothes, the knife he'd slashed across her chest had not penetrated her flesh.

The words he had uttered kept running round her head: *This is for not minding yer own business.* Horatia Strong.

She concentrated on the pathetic flame she'd managed to entice from her meagre fire. She should have got more money from Horatia, then called it a day. But she wasn't going to leave this. She'd damn well have her revenge.

Creases like the hairline cracks in an old jug radiated around her mouth. 'Then let's see what yer husband thinks of it all,' she muttered, gave the coals a hefty poke and spat a mouthful of phlegm into the flames.

The vast parkland around Marstone Court echoed to the sound of sticks beating against metal, shouts, whistles and the excited yapping of freckle-backed setters and spaniels with long tongues and short tails.

Men with weather-beaten faces and work-worn hands – labourers, tenants and gamekeepers to the Strong family – strode through fern, broom and elder, their steps steady, their expression resolute.

Ahead of them, apprehensive and confused, this year's pheasants moved closer and closer to the shorn stubble of an open wheat field, the biggest on the estate. Driven by the beaters through the rough cover and with an open space in front of them, they would have no choice but to fly into the clear air to gain the copse on the other side.

At the edge of the copse stood a row of men wearing velvet-trimmed tweeds, their guns raised at the flying birds. Among them stood Horatia Strong, hostess for a weekend of shooting, heavy lunches and long, drawn-out dinners.

An event to be remembered, said those lucky enough to be invited, and were grateful that they were, though wondered whether there was any particular reason for it. Horatia Strong was not known for socializing, unless a financial gain was likely.

Horatia cocked her weapon, closed one eye and took careful aim.

'I hear them,' said her companion, Martin Lodge, chairman of Webbers Bank. He laughed as the birds took to the air making their familiar clacking, chuckling noise. 'It always sounds to me as though they're laughing,' he said as he shouldered his shotgun.

Horatia controlled the urge to tell him to shut up, and squeezed the trigger of one of a pair of handsome Purdeys she'd had made to suit her. The sound cracked upwards into the sky and a soaring bird fell like a lump of lead.

Lodge was aware, by her tight-lipped silence, that he'd upset Horatia's concentration, but he brightened on seeing her jaw relax and hoped he had made a favourable impression on the wealthiest and most powerful woman in the city.

'God knows they've got nothing to laugh about,' she remarked with a cold humour as she let off another shot, checked as another bird fell to the earth, then swiftly exchanged her empty gun for one that was loaded.

'Your aim matches that of your husband,' Lodge said as he also took a freshly loaded gun, took aim and fired.

Horatia allowed herself the deplorable indiscipline of taking her eyes off her target long enough to glance at her husband. 'You flatter me,' she said with grim sincerity.

Tom was shooting with swiftly accurate precision. Her husband, and cousin by adoption, did everything well, although shooting was something in which she had hoped to defeat him. Eyebrows had been raised a few years back when the news leaked out that she was joining the men in a sport where few women cared to tread. Tom had not protested. He enjoyed her competitiveness, mostly because in sport at least, he easily defeated her. Business, however, was an entirely different matter.

Gun after gun was emptied and reloaded with frightening regularity. An avalanche of birds thudded onto the hard ground, retrieved by smiling dogs with lashing tails or trembling stumps. And still the guns blasted, the stink of spent cartridges hanging acrid in the morning air.

'I've never known a woman attend a shoot before,' Lodge remarked above the barrel of his gun. His shot rang in the air. The bird fell, only winged but put out of its agony by a beater.

'I do not merely attend. I shoot,' she countered. Her target plummeted to earth stone dead.

'And very well,' he repeated, a trifle disconsolately before expending his full concentration on the job in hand. This time his kill was clean.

'So to what do I owe this invitation?' He looked at her sidelong. 'It is a well-known fact in the city that Horatia Strong never does anything without a reason. I take it you have some business venture in mind? Perhaps it concerns your husband's plan regarding the redirection of sugar ships to London, and the refining, too? It might be you wish to persuade me not to back the proposed new dock at the Avon's mouth. Am I right? But if you need money for your London venture, I'm sure the bank can assist.'

He sounded amused. Horatia had never found anything remotely amusing about business. She took it very seriously. That's how you succeed, she'd told herself in the days when her father was still alive. Webber was a fool. The Board of the Bank had no confidence in him, though he did not know it. Horatia did. She had made it her business to find out. Gritting her teeth, her fingers aching with tension, she let off a shot. Yet again she had a clean hit, but even when she lowered her weapon, her jaw was still clenched, her eyes narrowed.

'I do not require any money for that particular enterprise, at least not in the short term. Isn't it possible I may indeed have invited you here purely for the pleasure of your company?'

The guns continued to rattle.

Lodge smirked. 'Come, come, Mrs Strong. I have been chairman of Webbers Bank for a considerable number of years. I know when someone requires my services, especially given that we are not averse to backing new ventures, though of course our funds would be limited. Backing a new dock is a very big venture indeed. By necessity, it has to be a joint venture. One backer alone could be ruined by unforeseen hold-ups.'

Horatia smiled over the barrel of her gun. Lodge, though he couldn't possibly know it, had hit the nail on the head. 'Yes,' she said after yet another bundle of plumage had fallen from the sky. 'You are quite right. I do indeed require your assistance and am aware of the bank's involvement in the new project at the mouth of the river.' Breaking the shotgun, she passed the empty weapon to her loader. Lodge was her next target.

He took aim.

'I've bought your bank.'

The gun barked, but Lodge missed. The bird he'd been aiming for flew merrily on its way to be bagged by the gun of Captain Tom Strong.

His face a picture of total amazement, Lodge turned to her, the muzzle of his gun dangerously close to his body. 'I'm sorry? Did I hear you right?'

Horatia smiled, raised her gun, squeezed one eye shut and fired. A pheasant fell to earth. She took aim again, the crack of the second shot following immediately. She'd let Lodge stew until she was ready.

'Yes. You did,' she said without taking her eyes off the dogs as they picked their way like ballerinas across the stubble, niftily lifted their prey and trotted back to their handlers, their tails spinning like windmills.

A cry went out for the guns to be silent as both dogs and handlers made their way across the field to retrieve those birds the dogs had missed, some of whom were dead, and some merely wounded. The men snapped the necks of the wounded and slid the heads between their fingers, leaving bodies hanging like bunches of limp cabbages.

Horatia kept her gaze fixed on the field. It wasn't that she had any fear of Lodge's response; she wanted him to feel the shock deep in his bones; to wonder how she had done it without him finding out; to realize that she was clever and based her moves on excellent inside information.

As she waited for him to speak she watched her husband exchange words with the beaters, who tipped their hats at him and smiled, not just with their mouths, but also with their eyes. The fact that they liked him was obvious by the way they continued to chew on straws, slap their thighs in response to a humorous quip and laugh out loud, or even to slap him on the back as if he were still one of them, one of the dirty, destitute and unwashed.

In a way he is, she thought. Beneath the fine clothes he's no different to any man. He could be rough, at times even vulgar, but always there was something about him that set him apart, that made her stomach clench and caused a tingling in her loins. And he's mine, she thought, and glowed with satisfaction.

'I'm astounded you had the bank in your sights, Mrs Strong,' said Lodge, his voice hollow and every bit of colour drained from his face.

She started and turned away from the sight in the field as he placed his hand on her gun and lowered it. She hadn't realized that her gun, as well as her thoughts, had been directed at Tom. It was unforgivable and embarrassed her.

'Do you have your husband in your sights, too?'

His choice of words was flippant and Horatia did not warm to them or him. Her lips were thin and her voice hissed with disapproval as she said, 'I bagged my husband many years ago.' The disapproving frown faded and a smile crept across her lips. 'But like all field sports, Mr Lodge, the fun is in the chase. Besides, even the best pheasant cooked in the best burgundy becomes poor fare indeed if eaten every day.'

Now she was being flippant. She liked to shock people, especially those she sensed felt a woman's place was firmly in the home.

Lodge turned red. 'It has been conveyed to me by the Board that other parties have already bought in—'

'*I* am those other parties,' Horatia interrupted.

Lodge was an experienced banker, and that was all he was. His life had been ruled by figures, by ledgers, the counting of money, the idea that he had served the bank well and in return they would serve him with equal loyalty. To find out he was not privy to all their decisions had cut him to the quick. It took him a little time to digest her news.

He knew someone had been buying shares in the bank and had not quibbled because the price had been generous, almost foolish. But the directors, the biggest shareholders in the bank, had taken the money.

'I thought there was more than one purchaser,' he said in a faltering voice. His shoulders slumped. He was not at all the big, bluff man he had been earlier.

But now he knows better, thought Horatia, careful to hide a small triumphant smile.

'I understand you are a gambler,' she said. 'Please don't deny it. I have had enquiries made.'

She turned swiftly and caught the look of disbelief on his face. Septimus Monk had been right. Her lawyer was one of the most useful people she had ever met. He knew those who inhabited the sinks and gutters of the city and how to use them; how to get information from servants, shopkeepers and those who controlled the vices to which a large city is prone.

'Please,' he began, his voice wavering, 'you won't tell the Board.'

Her expression hardened. Handsome as she was, when she looked at people the way she did now, her features seemed as if they'd been chiselled from marble. A more honourable man would have asked her not to inform his wife.

'Does your wife know the extent of your debt? Does she know you have mortgaged the house in order to pay off the immense amount you've stolen from the bank?'

She could almost smell his fear. Sweat beaded his forehead and ran into his eyes. That he should perspire was understandable, but she knew she'd shocked him and had meant to.

Her intention was for him to worry that his position at the bank, which he had filled for many years, might be at an end. In fact, the opposite was true. Offering that he should keep his position, though with greatly diminished responsibility, was a clever ruse she'd used before. Status to non-status and back again: he had to accept. That was the way she'd planned it, though she wouldn't tell him just yet. Martin Lodge deserved to be tortured a little longer for what he had done to the bank and to his wife.

And then I will tell him that he can keep his job, so long as he answers to me and me alone.

With ownership of the bank and the chairman in her pocket, the financing of the Avonmouth dock would be under her control.

Pies, cheeses, breads, cakes, jugged hare and thick custards, wines, sherries and spirits were set out beneath the trees for the benefit of the guests. Tom passed his gun to the gamekeeper. At the same time he wondered at his chances of slipping away. He wasn't too keen on these gatherings and had fancied having a quiet smoke alone for a few minutes, but a small hand suddenly slipped into his.

'Are we going to eat pie, Father?'

Resigned to his fate, Tom looked down at his daughter. She was wearing a dark pink dress with a lace collar and purple bows at the throat and on the wrists.

'Pie, cake, cheese and custard – though not altogether,' he joked.

Emerald laughed.

'Now, now, Miss Emerald. You know you're not supposed to be out here.'

Her nurse, Miss Potter, was right behind her, wearing an expression that was greyer than her dress.

Father and daughter exchanged a grimace.

The nurse curtseyed. 'Begging your pardon, sir, but Mrs Strong said Miss Emerald was to eat in the nursery.'

'All alone up there? Nonsense. Families who live together should eat together.'

Miss Potter attempted to protest. 'But—'

'No buts. You can come too, if you wish,' said Tom.

The nurse stayed rooted to the spot, her mouth hanging open.

Tom laughed as his daughter launched herself into his arms.

'Hurray!' she shouted.

He swung her round, her golden hair flying behind her, then hand in hand, father and daughter traipsed off towards the trestle tables, Tom's stride long and even, Emerald bouncing like a rubber ball beside him.

Horatia's smile – the one she reserved for events like this – tightened when she saw them. Ignoring her daughter's upturned face, she addressed Tom. 'I gave orders she should eat her meal in the nursery.' With a swift jerk of her head, she addressed her daughter. 'Go to the nursery.'

Emerald clung more tightly to her father, peeping out from behind his arm.

'She should be with her parents,' Tom said in an implacable voice, smiling as he nodded acknowledgement to their guests.

Aware they were being observed, Horatia spoke through a stiff smile. 'A child is happier in familiar surroundings, Thomas.'

'Were you?'

Her smile disappeared and she gave him that 'wait until we're alone' look. Their public image mattered. She would not force the issue, not in front of guests.

Tom bent down to his daughter and pointed at one of their servants. 'Get Mathilda to give you some cake.'

Emerald scuttled off happily, leaving her father to take the full force of Horatia's glittering gaze.

Tom took a sherry from a passing tray, and drained it. He felt like a butterfly about to be pinned to a card. 'I see I have made you angry,' he said quietly and avoided looking into her face as he reached for another sherry.

Horatia glowered. 'Sometimes I think you go out of your way to make me angry. I believe you actually enjoy undermining my authority!'

He nodded before swigging back his drink and slamming it down on a passing tray. Although she didn't seem to realize it, he'd been controlling his temper on account of her obvious sadness following the death of their child. Even when she'd told him about selling Rivermead, he'd merely pointed out to her that it might have been politic to inform her brother Rupert of her intention. She'd almost bitten his head off.

He kept his voice even now. 'And you, my dear. Have you made anyone angry today?'

Her frosty demeanour was suddenly replaced with a look of triumph. 'I have enlightened a man that was in darkness,' she said with a slick smile reserved for her more ruthless moments. 'I've spoken to Martin Lodge. I have told him he may not be in the bank's employ for much longer and that I know about his gambling.'

He looked at her incredulously.

'I just want him to stew a little,' she said defensively. 'It's what he deserves. Before he leaves I'll tell him that he can keep his job and that no one will be told about his gambling.'

Tom had only met the man on a few occasions, but had detected a little nervousness in his demeanour. Gamblers were sometimes like that, bankers and stockbrokers, too. Players for high stakes in a game of chance.

'Are you sure you haven't misjudged the man? You're threatening to destroy his life.'

For a brief moment, there was doubt in his wife's eyes, but it quickly passed. 'There is nothing wrong with my judgement.'

'I think you should let him off the hook, Horatia.'

'Why should I? It's only a bank.'

Tom shook his head and lit a cigarillo. 'Not to him it isn't. To him it's his life.'

Again, one of her looks. 'What's done is done. I'll tell him later.'

They parted, Tom to locate another sherry, Horatia to speak to her brother, Rupert, who had just returned to England from the West Indies.

'I'm selling Rivermead,' she said to him, glancing in a derogatory fashion at his tall, thin wife, who had chosen to wear a dress of deep saffron. Horatia was reminded of an overripe banana.

'Good,' said Rupert. 'I hate the bloody place.'

No prevarication, no hurt feelings, no pleas for her to retain the sprawling house and the cane fields surrounding it. The world of the eighteenth century, when black slaves and brute force had spawned their wealth, was gone. The children of the brutal men who had founded and advanced their dynasty were of a different mould. Fastidious in their tastes and keen of mind, they would look to new horizons and towards an expanding empire and a new century.

Horatia was pleased. Everything was going well. The hem of her dress turned wet as she made her way across the grass, smiling to herself and feeling triumphant at a job well done.

A flock of crows took to the air in response to the sudden bark of a gun. It was followed by a scream.

Tom recognized the voice immediately. 'Emerald!' Discarding his cigarillo, he ran in the direction of the sound.

Emerald was hurtling towards him, the dogs yapping behind her. Her pink dress was speckled with blood and she was screaming at the top of her voice. 'Daddeee! Daddeee!'

She was still screaming after her father handed her to her nurse, ran into the trees and discovered the body of Martin Lodge.

'I knows all about it, I knows all about it!'

Blanche glanced at the woman staggering on the other side of the road, but her attention was quickly drawn to the queue of people waiting outside the Workhouse gates: men, women and children, of all ages and sizes, their clothes threadbare and their faces lined with worry. She knew these were the people with nothing left in the world, all hoping to gain a place in the Workhouse. It made her ashamed to be wearing such a fine dress, such a rich velvet trim to her hat and kid gloves that cost enough to feed a family for a day, perhaps longer.

Her depression might have deepened if the woman making a ruckus on the other side of the road hadn't started shouting again.

'I saw that babbee! I knows what he was and where he went! I knows . . .' She waved her arms, upset her balance and fell flat on her face.

'Oh, my—' Blanche stepped into the gutter.

Edith grabbed her arm. 'No! Don't you worry. I'll see to her. You go on and do yer business in thur.'

Blanche heard the double gates open behind her as she watched Edith scurry across the road to the fallen woman.

'Well, 'allo thur,' she heard the woman exclaim.

Edith muttered something unintelligible close to the woman's face.

'Well, are ye coming in?'

She turned to face the Workhouse watchman, who was still attired in his mismatched uniform, his shoulders back and his stiff leg held to one side.

She apologized and headed for the main door, her gaze carefully diverted from the segregation signs.

'Take no notice of 'im,' said the watchman suddenly.

'What?'

It was then that she realized the stocks were being used. Her eyes met those of a bony-faced boy, his eyes deep-set and accusing, his jaw firmly defiant, though his body shivered.

'Why is he here?'

The watchman laughed and rubbed the boy's tousled hair. 'Been eating what he shouldn't be eating.' The boy jerked his head so that the watchman's hand fell away.

'I don't understand. What do you mean?'

The watchman sniffed and wiped his nose on his sleeve. 'Well, 'ee was s'posed to be crushing bones, but caught stuffing one in 'is gob!'

Blanche closed her eyes and swallowed the bile rising from her stomach. 'When will he be released?' she said.

The watchman shrugged.

Blanche glared at him as fiercely as the boy had done.

The watchman tried to laugh off her indignation. Taking a swipe at the boy's head he said, 'This un's a hard nut to crack. Don't you go worrying—'

Suddenly he howled as the boy's teeth bit into his hand.

'Bite me would ye?'

To Blanche's shock, he began to beat the boy about the head. 'Stop it,' she shouted.

The watchman continued. 'You brat, you little toe rag!'

'Stop it!'

When he still failed to oblige, she kicked out at the man's stiff leg. She'd half expected it to be made of tin or wood, but it wasn't. He tumbled onto one knee, his hat rolling in the dirt and a look of surprise on his face.

Blanche was still angry. 'Take care *I* do not bite *you*,' she said, her eyes blazing as she shook her finger at him. 'Unlock that contraption. Unlock it right now!'

'But the Reverend—'

'Will also experience the sharp edge of my tongue for allowing this cruelty. Now get that boy out of there, take him to the kitchen and see that he's fed. Use whatever is being provided for the Board's midday meal. They won't notice the difference.'

She stormed up the stairs and into the dining room where the Board was awaiting her arrival.

The Reverend Smart was as solicitous and sleazy as usual, but she was in no mood to be polite.

'Why has a starving boy been put in the stocks?'

His mouth broke into a leer, though he'd probably meant it to be a smile. 'My dear lady, the boy broke the rules.'

'By being hungry?' There were murmurs of condemnation among the other members of the Board, though she couldn't tell whether they were aimed at her or the Reverend Smart.

Mrs Tinsley jumped to his defence. 'How dare you come in here and accuse the Reverend of behaving in an unchristian manner!'

Blanche could barely control her anger. Taking a deep breath, she turned to Mrs Tinsley and wagged her finger in the way she'd wagged it at the watchman. 'Is it Christian that those in your care are starving, and that you sit here stuffing yourselves with hams and pies and all manner of good things? Is it right that they are skin and bones and you are fat as hogs that have been too long at the trough?'

A gasp of astonishment rose around her.

Blanche realized she had gone too far. What was she likely to achieve by alienating everyone there? If the inmates were to be treated justly and kindly, she had to have the majority of the Board on her side. She had to temper her words, accuse those who deserved to be accused, arouse pity and cause true Christian charity to beat a little more strongly in the Board members' hearts. It had never been her habit to use her appreciable womanly wiles, but she judged the time had come.

'Gentlemen,' she said, her voice quivering. 'Gentlemen,' she repeated, holding her hand against her breast as though she were likely to faint at any moment, and adopting a pleading expression, 'I ask you as a mother who adores her children just as your wives do your own. Would you see your own children suffer like this? Would you have your wives feeling as upset as I do now to see a child locked in a medieval contraption?'

Owing something to one of her ancestors who had been an actress, she got out her handkerchief and began to dab at her eyes.

'Mrs Heinkel,' said Sir Bertram, the rotund gentleman who only seemed to come for the port. 'Please do not distress yourself.' He took hold of her hand and patted it.

Colonel Barnes, a ramrod of a man wearing a monocle and bushy side-whiskers, came to her aid. 'Mr Tinsley. Release the boy,' he barked as if he were addressing a battalion. 'Never even treated me own men like that, and hard bastards they were . . . begging your pardon, ma'am.'

'Well, I don't know . . .' Tinsley slid a sly look in Smart's direction.

'Do it!' snapped the colonel.

Tinsley fled like a rabbit with a hound snapping at his tail.

As the colonel and the other gentlemen consoled Blanche, Smart adopted a sanctimonious look and said, 'Spare the rod and spoil the child.'

Colonel Barnes threw him a warning look. 'Spare the boy some food, and you wouldn't need a rod. In the army we always said that men marched on their stomachs. Feed 'em well and treat 'em with respect, and they'll follow you 'til the ends of the earth. Mark that well, Smart. Mark it well,' he said, pointing an accusing finger.

Mr Tinsley came back and reported that he had done exactly as Colonel Barnes had directed.

'There,' said the colonel, smiling down at Blanche like a doting father. 'Can't bear seeing a memsahib in tears. Now brighten up, my dear. The boy's been sorted. Dare say one of us should have said something when we first arrived. Shamed by a woman!' He stroked his moustache, a voluptuous affair that curled at the ends and tangled with his side-whiskers. 'Have to say, it's not the first time in my life that that's happened! What?' He leaned closer. 'Tell me, ma'am, and please forgive me for my presumption, but do you have Punjabi blood?'

Blanche felt her colour rising, but managed to hold her head high, and even managed to smile when she looked him in the eye. 'No. Spanish actually.'

'Ah!' he said, eyeing her appraisingly. 'That would explain it then. Must admit, always did like the native women.'

Thankfully, they were next to the window, and the conversation had not been overheard. The port had been replenished, and Mrs Tinsley was clapping her hands to attract their attention. After clearing her throat, she pronounced that they were gathered for a specific task before lunch.

'The new entrants,' she said. 'As you no doubt saw for yourself, we are quite full at present, but still they come.' She flapped her hands in a useless manner. 'We have to do what we can, which is not always easy.'

She smiled benevolently at the men and threw Blanche an odious look.

Blanche disregarded her and smiled up at the colonel as he led her to a seat.

Chairs had been placed on one side of a large refectory table. Courteously, the colonel held out one for Blanche. Once she was seated, everyone else took their places, facing the door and their backs to the window, the bottom panes of which had been filled in with green paint.

Blanche folded her hands in her lap. Today there was no need to fend off the roaming hands of the Reverend Smart. Colonel Barnes sat on one side of her, and Sir Bertram on the other.

But still she was filled with trepidation. She'd seen the city's poor lined up at the gate, willing to forgo their freedom and their self-respect in order to eat and have a roof over their head. There were too many poor and not enough places, even in such a terrible Workhouse as this.

By lunchtime, some people had gained entry and some had not. They had little room left. No matter how beguiling the food laid out before her, Blanche had no appetite. She'd seen so many pathetic creatures that morning, and had heard so many tales of woe.

The one face she could not chase from her mind was that of a young girl, probably no more than thirteen, who carried a child in her arms. She had insisted the child was her brother.

The Reverend Smart bore down on her. 'Tell the truth, girl, or it will be the worse for you. Who is this child? Who is his mother?'

Her bottom lip trembled before she answered. 'He's my brother, sir.'

Mrs Tinsley, standing in the corner and watching the proceedings, shouted, 'Liar. I heard you outside. That babe belongs to you. Go on, you little trollop, tell these gentlefolk the truth!'

The girl was one of those not offered a place.

Devastated by the proceedings, Blanche asked the Reverend Smart why she hadn't been taken.

'She's not married! The child has no father.'

Blanche felt her heart swell in her chest and only barely kept her temper. 'But she's so young. Where will she sleep tonight?'

Embarrassed by her question, all eyes became fixed on the tabletop in front of them.

It was Mrs Tinsley who answered. 'A shop doorway, an old cellar, or one of them old sheds the Charlies used.'

'What's a Charlie?'

The colonel answered. 'A night watchman's hut. They're not used any more, certainly not since this new police force came into existence.'

The memory of that first day of choosing who should come into the workhouse would stay with her for the rest of her life. It became especially piquant when Mrs Tinsley reported that a baby wrapped in a blue cloth had been found abandoned outside the gate.

'It must belong to that girl,' Blanche exclaimed passionately. 'We have to find her.'

Mrs Tinsley shrugged. 'So how do we do that?'

'A baby left out alone? Surely she'll be worried.'

Mrs Tinsley folded her arms and eyed her with undisguised disdain. 'And what about the other mothers? Do you think they're worried, too?'

Blanche frowned. 'What do you mean?'

'I mean, what about the other six babies left outside the gates this week? Will their mothers miss them? No! They won't. And neither will that one.'

Chapter Nine

The shooting party had broken up early, everyone pale with shock.

The bright day turned grey and it began to rain.

Once Emerald had been stripped of her bloodied clothes, she was washed and put to bed. She was already asleep by the time Tom went to her room.

He knelt at her bedside, the day a turmoil inside his head: flashes of golden feathers; the smell of gunfire; the sound of each shot – one louder and more terrible than any of the others; his daughter's dress splashed with blood. How much would Emerald be affected by such trauma?

Horatia had changed for dinner, and appeared at the table wearing a pale blue silk dress. The lace-trimmed neckline was cut very low, revealing her glisteningly white shoulders. Diamonds, fashioned like a chain of flowers, sparkled at her throat, with a matching bracelet at her wrist and earrings that flashed with borrowed light. Tonight they dined alone.

Tom was already in the dining room when she arrived, leaning on a lengthy sideboard where the handles dripped like chandeliers from drawers and cupboards of shiny satinwood. Each door was inlaid with a porcelain panel, hand-painted with shepherds and shepherdesses reclining amidst flowers and delicately outlined bluebirds.

The decanter was half empty. Tom eyed his wife over his glass as he swallowed another rum.

She smiled provocatively and stroked her waist as though inviting him to stroke it, too. Though her smile persisted, disapproval clouded her eyes. 'Thomas, haven't you had enough, my darling?'

All his compassion, his determination to be the perfect, honourable husband, seemed now a foolish dream. Nothing could change matters, but for now at least, he'd drown his sorrows in drink. His jaw was like iron as he slammed the glass down onto a silver tray where it shattered in myriad pieces.

'That's best Waterford crystal,' she said as though she really valued it. The truth was there were cabinets full of all manner of crystal, in all colours, from glassworks all over the world.

'You,' he said, his expression reflecting his anger, '*you* drive me to drink. You drive me to do many things.'

He tried to remember why he'd married her in the first place. The drink made his brain fuzzy, but his anger remained solid.

She turned away from him. 'The death of Martin Lodge was not my fault.'

'If you had assured him that his job was secure, he would never have done it. And Emerald? How do you think it's going to affect her?'

She turned away, then seemed to rethink her strategy and face him again. 'If she had eaten her meal in the nursery, she would not have been a witness to his stupidity. It was you who encouraged her to disobey me.'

Tom smacked the palm of his hand against his head. 'Of course, of course! If Emerald has nightmares following a man's suicide, it's my fault. My fault she was there, but *not* my fault he killed himself,' he shouted, his finger stabbing at her naked shoulder.

She stared at his finger, at his stance and at his face.

He read her thoughts, and knew they were his own. The fact that he actually felt violent towards her appalled him. Never before had he laid a hand on her; never before had he felt as angry as he did now. For a brief moment, he saw panic in her eyes; her complexion, silky smooth and as white as porcelain, now turned even paler.

'I'm sorry', he said, and turned away.

'Sorry?' Her voice was like cut glass. 'Oh yes! I know you're sorry. I can see it in your eyes when you look at me. Sometimes I wish I were Emerald. There's a different look in your eyes for your daughter. But me? You can't even bear to touch me, can you? You wish it was just you and Emerald, and if it wasn't for her, you would probably wish that you'd never married me.'

He stared at the thick net curtains that hid the parkland from view as though he were looking through their heavy pattern of roses and vines and lupins. He saw none of it. His blurred thoughts had cleared. A vision appeared: Blanche happily married to Conrad Heinkel. He felt again the pain of losing her.

'Disappointment,' he said suddenly.

'What?'

When he turned, she was frowning deeply, and looked confused. 'Disappointment,' he said again. 'That's why I married you. I was disappointed, and there seemed no better option.'

It startled him to see pain in her eyes. He'd actually hurt her and he found himself immediately regretting it. He had Emerald to think of, but he also had Horatia. She had never had a forgiving nature. She bore grudges, her mind was sharp and he knew it wouldn't end there. Although she rarely lost her temper in the way her stepmother, Lady Verity, used to do, she was vengeful. She didn't throw things or stamp her foot, or shout obscenities at the top of her voice. But at some point in the future she would find a way of getting even, of being as cruel to him as he'd just been to her.

Her glare was as cold as the marble statues holding up the mantelpiece and the sound of her skirts leaving the room was like a cold draught of air.

He would be alone in his own room tonight, but once the household had retired, the candles and oil lamps snuffed out, their pungent aroma still lingering in the air, she would knock softly at his door. He would not answer. She would creep in, softly calling him as if nothing had happened between them.

That was how his son had been conceived. They had argued just over a fortnight before. Horatia had made arrangements to send Emerald away to school without consulting him. Single-handedly, he had unpacked Emerald's trunks, called his wife a heartless bitch in front of the servants, and had then sat cuddling Emerald until dawn as she sobbed gratefully in his arms.

'You won't let her send me away? Promise,' Emerald had whimpered.

'I won't,' he'd said. 'I promise.'

Furious that he'd disagreed with her plans and called her names in front of the servants, Horatia had gone away to lick her wounds. The carriage had been brought round to the gravel drive at the front of the house in double-quick time.

She came back a week later and they had made up in the privacy of their shared room. He'd never asked her where she had gone.

Horatia sometimes needed solitude. He didn't begrudge her that, and had fully expected her to order the carriage round to the front door now. But he didn't hear it.

The clock on the mantelpiece made a whirring sound before striking ten, the gilt cherubs crouched against its marble sides hitting miniature hammers against miniature gongs, as if they were making the sound rather than the mechanism within. He looked at it despairingly, wishing he could turn back time and do things differently.

Catching a glimpse of himself in the gilt-framed mirror, he saw that nothing had changed. In the past he had sailed the oceans, relishing the freedom and the adventure of visiting many different countries and cultures. Along with his freedom, sailing was no more and the prospect of a lifetime with Horatia stretched ahead of him.

Emerald's resilience surprised him. So did Horatia's good humour, even though they had not shared a bed since their row.

I have to make an effort for my daughter's sake, he told himself and smiled as another thought entered his head unheralded. Absence makes the heart grow fonder and marriage more endurable.

Emerald recovered from her ordeal, but fell moody a few days later when her pet canary died.

'Will he go to heaven?' she asked her father with sorrow-filled eyes.

Tom smiled and smoothed her hair back from her forehead. 'Of course he will,' he replied.

'Miss Potter says that the man who shot himself wouldn't go to heaven,' the little girl said, a worried frown beetling her brows.

Tom made a mental note to have a word with the nurse. He didn't hold with children being indoctrinated with ideas that worried their souls. He'd long ago decided that it was best to leave religion until they were old enough to understand the options.

'Everyone good goes to heaven,' he said.

She looked up at him, her pert nose twitching as she thought it through. At last she said, 'Miss Potter says the good only go to heaven if they're buried in a proper churchyard – in consequential ground, I think she said.'

Tom smiled. 'I think you mean consecrated ground.'

'Will you take me there so we can bury Percy?'

He said that he would.

The day was bright, sunlight dappling the churchyard through the whispering branches of the poplars. The grass had been scythed around the family tomb. Tom lingered, his gaze drifting from one name to another:

THE REVEREND JEBEDIAH SAMSON STRONG
LADY VERITY ROSELLIA CRISPIN-STRONG
ISAIAH THOMAS STRONG

His eyes lingered on the last name. Thoughts of what might have been were as sharp and cutting as the glass he'd broken on the night he'd rowed with Horatia.

Emerald was running through the grass, and turned when she realized her father had stopped. 'Father? Come along. We have to bury Percy and say a prayer.'

Tom dragged his gaze away from the etched names and smiled at his pink-faced daughter.

'Over here?' she asked, coming to a sudden halt and pointing her towel at a shady place close to the hedge.

His first inclination was to dissuade her, to have her choose a sunnier spot unsullied by the sadness of past tragedies. But he changed his mind. Perhaps it was perfect that his daughter should pick a place between Isaiah's last resting place and the grave of Jasper Strong, the Reverend Jebediah's son.

Yes. It was perfect.

He managed to smile. 'Yes.'

Emerald began digging the hole and Tom bent to help with his hands, the dampness of the earth penetrating the good cloth of his trousers. As he did so, he watched his daughter, her pretty pink face screwed up in concentration. The thought of losing her terrified him. Yet if he didn't make amends with Horatia, she might use Emerald to hurt him, perhaps carrying out her threat to send her to a girl's school. He resolved to make amends, to eat humble pie, even to charm her into bed.

'Is that deep enough?' Emerald interrupted his thoughts.

He peered into the hole, which was only about six inches deep. 'A little more, I think. Here, let me.'

As he took the trowel, a cloud of rooks rose from the tops of the elms, cawing their warning cries. Tom looked up, wondering what had scared them.

Emerald was picking flowers. 'For his grave,' she said solemnly.

Tom placed the cigar box containing Percy into the hole and covered it. Emerald placed the flowers on the turned earth.

'There,' said Tom, presuming the funeral was over and brushing the earth off his knees. 'Percy is gone to heaven.'

Emerald looked up at him round-eyed. 'You haven't said a prayer.'

Tom searched his brain for something appropriate; certainly not any part of the burial service, just something light and right for the occasion. He cleared his throat and stood straight.

Emerald stood next to him, her hands clasped in prayer. She looked up at him pointedly, bringing her hands up so that he knew she wanted him to do the same. Resigned that he wasn't going to get away without doing things properly, he too joined his hands.

'Right,' he murmured under his breath. 'Dear Lord, we hereby commend our much loved Percy to your tender loving care. May he fly freely in heavenly skies for ever. Amen.'

'Amen,' echoed Emerald, her voice drowned by the resumed cawing of the rooks, as yet again they rose into the sky in a black mass. 'Why are they making all that noise?' she asked her father, her eyes as round as pennies.

Tom frowned. Perhaps a buzzard, he thought. 'They're calling for Percy,' he said. 'They're showing him how to fly very high so he can reach heaven.'

Head thrown back, her face bright with wonder, Emerald looked up at them; no doubt trying to locate the bright yellow of Percy's wings among the black of the rooks.

'There you are, Miss Emerald!'

Rustling like a flurry of autumn leaves, Miss Potter bustled towards them, the hem of her sweeping skirt leaving a trail of flattened grass. She dipped a brief curtsey to Tom. 'It's time for Miss Emerald's tea, Mr Strong.'

'Ah! The rooks,' he said, lifting his eyes to the high branches of the elm trees where dots of black squawked contentedly behind the leaves.

'You disturbed the birds,' he explained in response to Miss Potter's puzzled expression.

'Oh. Yes, sir. Of course.'

She didn't look up at the trees. He very much doubted that Miss Potter was ever in thrall to the wonders of nature. She was doting and disciplined, her mind totally focused on her charge. He doubted whether anything outside the nursery was of any interest to her.

As she fussed over his daughter, straightening her hair and brushing twigs and dirt from her dress, he found himself wondering whether the tight-faced woman had ever had a sweetheart. For a split instant, he thought about asking her.

Miss Potter's blue eyes, which seemed out of place with her dark hair and pale complexion, fixed on him. 'Are you coming back to the house with us, sir?'

Tom shook his head. 'No. I have done what I had to do, and I think the fresh air may have made my daughter feel hungry.' Purposefully, he took a cigarillo from the silver case he kept in the inside pocket of his jacket. He would smoke while contemplating his thoughts.

'We buried Percy and said a prayer,' Emerald explained excitedly to Miss Potter.

'And very proper too, Miss Emerald. You can tell me all about it on our way back to the house.'

Tom parked himself on a tree stump, one foot braced against a gnarled root. The tree had been felled many years ago to make room for the family mausoleum.

Everything changes, he thought, then raised his eyes to the treetops. Except for the rooks. They'd always been here. And the Strongs? Would they always be here?

He eyed the ornate columns, the gold lettering, the softly hued stone that was slowly turning grey and mossy. In time it would lose all its borrowed splendour and nature would return it to a mound of stone.

That will be when my bones are inside it, he thought, and found himself frowning. Somehow the prospect of lying beside Horatia for eternity was very disquieting. He couldn't see eternal rest with her as being very peaceful.

Suddenly he felt cold. He rolled his shoulders as if to shake the feeling off, but it persisted. Too many old ghosts, he thought.

Anyone who saw him would presume he was just a man enjoying a quiet smoke. He looked calm, at peace with the world. But he felt uneasy. Shadows thrown by the leaning tombstones ivy-covered walls and dense yew trees lengthened out of all proportion to their actual size. A silence descended.

Then something moved to his right, a shadow falling out from behind the family tomb. Raising his eyes to the treetops, he considered the rooks. Twice they'd cried out their warning. He'd presumed Miss Potter had disturbed them on both occasions. Now he knew he'd been wrong. Someone was watching him.

He continued to smoke, appearing to observe the façade of the tomb and keeping very still, waiting for whoever it was to show themselves. There'd been rumours of an escaped convict on the outskirts of Bristol, but surely he'd been captured by now?

Once, twice more he drew on the sweet-tasting tobacco. Only his eyes moved as he watched for the shadow to creep across the mossy mound around the tomb. When it did, the person it belonged to would step out.

The shadow lengthened, shrank, lengthened, shrank again. Whoever was there was undecided about whether to proceed.

Tom made up his mind to take the first step. Carefully, so that its sweet smell would not be snuffed out, he balanced the cigarillo on the tree trunk.

Stealthily but swiftly, he made his way around the opposite side of the tomb to the shadow. The grass was damp and clung to the hem of his trousers, and the moss around the mausoleum was slippery beneath his quick-moving feet. He flattened himself against the wall of the tomb and reached the corner. His fingers strayed around the stout quoins, the stone warm beneath his touch. A few more inches, a single glance and he would see who it was.

One step, two . . .

She had her back to him and was wearing a brown dress, a straw bonnet and clasped a shawl around her shoulders.

'Can I help you?'

The woman started. 'Ow, me God!' With the rush of her words came the smell of gin.

'Definitely not a ghost,' he muttered.

'What?' She looked shocked, but then appeared to collect herself. 'You gave me a fright, you did.'

'You gave me one. I'm not used to being spied on when I'm having a quiet smoke.'

'I was just making sure.'

Tom raised one eyebrow. 'Making sure?'

'That you were by yurself. I don't want to make a scene.'

Tom scrutinized the ruddy complexion, the pale eyes and the way she shifted from one foot to another, as if she were excited – or having trouble standing up. 'Why wouldn't you want to make a scene?' he asked. 'Are you sure it was me you wanted to see? Do you know who I am?'

Her expression altered. Due perhaps to the serenity of his voice, his courtesy and friendly manner, she blinked as if she were having second thoughts. At last, she nodded. 'You're Mr Thomas Strong. It was you I wanted to see. I weren't going to say anything, even when she refused to see me, but then something terrible happened, and I know it was 'er at the bottom of it! I knows it was . . .'

Tom's frown deepened. 'You have me at a disadvantage. You know my name, but I don't know yours.'

'Me name's Daisy Draper, and I know all about that baby your wife had.'

The cold he'd earlier felt around his shoulders now coursed through his veins. 'What are you talking about, woman?'

'See this?' she said, suddenly a flurry of activity, her arms waving and redressing her falling shawl as she charged around to the side of the tomb. 'See this?'

Tom followed.

'See this?' she said again, her voice shrill and her eyes glittering as she pointed at the inscription to his dead son. 'It's all a lie, and that woman,' she spat, her finger jabbing in the direction of Marstone Court, 'has a heart of solid stone!'

Beyond the lych-gate and the yew trees, the road meandered up to the house. His daughter and her nanny had disappeared from sight. Was there something to fear?

'Miss Potter? What do you mean?'

As she shook her head, a dozen iron-grey curls escaped from beneath her bonnet. 'Your wife! Mrs Strong! That's who I mean!'

Tom's feeling of foreboding was like a lump of lead in his stomach now. He saw by the look in her eyes that she was relishing the moment. 'Explain yourself.'

'He ain't here,' she said, jabbing her finger at the inscription to his baby son. 'She had that done, all nicely engraved as though the little mite was dead and put in 'is tomb. But the baby ain't here.'

'What do you mean, Mrs Draper?'

Sensing his surging anger, the woman took a step back, her arms crossed over her chest. 'She got rid of him before you got back. I want money to keep quiet about it. Just imagine gentlefolk finding out about it. Just imagine what they'd say, all the sniggers and the nasty remarks. Couldn't let you see him, could she? Couldn't let you see what *colour* he was!'

It was as though every drop of blood had frozen in his body. He couldn't speak. He couldn't move. His jaw hurt because he was clenching it fit to split bones.

When he at last found his voice, he wondered at its calm. Perhaps it's not mine, he thought. It sounded like that of a judge about to pronounce the death sentence: cold, calm and very far away. 'How do you know this?'

'I was the monthly nurse, brought in then discarded like an old boot. The wet nurse was annoyed too, though even if you're half blind, when you've got a breast full of milk, there's always someone wanting it.'

The history of the Strong family was peppered with stories of children sired by their forebears on African slaves. Horatia's own father had sired such a child, Blanche, and even Horatia's grandmother had been of dubious parentage.

'The fact that my child may have been darker than expected is of little concern to me. I only care that he is dead, though I wish most heartily that he were still alive. Now leave me in peace, Daisy Draper, and never, ever mention this to me again. Is that clear?'

'No, no, no!' Daisy exclaimed, shaking her head vigorously enough to part it from her neck. 'He ain't dead! He ain't dead! Or at least, he weren't when I took him away.'

Daisy's legs buckled beneath her as Tom gripped her shoulders, his eyes black with fury. 'He didn't die?'

She shook her head. 'No. After yer missus saw what colour it was, the doctor told me to take it away. Doctor Owen said he was a throwback and that a lot of plantation owners got a touch of black ink in their blood. It happens now and again.'

Tom swallowed his anger and forced himself to speak calmly, his teeth aching with the effort. 'Where did you take him?'

She opened her mouth to speak, then stopped, a conniving smile curling across her mouth. 'I was paid very well to keep my mouth shut.'

Her eyes narrowed as though she were weighing up exactly how much he was worth. The stench of gin and stale sweat seemed suddenly more acute.

Tom's nostrils flared and his lips curled like a rabid dog about to bite. There was money in his pocket; it would have been so easy to take it out and give it to her, but he stopped himself. He slid his hand across his chest and into the inside pocket of his jacket. 'I want to know where you took him.'

Her eyes followed his hand. 'I need money. I've got to go away. She tried to kill me. I knows it was 'er!'

Tom's blood could run no colder. 'You're talking about my wife?'

'I asked her for money on account that I'd kept me peace, but wadn't paid enough to keep quiet for ever. She refused, so I told 'er I would tell you. Only fair that a man should know the truth after all. But then someone tried to kill me. If the bobbies should ever hear of it . . .'

Tom took a handful of sovereigns from his pocket. 'Five!' he said, holding one between his finger and thumb. 'Five sovereigns.'

Her eyes followed the progress of each one as he counted them into her outstretched hand.

'Now tell me,' he said once her fingers had clenched over them.

'I took him to St Philip's Workhouse. They've got a revolving door there for foundlings. I put 'im in and turned the door. Brave little mite, he was. Didn't cry once.'

But Tom wasn't listening. Blinded by tears, his fists clenched in anger, he was striding off towards Marstone Court. As he exited the lych-gate, thunder rolled over the Mendip hills, the sky darkened and the first drops of rain began to fall.

By the time he got to the house, he was soaked through. Rain lashed against the windows and the frames rattled in the wind. It felt as though Marstone Court was being shaken to its foundations.

One of the footmen approached him with a Turkish towel. He brushed it aside as he strode past.

'Where's my wife?'

'She's entertaining, sir.'

'We weren't expecting anyone.'

'It was on the off-chance, sir. The gentleman was passing.'

He fully expected to find Septimus Monk, in fact he wanted it to be him. If there was one person likely to be behind the attack on Daisy Draper, it was Monk. Without bothering to knock, he swung open the library door.

Horatia was sitting in the leather armchair behind her father's desk, a huge piece of furniture that must have taken half a cherry orchard to make.

Sitting opposite her, and rigid with fury, was Max Heinkel.

Tom held out his hand and Max rose to his feet, but hesitated before he shook it. Tom was glad when he did and, for one dreadful moment, was tempted to outpour everything that was in his heart, everything that the dreadful Daisy Draper had told him, not just as one man to another, but as father to son.

Max looked far from happy. 'I've only just heard about Martin Lodge – and about Horatia's purchase of Webber's. I have a mortgage with the bank for ten thousand pounds. I have plans for expansion.'

'I assured him that everything would be fine,' said Horatia. There was a rustling of layers of gown and petticoat as she came out from behind the desk, a smile fixed to her face. 'No one is going to call in anyone's debts. My purchase of the bank makes good business sense. I'm also considering entering the insurance market. I think there are good profits to be made there.' With a sidelong look at Tom, she slid her arm through that of Max and began to usher him out of the door. 'You have nothing to fear, my dear boy. You may carry on with your refining for as long as you wish. We will not interfere. Now how is your mother? Is she out of mourning? I do think black is rather unbecoming on a dark-skinned woman. She'll be glad to wear something brighter. Is she keeping busy?'

Max looked perturbed, but answered politely.

'Yes. She serves on the Board of Governors for St Philip's Workhouse. She hopes to do some good there.'

Tom sat at his wife's desk, an open file in front of him, and watched her being the perfect hostess until the door was closed and Max had left. In the back of his mind he noted the coincidence of Blanche's involvement with St Philip's.

'What a nice young man – all things considered,' Horatia said, turning back to face him. 'He has your features; the same jaw, the same broad shoulders. I don't think Blanche has passed on many of the Strong family traits. He doesn't come across as a tenacious businessman. He's too sentimental and really believes that my bank will continue to pour money into that broken-down refinery—'

She stopped, suddenly aware that Tom was scrutinizing the papers in front of him. Something about his demeanour pulled her up short.

'What's that you're looking at?'

He flicked at the folder. 'Various household expenses over the last few months – including the expenses incurred for our son's funeral.'

'Oh, darling!'

She swept round the corner of the desk, positioned herself behind his chair and draped her arms around his shoulders, her chin resting on his head.

'Imagine how I feel,' she said, reaching over him and attempting to close the file, 'But what's done is done, and you really shouldn't torture yourself like this.'

Her perfume was heady, but although her cheek was warm against his, Tom felt as though he were swimming in an Arctic sea. He closed his eyes and thought of the child she had borne. How could she have done it? He wanted to strike her, to tell her he would never forgive her and the child must be rescued from St Philip's Workhouse. It felt as if he were drowning in a sea of power struggles, problems and disappointments. Like a swimmer, he struggled to the surface.

He picked up a piece of paper and waved it in her face. 'So this is the bill for the funeral?'

'Darling . . .'

She tried to tear it from his hand. He kept it out of her reach.

'Including the inscription on the family vault.'

'Thomas—'

'Why did you bother to go to all that trouble for an empty coffin?'

For a brief moment he could not hear her breathe. He felt her body go rigid against his back, her arms like iron.

'What do you mean?'

'I cannot believe the extent of your deceit. I cannot believe that you would have thought me so callous as not to accept our child.'

He turned and looked up at her. Her eyes were as round as Emerald's on the day Martin Lodge had shot himself. She was shocked that he knew, but more than that, she was afraid.

'Horatia, I know that there is African blood in the Strong family through your grandmother. And if he was a throwback to that blood, surely you knew I would accept that? He was my son, for God's sake. Our ancestry makes us what we are. We can't alter that. I understand your fears about what people might say. But me, Horatia? You could have trusted me.'

He knew his eyes were misty as he looked up at her. Horatia's surprised expression seemed to hold her speechless. She just looked at him, seemingly lost in emotions that she could not put into words. Her mouth opened and closed as she struggled to speak. Tom couldn't remember ever seeing her so tongue-tied.

'I had to do what was best,' she said at last. 'I'd had a long labour, but I was so looking forward to you coming home. When the doctor told me what colour he was I was devastated, even though he said he'd seen throwbacks in families before.' She fluttered her eyelashes, not in a provocative way like a young, silly girl, but because she was genuinely flustered, incapable of providing an explanation. She couldn't find the courage to tell him that she had actually seen the child herself, had held him in her arms and looked on his dark complexion. He would think too badly of her. At last she managed to quell her heaving breasts and gave him the only defence she could.

She looked at her husband pleadingly. 'I told him to do what was best for the child. I thought he had, Tom, I really thought he had.'

It was the closest he'd ever seen Horatia to hysteria. She clung to his arm, and bit her bottom lip as the tears trickled from the corners of her eyes. And she'd called him Tom, not the usual Thomas.

'I did what I thought was best,' she repeated, her voice small and her eyes screwed up, her cheeks pink. 'But I couldn't bear to tell you the truth, so I pretended he'd died. Doctor Owen took care of everything.'

'The child must be brought home,' he muttered.

'No!'

Her voice echoed around the room. He looked at her in surprise. How quickly her mood had changed. The pleading, the tears and the pink cheeks had all disappeared. There was fire in her eyes and her skin was pale.

'You must not do that, Thomas. I made the decision in your absence. I took great care in explaining his removal. How do you think I could possibly explain his reappearance?'

In one instant also, Tom's heart hardened. 'He's my son!'

'And would you ruin the lives of your other child – indeed – your other *children* for the sake of this one?'

The chillness of her voice cut him like a knife.

He took in the icy eyes, the unyielding set of her chin and the tightness of her pink lips. He recalled what he had just heard her say after letting Max out.

'You're going to call in his mortgage.'

The hem of her dress made a sweeping sound as she drifted to the window and stood looking out of it, head turned away from him.

'I want a new refinery at Avonmouth. I want one, sole refinery with the Strong family owning the controlling interest. I've already got a buyer for The Counterslip.'

It was like looking at a stranger, features you were used to hiding the real person within.

His tone was bitter. 'You want everything your own way, Horatia.'

Her shrug was almost imperceptible. 'It is the way I am. Born a Strong, always a Strong. Unlike you, Tom. You are a Strong in name only. That's what makes you so attractive.' She smiled. It didn't last, but froze on her face as her tone hardened. 'And that is what also makes you so vulnerable. Yes, Tom. I will have things my way. If you take it upon yourself to search for the child, I could not possibly contemplate keeping Emerald in this house one moment longer. You must see that. There would be no alternative but to send her away to school. The public shame would be too much to bear. Her prospects would be ruined, perhaps for ever. And then, of course, there is Max . . . I could reconsider his position, perhaps allocate shares in the Avonmouth refinery to him . . . Otherwise . . . his mortgage is large . . . I would have to review it. So do remember I might publicly proclaim my brother, who also happens to be his mother's half-brother, as his father. Imagine the shame. Imagine the scandal!'

'You would really do that,' he said, his voice little above a whisper.

She nodded. Her eyes glittered. She meant what she said.

Suffocated by her presence, and all affection for her finally torn from his heart, Tom left the room. He would not chance her using Max to get her own way with him. He would go to St Philip's and find the child himself.

It occurred to him later that she had not asked him how he knew.

'Because you know who told me,' he muttered to himself. Hands buried deep in his pockets, he watched the moon rise over the vast parkland that surrounded Marstone Court. 'Which also means that you are indeed the one who tried to dispose of Daisy Draper.'

The next day he rose at dawn, refused breakfast and made his way to the stables. A groom doffed his hat as he entered the stall of his favourite horse, Rangoon, a chestnut hunter.

'Is he fed and watered?' he asked, running his hand over the muscular neck, the veins proud of the flesh, rippling beneath his touch.

'Aye, sir. I was just rubbing him down,' said the freckle-faced groom, showing him the curry-comb.

'Good.'

The groom watched in amazement as Tom fetched a saddle and bridle and proceeded to tack-up the animal himself.

Tom hardly noticed him. His mind was set.

It was good to breathe the clean air of early morning. Although the servants were up and about, his wife was not. He'd stolen in and looked at his sleeping daughter before leaving. She was so innocent, lying clean and warm in her own little bed, safe in the knowledge that she was cared for and loved. But what of his son? Where was he sleeping? Who cared for him?

The birds were singing. Usually he enjoyed their song and looked for them as they twittered and chattered among the hedgerows, perhaps arguing over the surfeit of grubs and worms that slid through the wet earth of a ploughed field. Not today. Rabbits, squirrels and game birds dashed out of the way of Rangoon's galloping hooves. The traffic intensified as he neared the city: farmers driving cows or sheep before them, on their way to the slaughterhouses in Bedminster, Greenbank and St Philip's; dairy drays, heavy with milk churns, trundled their way to the city dairies where the creamy milk would be turned into cheese, butter or taken by smaller conveyances from door to door where eager maids or housewives came out with jugs and a penny for every pint.

To get to St Philip's meant crossing the city centre at the drawbridge, correctly known as St Augustine's Bridge. From there he travelled the wider alleys of the Pithay into Old Market and out towards the Bath Road, spurring his horse on to greater effort until the sweat flew up into his face.

By the time he got to the Workhouse, the animal's heaving sides were dark and wet. He pulled the animal to a steady walk, feeling guilty. 'Sorry, old fella.'

His attention to the horse was short-lived. The sight of the Workhouse walls shocked him and reminded him of Bristol Gaol. He grimaced as he remembered his short stay there before he'd been cleared of a false murder charge.

It was early, a little before seven. The labourers, who mostly worked at the cotton factory in Barton Hill or in the other small businesses in the busy little back streets, had already reported to work. Tradesmen, bakers, butchers and lamp oil sellers were out on their rounds. A milk cart went past. The measures used for ladling out the milk hung from a rack around the four churns and rattled against them as the cart plodded past.

'Won't see nothing yet,' shouted the milkman.

Tom turned to him with a questioning look.

'They does the entries on Wednesdays only. You won't see no queue today.'

Tom turned his horse's head and kept pace with the milk cart. 'They actually refuse people entry to that place? I thought anyone who was destitute could enter.'

The milkman had a weather-worn face, the sort used to rain, snow, hail or shine. He winked knowingly. 'The Reverend Smart keeps a tight ship. Places for three hundred paupers, no more and no less. It's always full.'

Tom asked the question that was on his mind. 'And what about babies?'

Bringing his milk cart to a standstill, the milkman pointed at a small doorway that seemed strangely made and oddly dark. 'See that? That there door revolves. Poor young women who have strayed from the straight and narrow put their babies in there and turn the door. The babe goes inside, and the young woman stays on the outside, her identity and her shame shielded from them on the inside. No young woman wants her good name destroyed, does she? No young man either, come to that.'

Tom thanked him for his help and the milkman went on his way, whistling a merry tune that the birds in nearby trees seemed to pick up.

Tom turned his horse again and looked at the grim building. The sight of it made him feel more melancholy than he'd ever felt in his life. The temptation to hammer on the door and demand entry was overpowering, but something the milkman had said lay heavy on his mind: *No young woman wants her good name destroyed . . . no young man either . . .*

If he did hammer on that door, take the child – if it was still there – and return to Marstone Court with it, Horatia would wreak havoc in all their lives, especially his but more importantly, those of Emerald and Max. He knew there was no chance whatsoever that Horatia would publicly admit being the mother of a coloured child and, no matter what he did with the baby, she would get her own back. Max would be her prime target and Emerald would be sent away. There had to be another way.

Thinking of Max reminded him that Blanche had joined the Board of Governors of this place. Could he dare to meet with her and ask her to help? If she did find the child, he wouldn't be able to raise him as his own, but he could at least find him a good family.

His mind was made up. Without Horatia finding out, he had to get Blanche to discover where his child was and bring him word. If the child had been adopted or boarded out to good people, at least then he could rest easy. But until then he could not.

He vowed to approach Blanche. He had to know. He really had to know.

Horatia was pleased with the way things were going. Her father would no doubt turn in his grave if he knew that she planned to sell Rivermead and diversify into property and machinery, new things which would have far-reaching effects in an expanding world.

Sugar had been his life, but he'd been raised in the days when far-flung cane fields had been a lucrative investment. Increasing shipping costs had diminished its importance and, although she'd respected, perhaps even loved her father, she was glad he was not around to stand in her way.

There was only one thing souring her achievements and there were dark lines beneath her eyes if anyone cared to look really closely. She snapped at the slightest thing. Her patience and her looks were marred by guilt. No matter how hard her husband and others might think her, giving away her son still lay heavy on her heart.

As the carriage slowed up Redcliffe Hill, the stunning edifice of St

Mary's rose on her left-hand side. The line of sycamores in the churchyard rustled as though whispering, *I know, I know, I know how you feel.*

'No, you don't,' she murmured under her breath.

She looked out at the trees. Sycamore seeds were flying from the branches with each breath of wind. The shadow of the church fell over the carriage like a large, black blanket.

Church was a pastime reserved for Sunday, so far as Horatia was concerned. Religion was something to which she paid lip service, something one had to believe in because everyone else did. But as the church's shadow lingered, Horatia found herself holding her breath. It felt like a rebuke.

Her next act was impulsive and completely out of character.

'Pull in,' she shouted to the coachman.

The church was huge, empty and silent. As the sound of her footsteps echoed around the ancient aisle and towards the altar, she thought of the thousands of people seeking solace over the preceding centuries. Some had sought absolution. Others had sought sanctuary or forgiveness.

There were few worshippers, their footsteps and whispered prayers also echoing. Did their hearts race as hers did? she wondered. Did they feel as weighed down with guilt?

'You look lost.'

She spun around. His face was kind and his hair as white as his collar of office.

'I suppose I am.'

His smile was warm and his eyes twinkled in understanding from within a wealth of wrinkles. 'Then you have come to the right place. I trust you will find what you are looking for.'

She turned back to the altar, then turned again to ask him what she should say, but he was gone, had left as silently as he'd come.

For the first time in her life, Horatia Strong knelt and prayed, not as she did on Sunday, but sincerely, straight from the soul and silently, her confession destined only for God.

Chapter Ten

The summer had been wet, and early autumn showed no sign of improvement. The damp air had heralded the return of her cough, so Blanche opted to take a respite before resuming her work for the Board of St Philip's. After due consideration, she opted to take the sea air of Clevedon rather than the waters of Bath. She wasn't as ill as she had been. She told herself it was merely the onset of an autumn chill.

The Channel View Hotel was much smaller and less grand than the Ambassador, but its plain lines and delicate colours lent it a quiet elegance. Mrs Jones, the owner's wife, confided that before it had become a hotel, the house had been home to a mistress of the Prince Regent.

'It's purely rumour, of course, and one should not always believe what one hears,' she said with obvious relish as she helped Blanche unpack.

'Of course,' Blanche replied. Mrs Jones, she judged, with her quick ways and merry face, loved a titillating story.

Her room was on the first floor and was decorated in a soft green. A glass-panelled door led out onto a wrought-iron balcony in the Italian style, its ornate casts and swirls smothered by a virulent climbing plant. It overlooked a garden where roses grew alongside a gravel path leading to a dark green gate. Beyond that, people walked along the promenade, children clambered barefoot over rock pools on the pebbly beach and the incoming tide crashed in creamy-topped waves. When the tide was out, light from a wide expanse of sky made the acres of mud seem painted with silver.

Because the establishment was small, the atmosphere was intimate. Mrs Carr, a widow with poor eyesight but a good income, smiled at her. Dr Begg, a clergyman accompanied by a rough-haired terrier, nodded and wished her good day as he fought his way through the hallway, his paints, palette and easel tucked beneath his arm.

Artists' materials brought Nelson Strong, Horatia's brother and Blanche's own half-brother, to mind, but there the similarity ended. Nelson had been a blond Adonis and had painted nudes; Dr Begg was angular, stove pipe thin and preferred landscapes.

Channel View turned out to be very agreeable. No one made judgements as to why she was alone and she found herself feeling quite at ease.

It was on the third day that she met Darius Clarke-Fisher.

He was outside the hotel, alighting from a Hackney carriage that had obviously brought him from the railway station. Blanche was walking along the promenade though the day was far from fair. There was a brisk wind and, just as she gained the gate, her umbrella was blown inside out.

'Allow me,' said a masculine voice as she struggled to turn it the right way.

From the moment he took the umbrella from her, she realized that Darius Clarke-Fisher liked to take charge.

'There! Knight in caped travelling coat and top hat rescues fair maid in distress.'

He gave a little bow before taking her right hand in his left and placing the umbrella in it with the other. It was a firm, no-nonsense action that made her feel obliged, as though reversing an umbrella was a feat only properly performed by a man.

First she thanked him and then asked, 'Have you come to stay?' Later, she'd chastize herself for sounding so friendly, and for asking the question in the first place. But it didn't seem wrong at the time.

'Indeed I have.' He thrust out his hand. 'Darius Clarke-Fisher.'

She thrust her hand forward in the same manner and mimicked his abrupt tone. 'Mrs Conrad Heinkel.'

He glanced searchingly to either side of her. 'And Mr Heinkel?'
'Deceased.'

'So I take it your name is not Conrad.' He said it cheerily, his eyes locking with hers and holding his head at an attentive angle.
'No.'

He failed to relinquish her hand. 'So what is your name?'

'Mrs Heinkel,' she said brusquely. 'Good day, Mr Clarke-Fisher. Do have a nice stay.'

She felt his gaze follow her through the door. He was interested in her. That much was clear.

That evening she shared a dinner table with Colonel and Mrs Hubert Simpson. The colonel was a quiet man unless the subject was of mules or horses. His wife, who had a girlish air despite her advanced years, talked of their life in India, the taste of boiled mutton, and of wrapping pillowcases around her ankles in order to keep the insect bites at bay.

'And we had wire over the bath drain,' the colonel piped up before shoving a forkful of Dover sole into his mouth.

Blanche looked to Mrs Simpson for enlightenment.

'So the snakes couldn't climb up.'

'I see. Were you very young when you first went to India?'

Mrs Simpson's cherry-red face nodded animatedly, her yellow curls like corkscrews around her face. 'Yes. I went with my father. We used to go up into the hills in summer when Delhi became incredibly hot. There was a hill station there – Simla – I expect you've heard of it.'

'I think so.'

'That was where I met Hubert,' she said with a modest smile.

The colonel folded his hands over his tidy midriff. 'Best thing I ever did in my life.'

His wife simpered like a young girl, patted his hand, then with a demure expression said, 'We have had a good marriage and a long one. It must be quite dreadful for you, my dear, to be widowed so young.'

'It isn't easy.'

'And you're still attractive, my dear. If it's not too impertinent of me to ask, have you thought of remarrying?'

'It's only been two years. I've just set aside my weeds.'

Mrs Simpson eyed the pink and cream striped silk of Blanche's tea gown. The cuffs were trimmed with Nottingham lace, as was the neckline. At her throat she'd pinned a cameo brooch, which was also tinged with pink and matched the freshness of her cheeks.

'Of course. But don't let the grass grow under your feet, my dear. There's still hay to be made.'

At the mention of hay, the colonel re-entered the conversation. 'And good horses to eat it! What?'

Sensing her husband was about to start talking horseflesh, Mrs Simpson steered the conversation elsewhere. 'Now there's a very handsome man,' she remarked, nodding and smiling an acknowledgement to Darius Clarke-Fisher as he entered the dining room. 'I hear he's a widower and has tea plantations in Ceylon.'

'Really.'

Blanche saw him smile and knew he was going to ask if he could join them. She was right.

'I hear you were in India,' he said to the colonel once the waiters had laid him a place.

The colonel's fine, sandy eyebrows rose with interest. 'Indeed I was, sir. I hear you were in Ceylon.'

'Tea. My family has plantations there.'

'How amusing,' Mrs Simpson exclaimed. 'You're in tea and Mrs Heinkel's family are in sugar.'

The colonel guffawed. 'All we need now is a farmer with a herd of Jersey cows, and we've got the milk as well!'

Enlivened by the presence of another male with some knowledge of India, the colonel took over the conversation and started talking about horses, much to Mrs Simpson's annoyance.

'Horses are all very well, my dear,' she said to her husband, 'but let us hear a little of the more important things of life. Did you meet your dear, departed wife in India?' she asked Mr Clarke-Fisher.

The colonel looked miffed. Darius Clarke-Fisher was unperturbed.

'I did indeed. She was just fifteen years old when she came out and I met her in Calcutta. I was finishing my army service before going back to Ceylon. I decided to marry her straight away.'

'She must have impressed you very much,' said Blanche, noticing for the first time that his eyes were hazel and that his hair was dark blond and very straight.

He had a knowing smile. 'I think you mean love at first sight. I sense you are a romantic, Mrs Heinkel, so I have no choice but to tell you the truth. It was indeed love at first sight. She also brought a sizeable dowry with her, but that, as they say in the more mundane literary circles, is another story.'

'So her money impressed you more than the girl herself?'

Clarke-Fisher rose to her challenge, a cryptic smile on his lips. 'No. I have plenty of money, Mrs Heinkel. This was an arrangement between our two families, the Clarke-Fishers and the Templegates. I loved Beatrice. I couldn't help but love her, and I duly provided for her as a husband is duty bound to do.'

Blanche raised his glass and smiled. 'To romance, Mr Clarke-Fisher.'

Clarke-Fisher raised his. 'To falling in love, Mrs Heinkel – and to beautiful women.'

Perhaps she was lonelier than she thought, but she found herself enjoying his attention and was sure her cheeks were turning red. It was something else that contributed to her later regret, though she didn't know that at the time.

She heard Mrs Simpson tut-tut and giggle. Clarke-Fisher was certainly a charmer, she thought, and couldn't help smiling herself.

The only one not smiling was Colonel Simpson. He was frowning at Clarke-Fisher as though he'd suddenly changed his mind about him.

'Templegate. Templegate,' he repeated. 'I'm sure I knew that family.'

'You probably did,' said Clarke-Fisher, his eyes fixed on Blanche as if she were the only woman in the room. 'They were a very large family with a long history of service in India all the way back to Robert Clive's day. But we are here,' he said, once again raising his glass. 'And we are in the company of ladies who deserve our full attention, so let us discard the past and talk of the present. Now ladies, perhaps when we have finished our meal and you've gossiped yourself hoarse, you might like to take the evening air. What say you, Colonel?'

The Colonel ceased frowning. He was not a man to dwell on vagaries. 'If that is what the ladies want, then I shall be happy to oblige.'

By the end of an evening strolling along the promenade, Blanche had told Darius how she passed her days now her family were grown and she had no husband to look after.

'Very noble of you, I'm sure,' he said. 'I believe every man and woman should dabble in at least one noble cause in their life.'

'I do not dabble, sir,' said Blanche, a little put out.

'But do you actually cater to their needs? Do you cook them their soup, scrub their clothes, or minister to them when they fall sick?'

'I . . .' She paused as she thought about this. She sat on the Board. She didn't actually work amongst the inmates. 'I see what you mean. Your comment makes me feel guilty.'

He cupped her elbow in his palm and leaned closer. 'The last thing I wished to do, Mrs Heinkel. Please accept my apologies. I have to say that I would not allow a wife of mine to stoop so low as to frequent such a place.'

'But I am not your wife, Mr Clarke-Fisher.'

'I would expect a wife to run my house in a thrifty and efficient manner,' he continued, as though he had not heard, 'though I would, of course, check the household accounts. Women, I have found, are not capable of handling the financial aspects of domestic management.'

Blanche was speechless, but her mind was alert. This was the true Mr Darius Clarke-Fisher. She suddenly found herself reading far more into the episode with the umbrella. To him a wife was a possession, a creature to be cosseted like a Pekinese and trained like a whippet.

Later that evening, she smiled at her reflection and considered the woman Darius Clarke-Fisher had gazed at with such interest. A few grey hairs streaked from her temples. There were creases at the sides of her eyes and at the edges of her mouth, but her eyes still sparkled and she still had a waistline.

'Will I see you soon?' he asked her on the day she left.

'Of course,' she replied, but had already made up her mind she would not be seeing either him or Clevedon again.

Samson and Abigail, with Desdemona wedged between them, looked up at the high walls of the place Aggie Beven had told them would give them food and a roof over their heads. Everything they owned had been destroyed in the fire at the boarding house.

They'd stayed on Aggie's boat for two weeks, traversing the canals and locks along the Avon and Kennet Canal, all the way to a town called Reading and back.

Although silent for most of the journey, engrossed in her own thoughts, Aggie had appreciated their help and, although she hadn't complained about sharing her meagre food, Samson couldn't bring himself to encroach on her generosity any longer. Besides that, the accommodation was smaller than the old slave huts in Barbados where you could at least lie full-length on the floor. The narrowboat cabin measured only eight by eight, a tight squeeze for five people.

During the journey, he and Hamlet had slept out under a canvas sheet on the roof, leaving the women to share the cabin. They'd supplemented Aggie's endless pots of tea, fried bread and fatty bacon with a few rabbits, wild ducks, pheasants and even a wandering chicken snatched from the water meadows along the way. Urged on by Aggie and supplied with a large enamel jug, they had also milked the cows that had watched lazily as they'd drifted by on the *Lizzie Jane*. He was a proud man and couldn't bear to put Aggie to any inconvenience, yet he felt that was exactly what he was doing. He'd told her they would leave, and because they had no money with which to pay rent, she told them of the only place that could take them in.

'But t'aint a nice place,' she's said, her pipe juggling worriedly at the corner of her mouth.

'Can't be any worse than some of the places I seen,' Samson had replied. It would do for now, he thought: somewhere to lay their heads until he got the lay of the land. Then he would look for Aunt Blanche.

'Let the boy stay. I could do with some help on this old tub, and he looks big enough to shift for himself. Ain't that right, Harry?'

'Hamlet,' his son had said with a grin and a shake of his head. 'My name's Hamlet.'

'What sort of name's that?'

'Shakespeare,' Hamlet had said with a grin.

'Too posh for the likes of me. Harry will do,' she'd said, turning her back and tapping out the bowl of her pipe on the cabin roof.

It had been a terrible wrench, but Samson was sure he'd made the right decision.

'I'm frightened,' whispered Abigail now, her eyes big and round as she looked up at the high walls, then at the dirty, desperate people gathered around them.

Desdemona began to cry. Samson attempted to comfort her, his heart full of foreboding and wishing that he'd never left Barbados. Perhaps he should have gone to another island instead of coming here. It was cold, unfriendly and so far he'd had little chance to try and find his aunt, or cousin or whatever she was.

'You bin in a fire?' someone in the queue asked Abigail. 'You stink of smoke.'

None of them answered. Samson wrapped his great arms around his small family like a protective barrier. If any of those waiting had considered pushing them around, they eyed the size of his biceps and thought again.

A woman poked at his arm. For a moment he thought she was being threatening, but when he looked he saw her eyelids were tightly shut and almost flat.

'Do you mind if I follow you in? I can't see where I'm going, but if I keep sniffing and smell the smoke on you, I'll know when we've moved forward.'

'Yes,' Samson replied. He found it hard to take his eyes off her, humbled to see that despite his own dire circumstances, there was someone here worse off than him and his family.

One half of the high wooden gate gradually creaked open. The crowd surged forward.

'Stop! No rushing, or you'll get no more than a look at that door, and be outside the gate.'

'I fought Boney, now I've come to this,' grumbled an old man.

'Sshh,' said another. 'Any backchat and he'll throw you out. I've seen him do it. So keep quiet and whatever you do, don't look at 'im.'

Abigail exchanged a worried glance with her husband.

A man in a mixed-up uniform eyed them up and down when they entered. 'Wass the likes of you doin' 'ere, then?' Samson curbed his temper as the man sniffed at his sleeve. 'You stinks of smoke.'

'A stroke of luck for me,' said the blind woman. 'I'm followin' me nose. This kind gentleman said I could,' she added, tapping Samson on the shoulder.

Raising the baton he carried until the end of it was an inch from Samson's chin, the man in the uniform fixed him with small, shrewish eyes. 'Just remember I'll be watchin' you, darkie. Got that?'

Samson tensed, looked away and kept his mouth shut. His jaw was as rigid as his body, but he wouldn't retaliate; he dare not.

The interview room was on the ground floor. It was as large as the one above it in which they dined, but the lower windowpanes were painted out with whitewash. Visible through the upper panes, the Workhouse buildings surrounding an open yard brooded like black cliffs casting long shadows. The slate roof tiles, shiny from recent rain, dulled to dark grey as they dried. The floor was also of grey slate and the walls were bare. The room was dark, chilly and forbidding. A row of chairs had been set up in front of the window and behind a long refectory table of dark, dense oak, on which were a large ledger, a zinc inkpot and a quill pen.

With a flourish of coat tails and a supercilious air, the Reverend Smart sat himself before the table.

Blanche, three other members of the Board, including Colonel

Barnes, and Mrs Tinsley ranged themselves in the other chairs provided, the latter making sure she was seated next to the Reverend Smart, and Blanche choosing to sit as far away as possible.

Taking the quill pen in hand, the Reverend Smart entered the date in the ledger. He took his time, his face rigid with concentration as he carefully wrote down the day and month in a fine copperplate hand, the figures in stiff Roman numerals.

Blanche sensed the impatience of her colleagues: the shuffling of feet; the fidgeting posterior against a polished seat; the polite cough behind a starched white cuff. She also sensed that the Reverend Smart knew exactly what he was doing. The Workhouse empowered him and being clerk to the Board made him feel important.

Once he'd finished, he turned to Mrs Tinsley. 'Mrs Tinsley, pray be so kind as to tell Corporal Young to make a start.'

'Certainly.' Pursing her lips in a self-satisfied manner, she got to her feet, self-importance shining around her like a halo.

Families, old men, young women and destitute children began to file before the refectory table, each telling a sad story, each face engrained with starvation and want. One old woman didn't know where she was, but insisted she used to work for a bishop. She'd thought she was going to the coal yard to purchase a bag of coal. No one could find out where she used to live. By a majority decision, she was sent to the lunatic asylum.

Blanche bent her head rather than watch her leave. If she was indeed telling the truth after a lifetime of work and loyal service, she now had nothing, not even her mind.

For the umpteenth time that day, she thanked heaven that she did not have to make decisions by herself. If she had her way, she'd let everyone in, even though she knew it wasn't feasible. There were only so many beds and a certain amount of food. But the strain was telling. Out of sight behind the brim of her bonnet, she closed her eyes and mentally counted to ten. She'd reasoned it would stop her running from this place, never to return. She kept her eyes closed as the door opened again and more than one set of footsteps clumped across the bare boards. At least this family had boots. So many had not. Some had worn cardboard shoes, the sound of their shuffling likely to haunt her dreams for some nights to come.

The Reverend barked. 'Name?'

'Sir, my name is Samson Marcus Rivermead though I used to be Jones.'

'Why isn't it still Jones?' asked Colonel Barnes.

'Because that was a master's name. I decided to take one for myself.'

Blanche froze. The accent itself would have been enough to give Samson away. The fact that he'd taken the surname of Rivermead convinced her that this was the boy she'd once known. But she didn't look up. Her heart raced. Inside her smart kid gloves, her palms were moist and her neck ached with the effort of holding her head down. She told herself she had to be sure, but at the back of her mind, other reasons spread like a malignant rash. If she acknowledged him here, both her and her children's lives in Bristol would be blighted. It was cowardly, it was weak and it cut her to the core, but she couldn't look, she couldn't take the risk. And anyway, cooed the smooth, silky voice of acquired comfort, you don't know for sure that it's the Samson you knew; Samson who was so proud of his learning that he scratched his name over walls, barrels and doors.

Smart bent over the ledger. Holding his pen as though it were a sable brush and he were a Dutch master, he slowly and carefully noted the name.

'Where are you from, Samson Marcus Rivermead?' he asked, looking up at long last after careful scrutiny of his entry.

'Sir, I am from Barbados.'

Yet again, Smart took his time noting the detail, his penmanship seemingly of more importance to him than the family standing before him.

Blanche felt herself flushing hot and cold. Of course it was Samson. Of course it was! Much as her conscience urged her to acknowledge him, her neck seemed to have solidified. She found it impossible to raise her head.

'Why, pray are you here?' asked Colonel Barnes, who was fast becoming impatient with Smart's laborious penmanship.

'I came here looking for a relative of mine. She's kind of an aunt, related to my grandmother who was half-sister to her mother.'

Blanche held her breath.

Smart, who was obviously feeling threatened by the colonel asking a question, snorted and rose too abruptly, his thigh knocking the table as he did so. A droplet of ink flicked from his nib and onto the unblemished surface of the ledger. His face turned bright red. Not brave enough to confront the colonel, he directed his ire at Samson.

'A likely story! And what is this aunt's name, and where do you expect to find her? Answer that if you can!'

Samson's head jerked high, the humility he'd been advised to adopt vanishing before the cleric's onslaught and the insinuation that he was a liar. His nostrils flared with impatience and his voice was big and bold. 'My cousin's name is Blanche and she married a man in the sugar industry.'

Smart leapt in. 'A moment ago, you said she was your aunt.'

Samson shrugged. 'Cousin. Aunt. She's a relative. My grandfather was half-brother of her mother. So she was only kind of an aunt, kind of a cousin.'

'A second cousin,' shouted Smart, slapping his hand down hard on the table so that the quill pen jumped from its well and, yet again, ink was flicked all over the neatly written ledger. He gasped in horror at the blemished page.

'Do you know the name of this man she married?' asked the colonel. At the same time he pulled Smart's sleeve so severely that the cleric had to sit down or lose his coat.

'No. I can't remember,' said Samson. He sounded devastated.

Blanche stared unblinking at the floor. It was hard to resist the impulse to proclaim she was found. But she couldn't. Foremost among her thoughts was the need to protect her children. What would happen if people – the powerful people whom Max was intent on impressing – should find out that their mother was of African blood, slave blood, and fathered out of wedlock.

The colonel bent his head and whispered to those on either side of him. 'It strikes me that in time this family might find this relative, or the relative may come to claim them . . .'

Smart was the colour of a ripe raspberry, his anger threatening to choke him.

'In which case,' said the colonel, blatantly ignoring the Reverend Smart's fury, 'I think he will not be here long enough to become institutionalized.'

Smart's jaw dropped. 'Institutionalized? What the devil's that supposed to mean?'

The colonel had the habit of closing one eye and turning the other more beady specimen on the subject before him. Officers and enlisted men alike had cringed before him in his army days. Smart slid back in his chair as the colonel pounced.

'Too long in a regimented place makes you forget how it is on the outside. And don't tell me I don't know enough about this place to say that. I've seen it in the army. Seen men of twenty years service unable to return to civilian life because they can no longer function without rules. Strikes me we should be looking to impress that this place is a temporary measure.' His eyes briefly took in their surroundings. 'Strikes me I wouldn't want to be in here too bloody long. I say we let the man in.'

Sir Bertram nodded in agreement over his port. Smart simmered. Blanche instinctively felt that she would not be asked for an opinion. The fact that the colonel had not apologized to her for his swearing made her think her presence was forgotten. It turned out she was correct.

'I think that's carried,' said the colonel, his right eyebrow returning to its normal position, shoulders back and a triumphant tilt to his chin.

Smart was still the colour of an infantry jacket. Acknowledging defeat, he nodded to the warden and Mrs Tinsley, and the Rivermead family were led away, mother and child through one door, Samson through the other.

Blanche sat perfectly still, hardly hearing the rest of the proceedings and feeling ashamed of herself. Nothing of her pedigree had been divulged, but she'd lost something of herself. My integrity, she thought. Samson came looking for me, and I denied him.

For the sake of your children!

Of course. But was it worth it? Was it for the best that they never knew their heritage?

Her heart lay heavy and, by the end of the proceedings, she ached all over and fine beads of sweat had broken out on her forehead.

'May I escort you to your carriage?' the colonel asked.

Blanche gathered her thoughts and quickly worked out what she would do next. 'I serve on this Board to visit as well as to officiate,' she said without sounding flustered. 'So today that is what I will do before making my way home. But thank you for your consideration, Colonel. It is much appreciated.'

Courteous as ever, he doffed his hat and left her to do as she pleased.

Mrs Tinsley, however, eyed her suspiciously. Ignore her, thought Blanche. Mrs Tinsley eyes everyone as though they're about to run off with the bricks and mortar.

'I'd like to visit the men who have just been brought in,' she said.

Mrs Tinsley pursed her lips and raised her eyebrows. 'The men?' She made it sound as though something lascivious had been suggested.

Blanche felt her face reddening. *Don't let that harridan see it!* With determined steeliness, she took out a lavender-scented handkerchief and dabbed at her upper lip. 'I do believe I have a cold coming,' she said in a casual manner before adopting a more assertive tone. 'I may be able to help them get jobs, especially those with families.'

Mrs Tinsley tried to look as though she wasn't really taking in the checked dress, the red trim and a width of skirt that barely squeezed through some of the doors. But even if Blanche hadn't noticed her scrutiny, she could feel her envy; it was like being pierced by a thousand tiny needles.

'They're having a carbolic wash first. Wouldn't want to see that, would you?'

Insult was intended, but Blanche pretended not to notice. 'Then I will see the women first.'

Mrs Tinsley made a sound that was halfway between 'yes' and a grumble. Keys rattling from the long chain attached to her belt, she led Blanche towards the women's quarters.

The corridor was long and cold. There was little light except that filtering through small, square windows set high up beyond eye level. This was not the first time Blanche had ventured along this corridor, but never had her body been so racked with icy shivers that seemed to begin at the nape of her neck and end in her toes.

What would she say to Samson's wife? What would Samson's wife think of her if she told her the truth now?

She pulled her shawl more closely around herself and told herself she must be strong. She coughed. This place is damp, she thought, and rubbed at the tickle she felt in her chest.

Her knees were knocking by the time they reached the last door that opened into the women's quarters. Just a few steps away, the door swung open and one of Mrs Tinsley's assistants, a one-eyed woman with no teeth, came rushing out. She was carrying a bundled blue shawl against her meagre chest. The smell of old food and mouldy clothes came out with her.

'We've got a dead 'un,' she squawked, her voice high-pitched and grating on the nerves.

Mrs Tinsley's wide nostrils dilated into small slits and she looked quite put out. 'Who's that then, Ethel?'

'Young trollop who came in with a big belly a few days ago.'

Mrs Tinsley jerked her head at the bundle. 'Is it dead?'

The shawl moved. A small pink fist waved in the air, accompanied by the weak cry of a newborn babe.

Blanche touched the tiny fist, which tightly closed around her finger. 'Poor little thing. To be born in such a place as this.' Concern for the child outweighed her own predicament. She addressed Mrs Tinsley. 'What will happen to it now the mother is dead?'

Mrs Tinsley sniffed. 'It will go to the nursery, of course, and a wet nurse will be provided.'

Blanche stared as Ethel tucked the baby's fist back under the shawl and bustled away.

'I'd like to see the nursery when I am next here,' she said, her gaze following Ethel until she disappeared from sight.

'Well, I don't know about that. You'll have to get the Reverend Smart's permission. I couldn't possibly let you in there without his say-so.'

Determinedly, Blanche tucked her handkerchief back into her reticule. 'Then I shall ask him.'

Mrs Tinsley looked like thunder. 'You do that! I've got a dead trollop to get out of here'. She flew into the room recently vacated by Ethel and slammed the door behind her.

Blanche tried to decide which was most immediately important. Perhaps she was a coward, or perhaps it was genuine concern, but she decided on the nursery. Put it down to guilt, she thought. My children had every comfort in life. These poor little mites . . .

She pushed the true reason, that she was not ready to confront Samson and his family, to the back of her mind. Another day, another ordeal. But for now she would confront the Reverend Smart and ask his permission to visit the nursery.

She caught him standing on a chair looking out of the window. He almost fell off when he realized she was there.

'Just checking on our charges,' he said with a slimy smile as he regained the ground.

Before she could ask him anything, Warden Tinsley entered and outlined the business of the dead woman, adding that they were bringing her through into the yard.

'Good man, Tinsley. Harness up the cart and do what you have to do. I'll come out and say a few words.'

'Shall I ask the usual fee, Reverend?'

With a sidelong glance at Blanche and a warning one to Tinsley, Smart ushered him to the far corner of the room where they spoke softly, heads almost touching.

Curious to know what Smart had been looking at, Blanche scratched a small hole in the thick paint that covered the lower windows. At first all she saw was a bare, brown back. Someone was standing in front of the window. As if at a signal, the body moved and she saw what Smart had seen.

There was a pump in the middle of the yard outside. The women who had just been given entry to the Workhouse were standing in a line waiting to fill bowls from which they washed themselves. Those without bowls washed beneath the pump. A large number of them, especially the younger ones, were stripped to the waist.

Blanche felt her face burning. At the sound of his footsteps crossing the room, she turned round, her eyes automatically rising to yet another of the texts on the wall:

'BY THEIR ACTIONS SHALL YE KNOW THEM'.

She struggled for her handkerchief as the tickle in her chest turned into a spasm of coughs.

'Mrs Heinkel!' The Reverend helped her to a chair.

'This is all too much . . .' she said, holding her handkerchief to her forehead, both embarrassed and annoyed that she'd been on the verge of fainting. 'The baby . . . upset me.'

'Very upsetting,' said the Reverend Smart, patting her hand. 'The Lord giveth and the Lord taketh away. Blessed be the name of the Lord.'

'And little children suffer,' whispered Blanche.

'I think you mean, "suffer little children",' said Smart.

'No. I do not.'

She sensed she'd confused him. The Bible excerpts that coloured his speech, the texts decorated on the walls and ceilings were just that, mere decoration.

Her head spun when she got to her feet and, although she was determined to visit the nursery, she knew she could not manage it today. Her obligation to Samson and his family would also be put aside for now. Somehow she would get them out of here, but had to be careful. Much as it grieved her to admit it, she would not hurt her family's prospects.

Despite her loathing of the man, she was grateful to lean on Smart's arm as he led her out through the gate and helped her into her carriage. As he did so, Blanche saw Warden Tinsley slap the reins across the rump of a sway-backed nag pulling a cart. The cart held one of the strange beds she'd seen in the communal dormitory, the lid now closed on its occupant who had fallen asleep for ever. The cart stopped a few feet in front of her carriage, causing the matching chestnuts to snort as if they knew what the cart contained.

'I bid you good day, Mrs Heinkel,' said the Reverend Smart, raising his hat. 'I'm just going to say a few words over the woman.'

Blanche found it impossible to drag her eyes away from the coffin. Twenty years had passed since she'd first come to Bristol. If Conrad had not married her, could she too have met a pauper's end?

'Will anyone say a prayer over her grave when she arrives at the churchyard?' she asked.

Smart shook his head and nervously cleared his throat. 'Oh no. No, of course not. At least, not for a while. She's a pauper, you see. First she'll go to the medical school. Those that die paupers always go to the medical school before burial.'

She did not remember what happened next. The carriage was moving, or perhaps she was. Her eyes were becoming unfocused, her surroundings seeming to swim before her eyes. Whether she gave the order to the coachman, or whether Smart did, she would never know. The shivers, the fever, the sweating and the faintness returned along with a new spasm of coughs.

By the time they arrived back at Somerset Parade, she was laid at full stretch on the seat. When she finally opened her eyes, she was in her own bed and it was the next morning.

Chapter Eleven

Throughout the meeting, Tom was aware of Max's hostility and felt helpless before it. Thanks to Horatia, the air between them was soured. Max was fiercely loyal to his father's memory and would never willingly relinquish his holdings in The Counterslip property. But Horatia was right. The site would become less and less profitable. How to persuade Max that it would be best if he sold and built a new property at Avonmouth, or move to London?

The meeting was being held in a room above the Corn Exchange. The sound of the city filtered in through the windows. Cabs jostled their way past the copper-topped corn nails outside the building where deals were still agreed and paid for 'on the nail'. Carts carrying hay, wood, pigs and beer pushed aside street-sellers and red-robed judges on their way to the assizes.

Tom watched the scene below, his hands folded behind his back.

Behind him, Max repeated, 'I will not shut The Counterslip. I owe it to my father.'

Tom understood how Max was feeling. He too had been stubborn in his youth.

The new chairman of Webbers, a man named Michael Forge, explained that it wasn't really up to him. 'You have to understand that the Strong family, through their acquisition of the bank, now have almost as many shares as you do.'

'But not enough,' snapped Max.

Tom frowned as he continued to eye the street outside where a beggar's dog was doing tricks with a ball and a hoop. Just as I have to, he thought. It was imperative he impressed on Max that he could lose everything if he didn't agree. Saying it sounded easy, but how could he explain Horatia's vindictiveness? Admitting the reason would surely lead to the truth, and now was not the time to admit he was his father.

One positive aspect was that a brewery was interested in The Counterslip site. Unlike sugar refiners, breweries were not reliant upon large ships crossing the Atlantic. The hops they used came from Kent via the Thames and along the Avon and Kennet Canal. More hops came from Herefordshire, brought down the Severn on large barges designed specially for the job. Horatia had changed her mind about calling in the mortgage, so long as Max agreed to the sale. So far, Max had resisted. But what were his options?

Tom turned and faced the meeting. There were six men there including himself and Max. Two of the others were shareholders. A clerk sitting next to Michael Forge took copious notes of the proceedings.

Tom slid his thumbs into the pockets of his waistcoat and blanched when he looked at Max. He saw himself in his eyes, but besides that, he saw his vulnerability. Max was trying very hard to act the part of the experienced businessman. For the first time he understood the weight of responsibility placed on the young man's shoulders. He had a widowed mother and a younger sister to maintain. It couldn't be easy, and his heart went out to him.

'It makes sense, Max. Ships are getting bigger. The cost of transferring loads from ship to barge is making The Counterslip unprofitable. A decision has to be made – and quickly.'

He saw the look of relief on the faces around him. No one had been willing to state the truth. They'd waited for him.

'This is very true,' said Michael Forge, folding his hands in front of him as though he were about to deliver a Sunday sermon. 'It makes sense to sell The Counterslip site, purchase land at Avonmouth and build a new refinery there.'

Max bowed and shook his head. Tom sensed his strain.

'The cost of a new refinery would be exorbitant. My portion of profit from the sale of The Counterslip site would only amount to a quarter of the cost. Your portion, too,' he said directly to Tom. 'I take it the rest of the money would come from the Strong family and, indirectly, from this bank. Therefore, whereas now I hold over half the shares in the refinery, in future I would only own one quarter. The controlling interest would pass to the Strongs.' He shook his head. 'Somehow I will hang on.'

Despite the fact that he disagreed with his decision, Tom's eyes shone with admiration. To the surprise of everyone there, Max had perfect understanding of what they were up to. The city that had once boasted over twenty sugar refineries had less than half that now and the figure would diminish even further. Those that were left must be larger and in the right position in order to compete in a shrinking market. Max understood that but was fighting to maintain control of his refinery.

The meeting broke up soon after that in an uncomfortable silence. As they made their way along the landing to the staircase that would take them out into St Nicholas Market, Tom took the opportunity to speak to Max alone.

'I understand your motives, and I sympathize.'

Max eyed him warily. 'You won't persuade me otherwise until I am guaranteed a fair share of any planned relocation.'

Tom nodded and noted the way Max's chin jutted forward, proud of his bottom lip. 'I understand that and will not try and persuade you otherwise. I think Conrad would have been proud of you.'

The comment was well received. Max's features relaxed a little. 'You and my father were friends.'

Tom looked down at his walking cane as he tapped it on the floor. 'Yes. We were friends. And of course, I knew your mother.'

'Indeed.'

They walked down the stairs in silence. At the halfway point, Tom asked, 'How is your mother? I haven't seen her for some time.'

Much to Tom's alarm, Max looked downcast. 'She has not been well. Damp and cold weather do not agree with her. She's taking the waters in Bath at the moment. I did offer to buy her a house there, but she says not to. She insists the Ambassador Hotel suits her fine and not to waste money. It's a comfortable place, though not so nice as being home, of course. I think the waters do her good.'

Tom briefly wondered whether Max could hear the thud of his heart. He had been trying to think of a suitable excuse for visiting Blanche at home. Now he didn't need to. All he had to do was go to the Ambassador Hotel in Bath. No one would know. He would make sure of that.

Penance, thought Horatia, gazing at the gleaming silver cross dominating the high altar, the tip of its shadow almost reaching the hem of her skirt. Penance, that is what people used to do in payment for their sins. That's what I should be doing. But what penance do I deserve?

It was the third time she had called in at St Mary Redcliffe. Each time it followed a successful meeting with her lawyer, Septimus Monk. Her plans for diversifying away from sugar were going well, too well it seemed. Unencumbered by children, she moved like a man in the business world, and knew she was lucky. Few women ever reached their full mental potential. Her mind was bright with possibilities, figures added and subtracted, plans memorized, potential examined and analysed.

Soon, the Strong family fortune would no longer depend on sugar. Selling the plantation would be the most difficult task. A large number of investors and owners had pulled out of the West Indies altogether. Her only hope was to find someone willing to reap less profits than would have been expected in years gone by. Someone would be found. She was sure of it. Things were going extremely well, and it troubled her. Where was the retribution for what she'd done?

Somehow, she was sure it would come. Success always came at a price. In time she would find out what hers would be. In the meantime she would continue to pray for forgiveness.

The clergyman caught her on the way out. 'You are becoming a regular visitor.'

His smile was disarming. She'd approached the exit telling herself that she need not visit the church any more. But there was something in his eyes that brought her up short.

'I had a need to come.'

He nodded sagely, as though he were looking into her soul and had picked out the barbs that were hurting her. 'Are you saying that your need no longer exists?'

It wasn't a habit of hers to fiddle with her fingers as some people did when they were wearing gloves, but she found herself doing it now. 'Perhaps.' She was unnecessarily sharp and regretted it. 'I'm sorry.'

He mistook her meaning. 'Then you should tell those concerned that you are sorry.'

She held her head pertly. 'Not God?'

His smile did not diminish. 'If you are telling those concerned that you are sorry, you are indeed telling God.'

Chapter Twelve

'You're love struck,' said Edith, and playfully pinched Max's cheek, just as she'd done when he was little.

He turned bright red and his serious expression was replaced with an irrepressible grin. 'Sometimes you forget you're a servant.'

Grinning broadly, she nudged his arm. 'And sometimes you forget that I've seen you without any clothes on and know what you've got to offer!'

'I was only a child then.'

'And you ain't now. It's time you was married.'

Most people of Edith's class would never have been so personal. But she wasn't just a servant. She was his mother's friend, was warm and chirpy and easily tolerated.

'Ooow! Look!' said Edith who'd spied a hansom pulling up outside the door.

Max moved so fast that he was at her side almost before she knew it. He didn't see her sidelong grin. His gaze was fixed outside the window. They both watched as Magdalene Cherry came tripping out of a cab with a hatbox dangling from one arm.

'I can't believe my mother's bought another hat.'

'She hasn't,' said Edith. 'She's having her old ones redesigned in the same style the Queen's wearing nowadays. Anyway, are you complaining? And don't deny it; I know a lovesick puppy when I see one.'

'She's only a milliner, Edith.'

He sounded sad and it touched her heart. 'Are you saying she's not good enough for you?'

'I have a position, Edith. That's what my family are likely to say.'

Edith crossed her arms and eyed him as if she were about to lay a cane across his backside. 'Don't you go making yur excuses to me, Max, my boy. Don't you go saying to me that she's only good enough for a dalliance. Do you know how many poor girls have been dallied with and ended up with a bundle and their lives ruined?'

Max tried to protest. 'I wouldn't do that.'

Magdalene disappeared from their view behind one of the potted trees standing on either side of the door.

'I'd better get that,' said Edith as the sound of the knocker reverberated through the hallway. She sniffed disdainfully. 'Can't expect you to open the door for a common little milliner, can we?'

'No . . . I expect . . .'

He was going to say that one of the other maids would answer the door, and that Magdalene should be ushered into the drawing room, but Edith was gone.

He listened as the door was opened. The sound of conversation filtered into the room, though he couldn't work out what was being said. Then he heard a light laughing, the sort that women do when they're sharing secrets.

He walked to the door and reached for the handle. No. He couldn't do it. His hand flopped to his side. But he listened, and if he listened very carefully, he could pick out Magdalene's voice from the muffled conversation.

'You can't do this,' he said, walking back to the window, hands clasped behind his back. From there he walked to the fireplace, to an armchair, to the door, then back to the window. 'She's just a milliner.' He thought of what Edith had said and repeated the same sentiment. 'You cannot take advantage of her.'

There! It was said. But he ached to run across the room and throw the door open, invite her in and insist Edith fetched them tea. It was torture standing there: his head determining that he stay fixed to the spot; his heart aching to do as it pleased.

He heard her laugh. He was sure it was her. His mind was made up. The door beckoned. How could he possibly let her leave without seeing her lovely face again?

Before he'd gone half a dozen paces, the door opened.

She was dressed in her usual uniform, but had added a red scarf around her throat. The effect, combined with her dark features and pink cheeks, was breathtaking. He was reminded of a painting he'd seen of a flowerseller by some Italian artist whose name he couldn't quite recall.

Edith stood behind her and winked at him. 'Miss Cherry has a little problem regarding your mother's hat. I said she'd better see you about it. I'll get some tea, shall I?'

Max opened his mouth, but no sound came out, which was just as well, because Edith was gone, the door slammed firmly shut behind her.

His heart hammering like a battering ram against his ribs, Max turned to Magdalene – and felt his legs turn to water. He cleared his throat. 'You have a problem with my mother's hat?'

'I need to try it on her, but I've been told by Mrs Blackcloud that she isn't here.'

'That is correct. Perhaps you'd like to leave it with me and I will make sure my mother attends to the matter on her return.'

Even to his own ears, he sounded priggish, like any upper-class man addressing a lowly servant or tradesperson.

A black, springy curl escaped from beneath her bonnet as Magdalene shook her head. 'Oh, I couldn't possibly do that. I need it to be tried on now. I need to see if the veil reaches the proper length.'

'I see.'

He didn't see at all. What difference did the length of a veil make to a woman's bonnet? Fashion had a lot to answer for and was something he'd never quite understood.

Magdalene cocked her head to one side. 'Perhaps you could try it on. I could see then whether the length was right.'

Max pointed at his chest. 'Me?' He felt himself blushing profusely.

'I think that would do very well,' said Magdalene, her nimble fingers already unfastening the ribbons that kept the box firmly shut. She folded back the silk-lined lid and, with a dramatic flourish, brought out a blue velvet bonnet trimmed with bows and a veil hanging down behind. '*Voilà!* As Madame Mabel would say. If you could just try it on . . .' She edged towards him.

Max held up both hands before his horrified expression. 'No! I don't think I could . . .'

'Oh!' There was a sparkle in her eyes that made him think she was enjoying his discomfort. There was also something else, a cheeky, secretive look that made him think she had already decided on the outcome of this meeting.

She set the hat back in its box. He noticed how narrow her waist was, how ample her bosom and how creamy her complexion.

'Then I think we shall have to compromise, if that's all right with you?'

'If it means that I don't have to try on that bonnet, then yes, I think a compromise is a very good idea.'

She wore dark blue kid gloves. Her hands were small. He watched, fascinated, as she undid her bonnet strings. 'I shall have to try it on, and you will have to judge that the length is correct. Does that sound a better idea?'

'It seems so to me.'

After placing her own bonnet on a small tripod table, she lifted his mother's bonnet from the box and walked to the mantelpiece. The mirror above the mantelpiece was large and gilded, bows and grapes intertwining at its apex, and small shelves standing proud at its sides.

Magdalene stood before it holding the hat above her head.

Max couldn't take his eyes off her. Her bodice was tight, the curve of her breasts accentuated by the raising of her arms. Posed like that, he was reminded of a Greek statue, voluptuous but perfectly formed.

As she tied the bonnet strings beneath her chin, he became aware that she was watching him watching her via the mirror's reflection.

She smiled. 'And now you will help me judge that the bonnet is right?'

He nodded and attempted to recover his poise. 'Of course. It looks very nice.'

'But the veil? Is it the right length?'

He shrugged. What did he know about veils? What did he know about bonnets either, for that matter? 'Yes. It looks . . . just right.'

She shook her head. 'That's no good. I can't see its length.' A smile flickered at the corners of her mouth. 'You see the place on my back where the veil falls?'

He nodded. His mouth had turned intolerably dry.

'Touch the spot. Run your fingers across my back in the exact spot to where it falls.'

As he moved closer to her, he felt as diaphanous as the veil itself, like steam or smoke, drifting lightly over the floor. The top of her head reached his chin. Her body was close to his. She smelled of violets. As he raised his hand to a spot about halfway down her back, their eyes met in the mirror.

'Trace your hand along,' she said softly. 'Just the tips of your fingers.'

He felt her back tense beneath his touch. She turned her head slightly and he trembled.

'You have a very light touch,' she said.

Her voice was hushed but the words were drawn-out, like an autumn wind blowing through sycamore leaves.

She turned a little more. The fabric of his waistcoat whispered against her sleeve.

All thoughts of resisting her vanished. His heart was pumping fit to burst when his fingers again crossed her back. For some reason he could not quite comprehend – her warm flesh was next to his; he could feel the heat of it through his clothes, through her clothes too – his arm snaked around her back. Her face was upturned and her eyes gazed into his. It was easy to kiss her. In fact, he wondered why he had never done it before.

Edith took her time with the tea, humming to herself as she smoothed a white cotton tray cloth decorated with red cross-stitches around its border. The cloth was particularly special. Her daughter Molly had done the stitching some time before she went into service in London. At the thought of her daughter and times past, she hesitated before placing the crockery on the tray. Running her fingers over the carefully proportioned stitches, she recalled how Molly had frowned over the task of decorating the cloth. It seemed such a long time ago now. All her children had left home, one girl in service, one married, one boy in the army in India and another sailing backwards and forwards out of Liverpool to America.

And me all alone, she thought. As her eyes filled with water, she bit her lip to stop from sobbing. If only Jim had come home from sea. But he didn't, she told herself, so make the best of things you can.

After wiping her eyes with her apron, she judged the time was ripe for taking the tea upstairs to the young couple. She had high hopes for them. She'd seen the look in Max's eyes, and she'd also interpreted from Magdalene's cocky stance that she was interested, but playful. Max will learn, she thought as she climbed the stairs.

Just as she'd expected, they were both flushed and sprang swiftly away from each other when she entered the room.

'Do you want me to pour?' she asked chirpily, her eyes shining.

It was Magdalene who answered. 'No, no. Of course not. I'm quite strong enough to lift a teapot, thank you very much.'

Edith beamed with satisfaction. 'Then I shall leave you to it.'

Once outside the drawing room her ear lingered a while against the door. She couldn't wait to tell Blanche about it when she got back from Bath. She was sure she'd be pleased. What did it matter that the girl was only a milliner so long as she made Max happy?

Chapter Thirteen

Bath was full of tourists taking the waters, walking in the sunshine around the Royal Crescent, across Pulteney Bridge and in the cloistered haven that was North Parade Gardens.

Blanche was feeling a little better, though much to Edith's chagrin, she was wearing black again.

'It's like wearing a suit of armour,' she had explained. 'There's no need to explain to anyone that I am a widow, and because it seems I am still in mourning, I am respected and left alone.'

On this particular visit, she did not desire company, but wanted time to think. What should she do about Samson and his family? How could she explain it to her children that they were relatives and, as such, she could not possibly see them destitute?

Perhaps it was the stout breakfast she'd been served, but courage poured over her.

I need to get back to Bristol, she told herself. I need to go to the Workhouse and face them, reminders of a past I had chosen to forget.

There was, for an instant, an echo of Viola, the strong-minded mother who had made sure her daughter was not born into slavery.

Determined she would do what was right, she'd made her way to the railway station. Running her finger down the timetable, she saw there were two trains going to Bristol that day, one in the morning and one in the afternoon.

Trembling slightly, she made her way to the ticket office, her fingers fumbling in her reticule for the correct fare. Half a crown for a first class seat.

There were other people ahead of her in the queue. An elderly lady with an ear trumpet was asking the ticket seller to repeat what he had just said.

'I said it's two and six first class, one and six for second, and one shilling for third. Which is it you want?'

Blanche didn't hear her answer. She was still rummaging for her money, and all the time thinking of how she would tell her children that relatives of theirs were currently residing in the Workhouse.

'Next!' said the ticket seller.

She took hold of her purse, let it go, pulled the strings of her reticule shut, then opened them again.

'Madam, I have not got all day.'

She suddenly realized he was talking to her. What courage she'd had sank to her boots.

'I . . . I've left my money back in my hotel. I'll get someone there to come along . . . and buy my ticket . . .'

She sounded unsure, and the ticket seller looked unconvinced.

'Next,' he shouted again, and the man behind her stepped forward.

She hurried away, her heart beating madly. What was happening to her? In the past she'd always prided herself on doing what was right, but it wasn't so easy now. Today's life was so different from her past. She'd never wanted for anything like some people had, like Edith for instance, but the one thing she had gained was the respect of her peers. Her children had inherited position and the respect that went with it. She didn't want them injured, but how could she help Samson at the same time as maintaining the status quo?

Accompanied by the warm sun and her thoughts, she wandered into North Parade Gardens, just a short distance from her hotel. The air was heavy with the perfume of late blooms and wet grass. A child ran past striking a hoop with a small stick. A caravan of nursemaids passed by, each pushing identical versions of a three-wheeled device called a perambulator, newly invented baby carriages for those who could afford them. The park had become crowded with a sea of colourful crinolines and smartly dressed gentlemen, their flamboyantly tied cravats, resembling seagulls with folded wings, nestling at their throats. Her eyes swept over them, not recognizing anyone . . . and then she saw him: Mr Darius Clarke-Fisher, head and shoulders above everyone else.

Hoping he hadn't seen her, she drew her veil down over her face and hurried away as fast as she could. She thought she heard him call her name, but didn't look back. She didn't want to see him, determined to be alone until she was ready to go home.

On her walk back to the Ambassador Hotel, she thought of her reaction. How different it would have been had she spied Tom Strong in New Parade Gardens.

They'd met socially on a few occasions, their exchange necessarily terse in the presence of their respective spouses, but she remembered when things had been different; long ago when she'd first arrived in Bristol and they'd lain together beneath the roof of Conrad Heinkel who had later become her husband. Other events had taken over, and Conrad had offered her security rather than passion. For the most part she had not regretted it, but even after all this time, the passion for one man above all others was still there, simmering beneath the surface. Thoughts of what might have been were perhaps the main reason she would not remarry, though there were bound to be offers, Mr Darius Clarke-Fisher for one.

She baulked at the thought of it and walked quickly despite the tightness of her stays and the thin heels of her canvas summer boots.

By the time she gained the hotel, her face was flushed but her breathing had returned to normal. She ran a gloved hand down the smocked panel of her bodice. Remember who you are, she told herself. Mrs Blanche Heinkel, a respectable widow.

The interior of the hotel was dark and cool, the walls panelled in walnut and a thick carpet covering the floor. A brass-faced floor clock stood against one wall. No gentleman could pass it without fetching his watch from his pocket and checking the time.

Sam the concierge met her in the foyer and asked her if she would like tea.

Blanche smiled at him. 'I would indeed. How is Mary by the way?'

'Doing very well, madam. She much prefers being a nursemaid to waiting on tables. Mr Devere, the hotel owner, is very pleased with her.'

'Good. I'm glad.'

She'd met Mary on first arriving at the hotel, too jolly and intuitive a girl to wait on tables, and Blanche had struck up quite a rapport with her. Sometimes Mary had got a ticking off for lingering too long after delivering Blanche her tea, almost to the point of being dismissed, and Blanche had had to intervene. But then she'd been given the job of nursemaid to the owner's child. Seemingly, it had turned out to suit her very well. Blanche liked to think that it was as a result of her intervention and continuing patronage. It made her feel warm and eminently satisfied.

She sought her usual table with the view of Pulteney Bridge, the table where Rupert had warned her that Samson was coming to Bristol. Would anything have been different if she'd heeded his warning? She didn't think so.

In the act of throwing her veil back over her bonnet, she inadvertently glanced towards the door, saw the concierge about to enter with a tea tray, but pause as if someone out of her view had spoken to him. She thought nothing of it, but turned her attention back to the view.

'Tea, madam?'

The sound of his voice caused her to start. Even before she looked round, she knew who would be there and who had caused the concierge to pause at the door.

Tom Strong smiled and, as his face relaxed, a lock of hair fell onto his forehead. His coat was a green-blue, his waistcoat grey and his cravat a mixture of the two. He wore it casually, yet strikingly. Tom had never been stiffly formal, sometimes verging on untidy but in an appealing, attractive way.

His presence caused a wave of interest. A woman with iron-grey hair and sporting a pince-nez put down her cup and left the room. A man rustled his newspaper and threw a disapproving look in their direction before hiding behind it.

'Widows should not entertain handsome men in hotel lounges,' she said.

His eyes narrowed merrily. 'Not even if they're very old friends?'

'Very old friends,' she said loudly so that no one was in any doubt, then in a quieter voice that was full of affection, 'I can't believe you're here.'

'I'm a well-travelled man.'

'And you never do anything without a reason. Tom, tell me what are you doing here.'

He set down the tray, flicked his coat-tails out behind him and took a seat, tugging at his trouser legs so they wouldn't cling too tightly to his thighs.

'Blanche. It's so good to see a friendly face,' he said, his hands clasped tightly before him.

The expression in his eyes told her he was glad to see her. The dark hollows beneath them and the tightness of his mouth told her that he was not here to swear undying love.

'Tom what is it?' Without thinking about what she was doing, she covered his hands with her own. They felt cold and hard, the knuckles white with tension.

He sighed and dropped his head. 'Please forgive me. I didn't know what else to do . . .' he began.

Blanche frowned. Tom had always been so strong, so dependable.

'Have some tea,' she said, releasing his hands. She poured milk and tea into his cup, and dropped in a large chunk of sugar, freshly cut from a loaf.

It surprised her to see his hand shaking as he took the tea.

He smiled nervously and wrapped both hands around the saucer. 'I'm sorry about this. I must pull myself together.'

'How did you know I'd be here?'

'Max mentioned it at a business meeting a few days ago. I would have got here sooner, but . . .' He shrugged.

'I think you'd better tell me what this is all about.'

He told her then about his child, about Horatia's lies and the terrible truth, imparted by Daisy Draper, that the baby, his son, had been placed in St Philip's Workhouse because of the colour of his skin.

Now it was Blanche's hand that trembled, the spoon rattling in the saucer as she placed the tea back on the tray. 'My God!' Her exclamation was low but full of emotion.

The horrors of her last visit to the Workhouse came flooding back to her; the tiny newborn being carried by the dreadful Ethel to the nursery, the mother of the child taken away in one of the terrible lidded beds, not to be buried, but to be dissected at the medical school, her options in death as grim as they'd been in life.

'Horatia sent your baby there?'

He nodded, his head seeming to sink into his shoulders with the weight of his sadness. 'His colour wouldn't have mattered a jot to me. I know that the Strong blood isn't as pure as they try to make out . . .' He jerked up, suddenly aware of what he had said. 'Not that I'm saying . . .'

'Oh, Tom. Tom!' Tears squeezed out of the corners of her eyes. His devastation was tangible, like bitter almond on her tongue. His grief was her grief, more so because she had seen that place and knew the child's chances of survival were virtually nil.

His eyes locked with hers. 'I can't enquire myself, Blanche. I went there, determined that I would demand the return of my son, but I couldn't.' He looked down at the floor. 'I spoke to a milkman out on his rounds. Something he said made me reconsider. Besides his skin colour, how could we suddenly explain the reappearance of a child Horatia had told everyone was dead?'

'It would be hard for both of you.'

Something about the way he lowered his eyes made her think that there was something he wasn't telling her.

'She threatened you with something, didn't she?'

He nodded, took both her hands in his and held them against his mouth. His breath was warm against her fingertips. His lips were soft. Although murmurings of disapproval travelled around the room, she bid them no heed. The moment was too precious, too long awaited. They were here, the two of them. Horatia might as well have been on the moon. The genteel and faded Bath society had little to do with the more vibrant commerciality of its sister city. The two rarely mixed. No one would know of this very public and intimate moment.

'She threatened to send Emerald away to boarding school . . .' He hesitated again.

Blanche knew there was more to come and guessed. 'Max?'

He nodded. 'She threatened to tell Max that I'm his father.'

'No! She couldn't.' She withdrew her hands as though they'd been burned. She saw the hurt in his eyes and shook her head. 'He'd be devastated. You know how much he thought of Conrad, how much he misses him.'

Tom nodded, opened his mouth to reassure her, but was suddenly interrupted.

The tall, lean figure of Mr Darius Clarke-Fisher threw a shadow over the proceedings.

'Mrs Heinkel. We meet again.'

Bowing stiffly from the waist, he raised his hat, his beady eyes shifting sidelong to Tom and then back to her.

'I trust I am not interrupting any mutual intimacy . . . ?'

Tom rose to his feet. The look in his eyes certainly wasn't amenable.

Blanche attempted to smooth the sudden prickliness of the air. 'An old friend . . . Captain Thomas Strong . . .'

She could have bitten off her tongue. Why hadn't she given a false name? Darius Clarke-Fisher knew Bristol society. Had he seen them so closely entwined?

'I do believe I know of you,' said Darius, and was slow to shake hands.

Blanche perceived an immediate animosity between them and it angered her. One had no call to presume on her affection. The other had every reason to but, by virtue of the fact that he was married, was not entitled to do so.

'I'm just leaving,' said Tom, reaching for his hat, gloves and stick. 'Anything I can do with regard to your charitable work, Mrs Heinkel, please get in touch. I have an office in the Corn Exchange.'

Their eyes met in one swift instant of understanding. 'I am deeply touched by your interest in my work, and am sure we can work together towards a conclusion that is satisfactory to all.'

His smile was tight and he left brusquely, not looking back, though Blanche's gaze followed him to the door.

Without being invited, Mr Clarke-Fisher sat himself down in the chair just vacated by Tom. He smiled at her. 'My dear Mrs Heinkel.' He leaned forward.

She felt threatened and sat back further in her chair. She did not want him too close to her, certainly not as close as Tom had been.

'I saw you walking in North Parade Gardens. I called out, but you did not appear to notice,' said Mr Clarke-Fisher.

'I do apologize. My thoughts were elsewhere, and it was very crowded in North Parade. In fact, it's always crowded there. I take it you followed me?'

He nodded, lit a large cigar, even though smoking wasn't allowed in the hotel drawing room, and looked around him. His gaze settled on the Caravaggio copy.

'Have you ever been to Venice?'

'Never, though I would like to one day.'

Swiftly, so swiftly that she hardly saw it move, his hand landed on hers. 'I could take you there, Mrs Heinkel.'

She felt immediately self-conscious. 'Mr Clarke-Fisher, I hardly think it appropriate . . .'

Her hand started to shake and she felt her face getting hot. What would the other guests think? Two men in quick succession, both getting familiar in a public place: one she welcomed, the other she did not.

'Mrs Heinkel, I would not be so coarse as to ask you to accompany me to Venice as anything less than my wife. From the first moment I saw you, I decided that I would marry you. Now I know you're not in the first flush of youth, but you're a fine-looking woman for your age. I think you would be good company, and not frivolous and wanting to be entertained all the time like some younger woman with no experience of running a household and understanding the extent of a man's needs. You might want some time to think this over, but may I suggest you don't take too long about it? After all, as I've just said, you're not getting any younger and not everyone wants to take on a widow. So there you are.'

Blanche was flabbergasted. Her mouth hung open in silence as he took out his watch. He frowned at it, almost as if he were timing the hours, minutes and seconds until she gave him an answer.

Bristling with indignation, she didn't look at him until her teacup was safely on the table. Her first inclination had been to throw it at him.

'Sir,' she said, her voice rumbling with barely controlled fury, her words uttered between closely ground teeth, 'please do not feel that you have to favour me with an offer of marriage. I am quite happy to remain unmarried to the end of my days. I am not in need of a husband. I was married to an incomparable man, a considerate and good person who treated me with the utmost respect. So please do not waste your time waiting for me, Mr Clarke-Fisher. The answer is no. Perhaps you should consider a younger woman. After all, she could be trained up to suit you, like a pony to a trap or a poodle in a circus!'

Judging by the rustling of papers and low murmurs of conversation, every single word was being devoured by the other people in the room.

Darius Clarke-Fisher looked very put out. He sat bolt upright, his eyes round and his chin receding into the opulent cravat at his throat. He raised his finger and wagged it at her as though she were a child. 'My dear Mrs Heinkel, permit me to say that I think you have made a very foolish mistake. But you have been a widow now for some two years or so, and I understand you haven't been feeling too well just lately. Therefore, I am quite prepared to give you a second chance and will keep my offer open for another month, but be warned – no more.'

Blanche slumped weakly into her chair, hardly able to believe her ears. He'd seemed quite bearable at Clevedon. Now he was quite the opposite, as if he'd considered the matter of marriage for a given time and had now decided the time was right to put in a claim.

'Please leave me, Mr Clarke-Fisher. I wish to be alone.'

'Well, you certainly shall be, madam, with that kind of attitude.'

He got to his feet.

'I will not reconsider,' said a resolute Blanche, her hands folded neatly in her lap, and her jaw aching with the effort of controlling her temper.

He tapped his hat onto his head and swallowed back whatever emotion he was feeling – if he was feeling anything much at all. 'Now, now, Mrs Heinkel. As I have already warned, do not be too hasty. I am a man who appreciates a woman's beauty regardless of her age. May I say before departing that black does become you.'

She ran her hand over the stiff silk and pursed her lips. 'Does it really? Then I think it's time I put on something a little brighter – once I am in amenable company.'

He shook his head and a mocking smile curled his lips. 'Captain Strong is amenable company? I wonder if his wife would agree?'

It was exactly as she'd feared. He'd seen them together, perhaps even holding hands, when the room had melted away. His palms had been warm and she had been glad she wasn't wearing gloves. Flesh pressed against flesh in the manner of old and very dear friends who could be more, much more than they were. She could give no excuse. All she prayed was that word of her meeting with Tom would not get back to Horatia.

She stood. 'Please go.'

'Just bear in mind what I have said. And don't be too long with an answer.' He doffed his hat and left.

The room was suddenly too hot to bear and she stalked out, aware that every pair of eyes was studying her, each person forming their own opinion.

The concierge was waiting for her outside. 'Mrs Heinkel?' he said, his face clouding on seeing her expression. 'Is something the matter?'

She shook her head. 'No. No. An old friend came to see me. His news was not exactly pleasant, but I was glad to see him. The second gentleman was not welcome. If he should ever come here again, please tell him I do not wish to see him. He makes me feel uneasy. He also causes . . . disapproval. You know how it is, Sam. Widows are fair game for gossip.'

The concierge smiled knowingly. 'I understand. I saw him leave. Your first visitor is still here. He asks if you would join him in the courtyard.'

Blanche was surprised. 'I didn't know there was one.'

'This way,' said Sam, opening a panelled door onto a long corridor with a flagstone floor and plainly painted walls. 'It's officially for the sole use of the hotel owner. The courtyard divides the rear of the hotel from the rear of his private house, but he allows me to make concessions for those guests who might find it useful. Your friend asked if there was somewhere private where he could talk to you.'

Tom's consideration made her heart beat more rapidly. Blanche followed the concierge down the passageway. The courtyard was a surprise, sandwiched as it was between the tall, Georgian buildings. It was an oasis of greeney and birds, larger than she'd expected it to be, more akin to a garden than a courtyard despite the lack of lawn.

The air was sweet and the leaves of silver-clad birch trees shivered in the slightest draught. Hosts of flowers jostled for space in raised beds amidst the flagstone paths and the air smelled of sweet-scented stock. Dividing the courtyard into two distinct halves, a mass of yellow climbing roses rambled over a row of arched trellis. Around the tangled roots the remains of a Roman mosaic floor glittered in the sunlight.

On seeing her, Tom smiled, and creases appeared at the side of his eyes and mouth. She couldn't remember him having those when he was younger, not that it mattered. His features were still firm and the sparkle in his eyes had not diminished with the years.

'Thank God we're all alone,' she blurted. Out of sight of curious eyes, she couldn't resist touching his cheek. 'You haven't changed.'

'A little greyer,' he said, smoothing his hand over the feathers of whiteness amongst the dark. A shadow seemed to pass over his eyes. 'You've considered our conversation?'

She nodded. 'I'm not sure if your baby will still be there, but I will do my best.'

159

His sigh seemed to encompass his whole body. 'That's all I want to hear.'

'Tom, if I can make you happy by finding this child, I will. But you know the news may not be good. Few babies survive in that place. I don't want to make you more unhappy than you already are.'

He shook his head as though what she'd just said shouldn't be uttered. His tone was almost defensive when he said, 'Are you happy, Blanche?'

The question was sudden and took her by surprise. 'I'm a widow. I'm not meant to be happy.'

'That's not really an answer.'

'It's not the answer you wanted to hear.'

Neither of them noticed that their fingers were touching until a sudden moment of silence that sits easily on old friends.

'The circumstances of us meeting are dire. But this is so wonderful,' she said softly. 'The world is suddenly brighter.'

His smile was weak, but at least it chased the sadness from his eyes. 'Now it's your turn to tell me about your problems.'

She began to tell him about Samson and his family, but he stopped her.

'That's not what I meant. I knew he was coming. I sent Rupert to tell you so, if you remember.' His face creased with concern and he held her hands more tightly. 'Let's talk about you first. Why do you come to Bath? How ill are you, Blanche?'

She chose her words carefully. 'I come here to take the waters. They taste foul, but I have a recurring cough and the waters do it good. Apparently it contains lots of iron. I also like the warmth of the baths. They remind me of home. I've always missed the Barbados sunshine.' She laughed lightly, as though her affliction was too trivial to contemplate. The opposite was true, but she wouldn't tell him that. She had resolved to bear her sickness alone. 'Remember when I arrived so wet and cold in Bristol? I thought I would never be warm again.'

He smiled at the memory. His fingers twisted and turned between hers. She looked round the courtyard, but there was no one there.

Snapping her fingers shut like a pair of scissors, she trapped his fingers between hers. 'We shall be the subject of scandal if we go on like this.' She kept her voice low.

'Would that worry you?'

She shook her head. 'But it would upset my family. And Horatia would not be pleased either.'

The mention of family steadied their reckless slide into intimacy. They sat on a wooden seat moulded to shape a curved frame. They talked of their children, their homes, their staff and the state of the city, the country and the world.

'I trust you are not finding Max too overpowering. He's taking the management of the refinery very seriously indeed.'

Tom grinned wryly. 'So I noticed. I expected him to be like any other young man, full of ideas though lacking in experience, which indeed he is. But he's also stubborn and fiercely loyal – to Conrad mostly.'

They exchanged a look that said everything. Max was like his father, though of course he wouldn't know it.

'And that man, he wishes to marry you?'

'Darius Clarke-Fisher. How did you know that?'

He shrugged. 'I couldn't think of any other reason why I should dislike him so much. I decided it was jealousy, and that he had serious intentions. After all, you are a widow.'

'I have refused him.'

'He'll be back.'

She frowned. 'Do you think so?'

'I'm convinced he will. *I* wouldn't take no for an answer.'

He took hold of her hands and clasped them tightly to his chest.

'I appreciate what you're going to do for me, Blanche.'

She felt herself blushing, but said nothing. No words were enough to express what she was feeling. What were her worries about family compared to his about the baby boy he'd never set eyes on? She decided not to mention Samson and walked with him through the foyer to the main door.

'Will you send me a message?'

She nodded. 'As soon as I know something.'

'Be careful.'

Blanche thought of Max. 'We both have to be careful.'

'Will you be coming to Bath again?'

'Yes.'

'We could meet here?'

If the circumstances had been different, she might have refused him. But life had become more precious than it had ever been, simply because she could see its end getting closer and closer. The doctor's latest prognosis was not good. Yes, she decided suddenly. They would be in Bath. Horatia would be in Bristol. No one would be hurt. That's what she told herself, though she knew deep down that she was straying into danger.

'I think we could.'

She watched him walk away, knowing that they would not resist temptation. Mortality and age altered one's judgement of what was important.

She was just about to go back into the hotel, when someone called to her. It was Mary, the concierge's daughter. She was pushing one of the new perambulators and about to disappear into the lane that ran along the side of the hotel to the owner's house at the rear.

She waved. 'Good day, Mrs Heinkel.'

Blanche waved back. 'Good day, Mary. You've been out taking the air, I see.'

'A quick circuit of the park, and now back home with Master James here.'

Blanche was tempted to dash along to the lane and peer beneath the tasselled canopy, but she didn't have time. 'I hope to see him on my next visit,' she called out.

A lucky child in a comfortable home with adoring parents, she thought. Not like Tom's poor child – wherever he may be.

Despite feeling short of breath, she threw herself into all the tasks that had to be done. Luggage had to be packed and a train ticket bought. She was going home to Bristol, to St Philip's Workhouse, determined to tackle both the issue of Samson and his family, and make enquiries as to the whereabouts of Isaiah Thomas Strong.

Chapter Fourteen

Soon it would all be gone.

Horatia smiled as she left Monk's office once more.

'You look pleased,' he said, escorting her to the door.

'Everything is going to plan,' she said as she prepared her parasol for opening. The season was mellow and the sun golden for the time of year. She would not countenance a sunburned complexion. A lady's skin must always be white and unblemished by sunlight. Perish the day when a woman wished it otherwise!

'You are indeed blessed,' said Septimus, then added, 'You think of him quite often?'

She looked at him sharply, so sharply that he apologized.

She sighed and shook her head. 'Yes, I do think of him often. I admit it. Even though I know he is being well looked after, I somehow feel that no one could look after him as well as his mother.'

Except his father.

The comment was unsaid, yet she could see it reflected in his eyes, just as he could see the words written in hers.

'Soon, a goodbye to sugar,' he said, emphatically changing the subject.

'A goodbye to sugar,' she said.

A pang of regret lay with her, though not for sugar. Its day was done so far as she was concerned. Only the Heinkel Sugar Refinery stood between her and her ambition, and soon even that would be gone. This was the nineteenth century. It was taking them forward at a rate of knots, just as she would take the Strong fortune forward. There were other things besides sugar.

*

Emerald was sleeping. Tom looked down on her, his heart heavy. It vexed him to feel so helpless. He was a practical man, a man who had sailed the oceans and survived situations where other men would have crumbled.

He remembered the time when he'd fought an opium-crazed Chinaman on a Macao quay. He'd side-stepped the pig-tailed man's onslaught, stuck out one leg as he did so and sent the little man flying. He'd cracked together the heads of two crewmen fighting over a dockside whore; he'd faced the fiercest hurricanes the weather could throw at him, yet had still come through. Despite the dangers, none of those situations had made him feel so weak and vulnerable as now. He'd set wheels in motion, knew Blanche would do all in her power to find his child. He'd also felt a subtle change between them. A little push and they'd both fall over the precipice. Where would it lead? He feared for them both. He feared for Max, and he also feared for Emerald.

His daughter still had nightmares about the day she'd seen a man blow his brains out. By day she was still the bright little thing he'd known and loved. Night times were different. Although the doctor had advised against it, Tom had ordered an oil lamp to be provided. If she did wake up in the night, it wouldn't be dark. It was the darkness that frightened her, and he did not want his little daughter frightened.

He heard the swishing of a heavy silk skirt brushing across the floor and knew by her perfume that Horatia was checking up on him.

'Thomas.' She kissed his cheek, her hand running down his arm. She rested her chin on his shoulder. 'I haven't seen you all day.'

'I had to go to Bath. I saw the plans for the new cranes.'

It was close to the truth. A large engineering firm in Bath had indeed drawn up plans for the huge cranes that would be needed at the new docks at Avonmouth. It was, of course, only a partial truth.

'Were they impressive?'

'Very. They'll be even better following some minor adjustments I suggested.'

'I think we should invest in a crane company ourselves.'

'Can we afford it?'

'Of course we can. We can use the money invested in the Heinkel Sugar Refinery. Once The Counterslip premises are sold to the brewery, there should be more than enough to form a financial base for a crane company. The remainder can be used towards purchasing more land around the new site.'

Tom frowned. Satisfied his daughter was sleeping peacefully, he guided his wife out of the bedroom, shutting the door quietly behind them.

Her features were made golden by a wall-mounted oil lamp.

'I thought we were going to use the money to build a new refinery at Avonmouth.'

She spread her hands. 'What for? Let someone else build the refinery. I've changed my mind. We can make money just by being landlords.'

'So where do we get our sugar refined – depending of course on when a buyer is found for the plantation?'

'At the refinery to whom we lease the land. I've spoken to Septimus about it. We insert a paragraph in the lease that ties the refiner to process Strong sugar in priority to anyone else – at a fixed price, of course. Until I sell the plantation.'

Tom could hardly believe what he was hearing. Horatia was pushing into new fields and changing her mind from day to day. He'd thought that Heinkel's Sugar Refinery, in which they had a large interest, would be transferred lock, stock and barrel to a new site at Avonmouth. He'd virtually guaranteed that to Max, who'd remained sceptical about the whole thing and totally loyal to his father's memory.

'I told Max that would not be the case.'

At the mention of his bastard son, a strange look stole over Horatia's face. 'Then he's not going to be very pleased with you, is he, and quite honestly, you can't blame him. I can't see him ever forgiving you for lying to him. How sad for you. How sad for him, if he but knew it. But not for this family,' she said, her voice deepening as her eyes blazed with a fervency that only came when something she wanted was within her sights. 'Oh, come along, Tom. Think!'

He stepped back, his expression reflecting the most bitter of his inner thoughts. 'I am thinking, Horatia. I'm thinking how I could possibly have been so naive to think we might be successful as man and wife. This is not a union between man and woman. I should never have believed that it could be. Why do you have to make so much money? Why do you have to trample over anyone that doesn't agree with what you want?'

Disinclined to slip into outright anger, he turned to go, grimacing as his fingernails dug deeply into the palms of his clenched fists.

Her face reddened with anger. 'I . . . am . . . ambitious! I do not feel I am living unless I am presented with a challenge. I cannot beg my way through life, or live it like a trollop, laid out flat on my back. Or end up in the gutter. Not everyone is as lucky as you, Captain Thomas Strong! Adopted son of the late Reverend Jebediah Strong.'

He walked on swiftly, knowing it would annoy her more, even though she was pouring insult after insult on both him and the man who had raised him.

Stiff with fury, she shouted louder. 'You're just the son of a whore, and the adopted son of an idiot who drooled into his necktie. How dare you turn your back on me!'

Spinning round to face her, he raised a finger in front of his mouth. 'Keep your voice down. You'll wake Emerald.'

The veins on Horatia's neck stood out as she fought to restrain her annoyance. 'I'll shout if I wish. This is my house, Thomas. My house, my father's before me and his father's before that. You are here by chance and have no say in what goes on here. You were born in the gutter. You weren't born in this house and you certainly were not bred to be a gentleman!'

His patience was at an end. 'And you, Horatia, sound as though your breeding is finally winning through. This house was built on the backs of slave labour. And they're very loud too, you know. I've seen the women, descendents of those slaves, selling their fish on the waterfront in Bridgetown, shouting at the tops of their voices. Yes, Horatia, your breeding is certainly shining through.'

He could see by her expression that the barb had hurt. He'd not meant to bring up the fact that somewhere in her background was an ancestor with the same colour skin as the son she'd borne. In a way, he could understand how she'd felt. For nine months she'd carried his child, had planned for its birth, suffered the debilitating discomfort pregnancy confers on a woman. There was no doubt in his mind that she'd been looking forward to the event, perhaps expecting a child of her own colouring, or perhaps the same as her daughter, who looked like her father.

The anger fled from her eyes and she wrapped her arms around herself. Suddenly, as her shoulders slumped and her head bowed, she looked smaller than she actually was, as though the hurt was making her crumple.

Despite the life he'd led, the boxing, the seafaring and the harsh existence of his early years, he couldn't bear to hurt anyone. He'd done exactly what she feared he might do on hearing about the baby's colour: he'd thrown it into her face. It was cruel. In response to the guilt he felt, he retraced his steps and folded her in his arms. Her head drooped upon his shoulder and she broke into sobs.

'I'm sorry.'

He had to say it. The guilt was all his. Regardless of the terrible things she'd done, that she would ransom his conscience and his illegitimate son if it meant getting her own way, he couldn't bring himself to be purposely cruel. After all, she was the mother of his beloved Emerald. They were married. The least he could give her was a little respect, a little compassion.

Without another word to each other, they made their way to the bedroom they regarded as belonging to both of them, even though Tom now had a separate bedroom of his own.

Horatia looked up at him with liquid eyes. 'Will you sleep with me this evening?'

He couldn't conceal his surprise. Despite her lack of passion, in ten years of marriage, he had never been unfaithful to Horatia – except in his dreams. There it was always the same dark-skinned woman with grey eyes. He knew her features well, knew her name, but never uttered it just in case Horatia should hear him and blight his dreams just as she'd blighted his life.

Meeting Blanche in Bath had heightened his sexual desire. The look, the feel, the scent of her was still vivid in his mind. He wanted her. He'd always wanted her, but he was tied to Horatia. There was no other option. She was his wife. He had to put Blanche from his mind.

After snuffing out the oil lamp, he got into bed. Horatia immediately eased herself against him. He put his arm around her, her head resting against his shoulder joint.

The darkness was welcome. At least she couldn't see his face. Her body was warm; her firm hip pressed against his. Her womanly smell was tinged with rosewater. She used it generously, soaked her underwear with it and smoothed it over her body after she had a bath.

Her closeness and her scent was enticing and he couldn't stop the throbbing in his groin. It hurt and he needed to get rid of it. Closing his eyes tightly, he pretended it was Blanche lying beside him and that she was murmuring sweet words of passion into his ear. But Blanche's body would be undulating, her thighs rubbing against his, her hands exploring his body just as much as he explored hers. Horatia never moved. She just waited.

He rolled onto his side so he was facing her, his eyes still closed as he brushed soft, sweet-smelling hair . . . If only . . . Her breast was warm beneath his palm, but larger, less firm than he knew Blanche's breast to be.

The vision was shattered. He stopped what he was doing and rolled onto his back.

'What's the matter?' Horatia sounded hurt.

'Nothing.'

Unfair, he thought to himself. Get her out of your mind. Horatia at least deserves to be in your head when you make love to her. It would be so easy to recommence if, just for once, she made the first move. But she wouldn't, and now his vision of Blanche had shattered, he couldn't bring himself to carry on until they'd cleared the air between them. With Horatia this was best done with talk of business.

'I was thinking about Lodge. You shouldn't have told him about the bank. It might have been best if you'd never bought it. We could have achieved our objectives without it.'

The bed moved as she raised herself up on one elbow and rested her head in her hand. 'No, we couldn't. There's such potential in a new dock, Thomas. Imagine the new warehousing, cranes and systems, all requiring finance. Now we have a bank, and its investors are at our disposal, nothing can stop us becoming the richest family in the city.'

He marvelled at the sound of her voice. Talk business and everything else that had passed between them was forgotten. He was forgiven for his outburst regarding her pedigree. Nothing mattered so much to Horatia as business, even her personal happiness, even, it had to be said, her family.

Although it was too dark to see clearly, he knew she was studying him in that forthright way of hers, challenging him to speak before she did. He never managed to beat her to it.

'If we own the land, we control the port. Growing and refining sugar is not as lucrative as it once was. You know that. All the bigger refineries and warehouses will transfer to Avonmouth. Those that don't will disappear. By the end of the century, not one refinery will remain in this city. You know and I know that they are struggling to cover their costs. Small ships cost money. Bigger ships carrying heavier payloads are the way forward. No refiner in this city can survive in the current economic climate without the new port. And we will reap profits from it, purely because we own the land on which it is built.'

Tom lay silently and thought of Max. The prospect of his son thinking him a liar did not lie easy on his conscience. He'd so wanted to cultivate a closeness with him without arousing Horatia's jealousy. Such a prospect was no longer likely.

Suddenly, his anger seemed inseparable from his desire. She gave a little gasp as he hitched up her silken nightgown and heaved himself on top of her. There was no preamble, no kiss or caress, just an animal desire to relieve himself of the tension caused as much by his mood as his sex drive.

Her back never arched as some women do, she never murmured sweet words, nor cried out in ecstasy. The only thing she did was to rest her hands upon his back, lying there until he was spent and had rolled over to sleep.

But this time was different. As he reached the zenith of his pleasure, she dug her fingernails into his shoulders. His cry of pleasure was mixed with pain and he felt a trickle of blood run warmly down his back.

He rolled off and lay there panting.

Horatia turned her back on him as she pulled the hem of her nightgown down to her feet. Her voice was cold as ice. 'Don't ever do that to me again.'

She was trembling. He could feel it across the space between them. The darkness was like a thick veil around them. He was glad of it. She couldn't see his expression, and he couldn't see hers. He didn't want to see the anger there, or the threat of reprisal.

Chapter Fifteen

The Reverend Smart had a private office at the Workhouse. It was situated on the first floor, just off the private dining room where the Board of Governors ate lunch.

It had been far from easy, but Blanche had persuaded Edith to accompany her.

'I don't have to go in, do I?' Edith had asked, her expression leaving Blanche in no doubt that the thought of entering that ominous place filled her with dread.

Blanche had pleaded. 'Just inside, within shouting distance, while I speak to the Reverend Smart alone in his office. Please?'

'Oh,' said Edith, suddenly getting the picture and pushing her sleeves up to her elbows. 'He's THAT type, is he? One hand on the Bible and one inside yer bodice given half a chance. Well, I've met the likes of him before. And don't you worry. I promise I'll be nearby.'

Although Edith looked uncomfortable with the idea, Blanche knew she wouldn't let her down.

The Reverend Smart kept a very concise record of all entrants. Persuading him to check those records for a newborn black baby should be easy: sweetly spoken words, a soft smile – hence the need for a chaperone. Blanche ran her fingers over the gowns in her wardrobe. Which should she wear? Which would be the most appealing to a man like Smart?

Her fingers darted between her black mourning dress and a bright yellow. It was one of her favourites and was decorated with green and mauve violets around each layer of frill. The black wouldn't suit. It might remind Smart of her widowed, and thus available, status. The yellow was too bright. She didn't want to give him the impression that she was frivolous and ripe for seduction either.

With Edith's help, she opted for a coffee-coloured dress with a tightly corseted top of fine lace that stretched from her neck to her wrists. It was elegant, attractive but neutral.

The day was warm and sunny. As they rattled out of Somerset Parade and down the hill, a host of down from late-seeding dandelions floated up from the grass around St Mary Redcliffe.

Blanche looked away. A few days before the death of Anne, her eldest daughter, from cholera the little girl had been standing on a common crowded with the fluffy heads of dandelions. It still hurt to see them.

A pensive Edith followed Blanche into the outer yard of the Workhouse, an amused smirk lighting her frown as she took in the muddled uniform and the awkward gait of Corporal Young.

'Looks as though he's bin in more regiments than I've 'ad hot dinners,' she muttered so only Blanche could hear. The smell of mutton stew came out to meet them and Edith sniffed disdainfully. 'Scrag end by the smell of it.'

Blanche wasn't fooled by her nonchalance. Edith was nervous, hating being inside these walls. Given half a chance, she would leg it out of the gate. Blanche was feeling something similar. Her heart was beating madly and her lips moved soundlessly as she rehearsed what she would say to the Reverend Smart.

Corporal Young told them to wait while he clomped up the stairs to tell Smart of their arrival. Blanche ignored him and followed, a reluctant Edith bringing up the rear.

'I don't like this,' said Edith. Round-eyed she studied the numerous biblical texts painted on the walls. Their footsteps sounded like iron-shod hooves on the bare boards. 'Fancy eating a meal in a drab room like this, poor souls.'

'Pour souls indeed,' said Blanche, chuckling. 'This is where the Board eats.'

Edith's eyebrows almost disappeared beneath her hairline. 'Really?'

Blanche could see she was appalled. 'It's only right that our surroundings are just slightly better than the inmates.'

'Thank God I'm not one of them,' Edith muttered.

Nervously, Blanche eyed the closed door of Smart's office. It was reassuring to hear the murmur of voices from within. It proved that if she screamed, Edith would hear and come running.

'Don't you worry. I'll be here,' said Edith as if reading her thoughts.

Only minutes after she said it, the door opened and Corporal Young re-emerged.

'You're to go in,' he said, his mouth hanging open in something akin to a grin.

To her surprise, Smart was not alone. The blackness of his suit was accentuated by the starched whiteness of his collar and cuffs. He was sitting behind his desk, his hands clasped before him. At his side stood Mrs Tinsley, her hands clasped at her waist. It was as if they'd been cast from the same mould, though not in the same position. Both looked pleased with themselves.

Blanche knew it wouldn't last once she asked to see the Reverend Smart alone.

'It's very important, and a very private matter,' she said, purposefully avoiding Mrs Tinsley's punctured expression.

Smart's smile almost split his face in half – just as she'd expected it to. 'Why, of course, my dear lady.' He turned to Mrs Tinsley, saw the impending anger, but chose to ignore it. 'If you would excuse us, Mrs Tinsley.' His teeth shone like a row of polished tombstones.

At first it seemed that Mrs Tinsley would not acquiesce. Her eyelids fluttered and her chin moved up and down as if she were chomping hay. With a sudden snort, she tossed her head, clenched her fists and headed for the door.

After the door had slammed on her exit, the sound of exclamation came from outside. She'd met Edith. Woe betide Mrs Tinsley putting on airs and graces with her, Blanche thought and almost smiled.

'I've come with a friend,' said Blanche on seeing Smart's puzzled look.

'I see.' Resigned that his actions were likely to be monitored, the Reverend Smart came from behind his desk and fetched her a chair. 'Do sit down, dear lady. Now! What can I do for you?'

Blanche had thought very carefully about what she would say. Too dangerous to admit to the baby's parentage, she had concocted a believable story.

'A young woman employed at my family's plantation in the West Indies came to Bristol, but unfortunately found herself with child and without a husband. Unknown to my family, the child was delivered and brought here. The young woman concerned then sought employment in London, but died there. Her married sister subsequently came looking for her, heard about the baby and where it had been taken. She also became aware that I was on the Board of Governors. Thus, she asked me to make enquiries.'

'Ah!' said Smart, and gave a single, momentous nod, acknowledging that he understood completely. 'And this child, was it a girl or a boy?'

'A boy.'

He held his head on one side as though there was something slightly distasteful about what he was going to say next. 'And it was of colour?'

Blanche stiffened, but tried not to show it. 'Yes.'

He reached for his register. 'How long ago was this?'

'Three months, possibly four.'

The cover of the ledger thudded on the desk. He licked his thumb and looked up at her between turning each page.

'Did she leave a name with the child?'

'A name – Draper – and two sovereigns, I believe.'

Smart fixed his attention to his beloved ledger. 'Boy child name of Draper . . .' he mumbled, as his finger followed a line of copperplate characters. 'My word. It would appear that the child was only here for a matter of two days. It wasn't me who signed the entry. I was ill at the time. my leg you know.'

Assuming the worse, Blanche felt the room beginning to swim around her. 'You mean he's dead?' Her voice was little above a whisper.

He shook his head and looked somewhat surprised. 'I don't know for sure, though I assume he must be dead. As I said, someone else made the entry – not correctly. That is why I prefer to write the entries myself. I am more precise than most people.' He frowned. 'Unless he's still in the nursery of course – though I can find no trace that he's still here. Either the poor child is in the arms of the Lord, or he is still in the nursery and has accidentally been omitted from the record.' With that, he slammed the ledger shut.

'We must look,' said Blanche springing to her feet. 'Will you take me there?'

The speed with which she got to the door brought on a tightness in her chest, but it was bearable. What wasn't bearable was the prospect of telling Tom that his son was dead. If there was the slightest chance . . .

The Reverend Smart didn't argue with her. Edith looked surprised to see her emerge so quickly. Suspecting the worse, she fixed Smart with a hard stare.

The cleric turned pale and stepped behind Blanche.

'Edith! We're going to see the babies in the nursery,' said Blanche before Edith had a chance to challenge the Reverend.

Edith allowed herself to be swept further into a building she'd prefer not to be in at all.

A small wooden door, with bars set into it at eye level, opened into a room that was as far from being a nursery as it was possible to be.

A small fire produced the only light and warmth in a low, dark room that vaguely resembled a cellar. It smelled of mould, gin and dirty backsides. For a moment, Blanche was sure they were in the wrong place. In the middle of the room was a wooden stage, the sort entertainers might use to dance, juggle or sing a song. What looked like three bundles of laundry were laid in a row. On closer inspection, they proved to be babies wound tightly in various shades of shawls, their little limbs almost bound to their sides. Two of them were asleep. The blue eyes of the third were wide open.

It didn't cry or gurgle like most babies of that age, but just looked, perhaps wondering what else this grim world had in store for the likes of them born poor and out of wedlock.

'Dear God,' she whispered.

Edith reached out a hand to the child. 'Poor little mite.' Warily, it curled its fingers around hers and instantly began to suckle at it. 'It's hungry,' she exclaimed.

Blanche turned to the Reverend Smart who had been exchanging a few words with the woman she recognized as Ethel.

'When was this baby fed last?' Blanche asked.

'The wet nurse came in this morning,' said Ethel and scratched her behind.

'And when does she call again?'

'Tomorrow morning.' Her scratching now transferred to her crotch.

Blanche looked at her in disbelief. 'You can't feed a baby once a day. And how many babies is she supposed to feed? Surely she hasn't enough milk for three.'

'Six is what she usually does. They all do, and then we gives a bit of porridge to the older ones if they're not full. See?' She pointed a dirt-encrusted finger at a black cauldron hanging in the fireplace in which something grey simmered like boiled mud.

'Six babies? And what do you mean, they all do? How many wet nurses are there? How many babies do you take in?'

Ethel sniffed and eyed her warily. She looked to the Reverend Smart, who was hovering nervously, unhappy with Blanche's re-action and unsure as to how he should handle it.

'Come along, Ethel,' he said in a mildly cajoling tone. 'Tell Mrs Heinkel how many you usually have to look after in a week.'

'Twenty. Thirty.' She shrugged. 'Depends.' She sniffed noisily then spat into the fire. A meagre flame flared up then disappeared. 'Not many survive. Sometimes six, sometimes more, most often less. We work out the ones most likely to live and put them on the tit. The rest get my porridge.'

Blanche ran her hand across her forehead. 'Oh my God!'

Edith was more vocal. 'You ought to be ashamed of yourself,' she exclaimed, directing her anger at the Reverend Smart. 'What's the matter with you, a man of the cloth allowing poor babes barely out of their mothers' bellies to be left in the care of this old harridan. Look at her! She's dirty, smokes like a Jack Tar and stinks of gin. So what are you going to do about it, I ask? What are you going to do?'

Unused to strident females of large proportion with no respect for the self-righteous, Smart backed away, his face reddening and his eyes almost popping out of his head.

Blanche looked at each baby in turn, hoping against hope that one of them might be Tom's son. But they were all white-skinned, too pale even to be healthy.

Ethel, who was now scratching her armpit, began to turn nasty and made the mistake of targeting Edith. 'Who do you think you are, eh? Think yer a lady or sommut? Think you could do any better than me, do you?' She spat into the fire again, one or two teeth coming out with the phlegm and landing among the coals.

Edith, who'd lived in some pretty disgusting places in her life and known some pretty despicable people, had a strong stomach. The old girl's head jerked back when Edith snapped her answer straight into her face, their noses almost touching.

'Yes, you old soak. You're more suited to be in charge of a flea circus than babies. You certainly seem to be keeping a few on board judging by the amount of scratching you've been doing.'

'I ain't staying around yer to be insulted.'

'Then out you go!'

Grabbing the old crone with both hands, Edith swung her round like a doll and propelled her through the open door, her feet barely touching the ground.

The slamming door shivered in its frame.

'Sorry,' said Edith, as the sound echoed around the low room.

The baby whose eyes were open looked startled, but did not cry. The others continued to sleep. Yet the sound of the slamming door was enough to wake the dead.

'Oh dear,' said the Reverend Smart, wringing his hands. 'Now who do I get to look after them? What shall I do? What shall I do?'

Blanche sniffed at the pot of simmering porridge and exchanged a quick glance with Edith. 'It smells of gin. That's why they're so quiet. But the Reverend's right. Someone has to look after them.'

Edith looked set to admit the error of her ways, but changed her mind. 'Anyone's better than that old hag! I wouldn't want her looking after my baby. I'd sooner be destitute.'

'Most women in here would be destitute if it wasn't for us,' sniffed the Reverend Smart.

Blanche leaned over the blue-eyed baby. Her heart was heavy and she certainly wasn't looking forward to telling Tom the bad news. His son was obviously dead. But what about these? Could some good come out of her prying?

Something about the exchange between Edith and the Reverend floated around in her head. The women in the Workhouse earned their keep smashing bones, stitching canvases and stripping oakum.

She peered from around the brim of her bonnet at the Reverend Smart. 'Why can't the women here work as nursemaids?'

His face quivered and his mouth worked as though he were chewing something particularly difficult to swallow. 'But they're paupers!' he exclaimed at last.

'Does that make them less acceptable than a flea-bitten drunk?' Edith demanded.

Unable to deny the logic of the idea, Smart floundered. 'Well . . . no . . .'

'Will you organize something, Reverend Smart?'

Blanche adopted an appealing expression.

'I know you're a good man,' she said, her voice oozing like molasses. 'I'm sure this can be arranged fairly quickly, don't you think?'

'Yes,' he said, sucking in his breath in response to the fact that she was standing very close to him. 'I can get Mrs Tinsley to choose some women—'

'I think that you and I are better able to choose suitable nurse-maids, Mr Smart,' said Blanche, swiftly slipping her arm into his. 'Edith will stay here and start sorting things out.'

'And this is first to go,' said a grim-faced Edith, using a potholder to extricate the cauldron from its hook.

I can't believe I'm doing this, thought Blanche. She flashed a reassuring smile at the Reverend Smart whose face was bright with joy. At last! He'd got her on his arm.

In the room where the women tore oakum into shreds, which was then recycled at the rope factory, the air was dusty and the light was not good. The women worked by a wan light diffusing through the small windows. Everyone turned to face them, looked tiredly at the Reverend Smart, but with more interest at Blanche.

'Now who would be most suitable?' said Smart, his words low so only she could hear.

Blanche searched the upturned faces for one that was darker than all the rest. They were all white except for an elderly woman who looked as though she'd been out in the sun too long. Her skin was as wrinkled as a walnut in contrast to her hair, which was snowy white.

'In order to save time, might I suggest that you make a selection here and I'll go into the bone yard and enquire there?'

She read a mix of emotions in his eyes. It was a sensible suggestion. On the other hand, he'd dearly enjoyed the feel of her arm through his and regretted its withdrawal.

'I won't be long,' she said with a parting smile.

Her heart pattered like a racing rabbit as she made her way along the dark corridor leading to the door that opened into the bone yard.

The smell was appalling. The sound of hammers smashing bone filled the air but ceased as those using the hammers turned surprised expressions on her. Men and women were segregated by a series of ropes and barrels. The ends of the ropes were tied onto drainpipes. The barrels contained piles of stinking bones and the air was thick with flies.

She found herself in the women's section. There was one dark-skinned woman there, a child standing beside her. Samson's family. It had to be.

In the men's section, intrigued by the elegant lady making straight for his wife, Samson approached the division.

Warden Tinsley attempted to stop him. 'No approaching the barrier,' he said in a high-pitched, panicky voice.

Samson brushed him aside. The woman was obviously not an inmate and looked vaguely familiar. He saw her address his wife, but her voice was low and he could not hear.

Then Abigail gave him a swift look, a sudden surge of hope in her expression. What was going on?

Joyfully Blanche led Samson's wife and her child to the nursery and discovered their names: Abigail and Desdemona. She did not introduce herself.

Smart was already back at the nursery with two other women. Both were young and had been put to work by Edith.

'These babes need decent clothes,' she said to Blanche.

'I'm sure we can find some at home,' Blanche replied.

Edith smiled smugly. 'I seen them up in that box you keep in the attic.'

'I've been found out,' Blanche laughed. She'd kept a lot of her children's baby things. It had been her way of hanging onto the happy times of their childhood.

Abigail was already engrossed in the babies.

'They need washing,' Edith pointed out to her.

'Yes, ma'am.'

'I'm not a ma'am,' Edith corrected her. 'I'm Edith, and don't you forget it.' She grinned and flicked a finger at Desdemona's nose.

The atmosphere of the dank room changed more quickly than the smell, but by the end of the afternoon, a decent fire was burning in the grate. Washed linen and cotton were drying out in the yard, and a few sheets had been ripped up and used on the babies' sore bottoms.

Edith caught Blanche staring at Abigail and her daughter, and whispered, 'Who is she?'

Blanche started. 'Is it so obvious?'

Edith remained silent, her pale eyes fixed on her old friend as she waited for an answer.

'I think she's a relative.'

'Does she know that?'

'Not yet.'

'Just her, or her and her family?'

'Her husband is a kind of cousin. They've come here looking for me.'

'So when will you tell them?'

'I don't know.'

Edith appeared thoughtful. 'You can't leave them here, you know.'

Still keeping her voice low, Blanche faced her. 'What can I do with them? They can't live with me. What would Max say? He has a future to consider.'

'Now come along, Mrs Heinkel. Think. This is your friend Edith, who is living alone in an empty cottage since her chicks are now all flown. Why don't they move in with me?'

If they hadn't been in company, Blanche would have kissed her. 'It never occurred to me to ask you. Would you mind?'

Edith shook her head. Her heart was bursting with happiness. She'd have someone to fuss over and, hopefully, plenty of noise. Her family had always been noisy. And perhaps the little girl would like a puppy, or a kitten, perhaps both, perhaps more than one.

But she merely said that she could do with the company.

Blanche turned over the pros and cons of the arrangement. 'Samson would need a job.'

'Surely you could find him something. The refinery perhaps?'

'Then I'd have to tell Max. I'm not sure I'm ready for that yet.' She hung her head, but lifted it swiftly when Edith nudged her.

'He's not that much of a snob. He's in love with that little milliner that delivers your hats.'

'It's not just infatuation?'

Edith winked. 'Do you think I don't know the difference?' She winked. 'Love don't care much about class, race or anything much else. Mark my words, Magdalene Cherry will end up as his wife.'

The fact that Max had a sweetheart gladdened Blanche's heart. It helped her cope with the death of Tom's child and filled her with hope that she'd see her son married.

She coughed into her handkerchief, crumpling it quickly so that Edith would not see the speck of blood.

179

She left it to Edith to offer a home to Samson and his family. Once they were out of the earshot of the Reverend Smart and Mrs Tinsley, safely settled in Little Paradise along with Edith and her three cats, she would visit and tell them who she was.

For now she would cope with her other problems. What was the best way of telling Tom the terrible news?

Sitting in front of her writing desk back in Somerset Parade, she composed letter after letter. No matter how she said it, the news seemed factual and cold, and each piece of paper was screwed up and tossed into the wastepaper basket. She couldn't hold him should he cry, she couldn't wrap her arms around him and tell him his son was in a better place. She couldn't kiss the tears from his cheeks. There was nothing else for it but to tell him face to face, so she arranged a trip to the Ambassador Hotel and sent a message to Tom telling him where she was.

Chapter Sixteen

Emerald came into his bedroom with her finger held tightly to her lips.

Tom smiled at her as he pulled on his riding jacket. 'Are you telling me I have to be quiet?'

She nodded and pursed her lips, letting out a fragile 'sshhh'.

He shook his head. 'Who told you to be quiet?'

'Mother did,' she whispered, then cocked her head to one side, her expression inquisitive. 'Where are you going?'

'I have a business appointment in Bath.' He felt guilty lying. It wasn't something he'd ever get used to, but since marrying Horatia, he'd sometimes found it necessary. 'I'll be back tomorrow.'

Emerald climbed on the bed, the springs squealing in protest as she bounced up and down. 'Can I come?'

'Not today, my pretty one. It's business and you'll get bored.'

'Mother doesn't get bored. She told me that business is the blood of life. Do you think that too, Father?'

Tom clenched his jaw as he reached for his hat. Horatia was indoctrinating the child, and he did not approve.

He was just about to reply that he most certainly did not, when Horatia entered the room.

She looked directly at him, merely glancing at their daughter from the corner of her eye. 'Emerald. Get off that bed this instant.'

Looking far less buoyant, Emerald obeyed.

Horatia took hold of the child's shoulders and steered her towards the door. 'Off to the schoolroom with you, or you'll be late for your lessons.'

Emerald dug in her heels, spun round and raced back to Tom. 'I want to say goodbye to Father.'

Tom smiled. Whether or not Horatia knew it, her daughter determined to have her own way as much as her mother did. He took her into his arms and kissed each cheek before setting her back down.

'Now run along, or you'll be over my knee and soundly spanked,' said Horatia, her expression and tone hardening.

Emerald knew when she'd reached the limit of her mother's patience, but she still had an air of defiance about her. 'I'll cry if I'm spanked. You won't like that, will you?'

'One more word, young lady,' said Horatia, bending down close to her daughter's face in order to emphasize the point. 'And remember what I told you. Be quiet. You know that Sears is not well. She must not be disturbed.'

Emerald nodded silently.

Sears had been sinking slowly for days. Much to her credit, Horatia had made sure that her long-serving personal maid was well taken care of.

'How is she?'

Horatia sighed and eyed the single valise Tom's valet had packed. 'Not well. I shall miss her. She truly has been a good and faithful servant.'

He knew his wife resented anyone except Sears looking after her clothes and her personal effects.

'So who takes her place?'

She shrugged. At the same time she beat a continuous tattoo on the windowpanes with her fingertips. He sensed she was agitated. He wondered why and feared she had seen through his ruse about his visit to Bath.

'I think you should see Max again.'

She didn't look round, so failed to notice his surprise. Why? he wondered.

'It would make things less difficult if he agreed to this sale.'

Ah, he thought. That was it. Septimus wanted a neat transaction. Max's continuous refusal to comply made the buyers jittery.

'Why me?'

'That's a stupid question.'

She turned and stood in front of him, her arms folded. He didn't understand the accusing look in her eyes, but feared it. Had she guessed who he was seeing today?

'Please remember, Horatia, Max does not know that I am his father.'

'The fact that you know influences your attitude. I would be less sensitive in my dealings if he were my child.'

Well, that was true, he thought.

'Can we discuss this when I get back from Bath?'

She seemed to think about it for a moment. Again, it worried him. 'Indeed. And for now, I shall walk with you to the carriage, where I shall kiss you on the cheek like any ordinary little wife.'

Tom smiled ruefully. 'You'll never be that, Horatia – ordinary, I mean.'

'Good. I'm glad you think so.'

The odd thing was, he didn't want her to see him to the carriage that would take him to the railway station and thus to Bath and the Ambassador Hotel. But he couldn't say so.

'Perhaps I should see Sears before I go,' he said instead. 'She might not be here when I get back.'

Tom mounted the stairs to the servants' quarters two at a time.

The curtains in Sears's room had been drawn right back and were billowing into the room. He found it chilly, and wondered if Sears felt the same.

Her face was as white as her pillow, her hair pushed out of sight beneath an old-fashioned mob-cap. Her hands were folded over her meagre breasts and her nightgown was buttoned up to her chin.

Instinctively aware that someone was present, she opened her eyes. 'I hoped you would come,' she said, her voice as thin as a reed.

He wondered if she could see him clearly, or whether she thought he was someone else. 'I thought I should,' he said softly.

At the sound of his voice, she raised a thin hand. Her skin hung loose on her bones and was speckled with brown spots. 'You have to know,' she said between shallow breaths. 'You have to know, if I'm to die in grace.'

Thinking she wasn't in her right mind, and feeling he should do his best to reassure her, he took hold her hand. 'Of course you will die in grace. You're a good woman. Why shouldn't you?'

Not having had much to do with her over the years, he wasn't sure whether she was a good woman or not.

'I never understood . . .' she began, her eyes fixed on him, 'I

183

couldn't believe the baby died. He was too healthy, you see. I used to hear him crying . . . he was loud.'

Tom felt his blood turning cold. Isaiah. 'You should rest,' he said, laying her hand down and patting it.

'I thought about the Post Office . . . Just after he died, she went to the Post Office all by herself to post the letter to you. You were in Barbados at the time, you see . . .'

Her voice drifted off.

Tom frowned. He'd never received a letter from Horatia telling him about the baby's death. He'd had a letter to tell him of the birth, but none after because they were already sailing for home. Horatia knew that.

'I think she was upset. That's why she went alone, why she wouldn't let me come with her.'

It was a small thing, but strange. Letters were taken to the Post Office by servants. Why had Horatia taken this particular one herself? And why not take Sears with her?

On leaving the room, he pondered on what he had heard. The woman's dying, he told himself. Her mind's not quite what it was. And what was really so odd about Horatia going to the Post Office and posting a letter by herself? There's nothing in it, he told himself.

By the time he was sitting in a first class carriage on his way to Bath, he'd pushed the matter from his mind. Hearing what Blanche had to say was far more important than the ramblings of a dying woman. Had she found his son?

In a bid to avoid attracting suspicion, Blanche had suggested in her note that they meet in North Parade Gardens. There were plenty of trees and people to hide among.

There had been a shower that morning, but by mid-afternoon the rain had been blown away by a sprightly breeze. Fluffy clouds gambolled in a blue sky, and spears of golden rod swayed drunkenly in the breeze.

They met by a fountain. Goldfish slid through the green water, and a solitary frog clung to the leg of a Grecian statue.

Tom knew the moment he saw Blanche's face that the news was not good. His body felt numb and there was a buzzing in his ears. Only Blanche's voice was at all distinct as she told him the probable shortness of his son's life. All the other sounds of the world were like so many insects, a drone of noise in a seething hive.

After she'd told everything she believed had happened, even her voice seemed to blend with the rest of the noise. The truth was unbearable. There never had been anything warm or soft about Horatia, but this, this was downright cruel, and he couldn't believe he'd married a woman who could be that callous.

Blanche touched his hand. 'I'm so sorry, Tom.'

Her touch brought him round. He blinked as if he had just woken from his worst nightmare, though in truth he was still in it.

The sight of his suffering stabbed at her heart. She trapped a tear with her finger and felt her own eyes turning moist.

'Do you know where he's buried?'

Blanche thought of the lidded beds and the pauper mother being carted off to the medical school. The thought of the babies ending up on the dissecting table appalled her. Yet she could easily believe it, though nothing, nothing at all, could persuade her to tell Tom. He was suffering enough already.

She shook her head and clasped his hand with both of hers. 'Come along, Tom. We'll go back to the hotel and have tea.'

She resigned herself that if anyone saw them together and jumped to a conclusion, then so be it. Tom needed her. She had to be there for him.

They walked close together along the path, winding through the throngs of people coming the other way. She hugged his arm to her side, her fingers clasped in his.

'I still can't believe Horatia could have done this,' he murmured.

Blanche was having the same problem. How could any mother see her child placed in a Workhouse where its chances of survival were less than bleak? Horatia was hard-headed, a tough woman who had always been determined to make her mark in a man's world. But even so, surely she possessed the same compassion as any other mother, despite the child's shortfalls?

Absorbed in their own worlds, neither Tom nor Blanche noticed the tall man with the jet-black eyes.

Darius Clarke-Fisher had still not forgiven Blanche for leading him up the garden path, or at least, that was the way he had interpreted her behaviour. He'd sincerely thought he'd been doing her a favour

185

in offering to marry her. After all, she was past the first flush of youth and did have a touch of the darkie about her.

The fact that she'd turned him down irritated him beyond belief. He didn't like being made a fool of, and he considered that was exactly what she had done. Those who slighted Darius Clarke-Fisher usually lived to regret it. He never forgave, and always took it upon himself to impart some act of revenge.

Chapter Seventeen

Max tried to tell Magdalene that he couldn't possibly marry her, but no matter how hard he tried, the right words never seemed to find their way to his tongue. One look at her cocky smile, and he resigned himself to the inevitable. He was hopelessly in love with her, and he didn't give a fig what anyone else might think.

It was a Tuesday morning when they met at a little coffee house he knew in Trenchard Street, just a few doors down from a black-and-white timbered tavern and at the back of the towering warehouse where Harveys stored their wines and sherries.

'You're going to have to marry me,' Magdalene exclaimed, taking him completely off guard.

He dabbed his handkerchief at the coffee he'd spilt on his jacket, aware that his face was reddening. He was panic-stricken in case someone had heard and presumed she was referring to a very delicate condition. He asked her nervously what she meant.

Both hands holding her cup, and a mischievous smile playing around her pink lips, she held her head to one side, an endearing action that he loved as much as her sparkling eyes and her wild, dark hair.

'Because you love me,' she said with the self-assurance of a woman who knows her man and knows what she wants. 'There's no denying it, and there's no getting rid of me, and there's also no taking advantage of my loving nature.'

'I wouldn't dream of taking advantage of you.'

In all honesty, the thought of making love to her haunted his dreams, but he liked her as much as loved her. And he knew without the slightest doubt that she was speaking the truth. He would marry her. He had to marry her and couldn't stand the thought that someone else might ask before he did. All that worried him now was how to break the news to his mother.

'So will you?' she asked pertly.

'Of course I will.' He sounded as if he were suffering from wounded pride. She'd put him on the spot, half-hinted that perhaps he would let her down. He hadn't.

'Then that's settled.'

She's right, he thought, and smiled, resigned that he could not refuse her.

Swinging his walking stick around in a circle as he bounced along, he whistled all the way back to his carriage. Magdalene had gone back to Madame Mabel's, and he was on his way to the refinery where a stack of paperwork and a problem with the sugar separators awaited his attention.

When he got there, he found he had a visitor, a man he'd never seen before. His hair was oiled flat on his head and his moustache was of the foreign sort, curly at the ends and waxed flat on his face.

Clarke-Fisher had already written to Horatia Strong and sowed the seeds of Tom Strong's undoing. Now it was Max's turn, though his intention with Blanche Heinkel's son was to sow a different field.

He began by introducing himself, stating his background and business interests, and mentioning meeting Blanche, Max's mother, in Clevedon.

He had no intention of blackening Blanche's name; on the contrary, he still wanted her as a wife, and that was exactly what he told Max, that he would like to call on his mother, but felt it only polite that he should report his intentions to Max first.

'Did she not tell you of our meeting in the hotel in Clevedon?'

Max eyed the pale face, the dark hair and the continental moustache. 'Are you implying that you and my mother are close?'

Clarke-Fisher used his hands to express himself. 'A lady alone in a seaside hotel; fresh air, good food, wine and company . . .' He smiled at his own cleverness. No family liked to have its reputation ruined by gossip. They'd persuade her to accept his suit rather than face that particular prospect.

Max took his business card, but although he listened courteously, he couldn't imagine his mother being attracted to this man.

'I'll mention you called,' he said in an amiable manner.

'Your father died a while ago?'

'Yes. Just over two years now.'

'And you are now a man of business, I see, a man well thought of among the merchants in this city. I have heard much of you as a man to watch for the future. Aim for the sky,' he said, the tip of his walking stick pointing at the ceiling. 'It's not enough to end up sitting on the roof, I'm sure you'll agree.'

'No,' said Max, his amiability faltering as he tried to work out what this man was getting at.

'Women, including mothers, should be well settled and provided for, leaving men to rule the world, don't you think?'

'My mother does not interfere with the family business. Her family has always come first.'

Clarke-Fisher ran a polished nail over his fastidiously groomed moustache. 'Commendable, very commendable. And thus our "dalli-ance" in Clevedon might come as a surprise to both your family and, of course, to your associates. I have asked your mother to marry me, but I think she feels it to be disloyal to your father. Perhaps that is why she has not mentioned it to you, feeling it might upset you.'

Taken aback, Max considered this. Was it likely she thought he would disapprove of her having a relationship with another man? On careful consideration, he decided it possible. Like the refinery, his mother had been part of his father's life. Out of loyalty to his father, he was loath to have things change. But it was wrong. He could see that now.

The two men shook hands.

'I will speak with my mother.' He glanced at the address on the business card and noted Clarke-Fisher's address as being just off Park Street. 'Perhaps I could send you an invitation to dine – with my mother's agreement, of course?'

'That would be very agreeable.'

He paused before taking his leave, tapping the head of his cane against his teeth as though he'd had a secondary thought that he might, or might not mention.

'I think I would make a very good husband for your mother. A very good catch, considering her pedigree.'

Max wasn't sure whether that was a smile on his face or a sneer. He tried to maintain an inscrutable expression. 'You wouldn't be insulting my mother's good name, would you, sir?'

Clarke-Fisher's side-whiskers were thick and curly. At times, and in a certain light, they seemed to have a life of their own, as though they had a secret to tell and would willingly give the same away. 'I would not dream of that, sir. But let's face it, Mr Heinkel, how many people from the sugar islands have not got a dash of African blood in their veins?'

After he'd left, Max sat alone with his thoughts. His mother had told him of Spanish blood and a sea captain. The fact that she might have some Negro blood in her veins was of little importance. Clarke-Fisher had spoken the truth; there were indeed a lot of sugar planters, refiners and shipping families with more than a dose of foreign blood. It did not concern him, though it might of course concern his mother, and he would not have her hurt.

Deep down, he did not much care for Clarke-Fisher. He'd left a nasty taste in his mouth, and the more he thought about the man, the more he marvelled at his own self-control. In other circumstances, perhaps after a few brandies, he might have hit him to the ground.

But his mother wished to marry him. Again he wondered at the match – though what could he do? It was her choice, just as he'd made his choice to marry Magdalene Cherry, come hell or high water.

It was hard not to feel protective of his father's memory and he had certainly shown it of late. No wonder his mother had not seen fit to tell him she had an admirer. He felt guilty about that, guilty and selfish. He thought of Magdalene, her warm eyes, soft hands and rounded figure. Everyone needs someone, he decided, and determined to be agreeable.

Horatia Strong acted with far less amiability to the letter from Mr Clarke-Fisher than Max had to his visit. Knuckles white with tension, she called for a carriage and went into Bristol. Silently, she observed the view from her carriage window, the mowing of hay, the lowing of cattle calling for their calves, but she saw nothing. Her husband in the company of Blanche Heinkel at a Bath hotel was etched in her mind, just like those photographs that were becoming all the rage. The main difference was that photographs were developed in subtle tones of sepia; her vision of Blanche with her husband was richly coloured with jealous outrage.

Throwing her head back against the leather upholstery, she closed her eyes and saw only a burning, red fury. The Ambassador Hotel!

Of all the hotels to be seen in! But then, they didn't know. They couldn't know, could they?

Concern at their reasons for being in the hotel was obliterated by jealousy. She imagined them looking into each other's eyes, holding hands, embracing in public as if they had every right in the world to do so. But they didn't. And she would make that clear, by heaven, she would!

Mr Darius Clarke-Fisher had done a very good job of stirring her jealousy. He had introduced himself as a great admirer of hers, not that she cared a jot about his reasons for telling her what Tom had been up to. She'd considered facing Tom with the letter, but had decided against it. Their marriage hung on a precarious thread, and a woman needed a spouse. Married women had prestige; they could go where the unattached could not and received respect where a woman alone would only invite intrigue and gossip.

No. She would not throw the facts at her husband. There were other ways to clean out the pond without making too many ripples.

On her journey to the offices of Septimus Monk, she decided she would ruin Blanche Heinkel's reputation and hurt both of them in a way they would never forget.

'I wasn't expecting you,' Monk said when she swept into the room. A questioning look turned one eyebrow downwards as though he disapproved of her arriving unannounced.

'What does that damn well matter? I pay you,' she snapped, uncaring of whether his schedule was upset or his feelings hurt.

Monk was unmoved. 'But you don't own me.'

It seemed she hadn't heard what he'd said. She sat there, staring at one spot on the wall, her body stiff.

He sighed and decided to take a different tack. 'The transfer of the hotel will be completed next week. I don't think there are any more papers to sign, but I will check if you wish.'

She nodded, just once, as though it was only as she had expected.

Monk rested his elbows on his desk, his smooth, beautiful hands clasped before him. It had been ten years since Horatia Strong first called at his office. She had engaged him back then to work on getting her husband out of prison. The poor man had come back from Boston and had been promptly arrested for a murder committed some years before. It was obvious the man had had enemies. Monk's agents, some of whom were the most dreadful, the most frightening criminals in the whole of Bristol, had got to the bottom of the matter. Horatia had appreciated his working methods and the fact that he could keep a secret.

He sat back in his chair now. In her own good time, she would tell him what she had come for. He didn't have long to wait.

'I want you to forge a legacy.'

Monk's expression was inscrutable. He'd been asked to do worse things in his time. 'I see.' He picked up a quill pen and unrolled a fresh folio of paper. 'And this legacy, I take it, is or was part of a Will. Whose Will am I to forge?'

'The Will of my brother, Nelson Strong.'

Her gaze remained fixed on the same spot on the wall. The coldness in her eyes was enough to make him shiver. Horatia Strong was a formidable woman. It was a foolish man who crossed her.

The pen nib made a scratching sound as he scribbled a note on the paper. 'And when was this Will made?'

'Ten years ago, just before his death. I want you to implement a codicil in which it is implied that my brother did not wish the contents to be known until now.'

Without making comment, Monk continued to scribble. 'And who is the beneficiary?'

He saw her swallow. 'Mr Maximillian Heinkel.'

'Might I point out that if the legality of this is to stand, there must actually be a sum of money available to bequeath. Where is that money to come from?'

'I will provide it.'

'And how much will it be?'

Her eyes flickered as though she were calculating the worthiness of her venture, evaluating what she could afford against her determination that her plan did the most damage possible. 'One hundred thousand pounds. I want you to word the document so that Maximillian Heinkel is informed that my brother was his father.'

For the one and only time in their acquaintance, Septimus Monk trembled. Once he'd pulled himself together, he said, 'You must have great affection for this young man to bequeath him such a large sum in your brother's name.'

Her eyes flashed like fire when she glared at him, as if he'd woken her from a deep sleep and she wasn't too pleased about it. 'Don't patronize me, Septimus. You know me better than that, and on this occasion the instructions I have given you are all you need to know.'

She left him without saying goodbye.

On her way back to Marstone Court, Horatia cried before the altar in St Mary Redcliffe. She was torn in two.

'Would you like to talk to me in private?'

Strangely enough, the minister's presence was not imposing in any way.

Rarely did Horatia share even her most humdrum thoughts with any other human being. Perhaps it was his smile. Perhaps it was his flitting presence and soft words said in the right way at the right time, as though he already knew of her problems, but she nodded and followed him into his private office.

'You can tell me what you like,' he said after closing the door. 'And I will make tea. When you have finished, I will give you the benefit of my advice.' He smiled wickedly. 'And hope to God that it is indeed of some benefit.'

Edith and Blanche had set up croquet hoops on the lawn and were laughing at their efforts to knock the balls through each spindly arch.

That was where Max found them when he got home. His head had been aching when he'd left the refinery, mostly due to the onerous task of going through the ledgers with his accounts clerk and finding that profits were down. The transport costs were eating up money faster than they could make it. It made good sense to move the refinery to Avonmouth, and although he had a certain amount of money to put into a new site, it would not be enough to give him autonomy. The Strong family would be the largest shareholders. He would cease to have much say in the running of the plant. Added to that, if he read their moves correctly, they were also in the process of gobbling up land at the river's mouth. Not only would they be refiners, they would also be landlords. He couldn't hope to compete without some other injection of cash.

A red ball rolled swiftly towards a hoop, hit it and ricocheted off beneath a laurel bush.

Edith shrieked with delight. 'I've won! I've won!'

He grinned to himself as his mother, in an uncharacteristic fit of pique, went down on all fours and reached beneath the bush.

Just as she drew back, the ball clutched in her hand, she bent from the waist, her hand flying across her chest as she began to cough.

'Mother?' He ran to her, dropped to her side and, with Edith's help got her to her feet. 'Mother,' he said, his face creased with concern. 'Come into the house. Sit down.'

She held up a hand in order to call a halt. 'Don't fuss, Max. I'm fine. I'm just fine.'

Max guided his mother into the house, hardly able to tear his gaze from her face. How long had she had those dark circles beneath her eyes? And since when had her complexion taken on that greyish colour?

The loving son guided his mother to a chair, noting that Edith was not with them. If she had been, he would have told her to fetch a hot drink or, better still, a brandy. The moment she appeared, he would do so.

'Now,' he said, kneeling at the side of her chair. 'Do I get you the smelling salts?'

He was relieved when she laughed.

'Certainly not,' she said.

He suggested she went for a lie-down.

'I'm not an invalid,' she protested.

'I wasn't suggesting you were, but you did give cause for concern out there.'

She shook her head as though it were nothing. 'It was the dust. You know what laurel bushes are like for dust.'

But there was a wary look in her eyes that he didn't like.

'Max,' she said, fixing her gaze on the polished fender where she rested her feet. 'I have something to tell you.'

He managed to convince himself that he'd been mistaken about the dark circles and the change in her complexion. Relieved and suddenly light-headed, he broke into laughter. 'And now we have your little secret. No need to fear, Mother. I already know. Mr Clarke-Fisher came to see me. I told him I would speak to you first, but I have no objection to you marrying him. In fact, Mother, I have decided to marry Magdalene Cherry, and all thanks to your love of hats.'

He stopped, suddenly aware of the look of horror on her face. He presumed it was with regard to his proposed marriage to a milliner and readied himself for confrontation.

'How dare he!'

Max frowned. He'd so wanted to make things right. This was not the reaction he'd anticipated. 'What do you mean, Mother?'

Her expression was one of outright amazement. 'He told you that I intended to marry him?'

'Yes, but he decided to see me first before pursuing you further. He said he thought it was only right that he should offer following your stay together in Clevedon, and the possibility of your reputation being compromised . . .' Something about the brilliance of his mother's eyes made him pause.

'Together? He told you that we stayed in Clevedon together?' Her pale cheeks suddenly regained a little colour. Her chest heaved in time with her quick breathing, with indignation rather than shortness of breath.

The man had duped him. Max had inadvertently insulted his mother. 'Was he lying?'

Blanche raised her voice. 'He was lying about Clevedon, and he was lying about my reaction to his proposal of marriage. I can't stand the man, and I have no intention of marrying him – not ever!'

'Oh!' Although Max looked perplexed, he felt mightily relieved. 'Thank goodness for that. It wasn't that I can't countenance you remarrying, he just didn't seem your type – nothing like Father.'

Max retrieved Darius Clarke-Fisher's business card from his pocket and tore it into tiny pieces.

'Well, that's the end of that,' he said, as the pieces fluttered into the fireplace, speckles of snow white against the polished blackness of the grate.

Blanche covered her face with her hands. It was bad enough that Clarke-Fisher had tried to blacken her reputation, but to use the lie in order to get her to the altar was unforgivable.

But she'd get over it. Nothing in life was as important as life itself, and she intended to make the most of the time she had left. Her family and those she loved – all those she loved – were what mattered.

Sighing with relief, she settled back in her chair. 'Thank goodness that's sorted out.' The absurdity of it all suddenly struck her. 'Imagine me marrying a man like that.'

'I'd prefer not to.'

'So tell me how you lost your heart to Madame Mabel's assistant,' said Blanche, reaching for her son's hand.

'Ah, yes,' said Max. Now it was his turn to blush. 'I hope you won't object, Mother.'

He turned his clear blue eyes on hers and she felt her heart leap with love and pride. Unlike his mother, who had married for security and also for his sake, he would follow his heart. She envied him that.

Smiling, she reached out and ruffled his hair, just as she had when he'd been a small boy. 'Follow your heart, Max. Always follow your heart.'

He took hold of her hand and kissed it. 'I was foolish to keep it from you.' He shrugged nonchalantly. 'I feared your reaction to me marrying a milliner.'

Her face clouded and her gaze seemed to drift off into the distance. 'A man named Conrad Heinkel also married beneath him. He married a nanny in service at Marstone Court.'

Max's smiled diminished as he remembered the rest of what Clarke-Fisher had said about West Indian ancestry. He now believed his mother was descended from slaves.

'And you came from Barbados.'

It hurt him to see her wince.

'Mother, have you any idea how many people in this city have interests in the sugar trade? Do you also have any idea how many of those have Negro blood in their veins? And what about the rest of us? Why do we all suppose we are of the same tree going back to the Battle of Hastings, that Englishmen have blond hair and blue eyes and all speak the same tongue. These islands have given shelter to people from all over the world since ancient times. Perhaps I was a little priggish in the past, but since Magdalene came along, I weigh up the worth of people as people, not by their station in society or their racial or cultural roots. Does that make sense?'

He couldn't quite work out her expression. There was surprise, there was joy, but there was something else in her eyes that he couldn't quite work out.

Blanche's thoughts were with Samson and his family. They were safely cocooned in Little Paradise with Edith and fending for themselves. She was ashamed that she had not declared herself their relative on the day they'd arrived at the Workhouse. The reasons had seemed perfectly acceptable at the time. She did not want her family's chances in life ruined by coloured relatives that no one knew they had. And yet, here was Max, the very person she had been trying to protect, telling her that he was not disposed to bigotry of any sort. It was refreshingly different, and a total surprise.

'Then I think it's time you met your relatives,' she said, and went on to tell him about Samson.

'. . . And my father was Sir Emmanuel Strong, though I didn't realize that at first. . . . Hard to imagine, really.'

Edith, who had lingered in the garden, listened in silence. In her hand she held Blanche's handkerchief. It was blood-stained. Her eyes moist, her fingers tightly clenched, Edith knew what it meant, was equally sure that Max knew nothing about it and that Blanche did not want him to know.

Later, she would get Blanche alone, and perhaps then she would learn the truth.

On the days she was at Somerset Parade, it had been Edith's habit to help Blanche off with her dress and unlace her corsets once she'd got out her nightgown.

Tonight was no different, but when she entered the room, she saw that Blanche was leaning out of the window.

The view was well worth studying. The night sky was studded with stars and a full moon bloomed like a rising loaf. The garden was spangled with silver.

'It's so beautiful,' said Blanche without turning round. Her voice sounded full of wonder.

Edith swallowed and swiped at her runny nose. She didn't have a cold, but it would be so easy to cry. I mustn't, she decided. I have to be strong for Blanche.

On receiving no response from Edith, Blanche turned round. 'Did you hear what I said . . . ?'

A single tear squeezed from the corner of Edith's eye, and she sniffed. 'Yes. I heard.'

She saw the expression on Edith's face, the outstretched hand and the handkerchief sitting in Edith's palm. The truth was out. 'Have you told Max?' she asked, her voice barely audible.

Edith shook her head. 'I didn't think you'd want me to.'

Blanche hung her head and turned back to the stars. 'Tom is the only other person who knows. He more or less guessed. And my doctor, of course.'

'And the rest of your family?'

Her eyes were big and full of pleading. 'I don't want any of them to know. You mustn't say anything. Promise me that.'

Edith took a deep breath and nodded. 'I won't tell.'

Chapter Eighteen

Little Paradise was becoming noisier than it had been in a long time, and Edith loved it.

Samson was a good carpenter and, thanks to Max, had been found a job as a ship's joiner at Charlie Hill's Shipyard. Both Abigail and Edith, accompanied by Desdemona, still visited the Workhouse to oversee the care of the babies.

It was Max who explained to Samson that his mother had not recognized him at the Workhouse.

'Little Paradise is the right name for this house,' Samson had replied, as Edith pushed yet another dish of mutton stew in front of him. 'And I'm grateful to your mother for getting us out of that place. I've left a message with the narrowboat people for my son. He's working on one of them pretty boats for a woman named Aggie Beven. She was good to us, she was. Seems there's a lot of people to be grateful to in this city.'

Max told Magdalene about his relatives and took her to see them. He was greatly relieved to see that she was as unconcerned with their origins and their colour as he was.

'You don't mind that they're foreigners?' he asked.

She shook her pretty head of dark curls. 'Of course not. I'm a foreigner meself, if you like to go back a few generations.'

'You are? I didn't know that.'

She clung to his arm, her chin resting on his shoulder. 'Would it matter?'

'Of course not. But I am surprised. Your name doesn't sound foreign.'

'Cherry. My mother picked it, just like you would a cherry.'

'Where did your family come from?'

'Prussia,' she said, her dark eyes still studying him for the slightest reaction for her to pick on and exploit, but only in fun. That was the way it was, like a game between them.

'So what was your family name?'

'Goldstein.'

'Isn't that Jewish?'

'Yes. My family were Jewish.'

'And are they now – Jewish?'

There were dimples at the sides of her mouth. 'Sometimes. Does it matter?'

He looked into her dark eyes and smelled her scent of crushed violets. He shook his head. 'No. It doesn't.'

Under pressure from the Board of Governors, who had learned of the conditions from Blanche, the nursery had been moved into a lighter room on the first floor. A number of inmates were now employed to look after the babies, but Edith and Abigail couldn't stop themselves poking their noses in. In effect, this was their idea, via Blanche, of course. They weren't about to let it slide now that conditions for the babies had improved.

Edith banned Blanche from visiting the Workhouse.

'We'll take care of everything. You catch something nasty if you goes there too often. So if you dare put a foot over the threshold, I'll tell Max just how ill you are. And I mean it!'

But Blanche insisted that she had to go into the Workhouse one last time.

'No,' said Edith, standing foursquare before the front door.

'This is ridiculous. You're the servant and I'm the mistress.'

Arms folded over her ample chest, Edith shook her head. 'I don't care.'

'I have a special errand to make,' Blanche pleaded. 'It's very important.'

'So's your son's wedding, but you're not going to be there on the day if you don't look after yourself.'

Blanche covered her face with her hands, then held them prayer-like before her. The records kept by the Reverend Smart had been surprisingly incomplete. She'd wanted to ask Mrs Tinsley whether she remembered the dark-skinned child. Doubtless, the warden's wife would be less than civil to her. After all, she had undermined her position at the Workhouse. There was much more of a self-help mentality among the inmates. The exploitation and bullying of the old regime had weakened considerably.

With a rustle of mauve silk, Blanche sighed and sank onto a chaise longue. Her head sank into her hands. 'There is something very important that I have to find out,' she said into her fingers. 'I have to ask Mrs Tinsley a very important question.'

'You? Ask questions of Mrs Tinsley? Well, a delightful baggage she is, and not well disposed towards you now, is she?'

Blanche shook her head. 'That's very true.'

'Right old cow, she is, or tries to be. Not with me, of course. She knows I won't stand any of her nonsense.'

'That's even truer,' said Blanche, looking up and wondering, just wondering, whether Edith might be more likely to get an answer. 'Edith,' she said, taking hold of her hand and pulling her down in front of her so their conversation could not be overheard. 'What I am going to tell you is very secret.'

'Ooow! I do like secrets.'

Blanche threw her a warning look. 'And it has to remain a secret.'

Edith's brightness dissipated, a sad look pulling down the corners of her mouth. 'I washed the handkerchief. Max didn't see it.'

They both fell to silence, Blanche because she was grateful to have such a friend, and Edith because she feared losing the best friend she'd ever had.

Once she'd recovered, Blanche went on to tell her all that had transpired with regard to the baby born to Horatia and Tom Strong.

'That Daisy Draper! I wouldn't put a dog in that place, let alone me own flesh and blood. Not that I'm saying it ain't improved, mark you . . .'

Blanche nodded impatiently. 'I know. There's a record of the child being admitted in the Reverend Smart's ledger, but no record of what happened to him. What I would like you to do is to ask Mrs Tinsley. She's sure to know. She makes it her duty to know all that's going on in that place. Do you think you can do that?'

Edith looked genuinely affronted. 'Do you doubt my powers of persuasion?' she said, getting to her feet. Rolling her sleeves up to her elbows exposed forearms the size of cooked hams. 'You leave that old cow to me,' she said, and licked her lips, relishing the thought of the confrontation to come.

*

Max was in his office, the door wide open. The heat of the refinery was thick with the smell of sugar. Furnaces throbbed with white-hot fire, metal scraped against metal. The pans that turned the sugar from muscavado to the finished product made a whistling sound as they spun the sugar so it separated from the impurities, the crystals to be formed into loaves and sold to a wholesaler, who in turn would sell them on to every grocer in the city.

I shall be sad to see all this go, he thought. He had accepted now that the refinery would move to Avonmouth. A businessman, he'd decided, needed to be flexible. He would, of course, still have a share, but it wouldn't be the same. If he could somehow create his own refinery there, he would still maintain control. To do that would take a lot of money, and he didn't have enough, not nearly as much as the Strong family.

By the time he was married, the brewery would be pushing hard to take over these premises. A year, perhaps two, and the site on which sugar had been refined for nearly a hundred years would give way to the brewing of beer.

Desperate to salvage control, he had gone to another bank for finance, but they'd been unhelpful. No Bristol bank was big enough to stand up to the power of the Strong family. His next course was to go to London. It was his last hope. There was a piece of land at Avonmouth that was ideal for development. If only he had the money. He wouldn't be destitute, of course, but he would have liked to improve on what Conrad Heinkel had left him. Limehouse and Hamburg could not be used to fund a bigger plant. Both needed money to upgrade. The Counterslip refinery had to survive or fall on its own merit.

I need to be lucky, he decided, but he wasn't the sort to believe that something would turn up, that luck was like Christmas.

Obsessed with his plans and his dreams, he did not at first hear his clerk.

'Sir? You have a visitor.'

Stubbins was a pompous little man with short legs and a shiny pate covered with freckles. He'd worked in the office for years and had been an overseer on a sugar plantation before that. He cleared his throat now and shuffled his feet. 'There's a gentleman outside,' he said in a louder voice. 'He seems quite anxious to see you.'

Frowning, Max said, 'Who is the fellow?'

Stubbins handed Max a card and Max looked at it. A smudged fingerprint was discernible on one corner. Stubbins sweated a lot. The card said, 'Morgan, Jay and Morgan, Solicitors, Commissioners for Oaths.' The address was Queens Square.

Max pursed his lips. He'd heard of them. He took a deep breath and told Stubbins to show the man in.

'Delighted to make your acquaintance, Mr Heinkel,' said a pale man with jug ears and a wide mouth that seemed to cut his face in half. His milky blue eyes were unblinking and his whiskers were like a halo framing his jaw.

Max bid him sit down, which he did with a flourish of coat-tails.

'How can I help you, Mr Morgan?'

'Mr Jay,' the solicitor corrected, swinging one grey trouser-leg over the other and placing a silk topper on the desk.

'Mr Jay,' said Max with a curt nod. 'How can I help you?'

His visitor waved a large hand as he extracted a sheaf of paper bound with ribbon from his bag. His wrists were thin and hung from his cuffs like gnarled twigs. 'It is I who am here to help you, my dear sir. I bring good tidings with regard to a trust fund settled on you by your father in the months following your birth.'

Max's mood lightened. 'A trust fund. I take it you mean money?' His thoughts went back to the plot of land at Avonmouth. Would it be enough? And why had he heard nothing of this bequest until now?

Mr Jay couldn't possibly smile any wider. 'Indeed. A lot of money, in fact.'

Max relaxed, slammed his hands on the arms of his chair, got to his feet and fetched a decanter of port and two glasses from a cupboard. He needed money to keep the Strong family from stealing his birthright, and here it was, provided by Conrad Heinkel, his father.

'Then we must celebrate.'

Mr Jay looked surprised. It wasn't often he was asked to celebrate even the largest of bequests.

The port gurgled into the glasses with unbridled generosity, some slopping over the top and onto the desk. Max didn't care about the mess. This was a special occasion.

Visions of a brand new refinery growing brick by brick inside his head, he proposed a toast: 'To my father's trust fund.'

Mr Jay spilt a little more as he raised his glass, as though he were nervous or at the very least surprised. 'Indeed, sir. To your father's trust fund, though I'm not quite sure I should be—'

'Drink, man,' Max ordered.

Mr Jay's Adam's apple moved against his stiff collar as he did so.

Max did the same then heaved a great sigh. 'Well, Mr Jay, I have to admit to being surprised, very surprised indeed. I never knew there was a trust fund. Father never mentioned it. How much money does it entail?'

Mr Jay paused, looked at him and blinked. The action seemed oddly out of place on his features, like a surprised owl. Regaining his equilibrium, he balanced a pair of spectacles on his nose, unfurled a folio of rustling paper and studied the wording.

'One hundred thousand pounds.'

Max gasped and sat back in his chair. 'Well I'll be damned! Well I'll be damned!'

It took a little time for it to sink in, but in his head the new refinery was complete from foundation to roof and the chimneys were belching smoke and steam, the sweet scent of sugar filling the air.

He took a deep breath. 'I didn't know he had such an amount?'

'Oh indeed he did, though he stipulated that you were not to receive your inheritance until you were twenty-one, which you were last September, I believe,' said Mr Jay, his eyes now fixed on the scrolling words.

Max agreed that had indeed been his birthday.

'However,' said Mr Jay, his eyes scanning the lengthy document as though he were searching for a discrepancy, a dropped letter or a misspelled word, 'there is just one modest proviso in order for you to claim this sum.'

Max nodded. 'Go on.'

Mr Jay pushed his spectacles up to the bridge of his nose and read again. 'In order for you to claim the said inheritance, your father asks that you adopt his name.'

Max frowned. 'I beg your pardon?'

Mr Jay coughed into his hand and avoided looking into his face as he repeated what he had just said.

Suddenly the room had darkened, or at least that was the way it seemed. Max sank into his chair and leaned across his desk. A dark foreboding that he couldn't explain flooded into his mind and made the room swim around him. He searched his mind for a plausible explanation. There was only one he could think of.

'He wishes me to be called Conrad?' he asked, though the idea seemed ludicrous. Why hadn't he named him Conrad when he was born instead of Max?

Mr Jay removed the spectacles from his nose and eyed Max with a cautious, almost fearful look. He shook his head. 'The money has not been left to you by Conrad Heinkel, who I understand was your adoptive father, but the man who claims to be your natural father, Mr Nelson Samson Delaware Strong, deceased. He also stipulated that no word of the source of your inheritance would be made public without your prior permission. I trust you think that fair?'

The vision of the new refinery became indistinct, as though a thick fog had descended on it. Things had been so good between him and his mother just yesterday. She'd told him so much, but not this. Certainly not this. He hardly dared utter the next question. It was too terrible. Surely it couldn't be right. His tongue cleaved to the roof of his mouth, but he forced it to move, to ask the dreadful question that made him feel as though . . . He couldn't get to grips to how it would make him feel, not until he knew it was so.

He asked the dreadful question.

'Nelson Strong was the son of Sir Emmanuel Strong. Is that correct?'

Mr Jay replaced his glasses and rustled a few sheets of paper in his search for precise details. 'Yes,' he said, his chin held high as he perused the document over the top of his glasses.

Max felt numb. If what this man told him was true, then that meant . . .

He shook his head and hid his face in his hands. 'It can't be.'

He caught Mr Jay peering at him quizzically and realized he was ignorant of the situation.

'I need your signature before I can hand over the cheque,' the solicitor said.

Max stared at the floor. If this lawyer was to be believed, then his love for the man he had all his life regarded as his father had been totally misplaced. He couldn't believe it. He didn't want to believe it. And how could Nelson Strong be his father? By his mother's own admission, Nelson Strong had been her half-brother, his uncle.

He shook his head. 'This is all too much.'

Mr Jay coughed nervously. 'As I have already indicated, if you are willing to change your name to Strong, the money is yours. But I will need your signature. Are you willing to sign?'

Max eyed Mr Jay through his fingers. His mind was reeling. The refinery, his mother, his father – or the man he'd always thought of as his father – and now this, this terrible slur. His anger rumbled to the surface, erupting full force into Mr Jay's face.

'Get out!' he shouted, springing to his feet. 'Get out!'

Mr Jay, surprised at being shouted at after bringing what he had thought was very good news, slunk back in his chair. 'I beg your pardon?'

'Get out,' shouted Max, grabbing him by the shoulders and flinging him towards the door.

Mr Jay scurried out along the passageway and into the street.

Max stared at the papers hanging from the desk. He didn't understand. If what Jay had said was true, then he could never look at his mother in the same way again. And what would people say? He'd been quite prepared to accept unusual ancestry. But this? What chance did he have of gaining the respect of the business community of this city should they find out that he was the result of an intimacy between his mother and her own brother?

The awful thing was, he couldn't tell a soul, not even Magdalene. He imagined her horror, a reflection of his own. There was nothing for it but to confront his mother. At present, she was in Bath for a few days. He would go there and speak to her in private.

There was a knock at the door. Stubbins entered. 'The bargees and boatmen are threatening to throw their cargo into the river if they don't get paid extra for waiting time.'

Max said to himself, 'Damn the boatmen!' To Stubbins he said, 'Get Robinson to deal with it.' Robinson was the foreman, a useful man with a brusque manner who didn't suffer fools or insolence gladly.

'They won't listen to him, especially that old crone, Aggie Beven. Right old dragon she is, frightens Robinson to death. Got a young darkie with her, too. Cheeky little sod. Reckons he's a relative of yours.' Stubbins chortled.

Resigned that he wouldn't be going to Bath today, Max fixed him with an icy stare. 'Then let's get on with it!'

He strode out of the office, brushing hard against Stubbins and pressing him against the open door.

Aggie Beven stood with arms akimbo, her voluminous skirts tucked up between her legs to aid her stepping from boat to quay. She was smoking a pipe and wore an old-fashioned bonnet with a broad brim and ribbons big enough to moor a galleon.

There was a boy beside her, his face as brown and polished as a conker, and his eyes bright and full of confidence. If this was Samson's boy, then he was no shrinking violet. He had an arrogance about him, a way of looking that said he would take no nonsense from any man. Max fancied Aggie might have had something to do with that. Aggie was a strong woman in more ways than one. She had a strong mind and a strong right arm, from what he'd heard from his labourers who'd run into her in dockside taverns and chanced a trial of strength over a beer-stained table.

'So what's the problem here?' He directed his question at Aggie, who appeared to be leading the rest of the boatmen and bargees.

'Robinson agreed, and you agreed, that we'd get an extra sixpence a hundredweight. We ain't got it, and we need it. Ain't our work worth that to you, Maximillian Heinkel?'

Max was in no mood to argue. He turned to Robinson. 'Did you agree that?'

Robinson squirmed. 'Well, I did tell them that, but I got so busy with the new separator and that, it slipped my mind to mention it to you.'

His face burning with anger, Max raised his fist and pointed an accusing finger directly at Robinson. 'Fail to inform me again, and you're sacked!'

Robinson looked astounded. It wasn't surprising. He'd been with the firm since Conrad's day. He was totally loyal, running the refinery as if it were his own. He didn't deserve to be vilified like this in public. He looked hurt, but today Max neither noticed nor cared.

'You'll all be paid,' he said, and aside to Stubbins, 'Pay them.'

He turned on his heel, but found his way blocked by Samson's young son, his upturned face too worldly wise for his years.

'Hamlet Rivermead,' said the boy, sweeping his hat from his head. With a pointed toe and an exaggerated flourish, he bowed like a prince. 'At your service, Mr Heinkel.'

'I haven't got time—'

'We are related,' said Hamlet, his face shining like the sun. 'How do you do?'

He extended his hand. Hesitantly, Max took it. A quick glance around confirmed no one was close enough to hear.

'And from which of the Strong family are you descended?' asked Max.

Hamlet shrugged. 'I don't know. Could be any of them. Could be all of them. They owned us. They could do as they liked.'

Max thought about it. It was the most chilling, the most calming thing that could have been said to him. That night he would think further on what had happened today. Tomorrow he would journey to Bath, go to the Ambassador Hotel and confront his mother.

Chapter Nineteen

They walked in North Parade Gardens, Tom kicking at an odd stone that happened to be in his path, poking his walking stick at a stray leaf, his eyes downcast.

Blanche stayed silent. His distress was her distress. His guilt was his own. At one time she would have felt the same about being in the company of a man married to someone else. Recent events had caused her to take a different view of the world. Time was precious, and so was love. Only someone who was facing death could understand how she was feeling. Tom, even loving her as he did, could not possibly understand, although he did his best to do so.

She had told him Edith was making further enquiries so they would finally know his son's resting place. And what about Horatia? He had told her of his discovery. Ashen faced, she'd swept away, locked herself in her room. On emerging, she insisted the matter was never mentioned again, 'it is too painful,' she said. It seemed it was literally business as usual. But surely she was feeling the child's loss to some degree, perhaps not as much as Tom, but even so . . .

She recalled a children's birthday party they'd both attended. The parents had been titled and lived in Cornwallis House. Whilst the children played their party games and ate their creamy cakes and sickly sweet jellies and blancmanges, the parents had been entertained to a piano recital in the drawing room. She had seen Horatia there with Emerald, smiling down on the child, wiping the cream from around he daughter's face, looking as though she really cared. And yet she had given her child up . . . it was hard to believe, but Tom assured her it was so.

'Edith is a very capable woman,' Tom said suddenly.

They continued walking, Blanche staring down at her hands. 'She will do her best.'

He sighed. 'It's a pleasant day.'

'Tom?' She touched his arm and they came to a halt. 'Can you ever find it in your heart to forgive Horatia?'

He blinked. She saw it and wondered what sudden thought had crossed his mind. 'I do my best. I tell myself that she can't possibly have done such a terrible thing, but I know that she did abandon the child. So, your answer is, no, I don't think so.'

Blanche hung her head. It was sad, but only to be expected. She knew that, but the feeling that there was more to this would not go away. 'Life goes on,' she said, and tucked a stray curl back beneath her bonnet.

He nodded and came to a halt beneath a tree that was heavy with orange and yellow leaves. The breeze blew and they were showered with petals.

He took her hands in his. 'My future with Horatia is doomed. But somehow, I don't think there is anything I can do – or care to do – that will make things any different.'

She didn't say a word in response. She just looked at him, wishing she could heal his hurt, that she could do something to make him feel better.

'My future is assured,' she said eventually.

He frowned. 'Blanche, I—'

She reached for his mouth and pressed her fingers on his lips. Her eyes sparkled when she looked at him. 'Let me finish what I was going to say. After Max's marriage, I intend going back to Barbados. It's been so long. I want to go home.'

He laughed and shook his head. 'Well, well.'

'I'm sorry.'

His amusement became a muted smile. 'There's no need to be. I never doubted it might happen one day.' He brushed a few dried leaves that had tangled in the fancy bits on her bonnet. 'Where will you live?'

A dreamy look came to her eyes. 'I'd like to live in the house where I grew up. I thought I might paint it white. It would be very pleasant to sit out there on an evening and watch the sun sink into the sea.'

'Yes,' he said thoughtfully. 'It would.'

His eyes stayed fixed on her, almost as though he were imagining her doing exactly that.

She looked away from him as she tried to swallow the tickle in her throat. It was making its presence known more forcefully. It still irked her to have it invade her precious moments, to upset the vital health she had once taken for granted. Deep inside, something had changed, and affected the way she saw the world and the things she wanted from it.

'Tom, I have to ask you something.'

'You sound very serious.'

'It is serious.'

'Goodness!'

She saw he was smiling again. 'I think I'm going to surprise you with what I have to say. I hope you won't think less of me for doing so.'

A puzzled, almost hurt expression crossed his face. 'I could never think less of you, no matter what you did.'

He clasped her hands and held them against his chest. The feel of his heart beating beneath her fingertips made her pause and reflect on what she intended to say. What would he think?

She fixed her eyes on his. 'My room is next door to yours. Did you know that?'

He hesitated. Blanche thrilled to the feel of his quickening heart-beat.

'Yes. I know.' His voice was a long, drawn-out sigh. 'I'm going to have trouble sleeping tonight. I shall be imagining I can hear you breathing.'

'Coughing, more likely.'

The concern came back to his face. 'I wish there was something I could do to make you better. If it cost the whole world, I would do it.'

She looked up at him in earnest, her eyes unblinking and her features quietly still. 'I'm not going to ask you for the world. Just one night. That's all.'

Tom looked astounded. 'Blanche, I don't know what to say . . .'

She was not surprised when he didn't jump at the chance. He had two reasons to be concerned: Emerald and Max.

'If Horatia should find out . . .' He shook his head, unwilling to tell her the lengths Horatia would go to should she discover that they'd gone to bed together. It wouldn't be just him who would suffer; she would get to both of them via the children. Emotional, long-lasting vengeance – that was Horatia's way.

You should have remembered what an honourable man he is, she thought as she withdrew her hands from the vicinity of his heart.

Perceiving she was about to turn away, he held her shoulders, forcing her to look up at him. 'Blanche, you cannot possibly conceive what is at stake here. There have been so many times in these past years when I have wished and wished that you were lying beside me. But fate didn't play us that particular hand. I can't do what you're asking of me, much as I would like to.'

Her eyes looked huge in her face. 'I should have known better,' she said, and attempted a weak smile.

'But I'll always be there for you,' he added.

His hands were still on her shoulders. She was still looking up at him. Being so close, the inevitable happened. The distance between their lips became smaller and smaller. They kissed like lovers, their hearts racing and their bodies seeming to fuse into one.

When they parted, she was breathless.

'Nothing's changed.' She did not mean that only the kiss had not changed. Their feelings for each other had never altered.

A group of children ran past chasing a hoop. Their nurse followed, pushing yet another of the new-fangled perambulators.

Blanche adjusted her bonnet. 'We'd better go,' she said, sheepishly lowering her eyes. She didn't regret having asked him to go to bed with her. She merely regretted the outcome.

She slid her arm into his. He stroked her hand and they continued walking.

'At some point you may have to go to a better doctor or one of the sanatoriums,' he said. 'I hear there are some very good doctors in Harley Street, and a good sanatorium at Clevedon.'

She laughed at the mention of Clevedon. 'I dare not go to Clevedon again. It seems full of unsuitable gentlemen in pursuit of respectable widows. Besides, I'm much improved. It's the sunshine. I'm always better in the sunshine. Have you heard me cough lately?'

Smiling, he shook his head. 'No, I haven't.'

'Well, there you are. You linger here on false pretences. I am not ill. You are here because—'

'I love you.'

She laughed. It had a beautiful quality, like the notes of a fine piano. 'But you won't go to bed with me.'

'I care for you too much to see you hurt by my wife.'

'Whatever your reasons, I will respect them. Besides, we're too old for those sentiments, surely.'

Her grey eyes looked up into his. She could read his mind by the expression in his eyes. He cared for her. He cared for her deeply and her present predicament ate into his soul.

'No one is ever too old to love.'

They came to a standstill at the top of the steps leading out from the gardens and onto North Parade itself where carriages, carts and cabs vied for space in the narrow, congested streets.

His body ached for her. There never had been another woman he'd desired as much as he did her. If only things had been different. But her suggestion had worked its magic. No matter how hard he tried to shove it to the back of his mind, it refused to go and sat there, simmering like a flickering coal about to burst into flame.

By bedtime, she was feverish. Alone with her thoughts, she stood in her nightgown before the open window, unheeding of the chill breeze that had come with sundown.

Leaving the windows wide open, she finally got into bed, closed her eyes and, with her head thumping, fell into a troubled sleep. In her dream, she shivered yet felt hot, began to see a scene: gaslights, stone doorways, alleys and moonlit roofs. A cat screeched as it ran out between her and a deep puddle. She started, slipped and fell face first. She didn't know how long she lay there, the dirty black water cool against her face. Someone, she didn't see nor care who, lifted her arm and slid off her purse strings, then lifted her head and took her hat, the brooch from her throat, a bracelet from her wrist. It wasn't until she'd struggled to her feet and felt sharp cinders beneath her soles, that she realized whoever it was had also taken her boots.

Their loss suddenly seemed funny, almost welcome, and she no longer saw her drab surroundings. Clenching her toes, she felt her way over the worn-out road, through the dirty puddles, the cold water gently soothing on feet that had not felt the bare ground for many years. A draught of cool air tossed her hair around her face. On tasting its tangy sea saltiness, she was transported back in time. Once again she felt the sand between her toes. Just as she had in Barbados, she began to run towards the source of the sea breeze. It felt as though she were flying, yet she staggered as she ran, slowed by the heavy dress she wore.

Cinders began cutting into her feet and the sandy beach was gone, her surroundings greyer and drab, rain soaking her dress to her body, her teeth chattering from cold. Her breathing rasped in her chest and her hair, usually so neatly fastened, flew around her face.

'I'm going home,' she cried on seeing a pair of double gates ahead of her, the branches of trees hanging over a wall. Frangipani, she thought, and sniffed the air. Their scent was non-existent except in her mind where the smell of the trees was as sweet as ever. She stopped running and spread her arms over the gates, closing her eyes . . .

The scene faded. Suddenly, she was inside the Workhouse, smelling the disgusting stink of bones, overcooked food and mouldy clothes.

She woke with a start, sitting bolt upright in bed. Someone was tapping at the door and calling her name softly.

She remembered where she was. Soaked in sweat, though shivering beneath the cool cotton of her nightgown, she swung her bare feet out of bed and went to the door. It was no surprise to see Tom standing there, a concerned frown furrowing his sweet, handsome brow.

'I heard you scream.'

'I had a nightmare,' she said, felt herself fainting and leaned against the door frame for support, but slowly, like melting snow, sank to the floor.

Strong arms picked her up, carried her to the bed and drew the coverlet over her. She saw the worry in his eyes.

'I think I should send for the doctor.'

She shook her head. 'No. I'm all right now. It was just a nightmare. I was in the Workhouse.'

She raised herself up on her elbow. Her hair was loose and tumbled over her shoulders. Her skin glistened and, although her cheeks were warm, he sensed her skin was cool. He imagined the smell, the feel, the taste of it beneath the bedclothes. His loins tensed in reaction to his thoughts, the longing he had hidden for years tightening his stomach, a throbbing and hardening that his wife had never aroused in him.

'I think I should leave,' he said gruffly, tearing his eyes from the sight of her, lest he allow his desire to overrule his sense of chivalry.

The feel of her hand on his sent his pulse racing. 'Don't go, Tom.'

The sound of her voice was like balsam to his troubled soul. She had risked her reputation in meeting him here. He had risked his marriage and the possibility of blighting the lives of Emerald and Max.

'Are you sure about this?' Tom said, his hand closing around her arm.

'What have I got to lose?'

'Your reputation?'

She laughed. 'Tom, what price a reputation to someone who sees eternity staring her in the face?'

He pressed a finger against her lips. 'Don't say that. Please don't say that.'

She reached for his dear face, her palm warm upon his cheek, her fingers cool as she delicately traced the shape of his eyes.

He leaned his head against hers so that their foreheads touched. She felt the wetness of his tears and knew he wasn't just crying for her, but also for the years they'd lost, years when they might have had children together and lived for them and for each other.

'I should never have left. Things would have been so different.'

'We have now.'

He shook his head, his forehead still against hers. 'It's not enough.'

'It has to be.'

She kissed his forehead, his nose, his cheeks and then his mouth. 'I'm not made of porcelain.'

He stretched out beside her and kissed her gently. She looked into his eyes and saw his hunger. It overwhelmed her. She felt lost in the intensity of his eyes. Although they were barely touching, she felt the deepest, most pleasurable sensation flood over her. She reached for him, closed her eyes, opened her mouth and pressed her body against his.

He kissed her more deeply, more passionately than she had ever been kissed before. Working his way down her neck and throat, he kissed her shoulders, his tongue and lips caressing each sensitive nipple, as his hand caressed her belly and moved down to her thighs.

Moaning and closing her eyes, she moved her hips, rolling them in obvious pleasure as his hand invaded the warmth between her thighs, a cry escaping her lips as he touched the ache he found there.

Sucking her nipple, he forced his leg between her thighs as he'd done with Horatia, but felt no resistance as he did with his wife. He struggled to contain his urge, slowly caressing and kissing until she was gasping against his ear, begging him to do once again what he had only done just once before.

Without any need to guide or impress, he pushed into her. Unlike Horatia who lay flat and unmoving, Blanche rolled under him, gasping and moaning in pleasure, her legs folded around his back, inviting him to dig deeper, to pleasure her more, to fill her with his seed just as he filled her with his love.

They cried out together, a fusion of ecstasy as spasms of simultaneous pleasure flooded over them; like the warm waves of the Caribbean, like the tropical breeze of an evening long gone.

Chapter Twenty

Edith decided that two determined women were better than one, so when she went to confront Mrs Tinsley, Abigail went, too.

They found her gossiping in the laundry room with a woman they called Big Bertha, who had forearms the size of tree trunks. She was presently wringing out a sheet by hand before feeding it into a cast-iron mangle. Very little water trickled from the wet sheet. Big Bertha's strength had done the job already.

'I'd like a word, Mrs Tinsley,' said Edith.

'Go on then. Have yer word,' she said with a snigger and an exchange of looks with Big Bertha.

Edith sensed there'd been gossip and that she, and possibly Abigail, had been the subject of it.

'In private,' said Edith.

'You can say what you want in front of Bertha. She's me friend.'

'Pah!' said Edith. 'You ain't got no friends. You just like to think you do. Even thinks yer a bit of a picture, don't yo? Give over! Seen yerself in the mirror lately? I've seen better features on a pig's rear end, and I'm sure that the Reverend Smart thinks the same, however much you might fawn over the dry old stick!'

Mrs Tinsley's mouth dropped open. 'Well, I never did!'

'Yes, you did,' said Edith with a grin. 'Makes a bit of a noise that Reverend Smart when he's rutting away like a prize pink boar. Anyone else want to hear more about it?' she said, raising her voice and eyeing the laundrywomen working on the other side of the room.

Not having heard what she'd first said, they looked up, their faces full of curiosity.

Edith had guessed correctly. Mrs Tinsley was suddenly all of a jitter. 'There ain't no need of that.'

They went into the Reverend Smart's office, which was empty.

'He's gone to visit a sick relative,' said Mrs Tinsley.

'The way that bloke carries on, they're likely to get sicker – dirty old man,' said Edith with an amused aside to Abigail.

Abigail grinned back at her. They got on well, these two, and had done since the moment they'd met. They'd both led a harsh existence.

The frills of her mob-cap flapping around her face, Mrs Tinsley moved behind the desk out of their way.

'So what do you want?' she asked, her small eyes darting between each of them.

Edith pushed up her sleeves again and Abigail stood behind her, hands firmly fixed on her hips.

'I want you to tell me exactly what happened to the black baby that was in here a while ago, the one Mrs Heinkel was asking about.'

Mrs Tinsley regained her nerve, folded her arms and sniffed imperiously. 'I don't know what yur on about.'

Edith rolled up her sleeves. 'The Reverend Smart had trouble finding out what had happened to the poor little sod. Now then, we ain't going to have the same problem 'ere, are we?'

Mrs Tinsley looked from one to the other, weighing up whether she should be awkward or not. She relished being difficult with those she considered her inferior. Being wife of the Workhouse warden had given her a status she'd never enjoyed all the years of her life. She regarded ordering people around and being obnoxious as part of her duty, but faced with a glowering Edith and the stern Abigail, she gulped and came to a rapid decision.

'It's no secret,' she said, the words tumbling out now as fast as she could say them. 'It's just that it wasn't recorded in the Reverend's book. That's all.'

Edith slapped her hands down on the desk. Both Mrs Tinsley and Abigail nearly jumped out of their skins.

'So what happened to him? Tell me. Tell me now or I'll take you back down to the laundry room and feed you through the mangle meself!'

'The father has him. He came and took him away.'

'What the bloody hell are you talking about?' Edith demanded.

Before Mrs Tinsley could make a move, Edith grabbed her long chin and used it to tilt her head upwards so she could see the hairs of her nostrils.

Mrs Tinsley pointed. 'There! In the drawer. There's a letter.'

Edith looked. Abigail tried the drawer. It was locked.

'I've got the key.' Mrs Tinsley fumbled with the chain that hung from her waist on which dangled keys of various sizes.

She caught her breath in a deep gasp when Edith let her go, and careered on shaking knees towards the desk. Fumbling at the keys with nervous fingers, she found the right one, cursed and swore until she could aim it properly into the keyhole, then wrenched open a drawer and pulled out a letter. She passed it to Edith who unfolded it and read it slowly. It hadn't been that long since she'd learned how to read.

Her knuckles whitened, and her face turned pale. Did she understand its contents correctly, or was her reading too bad to understand it at all? She passed it to Abigail, who scanned it quickly. On seeing her expression, Edith knew that she had read every word correctly.

'I have to go to Bath,' said Edith, tucking the letter into her pocket and heading for the door.

'I'm going with you,' said Abigail.

'That letter's Workhouse property,' Mrs Tinsley shouted out behind them.

Neither paid any heed. Silently they ran from the Workhouse and all the way to Temple Meads Station. From there they caught a train, the letter seeming to burn a hole in Edith's pocket. She turned over the facts again and again in her mind. In little under an hour they would be in Bath. Both she and Abigail were shocked to the core. Blanche would be shocked too, but goodness knows what Tom Strong would do once he knew the truth.

Max locked himself in the study and again perused the legal document left by Mr Jay, re-read the particulars and pondered what he should do. The horror of discovering his father was not the man who had brought him up was bad enough, but to find out he was the product of an incestuous relationship was far worse.

And yet I'm being asked to accept it along with the Strong name, he thought and frowned. His mother was a Strong, though born on the wrong side of the sheets. And one hundred thousand pounds was a lot of money. He thought of what he could do with it. *But you can't*, he told himself. *You can't*.

The study had a fireplace, an arched, iron affair with a slate surround. If there'd been a fire burning, he would have crumpled the offending document and thrown it in. There were two things that stopped him: one, he wanted to check the truth with his mother; and two, something about this whole thing was decidedly wrong. Why hadn't it been put to him immediately following his twenty-first birthday last September? Why now?

With one swift movement, he crumpled the crisp paper between his palms. 'Damn!'

Raising his head, he eyed the crumpled paper and took a deep breath. What would his father – he corrected himself – what would Conrad have done? Nostalgic memories of the big, bluff man who still spoke with a German accent, despite his many years in Bristol, flashed into his mind.

Think of it as business, my boy. What are its advantages, what are its pitfalls? What can you gain by accepting, and what can you lose?

Max smiled. Nothing could break the bond between him and the man who had raised him.

The last question was the most delicate, the most painful of all.

What will your mother say?

He had to know the truth.

Chapter Twenty-One

Leaving the train at Bath Spa Railway Station, Edith led the way to where a row of cabs waited for business, the horses' heads drooping and their eyes closed.

'Ambassador Hotel,' she shouted up at the first cab she came to.

The cab driver, who had also been dozing, awoke with a start. 'Half a crown!'

'One shilling or I'll walk.'

He chewed his moustache. 'One and six.'

'Done.'

The two women climbed into the cab, their hearts racing. The wheels nickered over the cobblestone streets and soon they arrived at the Ambassador Hotel, which was built of the same honey-coloured stone as the rest of the city. Its name was etched into the stone pediment above its wide door.

'I think he wants something else,' said Abigail after Edith had paid the cabbie. 'He doesn't look very happy.'

'One and six I said, and one and six I paid him.'

The inside of the hotel was cool and dark, a place of rich woods, damask-covered furniture and thick carpets. Maids and waiters bustled past with tea trays, newspapers, luggage and piles of newly ironed bed linen.

A man with a lofty expression, his hands clasped behind his back, stepped forward to greet them, at least that was what they thought.

'If you're looking for work, the servants' entrance is at the rear.'

Edith bristled. 'You misjudge us, sir,' she said in her most superior voice. 'We are looking for our mistress, Mrs Heinkel. We have been on an errand on which she is awaiting news.'

The expression of the concierge softened. 'In that case, perhaps you would like to follow me.'

They trailed behind him, taking in the surroundings and the clientele as they passed.

An old man with white side whiskers snored into a newspaper covering his chest. A woman adorned with enough lace to stock a haberdashery knitted furiously, her needles clicking at breakneck speed. Two ladies clad in black sipped tea from tiny cups, their smallest finger held away.

'Mrs Heinkel!'

Blanche was sitting in a chair by the window where she had a view of the bridge and the river. There was a tea tray in front of her set with Coalport china, a silver teaspoon and matching sugar tongs.

She started when she saw them. Edith fancied she turned quite pale.

'Are these indeed your servants, madam?' the concierge asked.

Blanche confirmed that they were.

'Very well.' He left.

'What are you doing here?'

Edith ignored Blanche's surprise, putting it down to her illness. People suffering as she was shouldn't be exposed to shock, she thought, and immediately took two jagged pieces of sugar from the bowl and dropped them into her mistress's teacup.

'You're going to need it,' she explained in response to Blanche's surprised expression. 'I've got a letter here. That cow, Mrs Tinsley, didn't want me to take it, but I persuaded her that she'd be doing the right thing – if you know what I mean.' She thrust the letter into her hand.

Blanche was in no doubt of Edith's persuasive powers. She might be a maid now, but she'd lived in the Pithay, one of the most notorious slums in the city. A woman that could survive there, and bring up a brood of children, had to be pretty resourceful.

Feeling her face grow hot, Blanche read and re-read the letter.

Dear Sir,

Would you please be advised that the dark-skinned child brought to you recently by one Daisy Draper is to be handed over to me, his natural father. Please take this letter as authority for his removal along with the sum of twenty guineas for your absolute discretion.

Yours most loyal,
Duncan Devere

Blanche stared at the name. Not the surname, Devere, but Duncan. *Duncan!*

Her hand flew to her breast and she felt her heart dancing.

'I can't believe it. Twenty guineas for Mrs Tinsley's discretion but not her efficiency. She never finalised the entry.'

'The Ambassador Hotel,' said Edith, spreading her hands and rolling her eyes as though to take in all the details of the room.

'Yes,' said Blanche, not comprehending exactly what Edith was getting at, and thinking it an improper time to consider the merits of the hotel.

Edith stabbed at the paper with a blunt finger. 'The address,' she exclaimed. 'Read the address.'

Blanche looked again. The Ambassador Hotel was printed neatly at the top of the page. Suddenly it all made sense. Mary, the perambulator, the newly arrived baby . . .

Her eyes went back to the name. Mr Devere, the hotel owner she'd never seen.

'Oh, my word!' she exclaimed, and sat back in her chair, her whole body turned to jelly.

It was all frighteningly, terribly clear. Horatia. Duncan. Now she understood how a mother could brave her husband's condemnation and given her baby away. The simple fact was: Tom was not the child's father. The child was coloured because his father was.

Duncan had been a footman at Marstone Court, brought over from Barbados by Sir Emmanuel Strong. He'd been besotted with Horatia, and she had taken delight in manipulating his adoration.

To Blanche it had always seemed as though Horatia was merely playing with the man, just as she would a pet dog. Now it seemed that was not the case. There had been more than a mistress–servant relationship between them.

She remembered Duncan as being over six feet tall, dark as mahogany, broad in the shoulders and fastidious with his looks and surroundings. He'd supervised the cleaning and maintenance of Marstone Court, as though he'd owned it. There was also the matter of the suspicious circumstances surrounding the death of Sir Emmanuel. He'd been found dead in an Egyptian style sarcophagus in a room resembling a pharaoh's tomb. The tomb had been built inside the house as his final resting place when he died. On occasion he'd slept in it, prior to occupying it for eternity. But one night the lid had slipped, sealing him inside. No one could know for sure whether it was an accident, but Duncan had disappeared soon afterwards, was said to have been seen emerging from the room. Blame was easily levelled on an absent suspect, but there was no proof and he was not charged.

It seemed Edith had come to the same conclusion. 'Of course, Duncan. Do you remember when—' She stopped when she realized Blanche was no longer listening but had turned in her chair. Curious to know who or what she was looking at, Edith followed her gaze. Her hand flew to her mouth. 'Captain Tom!'

Tom greeted her warmly and also acknowledged Abigail.

Blanche was a bundle of nerves. What should she tell him? How should she handle this?

'Tom,' she said in the end. 'I think you'd better sit down.'

Aware that something special had always been between them, and was more tangible at this moment in time than she'd ever seen it before, Edith nudged Abigail's arm. 'Let's get a bit of fresh air.'

With a rustle of petticoats, the two women rose from their chairs and exited the room.

Blanche remained clasping the letter with both hands as Tom sat down.

'Edith found out what happened to the child,' she said, her voice sounding small and far away, even to her.

Tom's look was intense. His eyes did not leave her face. 'Where is he buried?'

Blanche shook her head. 'He isn't. This letter goes some way to explaining why Horatia wanted to keep his birth secret.'

The paper of the letter seemed oddly sharp. A two-edged sword could not have felt more lethal. On the one hand, it told the truth. Horatia had not been as unfeeling as they'd thought. On the other hand, she had not been a good and faithful wife, the woman without passion that Tom thought he knew.

'You'd better read this,' she said.

Tom took it, looked at her, then dropped his gaze.

Now here it is, he thought, his hands shaking but steadying as the frown on his face deepened. At last he gasped and fell forward. Resting an elbow on his knee, he supported his head in the palm of one hand, the letter dangling from the other.

It had to have been inspired by another letter. The man could not have known where the child was without Horatia telling him. He remembered Sears's confusion about Horatia's visit to the Post Office, and understood now. She'd done the right thing as a mother in an incredibly complex situation, but she'd had no thought as to how her husband would react. He hated her for that more than for her act of adultery.

Blanche studied him and worried about the way his breath seemed to catch in his throat. Was he relieved or angered? She couldn't tell. Perhaps a mix of both.

At last he managed to find his tongue. 'Well!' His whole body seemed to heave up into his shoulders then diminish to its normal position. 'It appears I have no son, but I do have an errant wife.'

Blanche felt obliged to point out the same detail that Edith had pointed out to her. 'Did you note the address?'

He nodded. 'I don't think I will be staying here again. In fact, I don't think I will be staying in England.'

'You feel no urge to have this out with Duncan?'

He made a strangled sound, as if he should have known, as if he should have been more observant. Then he shook his head, and she fancied she saw a slight smile.

'Strangely enough, I feel more able to look Horatia in the face now. Before, I could barely do that. The thought of her putting a child in that dreadful place was too much to bear. The notion of her renewing her acquaintance with Duncan is more easily bearable. I presume she set him up with this hotel. A paid lover.'

Blanche eyed him thoughtfully, uncertain of the conversation's path, unsure of the truth and depth of his feelings.

'So you've no wish to see the child?'

He shook his head. 'No. He no longer needs rescuing. My conscience is at peace.' His eyes turned the most sparkling blue they'd been for a long time. 'But Horatia's conscience is about to be stirred. She has allowed herself to be compromised, and in a strange way she has set me free.'

It was as if his face glowed with reflected light. Many months had passed since she'd seen him looking so happy, so at peace with himself and the world.

What he did next took her by surprise.

Smiling, he cupped her face in his hands, the letter crumpling against her cheek. 'And now I can kiss you without feeling any trace of guilt whatsoever,' he said, his fingers delicately caressing her face as he brought her lips close to his, paused, then kissed her.

A hum of condemnation ran like a train around them.

'Do you hear them?' said a breathless Blanche.

'Yes, I do. And I don't care. In consequence of this recent enlightenment, I have decided not to go home on this afternoon's train. I'm going home tomorrow. With you.'

They had dinner that evening in a pretty little restaurant close to the Abbey. In view of events, their conversation should have sparkled. On the contrary, they ate their meal in silence as the truth sank in.

The future was going to be very different from the past. They both knew that as they fingered glasses of wine, each avoiding looking into the eyes of the other in case it wasn't true, in case leaving for Barbados was just fantasy, that nothing they really wanted would ever happen.

'Do you realize what we are saying?' Blanche said to him.

He took her hand and stared at it, his thumb massaging her palm as he considered their options: what they wanted to do and what they should do. He raised it to his lips and kissed it. He tried to bluff it out.

'Old friends planning their future together. And you'll be living at Rivermead. Horatia's transferred the plantation into my name. No one else wanted it – not at the price she was asking anyway. I think she felt that I needed something to occupy my time, even though it meant being away from her.'

'Once she finds out, she won't take kindly to our close proximity.' She shook her head and stared at her hand, willing it to pull away from his but finding it impossible. 'Two people who love each other are about to scandalize society.'

Tom's eyes twinkled. 'You say it so matter-of-factly. Most women would blush at the thought of it.'

'I am not most women.'

'No,' he said softly. 'You're not.' And he took her hand, kissed her palm and then each finger.

She looked at his bent head, the unruly dark hair, the way it curved into his neck. Casually handsome, confidently dressed, yet almost untidy, he sat easily in his well-cut clothes as she saved the moment to memory.

He'd seemed thoughtful all evening. She presumed it was the prospect of lying together again tonight. She would not stop it happening. What would be, would be. But she sensed there was something else, something he would tell her all in his own good time.

They took a cab back to the hotel, the harness jingling and hooves clip-clopping along the cobbled streets. She didn't feel guilty. Live life to the full. Gather ye rosebuds while ye may. Make hay while the sun shines. All those little sayings sounded as though they'd been made for her. She intended following their advice.

They alighted outside the hotel, the light from the door throwing their shadows across the pavement. Tom paid the cab driver then caught her by the waist before she could enter the hotel.

She laughed like a young girl, in love for the first time in her life. 'What are you doing?' His expression made her legs weak.

'We either go through this door one by one, preferably with a few minutes between us, or we go through together. Once we have decided which, that will be the way it will be – for ever.'

The night promised rain, enough to dampen the daytime dust.

For what seemed like eternity, but was no more than seconds, they looked at each other.

At last, Blanche said, 'Give me your arm.'

There was a moment's hesitation then Tom raised his arm. His sleeve was speckled with raindrops. Blanche slipped her arm into his, enjoying the smell of damp wool. Together they entered the hotel.

It was after midnight when he came to her room.

She watched him as he peeled off his nightwear and leaned to turn down the oil lamp.

'Leave it on.'

Her demand seemed to surprise him.

'I want to see you,' she said.

He understood her meaning and stood there, his body hard with desire, pulsating with every indrawn breath.

Having him there was almost like drowning. All the pent-up desires of the last few years flooded over her. The buried longings resurfaced. Taut with desire, breathless with pleasure, she was wanton beneath his hands, arching her naked body towards his, surrendering to his hands, his mouth, his body, her pleasure soaring like a swallow in summer, reaching high enough to touch a cloud, then diving slowly, languorously back to earth.

They held each other afterwards. After any ordinary day, Blanche was ready for sleep, but tonight it didn't come.

Tom also lay awake, his head resting on one arm. 'I meant what I said. I've decided to leave Horatia,' he said. 'I'm going to Barbados with you.'

Although he prided himself on being a man who never broke a promise, she couldn't help wanting him to repeat his intentions again, and again, and again.

It all seemed so simple. Horatia was in danger of having her reputation ripped to shreds.

'I won't divorce her,' he said, as if reading her thoughts. 'There's no need for that. We have a child to think of, but I'm certain she will agree to whatever I demand. She can threaten those that I love, but now I can ruin her more cruelly than she can me. So long as we are discreet, no one will be hurt.'

Blanche caught her breath, which instantly brought on a fresh bout of coughing. Tom helped her into a sitting position, his arm around her naked shoulder.

'You do want me to go with you, don't you?'

She nodded. 'Yes.'

He lay her gently down on the soft pillows and pulled the bed-clothes up over her so she wouldn't catch cold, then paused, his brow creased with concern.

'You're thinking of Emerald.'

He nodded and swallowed in a way that made her think he was fighting some inner turmoil. She knew he loved the child. Emerald was the one thing that might make him have second thoughts.

'Could . . . she come with us?'

'Would you mind?'

'More to the point, would Horatia mind?'

He frowned. 'She's always been threatening to send her away to school. Horatia was never meant to be a mother. Perhaps in a future world, no one would expect her to be if that wasn't what she wanted.'

'But this is now.'

He nodded. 'I think that, under the circumstances, she could be persuaded. There are new opportunities in the port and the sugar industry is expanding to global proportions. Horatia will want to be part of that expansion. I can see her eyes glowing when she talks of it. Yes.' He sighed and nodded. 'Yes. I think she might agree.'

'Good,' murmured Blanche, closed her eyes and dreamed of azure surf breaking on a golden beach.

They caught the train the next morning.

'I can't wait to tell her,' he said before kissing Blanche goodbye. 'And you must tell Max.'

'I don't relish your task.'

'Have a care. Perhaps Max will be less amenable to our plans than Horatia.'

She laughed. Max could never be as vindictive as Horatia. It wasn't in him.

Chapter Twenty-Two

Max had not thought to see Darius Clarke-Fisher again, but here he was, demanding to talk to him in private.

'They're still seeing each other,' he said, hardly giving Max time to close the door of his study.

Max felt himself colouring 'What do you mean?'

'Captain Thomas Strong. Your mother keeps company with a married man. She stays with him at the Ambassador Hotel in Bath. I've seen them there. But I'm willing to forgive and forget—'

Max exploded. 'Get out of here!'

'I am just trying to save your reputation—'

Max opened the door and pushed him out. 'Stay away from my mother!' He pushed Clarke-Fisher with such force that he bounced off the wall opposite, as though he were made of India rubber.

After slamming the door shut, Max sank back into the chair. First Nelson Strong, now Tom Strong! Whatever was his mother thinking of? He couldn't deny that he liked the man, but he was married.

Should I be that surprised? he asked himself. Childhood memories came flooding back: Tom Strong coming to the house, talking to his mother and his father; flying kites on Durdham Down with his mother. The more he thought about it, the more obvious it seemed that he had always been lurking in the background, a constant in his mother's life.

Usually, one brandy would have been enough to revive his spirits, but damn it, better drunk than feeling sorry for himself.

By lunchtime, he had consumed half a bottle and still his mother was not home. He needed air and he needed to go to the refinery where he had a meeting later that afternoon. I must get out, he decided as he caught hold of the chair arm in order to stop himself crashing to the floor.

The carriage was ready and waiting by the front door. His cane tucked under his arm and his hat slightly askew, he scrambled aboard.

'Avonmouth,' he shouted to the coachman.

The journey passed in total oblivion as he slept off the half-bottle of brandy. Edward, his coachman, was canny enough to know he'd been the worse for wear, and presumptuous enough to go directly to the plot of land overlooking the proposed new dock, a place he'd taken him once before.

There was a blacksmith inside his head hammering the hell out of an anvil, and the brightness of the water flooding in from the channel pierced his eyes. Narrowing them helped him focus both his sight and his thoughts. Despite his thumping headache, the sight of the virgin land, untouched by any building in living memory, was a joy to behold. Even as he looked, he could visualize a brick edifice with tall chimneys, row upon row of windows, and pulleys and jetties big enough to take the largest steamships currently afloat.

'I could do it,' he murmured.

Edward presumed he'd been addressing him. 'Begging your pardon, sir?'

'Nothing, Edward. I was just thinking aloud.'

Changing his name for the sake of a new refinery? The thought was both tempting and appalling. Desperate to chase the temptation from his brain, he clamped his jaw tightly shut so that his teeth ground tightly together. It served to make his head ache even more, which was exactly what he'd intended. He deserved the pain for even contemplating such a terrible thing.

'Call at Madame Mabel's on the way back,' he ordered.

The clock at Temple Church had not yet struck six. The carriage came to a halt outside. Young women were pouring out of other shops in the same rank. Haberdashers were pulling down shutters. A bell jangled from the pawnbrokers on the corner and the dust of the city smelled metallic in the tired dampness of the spent day.

A young woman came out of Madame Mabel's purple door, then a group of two, another single, then three. Finally, Magdalene, not rushing like the others, but serene and neat, her hands folded neatly over the black velvet reticule that she'd made herself.

She spotted the carriage immediately, opened the door and

climbed in. 'Max! What a surprise!' She was about to kiss him, but stopped herself. 'I'm not kissing a face that looks like that.'

'Like what?'

'As though you've found a farthing and lost a guinea.'

He sighed. 'I'm sorry.'

'You said that yesterday, and now you look twice as miserable as you did then and you smell of brandy.'

He shook his head and ran his fingers around the brim of his hat, which presently sat on his knees. 'My troubles have doubled since yesterday.'

Magdalene frowned. 'I've never seen you as down as this. What is it, Max? Come on. Surely you can tell me.'

He glanced at her as he tried to make up his mind. Could he bear the consequences?

'There must be no secrets,' blurted Magdalene. 'Now tell me everything.'

'I'll take you home,' he said, tapping on the roof of the carriage.

Drowned to outside ears by the turning of the wheels and the clattering of hooves, he told her about the codicil to a Will written ten years ago. 'If I adopt the family name, therefore declaring that Nelson Strong was my father, I inherit a very princely sum indeed, enough to clear my debts and enforce my plans.

'But . . .' he hesitated, his fingers rapping a nervous tune on his thigh. 'There's something terrible about it. Something truly sinful.'

She held her head to one side, her expression bordering on amusement, but also apprehensive.

'Go on, Max. What is it? Nothing can be that terrible.'

He spoke in a rush. 'It seems my father was also my mother's half-brother. Of course she didn't know at the time . . . she couldn't have, or she wouldn't . . .'

Her eyes were wide, her face still as she waited for him to continue.

He told her as much as he knew.

She sat silently after he'd told her.

He studied her, his stomach churning with worry. The likelihood that she might call off their engagement was uppermost in his mind, and who could blame her? Trying to read her thoughts was impossible. The tension was too much to bear.

'Well?' he said at last. 'Will you still marry me?'

'Are you mad?'

The look she gave him and the tone of her voice made his heart flutter.

'You still want to?'

'Nothing's changed, but, as I see it, we have a few things to sort out that will no doubt have a very great impact on our children's lives.'

'It will?' This was the first time he'd heard her mention their having children. But of course, if they were getting married, there would be children.

'Don't look so surprised. It's what married people do, you know; they produce the next generation. There's no going back with children, only forward. Now this is the way I see it: my family changed their name in order to improve their chances. It didn't hurt and my father didn't moan that he should be faithful to his father's name. And besides, look what you'd be gaining: a brand new refinery and more control over your own destiny. Don't you think that a fitting memorial to the man who brought you up?'

Max eyed her uneasily. She made it all sound so sensible. Rigid loyalty to the past was brushed aside. It all made sense and he found himself thinking that even if she hadn't agreed to be his wife, she would never have stayed a humble milliner.

'I suppose you're right.'

She hugged his arm. 'You have to think of the future.'

'And my mother?'

'Sign the deed first. Do you have it with you?'

'Yes.'

He took it out from his inside pocket. He'd been carrying it around for days, taking it out and looking at it, thinking about it, and putting it back again.

There was a brass ring at his side set into the upholstery. He pulled it and out came a small travelling slope complete with inkwell.

'Ooow!' Magdalene exclaimed. 'That's clever.'

Quickly he signed before he changed his mind. 'There.'

'We'll drop it off at the solicitors now.'

'Good heavens,' said Max after pushing the writing slope back into place. 'Do you know what this means? By lunchtime tomorrow I will have a hundred thousand pounds in my bank account.'

'Is that all?' laughed Magdalene.

'No. By mid-afternoon I will have purchased extra land at Avonmouth from under the nose of Horatia Strong.'

*

They ate supper together before he returned to Somerset Parade.

Alighting from the carriage, he looked up at the red-brick walls and white windows of the house he'd lived in for most of his life. That morning he had left it as Maximillian Heinkel. Eleven o'clock chimed in the new spire of St Mary Redcliffe. It sounded like a celebration that he'd come home as Maximillian Strong.

He was surprised to find that his mother had not yet retired. He found her sitting in front of the window reading, the moonlight filtering through the flimsy lace curtains and forming a floral pattern over her head and face. His heart missed a beat. When he was a boy he'd told her that he would marry a girl like her when he grew up. She had laughed and told him he would likely marry a pretty little blonde with a button nose who'd laugh when he wanted her to and wouldn't mind flying kites and climbing trees.

His mother's dress was a bluish grey some of which turned green when she moved and laid down her book to smile at him. The material reminded him of a peacock's tail. He noted the clearness of her eyes, the glossy hair. His mother was growing old beautifully.

She looked up on seeing him enter and presented her cheek for him to kiss. 'Max. I thought I would wait up for you. There's something important I wish to discuss with you.'

'And there is something I wish to discuss with you.'

'Then you shall have my full attention.' She closed the book as though it were made of the softest silk. A frown creased her brow momentarily and then was gone. 'What is it?'

Before entering the house, he'd felt quite light-headed, excited at the prospect of taking both the refinery and his life forward in giant steps. The matter regarding his birth, not to mention his mother's liaison with Tom Strong, was more delicate. Truth was, it embarrassed him. After all, she was middle-aged *and* she was his mother. The whole thing was terribly distasteful.

Max poured himself a brandy.

She cleared her throat. 'I'd like a brandy too. Will you pour me one?'

He looked at her, then at the dark, balloon-shaped bottle. 'Wouldn't you prefer one of Mr Harvey's sherries as you usually do?'

She shook her head. 'No. I need something a little stronger and less sweet.'

He did as she asked, filling the brandy balloon halfway. Still without meeting his eyes, she drained half the glass. He decided to tackle the issue of Tom Strong first.

'I met your old beau, Mr Darius Clarke-Fisher.'

Her retort was swift. 'He is not my beau. I detest the man. I hope you told him so.'

Max frowned and eyed the treacle-coloured liquid swirling in his glass. 'He offered to take you off my hands before your liaison with Tom Strong became widespread gossip.'

For a moment, she said nothing, but he could tell by the fiery look in her eyes, and the way her lips were parted, that she was searching for the right words and none would come. He came to the immediate conclusion: Darius Clarke-Fisher had been telling the truth.

'That's what I want to speak to you about,' she said eventually.

'Mother, before you say anything, I need to talk to you about something else.'

Max cleared his throat again, clasped his hands behind his back and began pacing the room. God, but this was damned difficult.

Blanche said, 'If it's about my trips to Bath—'

'To take the waters . . . yes, yes, I know and I do not begrudge you a moment.' He stroked her head and looked down into her lovely eyes. 'Mother, I understand that you've always had a relationship with Tom Strong.'

Kneeling down, he took both her hands in his and noticed that her eyes were moist. She drew a hand from his grasp and smoothed his hair back from his temples, a simple action, but one that spoke volumes about motherly love and duty.

'Don't ask me to give Tom up. I won't. We're going away together.'

'What?'

Max was shocked. This was not at all what he'd expected. He imagined the shame, the whispers, the outright sniggering as he was pointed out as the man whose mother had run away with Tom Strong.

'It won't be like that,' said Blanche, instinctively knowing what was in his mind. 'Horatia has dug herself into a deep hole that she cannot possibly get out of. Nothing she can say or do can damage our reputation as badly as hers can be damaged. We're going home, to my home. Barbados. Someone has to take care of the plantation, or what's left of it.'

He steeled himself for what he had to say next. He couldn't say it looking into her eyes. Gaze fixed on the floor, he began to pace.

'The other day I had a visit from a solicitor, a man named Mr Jay. Thanks to what I learned from him, I will now be able to build my own refinery at Avonmouth without being hampered by the Strong family.'

'That's wonderful, Max—'

Max began to chuckle. 'Mother, you cannot imagine how ironic it is. I am no longer at the mercy of the Strong family's business plans, and yet I am one of them.'

'Yes, but I did tell you about Sir Emmanuel and—'

'Today I signed a document that made me a Strong in name. The document was a codicil to a will made by Nelson Strong. He left me the sum of one hundred thousand pounds so long as I acknowledged him as my father by changing my name to Strong.'

He shook his head and covered his face with his hands. Now it was out, it seemed far more incongruous than when he'd talked it through with Magdalene.

His mother's silence puzzled him. On withdrawing his hands from his face, he saw she was frowning, as though she too were puzzled. She got to her feet, wrung her hands and looked away.

'That's impossible.'

'How is it impossible?'

She shook her head and brushed her forehead with the back of her hand. Her breathing quickened and, for the first time, he heard wheezing in her chest.

'I can't tell you without asking him first—'

'Without asking who?'

She was brazening it out; he could see it in her eyes. His mother, the woman he'd adored all his life, had a secret. Had she ever had secrets from his father?

'Mother, I want to know.'

He saw the tears in her eyes as she turned to face him. 'I would never do anything to hurt you,' she said.

The look in his mother's eyes almost took his breath away. It was as though all her most precious memories were betrayed in her expression.

'When I first came to this city, I thought I had all the time in the world and, quite honestly, I did. I thought those I loved would always be there, though I should have known better than to believe that. After all, I'd just lost my mother. But now . . .' She sighed then took a deep breath as if she were summoning up deep feelings or deeply buried courage. At last she said, 'Time is running out and soon those I've loved and those who loved me will be gone. People mean more to me than my reputation, Max, and it's only fair that you should know who your real father is.' She raised her hands, palms out and shook her head. 'We were the victims of circumstance and of our time. We love each other. We always have and always will.'

The truth hit him. 'Tom Strong?'

Max could barely believe his ears.

She shook her head, amused that the young could be shocked by the actions of those they regarded as beyond sexuality, beyond passion. 'Conrad knew we loved each other. He also knew that we would be together one day when circumstances allowed. We have much in common and our time together is precious.' She leaned forward, her eyes bright. 'We are making the most of the time we have left.'

'And what about his wife?'

Blanche flinched. 'There is much you do not know and do not need to know. But our time has come. We will live out our latter years together. Horatia will not object. Emerald, Tom's daughter, will be coming with us.'

Max slumped into a chair. 'I can't believe this is happening.'

'We won't be leaving until after your wedding.'

'Thank you for that.'

'There's no need to sound sarcastic.'

'It's not sarcasm, it's shock. I can't believe so much has happened to me in just a few, short days. First I'm Conrad Heinkel's son, then I'm Nelson Strong's son, and now I find that my real father is Thomas Strong.'

'Speak to him,' she said softly. 'Tell him that you know.'

Max left the room without saying goodnight. Blanche knew he was confused more than angry. The world he'd known had been turned upside down. His mind was troubled, but he had to find his own peace, she told herself, just as she and Tom had done. She decided to send Tom a note, warning him of what she had done. Max knew who his father was. She hoped Tom would understand.

Irritatingly, Tom had to wait to confront Horatia about her relationship with Duncan. She had gone to London to negotiate the price of some prime refineries in Limehouse. But he did have another job to do before he and Blanche left for Barbados. He had to explain himself to Max. In order to soften the blow, he had decided to hand over all his interest in the refinery. He didn't expect Max to be grateful for it, but at least it would help ease his own conscience. He decided to talk to him after the directors' monthly meeting that week.

He arrived late. The other directors were already seated in the room Max had named 'The Boiler House'. Summer or winter, the room was always warm. The end wall formed the outer skin of one of the chimneys that towered sixty feet into the air. Tom removed his coat and hung it on the back of a chair. One or two of the more liberal followed his example. The rest boiled, trickles of sweat pouring down their faces and into their stiffly starched shirt collars. 'That chimney needs sweeping,' he said, brushing cinders from the back of his coat.

'We can't shut the whole place down for one chimney,' Max said sharply. 'I've given orders to wait until the others need cleaning and to shut down then.'

Josiah Benson, who was there representing his wife, Caroline, Horatia's half-sister, nodded in agreement. 'Much more sensible and far less costly.'

'There is a fire risk—' Tom began.

'A small one,' said Max, surprised at his own sharpness.

He ignored Tom's troubled frown. In his heart of hearts, he agreed that the chimney should be swept, but he couldn't bring himself to agree with anything Tom uttered. He couldn't help being awkward because he felt awkward. It wasn't every day a man discovered his father.

'Can we move on?'

Everyone agreed, though Tom's nod was barely perceptible. Max took it that he had agreed and handed the meeting over to Woodbine Chester, who acted as company secretary and general factotum.

The main topic of the day was the future of the refinery.

Chester droned on about the costs of ferrying sugar by barge from ship to refinery. 'There are two proposed plans of action,' he said finally. 'One, proposed by Mr Max Heinkel, that we purchase land at the mouth of the river and build a new refinery, but maintain these premises as additional warehousing facilities, perhaps to be used for overspill refining. Two, proposed by Mr Thomas Strong on behalf of his wife, we sell our present site and move our total operation to London.'

Max looked around the table. Some shuffled nervously, but few met his gaze. A nod, a frown, a thoughtful stroking of whiskers or chin, as they all considered the matter.

Only Tom was looking straight at him. 'I understood that you did not wish for these premises to be sold. You'll not have such a big say in a refinery controlled by my wife's pet bankers.'

There were raised eyebrows. Never had he referred to his wife in such a derisory way. One of the implicated bankers turned a furious shade of puce. 'We were not ungenerous.'

'If dividing a man's cake into unequal parts is not ungenerous—' Tom continued.

Surprised at his off-hand manner, Max held his gaze. 'It doesn't really matter. I've changed my mind. Thanks to an inheritance, I have gone ahead and purchased the Avonmouth site in my own name.' He paused, his eyes scrutinizing the men, all of whom were older than him. 'My new name, I should say. Strong. Maximillian Strong.'

There followed a hum of gasps and murmurs of surprise. None was more shocked than Tom.

Fired up with a thrusting confidence, which seemed to shine from his eyes and glow in his face, Max went on. 'My mother, as some of you may know, is a daughter of the late Sir Emmanuel Strong, and widow of Conrad Heinkel. I will not go into the reasons for adopting my grandfather's name at this time. This is a private matter. My decision regarding Avonmouth was taken after listening to the sound advice of a valued friend. Gentlemen, I am looking to the future. Bigger ships mean bigger facilities. The days of sailing ships coming up the Avon are long past, but in honour of the man who brought me up, the refinery will retain the name of Heinkel. The new refinery will be a shrine to Conrad Heinkel, and a beacon of hope for the generations to come.'

Tom met Max's accusing glare and knew then for sure that Blanche had finally told their son the truth. He felt a mix of elation and surprise. Was that why he'd taken the name Strong, because he now knew who his father was?

Woodbine interrupted. 'So how does the meeting vote?'

Josiah Benson cleared his throat and clasped his hands on the table in front of him. 'Regardless of family sympathies, our first priority is to reduce our transportation costs, that is those incurred in transferring cargo from ship to refinery. With that in mind, I feel that we should back Maximillian's plans for the new refinery at Avonmouth – that's if he wants or needs our support,' he said, raising his bushy eyebrows at Max.

'Your investment is welcome, so long as you concede that I own the biggest share and am therefore in overall control.'

He saw Tom Strong look at him from beneath a shock of dark hair, greying now at the temples. What had he looked like when his mother had first known him?

Hezekial Carey, a merchant venturer and past mayor of the city, shook his head. 'Gentlemen. My honorable friend, Mr Benson, is right. There is no sentiment in business, and neither is there any age limit. Our young friend here is the best placed to take us forward with new ideas. We have had our day in the sun, but that doesn't mean we cannot bathe in some of his reflected rays. I for one have every intention of backing this venture, and not just with my shares. I will also put pressure on the planning authorities to speed up the process so that not a day of production is lost. I vote for supporting the move.'

Tom got to his feet, took a few paces to the window and eyed the view outside. 'The dock is no holy grail, gentlemen. Let's get that straight from the start. Although the proposed port at Avonmouth will take bigger ships, the tidal problem still remains. Ships waiting out in the channel for the tide to turn cost money. Should the port authority fix too high a fee for berthing, business could be lean indeed.'

He turned from the window, his presence dominating the room.

'This is an opportunity to build a modern refinery, not just to facilitate easier off-loading, but without the tidal problems we experience in the Bristol Channel. There is only a few feet differential between high and low tide on the east coast. Here on the west coast it's closer to forty feet – second only to the Bay of Tundy in Canada. My inclination would be to abandon the new docks and relocate to London unless you have no need of borrowing and can finance the scheme in its entirety.'

'I have the money to finance the complete venture,' said Max.

Tom nodded acknowledgement. Inside, he surged with pride. Somehow Max had broken the stranglehold of the Strong family. He truly was an independent man.

Hezekial Carey slapped Max's shoulder as the directors made their way out. 'We've made the right decision, my boy. I'm sure your father would have approved.'

'Well that's not for us to know, is it?' said Max, unable to veil the sarcasm in his voice.

Then it was just Tom and Max alone in The Boiler House.

They held each other's gaze, weighing up what the other might be thinking or be about to say. One of them had to break. It turned out to be Tom.

'I suppose your mother told you.'

'Yes. She did.'

Tom ran his fingers around the crown of his hat, looking at it searchingly before placing it on his head.

Max looked awkward. It wasn't every day a man found secrets bursting around his head like fireworks.

'I've always looked out for you,' Tom said at last. 'It was one of the reasons I stayed with Horatia and in Bristol.'

'And now those reasons no longer exist?'

'The truth's out, not just about you, but about my wife.' A look of puzzlement came to his face. 'The only thing I don't understand is why you took the name Strong. It's a great honour, though of course I wasn't born with the name myself. I was adopted, you see—'

'It wasn't out of respect for you. I did it for the one hundred thousand pounds left to me in Nelson's will.'

Tom was astounded. 'One hundred thousand? Are you sure?'

Max smiled triumphantly. 'How else do you think I managed to finance the Avonmouth site all by myself?'

'But that's impossible. Sir Emmanuel judged that Horatia was best able to further enhance the Strong interests. Nelson was only allotted a yearly income.'

Now it was Max who frowned, his mind whirling with possibilities. 'Tell me,' he said, closing the door between them and the passage recently vacated by those attending the meeting, 'have you heard of a man named Darius Clarke-Fisher?'

Tom nodded. 'We met briefly in Bath.'

Taking a decanter from a tall chest, Max poured them both a large brandy.

'It was Clarke-Fisher who told me that you and my mother were having an affair. He offered to marry my mother, take her off my hands like a load of dirty laundry – his insinuation rather than description,' Max added on seeing Tom's indignant expression. 'He also mentioned your wife. Do you suppose he saw her, too? Is it possible she could contrive this? I mean, giving away so much money just like that.'

Tom threw the drink into his mouth so that it hit the back of his throat and burned as it went down.' She would,' he said darkly. 'She can afford to. You cannot imagine just how much money the family have.' His face lightened suddenly. 'Just a minute. This wasn't just a matter of revenge, hurting Blanche and hurting me. She never expected you actually to change your name. All she intended was to sow seeds of doubt into your relationship with your mother, seeds that would reap a bitter harvest in years to come.'

Max looked surprised then burst out laughing. 'She would really do that?'

Still amused, Tom nodded. 'She usually reads people very well, but not this time. My dear boy,' he said, chuckling as he slapped Max on the back, 'you've beaten her at her own game. Not only did you react differently than she'd supposed you would, but you've also beaten her to the land at Avonmouth and control of the refinery. I can't believe it, I can't believe it,' he said, his laughter resuming and shaking his head.

Max was ecstatic. The difficulty he'd thought he would have in relating to Captain Tom Strong, his natural father, didn't exist. And he'd beaten the Strong family! He felt as though he could fly. Instead, he reached for the decanter again.

'Another brandy, Captain?'

Tom held out his glass. 'To a young man his father would have been proud of – just as I am,' he said as he raised his glass in a toast.

Max glowed. He understood that the toast was for Conrad, for him, but also for Tom.

The conservatory attached to the house had been extended in recent years to take in the old orangery built in the eighteenth century by

Isaiah Strong. The structure now boasted a huge dome at its centre, and iron arches in the Hindu style formed its sides.

Tom was sitting in a cast-iron chair smoking a cigarillo and surrounded by shiny-leaved plants. An Irish setter lay at his feet. It lifted its tail and wagged lazily at Horatia's approach.

Tom's smile was warm. 'Will you take a seat and a smoke?'

She looked taken aback at first; after all, she had always tried to keep her smoking secret, forgetting that the smell seeps into fabrics, hair and breath.

He indicated the chair next to him then took a cigarillo from his inside pocket. On this occasion, she declined.

'And how was your London trip?'

'Good.'

Her voice was clipped. He guessed that Septimus Monk, or Mr Jay from Queen's Square, had already told her that she'd misjudged Maximillian Heinkel and as a result she was a hundred thousand pounds lighter.

'I wanted to talk to you,' he said, getting up from the chair and standing with his hands clasped behind his back, his feet slightly apart. He was determined not to lose his temper. His spirits were soaring, his heart lighter than it had been for years. If she cared to notice the look in his eyes, she would see only warmth. But she wasn't looking. He'd already handed her the letter that Duncan had written to the Workhouse.

He drew leisurely on his cigarillo, blowing the smoke into the air in lazy, perfectly formed rings. He couldn't help imagining her in bed with Duncan. Had she been as cold and unyielding with Duncan as she was with him? He'd never know, and he certainly wasn't going to ask.

'You were very lucky to be born rich, Horatia. No woman contemplating adultery could afford to buy her lover a hotel. Duncan was lucky, too.'

Her face was turned away from him. Unusually for her, she said nothing in her defence. Her gaze seemed fixed on an India rubber plant, as though she were seeing something there that was invisible to his own eyes.

'Was it that you couldn't endure the whispers, the gossip, the nasty remarks of your male minions in the worlds of banking, sugar and shipping? Not to mention the adverse affects it could have on your daughter? I presume you'd envisaged a future role for her in the Strong business interests, as a pawn in a marriage contract perhaps?'

'I couldn't bear . . .' she began, half turning towards him, then turning away again.

'The gossip?'

Sighing, she closed her eyes as though a great weight had been lifted from her shoulders. 'I thought it best to tell you he died when I saw his colour and knew—'

'He couldn't be mine. You could have got away with saying that he was a throwback to African ancestry. But no. You took him to the Workhouse.'

'But I couldn't allow him to stay there,' she blurted.

Tom sighed. 'Never mind, Horatia. It's all water under the bridge. Now let us attend to the matter in a manner that suits both of us. I never had your business acumen, and you could never quite relinquish your ambition, no matter if you'd had a dozen children. Therefore, I suggest that we go our separate ways without any recriminations from either of us. You will stay here as queen of the Strong empire, just as you've always wanted – and, together with Emerald, I will go to live at Rivermead.'

She looked at him sharply. 'You're going with Blanche Heinkel, aren't you?'

He nodded and made no excuses. He could have lied and said that she was going along as housekeeper or nursemaid to Emerald. In a way, she was. Her own family were all grown up. Emerald would need the woman's touch he could not give her, and Blanche needed to be in a warmer climate. It all made sense.

Horatia's hands were clad in lace mittens trimmed with tiny seed pearls. Her knuckles showed white through the fine mesh as she clasped her hands tightly together and one or two pearls popped off in response.

So far, Tom was surprised at her composure. He'd expected anger before she saw the advantages – no ties to a child or a husband, her mind as well as her body set free – but still, it was unusual, in fact slightly surreal. After all, he was telling her that he was leaving her to live with another woman and, what was worse, he was taking their daughter. He braced himself for the onslaught that he was still sure would come. She had every right to be angry and he had every right to feel as guilty as sin.

'I think your proposal makes sense.'

He looked at her. Her eyes were downcast. Her fingers fidgeted nervously.

'Did you hear what I said?'

'Of course I did. You wish to live with Blanche in Barbados and you wish our daughter to live with you.'

He studied her more closely to make sure that this *was* Horatia Strong, his wife, he was talking to. He couldn't quite believe it.

'I was never suited to be a mother, Thomas. I love our daughter, please believe that.' She looked up at him and he could see by her expression and the moistness of her eyes that she really meant it. He'd never seen such sincerity in her face. 'I cannot help being what I am. There is within me this desperate hunger to succeed, to expand the Strong family fortune, to be better than my father and grandfather. Thus it is that my priorities are directed towards myself. Isaiah was conceived in a moment of careless abandon. It is rare that I am driven by lust, as I am sure you have noticed. Strange as it may seem for me to admit, I know that Emerald will be better looked after by another woman than me. Blanche has inherited the more congenial aspects of the Strong family, the gentler elements which my grandmother possessed. I cannot imagine a better home for Emerald than with you and Blanche.'

Tom found himself taking a deep breath as if it were the first for a long while. This was not at all the response he had expected. He'd anticipated a horrendous argument and a threat that she would do all in her power to stop him taking Emerald from her. Instead, she had injected an element of uncharacteristic unselfishness into the occasion. He found himself almost loving her for it.

'I didn't expect this,' he said at last.

Her smile was slow and had an element of pain about it. 'Whatever you may think in later years, please believe me when I say it was not an easy decision to come to. She is still of my body, but I know my limitations. Being a mother does not come easily to me, and I have no wish to end up like my stepmother, Lady Verity, who left the upbringing of her children to servants. I do not want that.'

She laughed as if she couldn't believe she had made such an incredible, and in most eyes, unnatural decision. 'I love you, I love her, but I also love the cut and thrust of business. I have been left a legacy that few women ever inherit. I intend to build on that legacy, those admirable foundations put down by my great-grandfather. I enjoy beating men at their own game. I am totally committed to what I do, just as you are committed to Blanche and to Emerald.'

Never in his life could he remember Horatia ever looking as serene as she did now, as though everything was exactly how she wanted it to be. There was one thorn that was bound to be hurting her, one unforeseen occurrence to a carefully laid plan.

'I presume you will now invest more heavily in the properties you purchased in Limehouse rather than Bristol.'

He had to admit, she tried very hard to stop herself from stiffening, but her shoulders turned rigid and, for one moment, her jaw looked as if it had been carved from ice.

'I think you should leave now. You no longer belong here.'

She looked forlorn, but he told himself it wouldn't last. Horatia would find solace doing what she did best, alone with the power she'd always relished.

He left her there, told his valet to forward his trunk to the Greyhound Hotel where he would reside until the time came to leave the city of his birth.

He declined the carriage, preferring to take a horse. The Greyhound had very fine livery stables where privately owned animals were lodged next to those used by the Post Office.

He felt happy as he rode the country road from Marstone Court to Bristol. The world seemed cleaner somehow. Low-lying mist feathered the muddy riverbanks. Cattle, full of cud, were picking spots in meadows where the sun had already warmed the ground. The feel of frost was in the air and the hedges were bursting with berries and the bustling of sparrows, blackbirds and blue tits.

There would be no divorce, no messy recriminations. So long as everyone's reputations were left intact, no one would know anything untoward had taken place. Captain Tom Strong was running River-mead Plantation. The sugar it produced would go to Limehouse. There would no longer be any connection between the Strong plantation in Barbados and the family in Bristol.

It would also be made common knowledge that, in the aftermath of a shooting incident she had witnessed, it was felt conducive for his daughter to live in Barbados. His wife, the head of a huge business empire, would stay at home. The fact that Blanche was ill would be made known to the biggest gossips in the city before she left. Edith would make sure of that. Servants in big houses followed the lives of their betters with keen interest. The whole of Bristol would know of her illness within day so of them getting the news. Thus, there would be no breath of scandal for anyone concerned.

Horatia cried after he had left. This is your penance, she told herself. Sacrificing yourself for those you love was the only path left open to you if you were to save your soul.

She'd been determined not to mention her visits to St Mary Redcliffe. Admitting what she was doing was an act of penance would have made him feel guilty at leaving her and she didn't want that. All her life she had sought the success that only wealth could bring. Much wrong had been done as a result of this. Now was the time to put things right, and she felt that was exactly what she had done. She had her world; they had each other. They also had Emerald. The fact that they did would hurt her for ever, but it was only right that she gave her up, just as she had her son. This was her penance. The pain would always be with her.

'I never thought I'd find myself thinking her honest and noble, but I do now,' said Blanche when he told her the news.

He shook his head. 'How many of us ever admit that our true self is not as righteously acceptable as we make out?'

'Perhaps because we don't dare.'

They decided to visit Edith, Samson and family at Little Paradise before their departure. Hamlet was home from the canals and full of stories about the water meadows, the locks and the cows they milked in the dead of night when the farmer wasn't around.

Abigail had prepared a spicy meal of lamb and vegetables, and baked a pie containing the few fruits left in the garden.

After dinner, as Emerald ran barefoot with Desdemona and Hamlet, Abigail washed dishes, and Edith and Samson sat smoking pipes on a wall beneath the apple trees, Tom and Blanche walked among the rhubarb, the gooseberry bushes, the winter sprouts and the potatoes.

They'd already told everyone that they were going to Barbados. Edith had cried. Abigail had passed her a large handkerchief and said that sunshine was the best thing for bad coughs.

They passed through the gate at the end of the garden and stood admiring the view.

'You look wonderful,' Tom said.

It was true. Her face was bathed in the golden glow of the setting sun and she was wearing a grey evening dress sprigged with tiny mauve flowers. She'd last worn it on the day her daughter Anne had picked dandelions on the common before she'd died of cholera. Accepting illness was all part of life and it was hardly the fault of the dress. She resolved to make out a Will leaving Little Paradise to Edith Blackcloud, and thereafter to Samson and his family.

Max brought his wedding forward to November and Emerald was a bridesmaid. Hamlet was almost a pageboy, but having discovered what he would have to wear, legged it to Aggie's narrowboat, pleading with her to accept a stinking load of creosote rather than have him suffer what most boys regarded as a fate worse than death.

'I ain't wearin' no knickerbockers and silky, lacy collars,' he protested.

Aggie, generous as always, duly obliged.

Horatia Strong sent a note that she was unable to attend by virtue of business commitments and trusted that her husband would represent the Strong family.

Two days before the wedding, Mr Darius Clarke-Fisher made one last attempt to procure Max's assistance to marry his mother.

'I don't believe the cheek of the man,' said Max who was getting fitted for his wedding suit in one room, while Magdalene was in another, complete with her mother, father and goodness knows how many of the girls from Madame Mabel's.

'*Ma cherie*, you look divine,' gushed Mabel, still affecting a French accent and fluttering around like a lost butterfly.

'Here,' said Edith as she heaved a bolt of cream cloth from where it was leaning against the wall onto a nearby table. 'Are you the Mabel Morris who used to live in Cock and Bottle Lane? Mabel Pudding as was?'

Madame Mabel went scarlet. 'Certainly not,' she snapped, but kept a low profile from that day forth until the wedding, hardly an accented word coming from her mouth.

The bride wore a cream dress and a silk bonnet lined with gold damask, acres of tulle hanging down her back.

'I'll remember this day for the rest of my life,' murmured Blanche against her son's ear as she hugged him for what she thought might be the very last time.

She wiped at her cheek, thinking they were her own tears.

'They're mine,' said Max, and hugged her as though he would never let her go.

Epilogue

The breeze eased the heat of the day. A red slash left by the setting sun made silhouettes of the palm trees.

Blanche and Tom were lying on a double-width wickerwork chaise longue. Her head rested on his shoulder as she lay listening to the encroaching sounds of evening.

Surf made a sweeping sound against the shore, and wooden doors and shutters, baked during the daytime, now creaked into the cooling air. The crickets fell to silence as a solitary bat flew into the matt black trees that separated Rivermead House from the growing cane and the tumbledown huts where the field hands used to live.

Tom's masculine scent, the warmth of his body was as good for her well-being as the Barbados climate.

A sudden scream disturbed their peace and made them both sit bolt upright.

Blanche clutched at his shoulder. 'It's just an animal.'

'I'll check anyway.'

Blanche let him go. It would be a while yet before he fully believed that Emerald no longer had nightmares. Barbados had eased that pain too, as well as the one in her chest.

He smiled when he came back. 'She's sound asleep.'

After he'd resumed his former position, Blanche snuggled up against him.

'I never want to leave this place again,' she sighed, rubbing her chin up and down on his arm.

Tom looked down at her. 'You're not going to. We're here for ever.'

'Is that a promise?'

'Yes. And as you know, I always keep promises.'

The breeze stirred the trees, and the moon rose above the sea and the white-painted house.